WHAT *THE HOUSE OF GOD* DID
FOR THE BODY,

FINE

DOES FOR THE MIND.

"THIS IS A PSYCHIATRIST? THIS IS ALL THAT
STANDS BETWEEN US AND MISERY? The truth
of Shem's portrait of the head doctor as a young man
should make customers out of everyone who's ever been
in therapy and everyone who's thought about why he or
she hasn't been. . . . INSPIRED . . . FASCINAT-
ING . . . OFTEN SCANDALOUS!"
—*Los Angeles Herald-Examiner*

"FUNNY . . . FULL OF DAZZLING, ZANY IN-
TELLIGENCE . . . ENERGETIC AND EXUBER-
ANT."
—*The New York Times*

"HILARIOUS . . . NOT TO BE MISSED . . . and
filled with the emotions and truths common to us all."
—*San Diego Tribune*

"ULTIMATELY ABSORBING . . . [a] mix of high-
toned philosophy, current psychoanalytic theories,
broad comedy, raunchy sex, and even the suspense of a
murder mystery . . . a story with metaphysical over-
tones about the eternal mind/body dilemma, the love/
hate conflict in human relationships."
—*Publishers Weekly*

Also by Samuel Shem:

The House of God, a novel

Room for One Woman, a play,
in *The Best Short Plays 1979*

Napoleon's Dinner, a play,
in *The Best Short Plays 1982*

Brothers, a play

FINE

A Novel by
Samuel Shem, M.D.

A DELL BOOK

Published by
Dell Publishing Co., Inc.
1 Dag Hammarskjold Plaza
New York, New York 10017

The author wishes to express appreciation to the following: Doctors Jordan, Kaplan, Miller, Stiver, and Surrey of the Colloquium series of the Stone Center, Wellesley College, Wellesley, Massachusetts, for discussions on theories of human development.
Grateful acknowledgment is made for permission to use:
"It Happens All Over the World." Copyright © 1957 by the Bourne Company. Used by permission.
"Carry Me Back to Old Manhattan." Copyright © 1955 by the General Music Publishing Company, Inc. Used by permission.
"John O'Dreams." Copyright © 1976 by Bill Caddick. Used by permission.

Dell ® TM 681510, Dell Publishing Co., Inc.

ISBN: 0-440-12510-3

Reprinted by arrangement with St. Martin's/Marek

Printed in the United States of America

September 1986

10 9 8 7 6 5 4 3 2 1
WFH

To Janet Surrey and Ben Heineman, Jr., again

(Enter Ariel, as invisible water nymph)
PROSPERO: Fine apparition! My quaint Ariel,
               Hark in thine ear.
(He whispers to her)
ARIEL: My Lord it shall be done.
(Exit Ariel)

                    —Shakespeare, *The Tempest*

Contents

I

BLIND

All love stories are about three people.
—Anonymous

1

TO BE ALIVE is to have an open mind. This is not easy to do. To be happy? Happy seems flawless. This is its great flaw.

Fine kicked open the front passenger door of Stephanie's old purple Jaguar and bounced out into the dark, thinking he was happy.

He was a man who imagined he saw things just as they actually are.

I feared for him.

The car hadn't come to a full stop, and the motion of Fine's foot against the asphalt spun him around, caromed him off the back fender, ripping the crotch of his black tuxedo pants, and dumped him on his butt. Still anesthetized by the champagne, he smiled. Chubby yet solid, he gave off an earthy aura, a sense of *thereness* that made him a natural leader. Through neck and shoulder, thigh and calf, he was thick, muscular. In his youth a prodigal *klutz*, he'd grown up to move with that contrapuntal agility often seen in big mammals—fat men, elephants, dancing bears. He'd freed himself from any and all attempts to control his physical being. On the contrary, years ago he'd learned, with Stephanie's help, to use his flesh for fun. She'd shown him that if *he* could laugh at himself, others couldn't. An effulgent chestnut-haired man with pink freckled skin, he was as corpulent as a fireplug. He had grown to love his shape. Loving it meant he could eat. Fine loved to eat. At twenty-seven, he met the world orally. He put things into his mouth. On those rare occasions when his body still attacked him, his falls had become fun, true surprise parties of the soul. Almost, he'd often thought, like the surprise of falling in love. Fine was big on surprises. Six months before, applying for his psychiatry training, in the blank marked "Hobbies" he'd written "Serendipity." A master of probability theory, he had a strong weakness for the laws of chance. His intuition was that chance, followed back far enough, became fate. And so he lay there on the cool dewy roadbed and chuckled.

"Oh boy!" Stephanie said, shutting off the headlights. He felt her rushing toward him through the ether. "Are you okay?"

"Okay?" he asked, delighted at her lapse, which fed him the setup, he said: "I'm—"

"Don't say it—!"

"—Fine!" Completing the circle of their oldest joke, he laughed. "Haha!" Balanced between drunk and hung over, he couldn't stop, laughing so hard the tears soon welled from his gray-green eyes, nudged his Jewish nose—he saw it as a capital "J" shoved roughly, against its will, forty-five degrees counter-clockwise on his face—and rolled down his round freckled cheeks.

"You split your pants!" Stephanie said. He kept laughing.

"Oh my dear little Falstaff," said their best friend John, getting out of the back seat, from Fine's point of view a supple blond giant looming against the bruised sky, "you've got to stop eating so much!"

"Why?" Fine asked. "I used to be ten pounds shorter."

"Shorter?" said John. "Oh Jesus!"

"Ha!" said Fine. "Haha!" His cheeks wobbled, his gut bulged all pink and fuzzy from his unstudded ruffled white shirt.

He minded being short as little as he minded being chunky.

Steph and John leaned over him, height foreshortened, heads together in a vertex, looking down. He sensed their puzzlement that he, the solid base of their pyramid, was acting so undignified. At a peak of his life—in terms of hope and happiness, and a usual peak of lives, daring—it all was flowing smoothly, wave upon wave.

"We did it!" said Fine, arising. "We are at The End!"

May Day dawn. The end of Cape Cod. He walked the few steps to the edge of the high sand promontory, more cliff than dune. As he always did upon first sighting the sea, he quoted a pun from Lewis Carroll: "The sea is but a notion unto me."

John punned back, as always: "Hey, big doin's, here!"

Steph said: "I have *got* to pee!" And disappeared.

"Good Christ!" said John. "Me too!" He unzipped, and Fine, catching a glimpse of his penis, marveled again at the length compared to his own, and, feeling strangely uncomfortable, turned away. He heard the two streams: the male sibilant, the female splashing. Still seeing the genders as more similar than different, he made nothing of this discordance at that time.

The offshore air hit Fine with the freshness of water. His tongue felt muddy and stale from the celebratory cigars and champagne, as if an army had marched across it. He opened his mouth to the ion-rich sea breeze, and looked east. As he'd predicted to the others, everything here—time, space, motion—was fitting together perfectly: the sun, a shaky old lady streaking rouge everywhere but on her cheeks, was nudging up from the edge between sea and sky. To the right and left, the long lines of dunes rolled up and down off into darkness, and behind, the asphalt road burrowed into sea pine, sea grape, locust trees, sawgrass, and heather, vanishing. Fine was a lover of shape. This one pleased him much.

Steph and John rejoined him. He looked up from one to the other, smiling. John was in black tie. Steph wore a white linen dress. Around her long slender neck was the black choker with the tiny diamond he'd given her a year ago for her and John's cabaret-act debut. John's diamond, a matching present, was pinned into his tie.

John raised the last bottle of champagne, and said: "To the end of the beginning." He drank, and handed it to Fine.

"To the beginning of the end." Fine passed it to Steph.

Steph drank, gave the bottle back to Fine, and formed an "O" with her mouth. "Listen!" They heard the wind sing through.

Fine put the bottle to his ear: "I can hear the ocean!"

"In the bottle?" asked Steph.

"Nope. In my other ear! Ha!"

Twirling with the lithe grace of a discus thrower, John hurled the bottle over the slatted fence into the scrub.

Silence, but for the crash and suck of the waves, and for the wind. Fine felt a twinge of emptiness, and filled it with a sudden urge to submerge. To invert himself, turn all inner membranes to the fresh air and water. "I want to turn myself inside out."

"Cold!" said Steph, pulling John's jacket tightly about her.

Fine spread his arms up, and his tuxedo fluttered out behind him like a cape. "Look—it's a bird, it's a plane—"

"—it's Superjew!" said Steph.

"Yes!" said Fine. "I can do anything, everything—even fly! That settles it! I'm going in!" He handed John his tuxedo jacket and sat down to take off his shoes and socks.

"Don't be ridiculous," she said, "it's freezing—"

"Sissy!" He got up, barefoot, sizing up the runway, envisioning the takeoff and the flight.

"Fine," she said, apprehensively, "don't!"

"Just like my mother—don't don't don't!—story of my life!"

"Be careful!"

"Been careful enough for one lifetime already!"

"But there's an undertow—"

"What's an undertow to an *Übermensch?*"

"Come on, man," said John, soberly, "listen to reason—this is how people get killed—at my high school prom in South Boston—"

"What better time to die? In the long run, life is short!" Fine swooped back around the car to get a running start and then before they could grab him, with a shout he ran straight off the edge of the cliff, and tumbled head over heels down the slope, everything sandy, sandpapery, gritty, and yet somehow clean and fresh. Like a total body manicure, he thought. He hit the bottom rolling, and up on his feet he clunked along sinking deep into soft sand and then, gathering speed on the harder stuff and desperately out of breath and knowing that if he stopped he'd never do it, closing his eyes he hit the water full tilt, splashed with his right leg, staggered with his left, tilted forward, bounced off the flat ebb like a snub-nosed torpedo, plunged smack into the first big wave and, buried by six feet of solid saltwater, was sucked on out toward Iceland.

He could well have been drowned. Such, at that time, was the

Fine exuberance. Four years earlier, when asked on his application to Harvard Medical School to "give a brief candid description of your personality," he'd written: "Fine is trustworthy, loyal, helpful, friendly, courteous, kind, obedient, cheerful, thrifty, brave, clean, and reverent." The Boy Scout Oath. Knowing from his years at Yale that universities revered style over substance, knowing that he looked great on paper, he knew they couldn't refuse him.

Fine emerged bellowing, skin afire with pain. They were running toward him, John carrying the red blanket that Fine had bought off the back of an Arab in Marrakech, on his trip to Morocco with Steph during college. Fine had never felt colder, and yet later he would recall that he never felt better. More than anything in the world he wanted to be curled down into the warmth of that blanket. And yet, strangely, part of him wanted it never to be.

"Hold me!" he cried through his pain, eyes tearing.

They stripped off his wet clothes, wrapped him in the blanket, and sat huddled with him, cuddling.

"Didn't we tell you it'd be cold?" said John.

"C . . . c . . . cold, hell," said Fine, teeth chattering, shivering, "c . . . old enough t'make me . . . ee cry!"

"Know what that water is?" asked Steph, teasingly. They did not. "Cryogenic!"

They groaned. Fine was sure he'd never be warm again.

The earth spun on. Like magic, it got hot. The sun broke through the mist, pulling a furry warm rabbit out of the hat of the day. Everything went golden. A soft humid breeze lifted up off the Gulf Stream and chased the gravelly North Wind away. Steph, the world traveler, acutely sensitive to smell, swore she could pick up auras of the tropics—orange blossom, yellow jasmine, coconut. As the tide retreated, the heat steamed up from the drying beach. Warming, Fine said: "A magical day!"

His usual effusiveness. And yet, it was truly a seam in three lives. Each was about to graduate: Fine from Harvard Medical School, Stephanie and John from Harvard College. They'd lived side by side in Adams House for three years, Fine as resident tutor for premeds, they as undergraduates. Steph and John, having written a joint thesis ("The Psychohistory of George Washington"), were getting a magna in History. Fine, the scientist, in med school had done research in neurophysiology: he taught grasshoppers to lift their legs. He was copping a med-school summa for his surprise winner: "Higher Knowledge in Lower Forms: The Biological Basis of Learning in *Schistocerca gregaria* (the Grasshopper)." They'd had an all-night graduation and good-bye party. John was off to Ireland to study acting at the Abbey Theatre, Dublin; Steph was off to Paris to learn her father's import/export business (her childhood years in Europe accounted for her graduating Radcliffe at twenty-five); Fine was diving into his psychiatric training at McLean Hospital in Belmont, just outside Boston. The party had melded into May Day, John's twenty-third birthday. On impulse, Fine insisted that in this ending of things they must drive immediately to "The End" of Cape Cod to see the sunrise together.

What hadn't they done together, this tight threesome?! Steph and Fine had fallen in love the summer before Fine's final year in high school. She'd entered Radcliffe when he'd entered Harvard Med. Their sophomore year, they'd had neighboring rooms in Adams House. Directly across the hall was a tall, sandy-haired, and graceful fellow named John James Michael O'Day, Jr. As John put it: "Of the O'Days of South Boston and two trips to Ireland."

The two Jews befriended the Catholic. His presence gave all three a sense of completion, as if each alone, and any duo, was unfulfilled. Each seemed to hold a hidden missing part of each other. And so each provided, and all provided, for the three. Yet it was not an equal providence—Fine, the oldest and most mentally intimidating, was always the rock-solid center of it all. In his own family an older brother, Fine was like an older brother Steph and John had wished for. As center, he kept them all centered. And so they'd been together constantly, a troika filled with the crazy daring, the sudden blossoming, that comes only once, with the daffodils of a life.

At two that morning, as the party was dissipating, they'd piled into Steph's elongated grape of a car and raced the receding dark down Route 3, to the great dunes at Wellfleet, Newcomb Hollow Beach. They'd sung much of the way—Stephanie and John doing their twenties cabaret act featuring Mabel Mercer. They'd made it on time, just as the line between sea and sky had begun to crinkle into light.

And so the threesome sat, huddled together, toasting on the deserted beach.

"The rising of the sun," said Steph.

"Nope," said Fine, "the turning of the earth itself."

"How can you know that for sure?"

"Accumulated knowledge—'Thirty days hath September.' "

"Just think," she said, "half the world is getting up and half the world is going to sleep."

Fine felt John's body sagging heavily against him, a rough snore rattling in his ear. "Right—help me put John James to bed."

They often played parents to John. As Fine supported John's head, Steph rolled together Fine's wet clothes into a pillow. She bent over, and Fine found himself looking down her swoop-neck dress at her breasts. He thought himself a "breast man," and hers had always been, for him, exquisite. There was something ultra-erotic about looking down her cleavage—as if he could dive in, tongue first, pull the smooth elastic skin around his ears and muffle out all but the quintessence of the sensual. Boobies! Slick, smooth, soft. He yearned to have breasts—no—to *be* breasts, and in seeing and touching and sucking them, he felt almost one with the special fullness, the nurturant curve, of the woman he loved. He followed the swell to the brown rim of areolae. She knew that he loved watching the free movement of her breasts and the way that the rub of nipple against cloth would often bring them erect, and she rarely wore bras anymore. Fine said: "Oh my, my 'natural girl.' " She looked at him looking, and laughed. Her breasts swayed.

She was a closet exhibitionist; he a closet voyeur. Oh, the day they'd found that out! Bliss, Fine recalled, and bliss!

Fine the peeper was expert in sighting mammary tissue through clothing—in through the armpit, across through the billowed blouse between buttons, down through the top in a multitude of sight-paths and, occasionally, up through the bottom. Peeping down any dress drove Fine nuts. Peeping down hers was unbearable.

Together they lowered John's head to the soggy pillow.

"Steph, I'm wild about your boobies!" said Fine.

John opened his eyes, bloodshot and dazed, and, feigning "gay," mumbled: " 'Boobies'? Oh Fine, you sweetie, you just will

not be one of the boys!" He smiled, snuggled into the makeshift
pillow, and sighed, the cool damp a relief to his booze-fevered
brow. He kept his eyes open, looking from one to the other, for a
while.

While not unusual, his intrusion was startling.

Over the years, John had often been present when they'd gotten
physical. Like a gangly brother, he'd seen various degrees of nakedness of each and both. Stephanie, proud of her body and relaxed about her dress, sometimes caught him looking—knowing
he was seeing an edge of breast, a high inside of thigh—once,
even, when, in her rush to get ready, Fine's bathrobe slipped
open, the whole frontal view, boobs to bush, and when she turned,
buns; "boobs, bush, buns"—it had become a joke between them.
They'd handled it like family seeing family. It wasn't sensual, it
just was. When she and John had acted together, they'd seen each
other naked in the dressing room. Once, early on, John had
barged in on them making love. Embarrassed, muttering, he'd
backed out. They'd been in the orthodox missionary position.
John's view was mostly of Fine's big pumping butt. Turned on,
they were going at it hard. Steph, close to orgasm, was whimpering—she knew John had heard her sharp cries. Yet she was relieved—ten minutes sooner, he'd've found them in their latest
discovery: *soixante-neuf.* John referred to it thereafter as "the
beast with two backs." In the time John had known them, their
sex had come to bloom, each year richer. It had been the greatest
of erotic experiments, for it had been fueled by love. They tried
just about everything that two could try. They'd wondered
whether it was bothering John. Fine, with his usual boldness—he
felt if he knocked, rationally, on the door of Truth it would open
—asked:

"Does it bother you?"

John laughed, and said: "No."

It did.

An actor, John lived and breathed affectation. His latest was to
act gay. They knew he was at least hetero; they had no evidence
for homo too. It had started with his fey portrayal of Sir Andrew
in *Twelfth Night.* John the star had always had all the women
he'd wanted. Each affair was theatrical, florid, kinky, infantile,
and tragic—sometimes all in a single afternoon. John James had
told Fine about how as a teen, masturbating, he'd always turned

the statue of the Virgin around to face the wall. As a joke Fine had presented John with a monograph by Freud: *Zur Onanie-Diskussion,* 1912 *(On Masturbation).* John, unamused, asked: "Is this above my head?"

Fine, delighted, replied: "No, it's between your legs."

To recoup, in his best Viennese accent, John read:

"We are at all events confronted in the neuroses with cases in which masturbation has done damage. . . . On the basis of my medical experience, I cannot rule out a permanent reduction in potency as one among the results of masturbation. . . . This, however, cannot be classed unhesitatingly among the injurious ones. Some diminution of male potency and of the brutal aggressiveness involved in it is much to the purpose from the point of view of civilization. Virtue accompanied by full potency is usually felt as a hard task."

"*Hard* indeed," John had said, laughing too hard. "Sounds like he stole it from the Church—listen to the ending: 'We are all agreed on one thing—the subject of masturbation is quite inexhaustible.'"

Now John looked from Steph to Fine, his eyes riveting them in turn. "Still in love?" he asked, and then, turning on his stomach with a sigh, muttered: "What a goddamn relief."

As he often did, an actor bored with the *mere*-ness of the world and living at a slight tilt to it, he'd put a spot light full up on them. Steph and Fine sensed he wasn't just playing this time; this was a rare straight shot from his heart. Fine's skin crawled—the moment felt omenic. Like a hologram, all—all, all, all—was encoded in the feeling as Steph and Fine nuzzled above John. An enchanted pyramid had tipped, fallen on its side, freeing some force set in motion long ago to gather speed, just past the edges of their sight. It was nebulous but inevitable, flushed with power and nostalgia, like melancholy music from an unseen flute.

John conked out. Fine the *schtupper* was not to be denied. He looked from her long lashes into her dark blue eyes—"lacustrine" someone once had called them—eyes so chillingly dissonant against her raven hair and Modigliani face—and stared at her perfect imperfection, her right lip and cheek pulled ever so slightly down (from a mild childhood Bell's Palsy) into a charm-

ing pout. He bent across John and kissed her wetly on her right
shoulder, where the trapezius met the deltoid rim. She looked
down, saw, in his bushy red curls, his penis growing bigger,
thicker.

"Look at Fine," she said, "oooh! Cute!"

"Stephanie Dear"—their second-oldest pun, on her last name
—"I really want you!"

"Now?"

"Yes!"

"Can't you wait?"

"No! Come on—the dunes—hurry!"

He held out his hand and she took it, and they half-walked,
half-ran down the tideline. She, taller than he, had her arm
around his shoulder. His curly brown-red hair brushed her jaw.
He was the proud possessor of an erection that wouldn't quit, and
even as he walked, naked under the red blanket, his anticipation
was such that his penis stuck out from his body like a stick from a
candy apple. They turned up the steep water-etched slope to a
break in the high dunes and followed the curl of a path up into a
hollow, shielded from the morning wind by a gnarled and fragrant pine.

Fine spread the blanket, lay down on his back. Stephanie stood,
facing away. Through the diaphanous white, as if the cloth had
evaporated, came the sharp outline: legs thin, broadening in an
inverted V to meet at the top; rump flatter than one would have
thought, yet still rounded, and then, his favorite, her breasts. She
turned, looking up toward Provincetown. Her breasts swooped
out with the relaxed curve of a chain hung between posts—cate-
nary—and then up, up, to the conical perky tips. Her long dark
hair splashed over her shoulders. She turned her head, saw him
staring, a turn-on. He watched, bursting with anticipation, as her
nipples—his favorite of favorites—rose to bud. Big and nubbled,
they stuck out like antennae, now, lifting her light dress higher.

Slowly, she unbuttoned. She wore pink satin panties, imported
via daddy from France. Enjoying the moment, she bent, breasts
hanging, and pulled the panties down, rolling them up into a rope
of pungent satin, stepping out, straightening, arms high to the
sky, breasts up. As fresh a moment as life can hold, Fine thought,
she has become my wish, my sweet dream. She laughed, and,
twirling the panties on her index finger, whirled around, a

chanced-upon dancer moving with all the lost grace and clumsy freedom of a little girl. And yet, big girl—her thighs so lithe, her breasts so many-shaped: as she bent down, full and hanging, and as she twirled, head back, so pointed, and as she stretched, so small, almost boylike. A whirling dervish. Fine said: "A sufi!"

"Yeah!" She laughed: "*Ça suffit.*"

Her body stopped spinning. Almost palpably, their shared wish —a life together—as if to balance, in the opposite direction, spun on. Dizzy, she fell. She grabbed the trunk of a scrub pine, holding tight, as if the revolution of the earth itself would throw her off.

On his back, he reached out his arms to her. His penis was so hard and thick, it seemed that, rather than it being part of him, he was part of it. All his being had flowed into that tight-packed cylinder—the essence of lust, bursting. Straddling him, she lowered herself, arms akimbo. Eye to eye, warmth and caring flowed between them. He looked down and saw a remarkable sight: above his penis, below her cunt, the sun. Her hairs were a little goatee, backlit, almost aglow. A shape so concordant it must mean that it was meant.

And then it was gone, and he rubbed once against her lips and, with a little sigh of pleasure, she eased down to him and he eased in to her. She held him, skin to skin, wet. Home, home, homefree. Given each of their families, their home away from home.

They made love. Fine, averse to inferior positions, was soon on top. Totally out of control, he was wild, veins bulging, face reddened, puffing like a flat-out pony.

Fine's eroticism was quite adolescent at that time.

Their lovemaking became edged, sharp, almost angry—hissing and slashing at each other like animals, crying and gasping—as if there were something out there, something so mysterious, threatening, and desperately wrong that they had to use all their joint sensual power to keep it at bay.

Afterward, the gentleness was commensurate with the savagery. So quiet—as if the wind itself was holding its breath.

Stephanie began to cry. Fine asked: "What's wrong?"

"We've loved each other a long time, kid."

"Kid" was what her father called her. "Yeah, kid," Fine answered, "like we were imprinted on each other."

"My buddy. I feel like I awoke from a dream, and there you were! I love you as much as I can ever love anyone. As much as

God must love this day." She cried hard. "Out there, love, is France."

"So?"

"Anything could happen to us."

"Hey, kid, come on—nothing will."

"I'm scared! Help me, Fine!"

Having learned from her that feeling, heart to heart, is the only comfort, ever, he held her: "I'm here, love, I'm here."

Yet his attention wandered, to a lone gull hanging low over the edge of the dune. Facing into the sea breeze, it was balanced exquisitely between the lift of wing on sea breeze, up, and the drag of gravity on mass, down. From the rear the gull seemed suspended, motionless, the head swinging back and forth, culling the unseen beach for food. The beak went this way, then that, a pendulum slung from the bullet-shaped body, silent but for the flutter and rush of wind. Closing his eyes, Fine could see the equations that held it there.

After a while, soothed, she rose. Wordlessly, she unrolled her panties, wiggled them up. Shaking the sand from her dress, she balanced precariously, and stepped into it, sliding it up, slipping thin straps over her smooth shoulders. With her fingers, she combed out her hair, the strands floating freely on the quickening breeze.

They sensed it was time to go back to their lonely friend.

She reached out her hand to Fine, palm up, and, with a somber and quizzical look, did the strangest thing, something she hadn't done in years: she called him by his first name.

Fine blushed. Feeling surged up, rushed through him, smacking against bone and splashing into cavities so that he felt almost seasick, finally pooling in, of all obscure places, his left leg?

Of course his left leg! The unconscious never lies!

In an avalanche of emotion he remembered the first time he'd feared his first name.

2

ON A STIFLING hot August day when he'd just turned four, Fine was peddling his tricycle along behind his mother. She was eight months pregnant with what would turn out to be his brother, Moe. They were on the one main street of Columbia, New York, a backwater town on the Hudson River. It was just about the time he was becoming aware of the existence of God. Fine asked his mother:

"Do you love me?"

His mother Anna, in four years of doing her best to feed the ravenous curiosity of her strange firstborn, had settled into a passionate, loving bewilderment. That afternoon she—enormous, hot, varicose—answered without turning around. He didn't hear her. Wanting desperately to *know*, he asked her again, peddling his tricycle furiously, awkwardly, to catch up with her.

He rammed her from behind, buckling her knees. She screamed out his first name and toppled down upon him, snapping his left leg below the knee.

He never recalled the pain. But for the violence of her shrieking his name in warning—twisting it all out of shape—his memories of the event were pleasant: a tactile and fleshy landslide. Anna was beside herself with fear for him and her unborn. She called to him, tried to bend to him. One hand palpating her own belly, the other reached down toward him, urging him to rise. He took her hand and was propped up. But then, more to his amazement than distress, one leg went all watery, light and weak, and he fell down.

As often the case with accidents, orthodox samaritans were right there: two painters, Ben and Curt, touching up the marquee of the town's only movie theater, the Columbia.

And then the most extraordinary thing happened: as if by a miracle, he was lifted up, high, high, high up over the hard scratchy concrete where he had fallen, cradled on the shoulders of these painters, arm around Ben's neck, legs straddling Curt's shoulders. And then, painlessly and smoothly and higher than he'd ever been before, he floated along high above the gravity of his former world, home. In one fell swoop, the clunky spasticity of the child metamorphosed into airy gossamer, as delicate yet as purposeful as the million seedlings of the fuzz of a dandelion. Like magic—religious magic ("Let there be . . .")—heavy had been transformed to light.

Thus began Fine's lifelong love of the smell of turpentine and the pursuit of flight. Carved into his unconscious was a sort of law of divine flotation: If one cannot walk, one will be carried.

As often in life, what seemed at first a disaster was in fact a blessing. Like the broken bones, the psyche, healing, knit together more strongly for the breaking. Calcium—which was to become the obsession, the lodestone in Fine's later, medical life—thus entered, here.

Fine's father Leo, a kosher butcher, instead of attending to the birth of the second child—Moe, having had enough of these screams, these bends, these painters, bolted for his own light twenty hours later—attended to the injury of the first. He took Fine to the hospital for X-rays—for the rest of his life Fine had the recurrent nightmare of being strapped down to an icy metal sheet, shapes tilting and sliding with no solid landmarks, he trying to escape and yet being trapped, pinned, immobile—and, when old Doc Levine put a detachable hinged cast on Fine's leg, every night the grizzly butcher would take off the cast and spend hours rubbing, on his little calf, cocoa butter (another enchanted scent). Father, a simple, straightforward man also bewildered by his pre-cocious, already complex son, would read to him for hours at a time while mother tended to the shaken baby. And so son, rather than competing against father, formed a close, deep bond with him. Without malice, through love, from Leo, he got it all.

And his strength—his ballooning self-esteem evidenced in his solidity, his *thereness*—his strength that would eventually be his weakness and unravel him before it was enlisted again to try to ravel him back up, was molded. His first awareness?

Number one, a magical sense of himself, a feeling of being *meta*mortal; like a Superman of the mind, from another planet.

Number two, his pathological aversion to his first name.

Everyone noticed it and no one understood it: whenever he was called by his first name, he would scream, shield his head with his hands and scuttle backward, as if a ton of bricks—(later, "an atom bomb")—were about to fall on him. His parents and relatives avoided using his name. What to call him? Immobile at a crucial eating age, with his dedicated, perplexed, and guilty mother showing her love through food, he ate. He got fat. He was nicknamed "Bubby."

Like most people of greater mass, he began to fall prey to his greater inertia (mass times acceleration). If he was stopped, he stayed stopped. Once started, he persevered. His heritage was Ashkenazi—Eastern European Jewry. Many of his forebears, including the two luminous males—a wealthy fruit peddler named Fuchs, from Pinsk; a poor Rabbi Leazar ben Epstein, from Kolomea—had been just as thick ankled, built low to the ground for solidity, for speed. The women were tall, fair, red haired, and attractive—as his mother still was. Columbians often wondered how plump, balding, dark little Leo had gotten buxom Anna. Born in Europe and growing up in New York City, they'd come to Columbia after the war, a distant carom off Hitler. They were American, consumingly: they used Ajax, slept on a Sealy Posturepedic, saw the USA in their Chevrolet. Their past was known and yet, being un-Columbian, mysterious. Fine was born in Columbia Memorial. Myths of Leo's potency suffused the town.

One day soon after his leg was again sound, Fine came down from the living quarters into the butcher shop, quizzical look on his face. There—standing in the light, blood-speckled layer of sawdust, before the hanging rubbery-necked chickens and the glassed-in slabs of bloodless red meat nestled next to displaced viscera in a true cornucopia of offal, all permeated with a musty-rich effluvia of life-meat-sawdust-death—there in the shop where

Leo hacked and carved and Anna rooked customers by weighing a piece of her hand with the meat, Fine asked his father: "Poppa? Is God everywhere?"

"Yeh," said Leo, absentmindedly. He was stripping brisket for Mrs. Flora ("Faith") Geiger at the time.

"So when I came into the shop I squeezed some of God out?"

"What?" Fine repeated the question. "Oh boy!" said Leo. He knew enough to know this was "smart."

Before he was five, Fine had, de novo, rediscovered the Theorem of Pythagoras. Soon thereafter, a "prodigy," he'd begun to see the harmonic shapes in math, chess, and music. And then in the world itself. Set in motion by an insatiable curiosity, the onslaught of his "strange" questions accelerated: "Poppa, what is 'real'?" And: "Poppa, how do I know I'm not dreaming?"

They sent him to the rabbi, an ancient, yellowing, kabbalic refugee, for instruction. On the first day, the rabbi tried to teach Fine the phonetics of the Hebrew alphabet: "Aleph—Ahhh," said the rabbi. He had very bad breath. Fine, thinking he meant the letter A, repeated: "Aleph—Ay."

"Aleph—Ahhh." The rabbi reached for the Ping-Pong paddle.

"Aleph—Ay," said Fine, not grasping the phonetic/nominal distinction, turning his head from the yellow-toothed stench.

"*Oy!* Not the letter A, the sound Ahhh," said the rabbi, in his voice the thought "What kind of idiot they send me now?"

"Aleph—Ahhh," Fine said, but, never one to leave well enough alone, adding, "but it should be Ay."

"Ahhh! I'll *creeple* you!" The rabbi slammed Fine over the head with the Ping-Pong paddle.

"Ah-HAH!" cried Fine, secretly thinking Ay.

He cried his way home. He burst in on Anna as she was sitting in bright sunlight nursing Moe. Shocked by his tears, she put down the happy baby and held out her arms to him. Fine felt her offering her love and wanted desperately to open up to her, but could not respond. Something about her lush beauty, her huge bared red nipple still oozing milk, the baby—no! Shapes came between them—venetian blinds skewed just enough so the light, sectored, obscured her from him. To open up would mean to be showered with unbearable light. Even keeping his distance, feeling her love, he was paralyzed by the imagined glare, almost blinded. He stared at her and then turned away. She called his name but he, ashamed, went up to his room and cried, feeling the pain of repudiation, the mutual wrench of hearts, and—fleetingly—a shadowy, excited anger. He suffered alone. The mystery between them deepened, prevailed.

Fine became a small-town misfit. Many thought him retarded. In his early growing years his creative vision was buried under layers of puzzlement and ridicule. His first name, in any form, could be used for this ridicule. Any who cared for him dared not use it.

I will refrain from using it here.

He fed his despair with food. He became addicted to Sunshine Mallopuffs: pink, rubbery, elastic things "With Real Coconut Topping." He grew a blubbery body, which led the schoolgirls to walk along behind him, making fun of his fat *pupik.* The town was blatantly anti-semitic. The public school, staffed by well-meaning provincial dolts straight out of Chekhov—or even Gogol —was a constant source of boredom for Fine. Deadened, he took to counting his pulse. At times he thought his heart had stopped —bored to death. From grade-two roll call, Fine's first name brought great eruptions of laughter and mockery. Bubby was soon used in classrooms as well as home. In sports, the local currency for boys, Fine was a prodigal klutz. In a down-at-the-heels town where Jews were a well-off, civic-minded minority, a blubbery daydreaming *schlemiel* who was the class "brain" was a prime target, and he was hounded, hit, pants pulled down and taunted—his student government election posters defaced with swastikas—with all the ruthless sadism of that Third Reich festering within every child. He learned, in school, to make a 100 while playing dumb, hiding his grades from the others. He never spoke in class. If he spoke in public, it was to sound stupid. In junior high in particular, a slew of ruthless Lutherans caucused with some tough Catholics and came out punching the two Jewboys, Fine and Eddie "Nose" Cohen. Nose was dumb and athletic, street-smart enough to ally himself with the other basketball wizards, the blacks. Fine followed Nose and the amazingly graceful blacks like a shadow, feeding countless lay-ups and jumpers in return for protection on the walk to and from school. Outside the house, Fine was afraid. He assumed everyone felt the same way. To be alive meant they could get you. He grew paranoid.

And so Fine retreated further, from his vicious schoolmates

and from his perplexed family. Younger brother Moe was turning
out to be his opposite in many ways: with Anna's height and
handsomeness, slow to learn and slow to argue, blindly affection-
ate, curious about meat, a joy to have around. Leo, Anna, and
Moe made sense; the space invader did not. And so Fine would lie
on his bed, earphones over ears, reading everything: *Talmud, Ge-
mara, Kabbala* (on the second day he'd grasped phonetics and on
the third the whole Hebrew alphabet as well as the doctrine of
metempsychosis [Pythagoras again] and from then on joined the
long tradition of Jews with photographic memories sucking up
knowledge), Aristotle, Newton, Einstein, Frege, Morphy,
Riemann, Gödel, Gauss, Bach, Spinoza, Beethoven—the last
shapes of Beethoven so much more difficult to see but definitely
there, and even more pleasing, eventually, for their asymmetry.
He sensed the Beethoven-shapes going past the Bach in the same
way the Einstein-shapes were a going-past Newton. Reading was
a way of focusing the shapes inside his skull, clicking his into
theirs.

From an early age he tried to engage Leo and Anna in his
world, encouraging them to debate. They, amazed, in awe, encouraged him as best they could, with food, and with love.

One bright moment came at age eleven. Fine published a paper
in *Gen. Relativ. J.:* "Wave Motion Through a Torus—Using
Quantum Gravity Theory to Show Blurring Between Past and
Future." Soon thereafter, on a Friday, a cheery crew-cut fellow
named Ron from NASA showed up at the Fine home, aeronauti-
cal problem in hand. Fine, racing against sundown—the shabbas
ban on writing—solved it in time. Ron from NASA said: "Bub,
you're a great American!"

Fine felt good that at least his country appreciated him. And
Ron from NASA returned, carrying his "stumpers," many times
more.

At puberty, on the eve of bar mitzvah, things exploded. First
came the volcanic eruption of testosterone. Fine bought binoculars. By night he peeped from his darkened bedroom window at
the detonating Bertha Schlagel. By day she shunned him. And yet
an even worse rejection was from Leo: realizing that staying kosher meant staying poor, he decided to open up half the shop to
nonkosher meats. What a storm among the Jews! The family
fought ostracism. Leo, pride on the line, worked like a demon,

night and day. Fine Meats soon began to prosper, as the son, abandoned by his father, withered. The new Kitchenaid made no difference to Fine.

One day, soon after he'd begun to shave, as he raised his Gillette double-edged razor to the lather, half his face slammed shut! Shocked, he stared. Again! The whole right side—scalp, eye, mouth—scrunched together as if yanked by a wire tied to his left ear! Appalled, he watched himself convulse—a mix of grimace and wink—out of control. He had developed a tic!

One can well imagine the taunts. The family, sympathetic but unaware, took him to old Doc Levine, who found nothing wrong. Fine felt it was his own fault—punishment for peeping at Bertha? —something willful to be willed away. No one disagreed. With attention, it worsened. Soon it became unbearable, but for it being borne.

Fine despaired of ever being able to see the shapes in human beings. People were unpredictable, emotional, chaotic, a puzzle. As he read the biographies of people like himself, he discovered, to his despair, that he was halfway down the road to a comforting yet dread isolation, perhaps leading to madness. He—and everyone else in Columbia, New York—knew about madness. The New York State Facility for Mental Hygiene was a mile out of town, up the Germantown road. A "shock box"—ring the doorbell, you get your first electroconvulsive treatment—it played an important part in the life of the town. The insane had been a vital part of the Fine boyhood. He'd often see them on outings on the main street, linked together fearfully, a human crocodile. He recognized their tentativeness and fear in the world—and their spasticity—as quite like his own. He would follow them along at a safe distance, fascinated—even talk to them, enchanted by their skewed view of the world, and their friendly acceptance of him. Bored to death, he was astounded to find that of all the people in his life, the lunatics were not dull! Later, Nose and he would sneak over the stone walls of the Facility to watch free movies with Nose's weepy father, a shell of his former self after all the ECT, a man in "Lady's Foundations" fallen quickly and astoundingly low. Given the stifling, cruelly bigoted small town and given the lunatics, Fine preferred the lunatics.

And so, after the third year of high school, ostracized by all but Nose and the blacks, yet to have his first date, Fine feared he was going mad. He told no one. Silence became his ken. There was no treatment except the short hop out to Mental Hygiene in Germantown. Columbia, rich in doctors for the body, never took much to doctoring the mind. Repression being dominant, psychopathology was florid. Like all small towns, Columbia was brimful of lunacy. All-American wholesomeness, far from being part of the cure, was part of the disease. Such, he grew to think, was the effect of close human contact: the friction, ignited by gossip, blazed into a grand inhumanity, featuring brutality, immorality, decay, madness. Fine became obsessed with a fact he'd read in the biography of another brain: Turing, the Briton who cracked Enigma and saved the free world from the Nazis, had committed suicide with a bite from a cyanide-laced apple. Fine willed himself on.

But then . . .

3

BUT THEN IN June after his junior year, at Tanglewood, the summer home of the Boston Symphony, by chance, each on the little island of each family's blanket, side by side on the great lawn in the softest part of the twilight, he met her.

Just before the start of the concert, final soggy strudel of the picnic consumed, Fine edged away from Leo and Anna to the far side of the blanket, full of dinner and anxious to escape the heavy grand opera of the family Fine and wrap himself in one of his few pleasures, classical music. It would be Van Cliburn and Brahms. The lawn was crowded with blanketeers. Fine, ever alert to food, knew that the couple on the next blanket had done the gourmand trip: as opposed to his family's greasy chicken, cement latkes, seltzer, and beer, they were finishing their pâté, salmon, endive salad, and Macon. In place of Anna's acrid anti–mosquito bomb, they'd erected two long tapers in silver candlesticks. Fine watched them nibble a fresh strawberry tart, washed down with Barsac. His mouth watered.

Suddenly a girl dressed in black rushed up and sat down on the contiguous edge of the blankets next to Fine, facing away. Something about her—the black of her dress, the flow of her hair, the scent of cherry, or the shape of the curve of her back from thigh

to shoulder—or perhaps something biochemical, a pheromone—
something pulled him toward her. He half-wanted her never to
turn around, for she would be certain to spoil his fantasy in either
of two ways: if she were ugly, the reality would spoil the imagined
face, the imagined breasts; if beautiful, she would take one look
and turn away.

She turned, settling herself down with a wide wedge of tart.

Their eyes met. Fine felt his heart break loose from its moor-
ings and float up to his throat. It was love at first sight. And with
the surge came the ebb, the expectation that this beautiful face—
with its slightly dragging lip?!—would see him and fall.

But no! She smiled! More—she spoke: "Hi—who're you?"

Fine, flummoxed: "Who, me?"

"Yes."

"I'm Fine."

"Really?"

"Yes."

"Just Fine?" She chuckled.

Fine had never seen anything so glowing, so alight in the twilight, as her smile, and he did what he'd never done before with a
girl, told the truth. "Not really. Actually, I'm miserable."

"Join the crowd."

"*You?!* You too!?"

"Call me Steffy."

"You too, *Steffy?!*"

"You bet."

"Why?"

"Just broke up with that jerk Jason—he's over there."

For the first time in ages, Fine answered spontaneously: "But
you're too good-looking to be beautiful—I mean, miserable."

She looked at him as if he were from Mars, and laughed. He
had never heard a shape so melodic. Applause. Van Cliburn had
arrived. In the expectant hush they fell silent, laughed, tuned in.

Van spread "the trapezoids of Brahms" (Fine) out over the cool
mellowing Berkshires. By the end of the first movement she had
slipped him a wedge of tart, a sip of sweet wine. The strawberry-
Barsac on his tongue mixed with the cherry and skin-scent of her
body. Happy, Fine waited for the ax to fall. For all he knew, given
her skin, eyes, and sparkle, she was Italian. Her brother would
beat him to a pulp. The music ended, the applause began.

"I'm bored!" she said.

Fine knew this was his big chance, but he was terrified. Pheromone, fear a moan. He blurted out: "Would you like to have a drink of water?"

"Our first date! C'mon!"

They got up. For her parents this was nothing new. For his, it was a miracle. They watched him walk off, mouths agape. Well, thought Fine to himself, at least once in my life I will have walked across a lawn with a beautiful girl. If Nose could see me now! His hope rose higher, and, sensing that he now had a greater distance to fall, he itemized once again his plans for suicide.

Fine walked her to the water fountain. After two clumsy tries, he managed to hold the knob down while she drank. On the way back, she held his hand. No one within living memory had held the Fine hand before. It tingled with life, as if just born. And then it sweated. She asked: "What's your first name, Fine?"

"I'd rather not say at this point and what's your last?"

"Caro."

" 'Caro?!' "

"Don't worry, I'm not Italian."

"I know."

"How do you know?"

Fine said he knew Caro to be an eminent Sephardic Jewish name. He had just finished reading the Gordon biography of the most famous Caro: *The Maggid of Caro—The Mystic Life of the Eminent Codifier Joseph Caro (1488–1575) as Revealed in His Secret Diary.* "Of course, I don't mean to imply that there's any direct link—"

"But there is!"

"Yes?" She nodded. "Gosh!" She laughed. "What's funny?"

"You! You're funny!"

"That's not funny!" he said, bursting out laughing.

"Then why are you laughing?"

"Who knows? 'Cause you are!"

"You are a dummy," she said, kindly, "aren't you?"

"I am very sensitive to people laughing at me."

"Why? It's the way Jews are!"

"Who says?"

"My grandpa Al—he's a Yiddish comic—he says: 'Show me a

Jew, I'll tell you a joke!' " They laughed, together. "New York's full of laughing Jews. Miserable, laughing, Jews. Millions of 'em!"

"In my town, I'm the only Jew my age."

"You're joking!"

"Well, there's one other: my friend Nose Cohen."

"Nose Cohen! I love it! That's funny! You're funny!"

"I am?"

"Yes! Wait'll Grandpa Al meets you—he's coming up next month—we've got a house on Copake Lake for the whole summer, and—"

"Funny-haha or funny-queer?" said Fine, perseverating.

"Funny-haha! Whydja get upset when I said you were funny?"

"It's a long story. It has to do with funny-queer."

"Great—we'll forget about the rest of this dumb music and walk around and you can tell me all about it. C'mon—"

At that, Fine's tic attacked.

Startled, she stared at him. "Was that a wink?"

"Nope. It's . . . a . . . my tic. Nerves, you know?" He cringed, awaiting the ridicule. But then, to his surprise her face filled with sympathy, her lower lip pouted out—crookedly!—as if furious at the cruelty of fate, and, eyes glistening, she said: "Oh, you poor kid! You poor, poor kid!"

That did it. As they walked in the dark hand in hand, Fine opened up. Her comments were a revelation: if he could laugh at himself, others would join in, *with* him; like a stand-up comic *(her* dream), he'd have to learn to make fun of his own ass. "It's big enough, isn't it? Ha!" He asked about her parents, the two on the blanket. Her father—a tall slender dark-eyed man born in Paris who could've passed for a count—she adored. She'd been battling her mother—a glamorous, elegantly dressed blonde who worked as an editor at Vogue—"forever." By the end of their walk she'd told him her first Yiddish *shtick* joke—("Two Jews are in Jersey . . ."), and they'd begun to fall in love. As they parted, she said: "Besides, kid, it could be worse—*both* sides of your face could tic out, okay?"

And the larger revelation, keeping Fine awake all that night: someone had listened to him, taken it in, and responded. It seemed to him that no one had ever done that before in his life.

That short full summer they were together constantly. Fine's life began to run more smoothly. She became, for him, a link to

others, a lifeline to life itself. His family had an initial suspicion
about her lineage—solved by the parchment-skinned rabbi who,
when he found out that she was "a descendant of the 'Maran *Beth
Joseph*'" (Caro's famous commentary that, from 1542, was *the*
source for rabbinical judgments), got so excited his blood pressure
went up and he went blind in one eye for five days. After that,
Anna, conquering the inferiority the Ashkenazim felt in the presence of the Sephardim, welcomed her into the Fine home. Her
humor enlivened Leo, and her glamour relit Anna. She insisted on
meeting Nose Cohen. Fine delayed, but finally the meeting occurred. Nose went nuts. He tried all his tricks. For a few tense
hours Fine thought he'd lost her to Nose—Nose the Athlete,
Nose the Charming, Nose the Stud (a year before, first on the
block to catch the clap)—but no! Steffy chose Fine! The nerd got
the girl!

And did something even better: hearing that Fine had been
hanging around with the basketball players for protection, Stephanie suggested that Fine become the manager, next year, of the
team.

"Oh come on," Fine said, "that's a nerdy job."

"Fine," she said, laughing, "you'd be perfect for it."

And Fine did it. A real turning point in his life, like the day he
learned to put on his socks *before* his shoes. Fine was perfect for it
in another sense—strategy. He discovered how to steal basketballs
from Pressman's Army-Navy (deflate, slip beneath shirt, walk
out), and he was fantastic at deciphering the shapes of the ongo-
ing game, sensing in the topological patterns, the flow. His scientific analysis complemented Coach Ryan's tough pep talks:
"Cohoes thinks they're so good they think their shit don't stink!"
On the recommendation of Roosevelt the black center who
could've won a beauty contest in Senegal (Fine was doing his
homework), they gave Fine a uniform, number 34. The
Bluehawks came home Class-D champs. Nose and Roosevelt got
scholarships to Oneonta Community and Texas Western, respectively. Fine joined the human race.

And so by the laws of chance she saved him. He, by the same
laws, saved her. He showed her the shape in the world; she
showed him the free-form of a woman. She made him see the
limits of his seeing; he made her see her own. Each the obverse of
each, they mirrored, matched. The core of their love was humor.

Fine was so different from his world, he only needed her permission to see the disjuncture as funny. She said: "You don't have to be the same as those clowns who reject you—just be yourself."

"*Me?* It's not enough."

"It's more than—it's plenty—stop worrying about it, okay?"

Stephanie, for almost opposite reasons—her beauty, upper East Side sophistication, and mostly smooth family relationships made her *too* easily accepted into her world—felt the same disjuncture, and tried to will away her despair with jokes, needing desperately to share her true self with someone fresh, far from home. Outwardly so different, they made the journey in, uncovering a likeness. "The city slicker and the hick," making fun of themselves, using puns and riddles and sick and corny jokes and *tummler* pratfalls, in relief fell in love.

He loved her for her beauty, her laugh, her shtick jokes, her worldliness, her palsied lip, her "knockers." He failed to see why she loved him. He asked. She said: "You're a kook! You bring out the kook in me. I'm seeing my folks from the *outside,* at last!"

"That's hardly it," he said. "You're an only child, I'm two years older—maybe I'm just the big brother you never had?"

"Nope," she said. "If it's anything, I think it's brains."

"Brains?"

"Raw brains. Brains is power, and power, kid, is sexy!"

Every love has a secret place, and they soon found theirs: Kinderhook Crik, in the horsy Chatham Hills. They happened upon it one steamy day that August, exploring a dirt path blocked by a log. Walking along amid the high wild-flowered grass, they came out on the high edge of a ravine, looking across the stream to the stone foundation on the other side. Knowing that its mate stood under their feet, they spanned the gap in imagination, the old bridge long gone. The stream curled down from the greening hills to the right, pooled, and gurgled off down to the deep chasm to the left, bending sharply away. They held hands and walked down the abandoned road to a pine grove on the bank, and sat in silence, overwhelmed with the vital peace of the spot. The richness of the season and land assaulted their senses: the clean sound and earthy smell of slow-running water, the raucous blackbirds in the scented pines, the wild-flowers, ruins, shadows, hot sun—even the human detritus seemed endearing: like found art, the resident

Clorox bottle, unbiodegradable, would outlast any stone. Fine thought the light to be like that given off when calcium burns: limelight.

Awed by the harmonic shape of place, Fine took off his shoes and socks and waded out on the slippery stones to the middle. She stayed on the shore. When he looked back at her, she was taking off her clothes. The seer and the seen. Bliss! She stood there naked. Her nakedness in the lush hot noon made her seem so vulnerable, tears came to his eyes. For a month they'd been "fooling around." She, though more expert than he, was remarkably unaware. Both virgins, they'd stopped short of making love.

She held out her hands to him, and smiled. He knew this was it. The moment started out somber and deep, but as Fine walked toward her on the mossy bottom-stones, he slipped and then, sole stung by a pointed edge, tumbled into the water. Wet and flummoxed, he crawled out up to her. Laughter broke the tension, for a while. He undressed, they lay down on the soft pine needles. Seeing the welcome in her eyes, feeling her soft breasts, he got big and hard.

And yet neither really knew how to go about it. The strange mechanics made it utterly unromantic. For the longest time it was so bad, so at odds with the fantasy—the erection, the try, the loss of erection, the sharp jab of rock into kneecap, the mosquito bite on the exposed rump, the distant distracting voice, the intrusive idea of how ridiculous they must look—they had to stop. They looked each other up and down, full of doubt and embarrassment, and then, sensing the ultrareal and mere human frailty of it all, they laughed, and then, laughing, he got hard again, and without much thought he got on top, he pushed, she guided, nothing happened, but she then gave a sharp hard thrust and something gave and he slipped in. Carried along on passion flowing from love, he lasted only seconds. She held him tight. He went limp. Done. Blood.

"Do you hurt?"

"Yes and no, love. It's strange: a sweet pain."

They held each other close. He said: "I love you."

"Now, dear Fine," she said, a sober look in her eyes, so he couldn't tell if she were joking or not, "now you *have* to marry me."

"I will!"

They lay together naked in the shadows, watching the movement of that grand master of shadow, the sun. Fine thought he knew what love was: two, entwined as one, *meta* to life, looking *at* it, together. "What a day!" Fine said. "A holy day—everything's so clear, sharp, like life's been distilled to essence, revealed—"

"Refined?" He laughed. She said: "Or confined?"

"If anything, kid, unconfined. Unconfined at last!"

That fall, Fine had to decide where to go to college. He went to his father and said: "I want to be an architect."

"Jews are not architects. To a Jewish architect who would come?" His thin black moustache twitched, his slaughterer's dark eyes seemed mournful in the white tired face. "And don't start with 'philosopher' again—starving geniuses make for starving families."

"You want me to be a butcher?"

"You I should trust with a cleaver? Be a doctor."

"Me you should trust with a scalpel?"

"So who eats people? Where do you want to go to college?"

Thinking of nice guy Ron from NASA, knowing that from Columbia, the only place to go was downriver, Fine said: "West Point."

"Oh boy!" Leo slapped his bald head with his palm.

"Why not? They say: 'The Army will make you a man.' "

"If you're *meshugge* enough to ask why a Jew would join an army, maybe college is not for you. What's the best college?"

"Steffy says Harvard, then Yale."

"OK. So go to Harvard." But when the catalogues arrived, and Leo saw the Hebrew letters on the Yale crest, it was dark blue and bulldogs from there on out.

During his senior year, he and Steffy visited each other, their intermittent separation deepening their attachment. Yale would be a mere two hours by train from Dalton School in Manhattan.

By the time he left for Yale, his tic had disappeared.

He flew through Yale in three, she finished Dalton, their love fed by illicitness and risk. Their special place at Yale was the Noguchi *White Marble Garden* of the Beinecke Library—the three asymmetric shapes on a tilted grid of curves a skewed, obscure, funny comfort. Holidays were swapped between Columbia and Manhattan, summers were spent together, he working as toll collector on the Rip Van Winkle Bridge—the graveyard shift so

he could read—she at her family cottage on the lake. On the
bridge, without knowing it, he began learning something about
the nature of human nature, as well as how short the night really
was. She would drive by in her Mercedes convertible, making fun
of him in his Bridge Authority uniform. He'd flash his Bridge
Authority gun. Working nights, playing days, he was nicknamed
by her mother "Iron Man Fine." At Yale he began in philosophy,
but finding the academic version as sterile as his childhood,
switched into science—first pure, then applied—climbing down
the reductionist ladder from psyche to mind through brain to cell.
He decided on going to medical school to get his "meal ticket,"
planning to become a brain/behavior researcher. In the same
year, he started Harvard Med and she started Radcliffe. Despite
the load of schoolwork, their being together alone and without
parents in Cambridge that first year was novel and thrilling.

"Know something?" Fine asked one sunny afternoon as he lay
in bed in Vanderbilt Hall memorizing *Gray's Anatomy,* peeping at
her. She'd slipped off her white silk blouse and was about to
unhook her black bra. His skin tingled. The fat book made a
mouthy warp of his tummy, a reminder of the dimpling power, in
spacetime, of gravity.

"Mmm?" she responded, hesitating, her hands at the front
clasp as if folded in prayer.

"When the Big Guy invented eyes, he did a very nice thing."

"You bet!" She jumped him, dumping the book to the floor.

"Sex without gravity!" he said. "My dream come true."

At the start of their second year they moved into adjoining
rooms in Adams House. Although neither of them was aware of
it, both had begun to sense it: the shadowy claustrophobia of the
dyad.

4

ONE MORNING EARLY that September as they came into the hallway to go down to breakfast, they met a tall sandy-haired young
man intimately connected to a shiny, stripped-down racing bicycle. The frame was slung over his shoulder, a rat-trap pedal was in
his hand. He was so tall and the bicycle so imposing, it was hard
to separate the two. Fine and Stephanie introduced themselves.
With a twinkle in his eye he said: "O'Day. John James Michael
O'Day, Jr."

"Aha!" said Fine, grinning, *"also* Jewish! Are you premed?"

"Jesus!" said John, startled. "No way!"

"Into metal, hunh?" asked Stephanie.

"Irishmen love bicycles," said John, "and words."

"Words love bicycles?" she asked. *"Quel* bizarre!"

"That's my girl Steffy," said Fine, proudly, "always the one
with the *bon* 'mote.' " It was one of their old puns.

John stared down at Fine as if at a visitor from space. Glancing
up from Fine to Steph, he said: "Weird!" and laughed. His laugh
surprised them: a loud outburst, a sharp, in-sucking chortle.

"Where are you going?" asked Stephanie.

"To Southie—the first day of school there—the start of another
year of forced busing—somethin' to see. Wanna come?"

Steph hesitated; Fine said: "Yes!" He offered Steph's car, but John said he'd make it faster by bike. It was one of the first fall days—crisp, football weather. They drove the purple Jag through Boston, across the Fort Point Channel into "Southie," the poorest white part of the city. They heard the fighting before they saw it. Parking, they hurried up the hill toward South Boston High. There, three bright yellow buses were trying to make their way through the crowd to the school. In the windows, in the children's black faces, eyes showed white with fright. The police cordon was leaking. The all-white mostly Irish crowd was closing in to block the way, carrying signs protesting the forced busing of blacks into Southie and whites out, featuring the word *nigger*. As Fine and Steph arrived, the first rocks were being thrown through the school-bus windows. The crowd wanted blood. The police cordoned off a corridor for the black kids to walk through to the school. Insults and missiles flew through the air. And there in the middle, trying to keep peace, was John.

It was hopeless. He was arguing with a black-haired woman who stood as a center pole of a linked chain of other women, barring the way. His pleas were useless. Pushed aside, he caught a beer can on the chin. He staggered. Fine barreled through the crowd to him, Steph in his wake. John's eyes were glazed. They pulled him away, off down the hill. In a doorway, Fine tended him. The cut was superficial. Shaking his head in shame, John said: "Welcome to me."

Steph asked: "Who was that fanatic you were arguing with?"

"That was no fanatic," he said, "that was my mother."

He led them to the Bellevue, a seedy bar near his house. The bartender, his uncle—called "The Uncle"—a fat, balding, gummy-breathed man whose skin seemed never to have seen the sun, greeted John with: "Begob! Up before noon? Whazzamater, lad, they paintin' yer bed today?" John blushed. The Uncle served up beers, and listened. Fine and Steph were shaken (Pogrom! thought Fine). Detective O'Herlihey from Boston Homicide stopped in. A maggoty-skinned, almost black-lipped emphysematous chain-smoker, he ordered Bushmill's whiskey. When John said he'd seen who'd thrown the beer can, at the riot, and wanted to press charges, O'Herlihey said: "Riot? What riot? I din't see nuthin', lad, nuthin' at all." Soon after, they left.

Physically John was, to Fine—and even to the taller Steph—a

giant. Six-four, lanky and muscular, possessed of the natural
grace of the athlete, he'd starred in hockey and baseball from
Gate of Heaven Grammar through South Boston High. He had a
classic Irish mug: light blond hair giving way to a high forehead
bulging slightly out and then ducking down under bushy blond
eyebrows. The eyes were light blue, the nose a great brawling
challenge to the eyes, yet delicate compared to the jutting jaw. Yet
his mouth was a woman's, the lips small and rounded—almost, at
rest, pursed.

That first day, on the drive back, they first talked about how
the world was coming apart at the seams and then John talked
about himself. Son of Irish immigrants, he'd grown up in a three-
decker directly across from Carson Beach, down the street from
the L Street Recreation Center. His "da" had owned the Bellevue.
John was the last of four children, the only boy. He'd often been
called on to amuse. His father had been one of the L Street
Brownies, swimming a mile in the Atlantic every day of the year.
The daily watery expiation for the nightly turgid beer. When he
was six, his father had died of cirrhosis. Trapped in a house of
four women, he'd run. He lived the restless search of the fatherless, hungering, in life, for fatherly contact, alert to every detail.
Encouraged by his father's brother The Uncle, he joined the
Brownies, every morning swimming repetitive laps between the
fences reaching out into the sea, eight times equals a mile. In
winter sometimes you had to break the ice, but Vaseline protected
you from the cold, the water warmer than the air. He got tough;
his mind tender. He had an uncanny ability to pick up the out-
ward essence—words, moves, aura—of another, and mime it exactly. If arthritic Father O'Herlihey sat black clad on a bench in
the white sunlight outside the Rec, John would observe him, noting how the priest's whole being was expressed in the movement
of one shoe on pavement forward—"scritch"—and—"scritch"—
back; later, for his sisters he would *be* the O'Herlihey!: "scritch";
"scritch." He discovered a remarkable ability to mimic, to repeat.

Poor-Irish, athlete, brain—full scholarship to Harvard! Pride of
Southie! His freshman year he tried hockey. He played his heart
out for "Hahvid," slashing the puck with all the blind rage of the
fatherless poor—and no one cared. In the crush of talented others, each searched frantically for a niche. His freshman room-
mate, a despondent Kansan goalie who'd been tops in his school

at math, found he could barely place out of the most elementary math courses, and so joined the Mountaineering Club, proceeding to pound four pitons into the ceiling and hang his bed from them. The next summer—which John, confused and gloomy, spent as a lifeguard on Carson Beach—back home in the dull underbelly of the country, the Kansan proceeded to use his Harvard education to pound two more pitons, sling a pulley, and hang himself. Alone, John was thrown into a ratty small single room in the "intellectual house," Adams. A lackadaisical student lost in the crowd, his athletic prowess discounted, he arrived to start his sophomore year brooding and lost, yearning for applause, not having the faintest idea how to get it.

Until they showed him. The two zany, daring Jews opened up a whole new world! Thrown in with them, he stuck tight. Enticed by Fine's weird free creativity, his exuberance, and his wit—and above all by his *sureness*—John aped him, dressing like him, talking like him, joking like him, gesturing like him, *acting* like him. Four years older, Fine—or, rather, the *dasein* of Fine—permeated John's sense of self. Fine became more than best friend; he became idol. At first Fine—almost a foot shorter—was puzzled at being lionized by this powerful, well-coordinated giant. Sure of himself as he now was, Fine couldn't figure out what John saw in him. Thus Fine's blind spot: the unconscious. Fine refused to believe in the unconscious, his own or anyone else's. Once when Steph was trying to point out a possible unconscious motivation for a floridly kooky Fine behavior, Fine, eyes wide with disbelief, said: "You mean sometimes I do things for reasons I'm not aware of?!"

"Yes!"

"Prove it! An 'unconscious' is only defined by what it's *not*: 'conscious.' The only valid proof is when something is 'falsifiable' —when you can conceive experiments to prove it false. Can't do that to an 'unconscious.' Don't believe it exists at all!"

But then Fine was Fine, plowing ahead, course unaffected by what lay in his wake. He welcomed John paddling along behind. And John found, in this short, chunky, unrestrained sure-of-it-all Jew, the father-brother of his dreams.

In life, as opposed to art, one often finds what one seeks.

Having had a deep close bond with his mother and sisters, John's attachment to Stephanie took a different form. At first, it was warily intellectual. The one part of Fine that did not interest John was Fine the Scientist. John could care less about Fine's passion—grasshoppers; he thought Fine's experiments quaint, but too close to roaches for comfort. Stephanie filled the intellectual-cultural gap: she introduced him to philosophy, via Kierkegaard's *Crisis in the Life of an Actress.* Stunned, John read *Repetition* and became obsessed with it—and with Steph. She, a history major, got him to read Isaiah Berlin's *The Hedgehog and the Fox.* He discovered that Fine, seeking a unitary inner vision and making order out of chaos, was a hedgehog (like Plato, Dante, Pascal, Dostoevsky, Proust, many Germans); Steph was a fox, accepting the variety in the world (like Aristotle, Homer, Shakespeare, Rabelais, Joyce, many Mediterraneans). John thought of himself (like Tolstoy) as seeing only the many while searching to see the one. He said to Steph: "I'm a fox yearning to be a hedgehog."

"Nope," she said, "you're a chameleon."

Soon after he quizzed her: "Who said 'If a tiger could talk, we wouldn't understand'?" She hadn't read Wittgenstein, didn't know. Thus he'd outstripped her. In philosophy. So he switched to history, took courses with her, and began his obsession with George Washington. He saw his own life as a repetition—(family, "schizoid" personality, loves)—of the early life of the "Father of His Country."

And yet the intellectual attachment to Stephanie was the least of it. She took care of him. She led him along. That Thanksgiving, she and Fine took him on his first trip to New York. Fine and John stayed with Steph's Aunt Belle on the West Side. John was overwhelmed by the City. Feeling insignificant, he needed to assert himself. The morning of their sightseeing, he bought an eggplant from a vendor on Broadway. Holding it by the stem end at head level, he spoke to it as if it were a purple-skinned pal: "Now, Eggplant, now we're in the crowded elevator in the Empire State Building. And the lady in front of us, Eggplant, is wondering why I'm talking to you." At dinner that night with Belle, on top of the G&W building, watching the red and white snakes of carlights wind reciprocally up and down Central Park West, John had Belle in stitches. Fine said: "This is nothing—you should've seen the show he put on today—"

"John James!" Steph said excitedly, grabbing his arm, "I've got it!—listen—I finally found out who you are! And—"

"God! I didn't know I didn't know who—"

"—and what you're going to *be*—listen!—" And then, turning both palms up like a magician, she said: "An actor!"

She got him to act, with her. After a few rehearsals of a house play, he came back to the room and, eyes wide, said: "Unbelievable! For the first time in my life I'm doing something that's easy! It takes no effort, no effort at all! I've found my calling!—to act as if I'm somebody else!" Only later, reading Borges on Shakespeare —*Everything and Nothing*—did he see that acting legitimized a falsity, masking his despair at not knowing who he actually was.

That year he went from spear carrier to Hamlet. Undiluted by training, his spirit soared. He exploded onto the Loeb stage, an overnight sensation. In raw talent, hunger, and openness, he was unrivaled. Theater consumed him, and he it, like first love. He tried everything—even those he called "the two great frauds: Brr-*echt* and Sh-aww." A milestone was *The Taming of the Shrew,* with Steph as Kate to his Petruccio. The lonely six-year-old had tasted applause. The hunger for love would never abate, but now it would often—desperately—be fed. Like many, he fled the crippled relationships of his life to seek a reality in the fantasy of theater. In the fakery of players he found family. Someone stuck a label on him: *wunderkind.*

All three bloomed. They lived life to the hilt, with a glorious disregard for restraint. Offstage, out of classroom and hospital, the three shared two activities: they often went with John into Southie—to the beach, the Rec, the bar. Steph became interested in grass-roots politics. Boston, the most racist city in the country, was also the most corrupt. The mayor, in his second term, was afloat on sewerage. John introduced them to the pols. Detective O'Herlihey, the "go-through," fixed parking tickets for the Jag. Fine laughed; Steph listened, and asked the liberal questions: Who pays if we don't? What about the blacks? The poor should all join together: Workers of the world unite! To which John said: "Who works?" She thought of becoming a pol herself.

Their other shared activity were the Fine "letters."

Like Bellow's Herzog, Fine wrote letters. At least weekly, he was moved by an uncontrollable desire to pen a letter, often to a celebrity. One week it would be an idolatory missive to reclusive Henry Roth—Fine loved *Call It Sleep;* the next week, Frank Sinatra ("Our studies have shown that two million dollars cash *will* in fact fit into an attaché case"); the week after, a starlet with large pneumatic breasts, inviting her to accept "The Suite D-38 Award." Occasionally a letter was serious—to the widow of the poor guy who, commuting by car from Staten Island on the ferry (having overslept, he'd just made it, the last car on), fell asleep in his car and when awakened, frantically shoved it into reverse, flipping it off the boat into New York harbor—and philanthropic (Steph sent a hundred bucks with that one). Each sent letters to their idols: Mel Brooks, Simone de Beauvoir, the Rabbi of the Actors in NYC (Steph); John Updike, Flann O'Brien, and the Boston Celtic Larry Bird (John); Samuel Beckett, J. D. Watson, Blaze Starr (Fine). Sometimes they mailed the letters, sometimes not; sometimes they got replies (Beckett, for one).

Their major collaborative letters were three: to the makers of their favorite movie, *Morgan;* to the Pope; and to the President.

The letter to the Pope was their best to date, featuring, from Fine, heated, tenebrous, and lurid philosophical passages:

. . . and isn't it so, Holiness, that the Crucifixion was the most primordial forbidden act, a human sacrifice? How could God allow this? Why, if Jesus was the Messiah, did he have to die, becoming a symbol of redemption? If God is Good, wouldn't He give us not the symbol, but redemption itself? The Old Testament says that when the Messiah comes, we'll be able to look out the window and see that the world is in fact better. This world, not the next. Isn't it possible that, rather than the arrival, the crux is how we live waiting? That the arrival killed off the morality of waiting? How often, growing up, did I hear not only "Christ Killer!" but also: "Yeah it's a sin to beat you up—but it's okay, 'cause I'll confess it Tuesday." Morality's not in someone dying for us, but in us; not in someone who's come and gone offering us a kind of "futures market" on the "Good." During World War II your predecessor Pius stood on his balcony waving while below they marched Jews off to the ovens. After the war, your Vatican helped Catholic Nazis resettle in South America. How do I reconcile this with Jesus, let alone the Big Guy? I am tormented. RSVP

Steph thought this too heavy: "You've got to make him laugh—
here, put this in—it's a routine Grandpa Al did every year at
Passover:

> Jesus? Nice boy. Cute beard. Kept kosher, kept *very* kosher.
> But no sense of humor, none! You could *die* before you got
> even one little chuckle outa dat fella Jesus! For the Jews,
> when the Messiah comes we'll know 'cause we'll laugh.
> He'll come rolling in on a belly laugh, you just wait and see!
> The closest yet was the Marx Brothers, or maybe the
> young, pre-Hollywood Mel Brooks.

And John said: "Hey, tell Him this, for me":

> I was brought up Catholic, and lapsed, and never came
> alive until I met these two loopy Jews. My questions: 1)
> Why is this? 2) A. Do you actually talk with God? 2) B.
> Does He actually answer? 2) C. If so, about my da—where
> *is* he?

Fine wrapped it up:

> Well, Your Highest Holiness, a long letter but, I think, a
> good one. It's important to "dialogue"—that Harvard and
> Rome keep on "impacting." It draws the strings of this
> crazy world just that little bit tighter, no? Adams House
> has a Monday night seminar series on "Great Personalities
> of the World." Interested? As they say in showbiz: ciao!

To this one they got no response. The last letter of their college
career was to the President. The night of the graduation party,
Fine sat in the living room of his suite, smoking his pipe, inviting
suggestions from the other two, composing:

> Dear Mr. President:
> In your newscast you said you wanted to hear from all
> "great Americans." Here goes. While I agree with you that
> the "Nuclear threat is the gravest issue of mankind," I
> think it might be a little more complex than you made it.

Do you really believe we are "good" and they are "evil"?
Are there truly no shadows in your sun? . . .

And yet writing to the President soon sickened them. JFK's and King's assassination, Vietnam, Watergate, the resurrection as elder statesmen of Nixon, Kissinger, Haig (the news: Ford, through Haig, *had* traded the Nixon pardon for the presidency)—like most of their generation they'd lost faith. Seeing the circus of corruption in Southie, they extrapolated, agreeing that to get elected President there could be no human qualities left. It would be exquisitely timed: as the polls opened, the person would be all leached out, like a man's shirt washed too many times. The world was coming apart, hidden in a haze of unreality: people were beginning to act as they thought they *should* act, their "shoulds" coming from TV. The TV commercial in particular—the modern equivalent of myth—told moral tales about how to live. Soon the nexus of crime in the streets and cable at home would keep all inside, birth to death. They gave up.

They went to the party. The common room was packed. Fine sat beaming in the front row as, up on the long mahogany bar, with top hats and canes, all ebony and ivory, Steph and John sang and danced their last cabaret, closing out the show, as always, with their favorite, Mabel Mercer:

"Carry me back to old Manhattan,
    That's where my heart belongs;
Give me a show spot to hang my hat in,
    Sing me those Broadway songs . . ."

5

WHEN THEY CAME back down the dunes to the beach, John was up on his hands, walking—as he'd done onstage as Hamlet *(up* on "What a piece of work is man! . . ." *Walking on hands* through speech, *slow cartwheel down* on ". . . And yet to me what is this quintessence of dust?"). As they approached, he faked a fall, laughing. But eye to eye, Fine sensed that something inside him was not laughing at all. With a sweeping melodramatic bow, John said: *"Fine Rux."*

Or perhaps *"Rox"*—his accent always masked the vowel. The word—coined by John, claiming it to exist—a mix of "rut" and "lox," had come to connote Fine the Horny/Crazy. To Fine now it seemed a challenge, even a taunt, as if to say: "You think she's *yours?!"*

Steph and John decided to take a walk down the beach. Fine watched them diminishing in haze until, bone-tired, he napped.

A florid daytime dream wrenched Fine awake. Or half-awake, for he was as drowsy as if drugged, and the hot sun slamming down on the seawater had pounded up a dreamlike mist. At the vanishing point of his vision he saw—or thought he saw or might have seen—John and Steph walking hand in hand up the beach toward him. And then something happened that made him shiver.

Or might have happened, for it was only dimly seen, so dimly seen as perhaps to exist only in imagination: they stopped, turned to each other, embraced, kissed! Their bodies seemed to press against each other, squirming! But as suddenly as the vision had appeared, it was gone, obscured by a curtain of fog. Fine was shocked, awash in suspicion. His best friend and his girl, kissing?! What does this mean? Sure they're fond of each other—"love" each other in a way—but this?! She's mine! How long has this been going on behind my back? They've had plenty of chances, with me busy at med school with my patients, in the lab with my grasshoppers. Is it possible?!

No, couldn't be. Hold on, Fine. Use your head: she loves me. I know she loves me. She could never love anyone as she loves me. She's said it—just proved it, up there in the dunes. They aren't lovers, they're pals. Look—here they come—what?!—holding hands?! Of course holding hands. The fact that they *are* holding hands means they've got nothing to hide. Bonehead!

Fine flashed on his recent decision, the first of the two surprise announcements he was about to make to them, and he calmed. And, calming, he thought: this is familiar, the side of me that's always been a little paranoid. Boy, am I going to be able to handle this better after June second! Thank God I made this decision! I'm a scientist, I don't know all that much about human beings, but dammit I'll learn. I can hardly wait to tell them the news!

Yet when they came back, he searched their eyes for clues, almost wishing to see what he feared seeing, and it seemed to him that, in the elusive shapes of their glances and banter, something had slipped, something was lying not en face, but aslant. As if there were something to hide. They sat down together, Steph in the middle this time, and Fine and John with their arms around her. Fine felt fatherly toward her; he felt jealous of John's arm around her, touching his own, even though she was (because she was?) his. And like a last point stuck into a high school debate after the bell has rung, Fine the Suspicious said to Fine the Trusting: Hey, *schmuck:* these two are about to go off to Paris and Dublin! For a whole year! Long weekends together in Europe while you slog through hospitals up to your ass in grasshoppers and lunatics! Again his paranoia rose. But then he thought of his other imminent announcement—which would take care of that fantasy once and for all—and sighed with relief.

Compared to the glamour of night and the magic of sunrise, the daylight seemed dull and sad. They fought to maintain their good cheer as the light swept lightness from the day. And yet it was, now, clearly an ending, as full of hopelessness as all endings.

Stephanie, in the middle, said: "None of us really fits in our families. And so each of us has been family to each other. We've grown each other up. Sometime in the future, one of us or two of us or all of us will be shaky, on a shaky edge, on the verge of falling, and in need of the others again. So we must vow never to abandon each other no matter what. 'Cause there's hope, you idiots, in that, see?"

Tired, they mumbled that they did. Fine, suspicion on a roll, heard in this a threat.

"So we make a vow," she said.

They vowed. Then, turning to Fine, Steph pointed a finger at his tummy and said: "Man." Pointing to herself, she said: "Woman." And turning so it seemed that she and Fine together were facing John, she stuck a finger in his ribs and said: "Both."

"Both?!" yelped John.

"Both." Firmly, she repeated: "John James is both."

"He's not both," said Fine, "he just wants us to think he's both. It's 'theatrical.' If anything, he's neither."

"Neither?!" squawked John. Faking his best imitation "Dooblin" accent, he said: "Ah fer Jayzez sake, fook off!"

"Both," said Steph. "There's a woman's soul inside."

"Okay," said John, "that settles it: I won't go to Ireland to become a great actor, I'll go to Ireland to bugger all the priests!"

"Why not join the U.S. Army!" said Fine.

"Why should I do that?"

" 'The Army will make you a man.' "

"Hey," said Steph, "I got a new joke: Two Jews are in Miami . . ."

Fine tuned out. He was trying to figure a way to dramatize his two surprise announcements. He didn't want to blow it. He rehearsed the words over and over in his mind. It was clear that soon after this last joke of hers, they'd get back into the Jag and head home. Or, rather, back. And this was serious stuff.

Unbeknownst to either of them, in the past six months Fine had undergone a conversion: he had discovered Sigmund Freud.

It had happened early in his psychiatry elective at Mass.

Mental Health. His interest in psychiatry until then had been
dalliance, the "psyche" at the top of his slide down the reductionist pole to grasshopper nerve cells. The theme of his quest was
calcium. Fine had the intuition—based on hard scientific data—
that calcium was the key element in learning and memory. (His
Yale senior thesis: "Macro-molecular Hypotheses of Information
Storage in the Brain: The Effect of Calcium on Memory.") He'd
found human beings and "mind" too complex and chaotic for the
scientific method—and had run from the study of both. He was
on the verge of cracking a major puzzle: identifying a single nerve
cell in the grasshopper that "learned" and "remembered." His
next project would be to look at the effect of calcium on this
learning process. Already there were two sets of rumors: Fine was
grandiose and crazy; Fine was tracking the fast lane to the Nobel
Prize. And so Fine, the final six months of med school before
starting his general medical internship, searching for a "gut"—a
last easy clinical rotation—was dabbling in psychiatry, filled with
the logical positivist's blind disdain.

When Sigmund Freud reared up and bit him in the ass.

It happened this way: an inpatient at Mass. Mental was being
interviewed before an audience of psychiatrists and social workers. The interviewing analyst was the legendary Dr. Sean Vergessen. Protégé of the recently deceased "master," Dr. Semrad,
Vergessen was president of The Boston Institute (TBI), the training ground for the crème de la crème of psychiatrists, Freudian
psychoanalysts. Vergessen was an albino, a short dumpy pink-
eyed scion of Jewish-immigrant Midwestern stock. This first interview Fine saw Vergessen do was one of the most remarkable
things Fine had ever seen.

The patient, a tough, shrapnel-laden Vietnam vet who'd been
hospitalized against his will for threatening to kill his third wife,
started the interview raging, ready to kill. Vergessen sat next to
him, pale chin on pudgy white fist, listening. Hearing the details,
Vergessen began grinning. Somehow, soon the vet—and the others in the room—were laughing. At what? The third wife's strewn
bras? The acrid smoke of the burnt string beans? The traffic jam
on the Southeast Expressway? The shared human predicament?
The folly of stubborn purpose in the face of the chance of our
lives? And then, imperceptibly, with such subtle skill that no one
could've pointed to what the skill was, the tone turned, and there,

before everyone's eyes, this trained assassin was bawling like a
baby. As were others. Vergessen sat silent, letting the weeping go
on; the mourning of 'Nam. It ended. The patient thanked him,
said he'd never told anybody what he'd just told him, and left.
Fine—wiping away his own tears—sat, stunned. After the power
of the epiphany, he barely heard the exegesis. He recalled Vergessen, smiling, saying:

"All jobs are boring, except this one."

The next day, Fine rushed to arrange a tutorial with Vergessen.
That first interview, as Fine told his story, Vergessen said almost
nothing. And yet Fine too laughed and cried, and felt almost
transparent, seen at his deepest level, and, despite his frailties,
accepted, understood in a way that no one—not even Steph—had
done before.

"How do people change?" asked Fine.

"How do you imagine people change?" asked Vergessen.

"By will power," said Fine, "by wanting it bad enough." A
bemused look spread over the albino's face. Fine asked if he
would supervise him, and Vergessen, even more bemused, asked:
"Why not?"

Fine went weekly to his new idol. At first they laughed. Humans were so ludicrous! Yet Fine had often found idols, just as
often lost them. He'd soon have tired of V. but for two things:

V. always made Fine feel inadequate.

V. always made Fine feel that he *accepted* Fine's inadequacy.

Never clearly saying it, Vergessen led Fine to believe that Fine
had serious psychological defects. Defects that V., smilingly, *accepted.* With alarm, Fine began to see that he often did things that
were bad for him. And then, riffling through these "self-abusive"
acts, he felt shocked—as if a harsh spotlight had been snapped on
inside: unconscious forces were in fact at work! Alone, puzzling
over the conundrumical nature of their interactions, Fine envisioned himself: huge, brainy head; sore, blocked-up heart; constricted tube between the two. Seldom aware of specific feelings,
Fine felt lost. If, as Vergessen implied, being human was nothing
more or less than integrating feeling *(affect)* and thought, Fine felt
less than human. This chilly "spaceman" feeling rang old bells:
"Brain!"; "Egghead!" But now he was getting it from Jews?! It
hurt! Fine felt weak.

Yet weakness was his strength. For Fine, inadequacy meant

challenge, challenge meant action. All that was needed was a little superhuman effort, and everything would be cleared right up. He'd soon conquer this latest peak of himself. Besides, this was nothing new. All he required was a little help.

Freud helped. Fine sucked up volume after volume, delighted to find that Freud too had come to psychiatry from science, spending a summer in Trieste dissecting out the sex organs of four hundred electric eels ("No one," Freud wrote in 1876, "had yet seen the testes of the eel, in spite of innumerable efforts throughout the centuries!"); that Freud for a time worked on human bodies (embracing his pal Fleiss's notion that the key to unlocking human sexuality lay imbeded in the mucous membranes of the nose—what a sight: Freud and Fleiss [the famous photo: two intense, bushy-as-beavers, bearded Jews] peering up each other's cavernous honkers, thinking sex?!); that Freud too seemed cold-blooded, obsessive, suspicious, often walking the cliff-edge: paranoia. Fine raced through, reading everything. One day he burst in on the placid albino, shouting excitedly: "About Freud!"

"About Freud?"

"I think I understand!"

"You think you understand?" asked Vergessen, and then, through a series of innocuous-seeming questions, managed to convey to Fine the feeling that he was even a bigger *dummkopf* than before but that despite this—or even *for* it?!—Vergessen *accepted* him. Fine left him as he often did, brain feeling like a scrambled egg, with the impression that the understanding he sought was not to be found by reading a book. Rather, that it had to do with a special, rare, deeper, yet elegantly simple understanding of himself.

Fine foundered. He failed miserably to understand his psych patients. They got worse, some refusing therapy. Facing the chaos, Fine used old patterns—isolating himself, reading. Inept, he got depressed. He saw, rising from his past, an old, atavistic despair.

He told Vergessen about his despair. Much to his surprise, Vergessen seemed delighted, as if for Fine despair were the best thing since blintzes. He smiled, and asked: "Despair?"

"Despair. Profound despair!" Vergessen smiled, all-wise, and, knowingly, winked, nodded. Fine asked: "What should I do?"

"What do you *think* you should do?"

Fine quoted the famous Vergessen saying: " 'Connect upstairs with downstairs, head with heart'?"

"Is that so?"

"How do I do that?" Fine asked, knowing that V. seldom made direct statements, mostly answering questions with questions. And so he was surprised—floored!—when V. for the first time replied with a simple declarative, in its *sureness* as compelling as a command:

"Get yourself into analysis. Fast."

It hit Fine like a punch in the gut. Some deep thing within him doubled over, gasping, groping blindly for the ropes.

And yet at the same instant it was as if a curtain had been lifted, a first scene seen. Feelings rushed up, bridged to words: There is more to life than meets the eye. I'm running the fingers of my mind over the world as if it were made of braille. Through analysis I will understand my "self." Through understanding my "self" I will understand others. And the world. The whole wide world! The universe too, why not? My paranoia has deep roots that I will understand through psychoanalysis. I must unearth my childhood. I will see once and for all whether or not I am mad. Analyzed I will finally be able to see the shapes in humans. Yes!— see the world that's been dark to me: the world of the human beings!

Fine gulped. I should become a psychoanalyst. I'm so bad with my hands, and analysts need no manual dexterity! I'll be in control of my hours, and clear time for my grasshopper research. And what elegance: to have, as your only tool, your self!

"Can I do it?" Fine asked Vergessen.

"Can you not?" Vergessen asked Fine.

"Isn't it innate? Isn't understanding other people a gift?"

"Hmm. And what are your fantasies about this 'gift'?"

Fine began to tell him just how ungifted he felt.

Too late for a psychiatry residency at Mass. Mental, Fine was accepted by another Harvard hospital, McLean. He would become an analyst like V. He would succeed where Freud had failed: he would create a grand synthesis of biology and psyche, science and art!

Such was the Fine humility at the time.

* * *

John got up, reached down two hands, one for Steph and one for Fine. This was it. Fine's heart was in his throat.

"Let's go," said John, pulling her up, "I've got rehearsal."

"Wait!" said Fine, sitting tight, holding their hands. "Sit. I've got to tell you two unbelievable things—things that'll change all our lives!" Stunned by his somber tone, they sat. To his surprise, Fine was trembling. "First: I'm starting psychoanalysis."

Stephanie looked at him as if he were nutty: "You, analysis? You, who not long ago told me you didn't believe in the unconscious?"

"See?" said Fine proudly.

"See what?" asked John.

"See how much I need analysis?" They groaned. "Vergessen found me an analyst, a good—no—a *great* analyst, perfect for me. I have my first session next month. June second, at six in the morning."

"Six in the morning?" asked Steph. "Why so early?"

"That's how great an analyst he is! The only time he had!"

They looked from one to the other, Steph rolled her eyes, John suppressing a laugh.

Steph asked: "What's the second surprise?"

"I'm getting married."

For a few seconds no one said anything, each glancing around the circle of eyes, and away. Steph asked: "To whom?"

"You."

"What?" she said. "But—"

"June first. The day before I start my analysis."

"Why now? Why not wait till—"

"It's got to be before I start. I hear they don't like you to make any decisions during the analysis."

"But what about my year in Paris?"

"You can still go to Paris—do whatever you want—as long as we're married before I hit the couch. I can hardly wait!"

"Why should I get married just because suddenly it's convenient for you?" Steph asked.

"Because you love me," Fine said.

"But *marriage?!* Suppose I say no?"

"I'll wait."

"For me or for the analysis?"

"Yes," said Fine, laughing.

"What do you think, John James?"

"Me?" he said, quickly, as if startled.

"Yeah, you," said Fine, "the best man."

"Why," said John, coolly, "I thought he'd never ask!"

"Oh I don't know, I suppose it was inevitable," Steph said. "Maybe I'll have even more freedom, married."

"What are you talking about?" Fine asked.

"You said I could still go to Paris and do whatever I want."

"I don't get it," Fine said.

"Join the crowd," she said. "Oh boy! I've got to think it over— it's a big decision now that it's real." And then Fine could see his proposal sink in. She blushed, her face flushing dark. Her voice catching the rising edge of her happiness, she said: "Oh Fine— what a wonderful idea! Yes!"

On June first, they were married. John was best man.

On June second at 5:30 A.M., following instructions, Fine drove to Brookline, parked on the street, walked up the driveway to the back of the gray wooden house, and—noting the basketball hoop, hearing the barking of a big dog—found the entrance to the home-office door. He obeyed the sign (DO NOT RING BELL AND ENTER), and sat in the waiting room, waiting.

His analyst-to-be entered, introduced himself, and led Fine to the couch. He was an elephantine, graying man in a dark three-piece suit.

Fine told his story. The analyst listened, saying little. At the end of the session, Fine asked:

"How long will it take?"

"What are your fantasies about how long it will take?"

Fine told him his fantasies, and then asked, again: "So how long you think it'll take?"

"How long does it take to read a book?"

"It takes as long as it takes."

"So," his analyst said, in a warm, friendly voice, "it takes as long as it takes."

The one fact Fine knew about his analyst was that he'd played football in college. On the way home, Fine nicknamed him "Fumbles," trusting that Fumbles would not "fumble" Fine. He felt optimistic, and then, exhilarated. "Out of sight!" he cried, in the privacy of his car. "I love being a human being! I am leading one charmed life!"

II

CAGED

I am at the moment tempted by the desire
to solve the riddle of the structure of the
brain; I think brain anatomy is the only
legitimate rival you have or ever will have.
　—Sigmund Freud, letter to
　　Martha Bernays, May 1885

6

SEVEN YEARS LATER, on May Day, Fine lay in bed in the red dawn light, thinking he was happy.

Having just finished his analysis, he now was a man who thought himself "a perfectly analyzed human being."

I feared for him even more.

Analysis had taught him to "de-repress" his dreams, and he now recalled nearly every one of what Freud called "the royal road to the unconscious." Strangely, almost every night he had nightmares. He'd "worked through" them, *accepted* them, and Fumbles had allowed him to terminate with the remnant. One good thing about nightmares: each day Fine awoke relieved, as if to a happy dream. Now a full-fledged psychiatrist, lying in bed felt like lying on the analytic couch. After all, hadn't that very hour—6:00 A.M.—five times a week except for August vacation for seven years been his? He'd become expert in "free association," the remarkably difficult skill of "saying whatever comes to mind." As his idol Vergessen put it: "Let your mind float, like a rubber duck in an infant's tub." This, Freud's "fundamental rule" of analysis, the only instruction he ever gave *(On Beginning the Treatment,* 1913. ["Think it's easy?" Fine had said to Steph. "Try it.(!)"])

Such elegance, Fine had thought, such a simple tool with which to unlock the mind! In silence, to avoid disturbing his wife, he associated: Freud. Mother. Nightmare about Sigmund Freud reincarnated as my mother. Bye-bye Fumbles last Tuesday—oops!—*Monday!*—incredible slip! To mix up such a landmark day! Why do patients nickname therapists? Fascinating question! What a last session we'd had!:

"Err," Fumbles had said, "perhaps your dream refers to your noticing my drooping basketball net, on your way in here?"

"Who saw your net?" I'd replied. "I was keeping my eyes on your path, for the dog poop."

Oh how we'd laughed! Real man-to-man laughter, that last session, yes! Classic!

At the memory, Fine laughed.

Stephanie stirred. She slept with her belly to his back, her right arm around his neck, her left arm on his rump, always. Fine had analyzed this right out: it came from her being a needy only child, holding him tight as if to prevent being abandoned ("Don't go!"). He slept on his right side, legs cartwheeled out as if caught in a freeze frame of running away ("Lemme out!"). A student of statistical probability for a healthy life and heart, Fine had slept this way ever since his brother Moe, a phys. ed. major at Albany State, told him that sleeping on the right side was healthier, elevating the heart, freeing it from mattress pressure, increasing venous return, stroke volume, etc. They had not emphasized these things at Yale. He felt his wife's breasts through her silky nightgown and his pajamas, smooth against his back, and wondered if that stubbly prickly brush was a nipple. He associated out loud:

"Kumquat."

Until the analysis, Fine had never realized that deep down he saw sexual parts as fruits. At the beginning of his analysis this had been an embarrassment to him, but Fumbles had cleared it all right up with a single incredible interpretation:

"If you see fruits, so see fruits."

So Fine saw fruits.

In his fourth year of analysis, it was revealed: fruits = mother, both beloved; in his fifth year: fruits also = mother's mother's father, the peddlar Fuchs ("Beautiful Fruits," Pinsk).

As he felt his wife close in, Fine set himself for the wake-up lunge, but, like a car motor firing on after the ignition has been turned off, his association fumbled out:

I am happy. I was a fat man, and now am a meaty man. Thanks to my wife's fanaticism about exercise, and mine about calcium and tryptophan-rich food. Pop has high triglycerides and cholesterol. I am thirty-four. My lucky number. Age thirty-four is *the* turning point in great men's lives: Buddha, maybe Moses, Christ, Shakespeare, Chekhov, Proust, Einstein, Freud—*all Jews!* (Freud's period of "splendid isolation"). Mine? The possibility of greatness exists. Although I am quite short, inwardly I am quite tall. I am halfway through my training to become a Freudian analyst at The Boston Institute (TBI; there is now a rival institute, and so we analytic candidates must face the choice: "TBI or not TBI, that is the question"—and my wife thinks I'm not funny?!)—only six more years to go!—and am considered a rising star, protégé of the great Vergessen himself! I do research. I see patients. I am a wooden peg, fitting snugly into a wooden hole in the world. At the peak of my life, into a nest smooth as gumwood, solid as oak, why not? I've grown a chestnut-red mustache and beard. Wear a fat necktie around my neck. Tuck my tie into my vest. This vest, matching the suit, is pin-striped and custom-made for a reasonable price in England. Five minutes they measure you up. You select the cloth. Five months later it arrives: perfect fit. A metaphor: the life of a perfectly analyzed human being is measured. Day in, day out, year in, year out: perfect fit. "Constant object" for my patients, and for my wife too. Analysis has brought me a settled life and will soon bring me a high income. Analysts like me aspire to be, more than anything else, settled. *Per aspera ad settled.*

Stephanie was rising from deep sleep. Fine tried to ease his right leg toward the edge of the bed, and she, with a late–REM murmur, hooked her left leg over his own. Trapped, he lay still.

Stephanie. Wife. Body. Expert in body, as I am in mind. Works for the senator, on "fitness." Claims she "grew me up," and that analysis has "shrunk me down" again. It's difficult on spouses. Left-handed females, because of their weirdly bilateralized brain wiring, are bizarre. Diagnosis of wife?: "hysteric." I wish she'd get herself into analysis, the most powerful tool of the century. As a boy I'd loved outer space, Einstein; as a man, inner space, Freud.

Stephanie rubbed, leg and nipple both, a seesaw.

Our sex life has tapered. This is normal. We know each other's moves. Time to have a child. A Fine baby. I have been clear: I am ready. She is not. What the hell is wrong with her! Careful. *Think* about that. She should get analyzed, work through her infantile conflicts preventing her from having a baby. My six o'clock patient, my TBI analytic "control" case, my hysteric, is in the midst of an erotic transference neurosis that would knock your socks off! *Very* sexy! In a few minutes she'll lie down on the couch and I'll be gazing down her dress at those round young terrific braless tits! Muskmelons, oh yeah, real boomers! My penis stirs. An erection blooms, as *there* as—well, yes: a banana!

Stephanie's hand found Fine's penis. She muttered, sleepily: "Oooh! What've we here?" Fine lunged, which brought about the usual reflex tightening of her arm around his neck. He began to cough. A second lunge usually broke her hammerlock, and he tensed for the effort. "Mmmm," she said, warmly, "how 'bout a cuddle?"

"You know I can't. I've got my Six o'clock."

"Time f'r'a cuddle. Seize the day 'n my tush, mm?"

"I think," Fine said, remembering the rule of analysis about the two cardinal mistakes an analyst can make—to be seductive (promise more than is delivered) or to be sadistic (deliver more than is promised)—"that for you to be seductive when you know I don't have time is to be sadistic."

" 'Nuf time f'r'a cuddle, before your sexpot at six."

A hostile referent to my hysteric. *"Think* about it." With a lurch Fine broke free and tumbled facedown onto the rug. What a way to get up out of bed, every single day!

"Ahhh!" Steph screamed, and jumped up standing on the bed, kicking at the pillow, nightie raised thigh high. *"Yoww!"*

"What?!" asked Fine, marveling at the delicate black fan of pubic hair, seen through the nightgown as through a window shade—clothes the erotic prod for the voyeur.

"A roach!"

"No, wait—stop!—it's a hopper!" Fine leaped onto the bed, and cornered the poor frightened little invertebrate. From its markings, he knew it was one of his high-calcium, intelligent ones. He put it gently in his pajama pocket, buttoning the flap.

"You and your dumb insects!"

"This is a smart one! Maybe even genius—*Yeoww!*" With a scream, Fine lost his balance, flung his arms out, hitting Steph in the back, and fell again onto the rug. She, with athletic grace, somersaulted, a perfect roll, stopping just short of the TV.

"First fall of the day," she said, happily, "a conjugal double! Forget the grasshoppers in the bed, the psycho-paralytic party last night—let's just keep 'falling' in love!" But then, grimacing, putting hand to forehead, she said: "Ow! Hung over!"

"What you did at that party is going to torment me at the Institute for the next three months!" Fine said, angrily. ("If you're angry, so be angry"—Fumbles.)

"What'd I do? I can't remember."

"You were drunk!"

"That's why I can't remember! Oh tell me, what?"

"You know that they're all having trouble working through their Oedipal envy at my being the first in my class to finish my analysis—how could you have said that?"

"Said what? Oh, please—tell me!"

"*The penis is a red herring,* that's what!" She let out a sharp crackle of laughter, which made him even angrier. "Too loose, Stephanie, that's what they all said, you're too loose!"

"*Me,* loose? They're all so tight, Hitler would've been too loose! My pulse started to stop—I had to do something!"

"Much too loose," Fine said, heading toward the bathroom.

"And that albino Santa Claus, that Vergessen—"

"*Think* about it!"

"You know, Fine, you really are turning into a man they all love to laugh at."

Fine disappeared into the bathroom. His analysis being the understanding of self (mind-body), Fine took great pains to control his physical being. Freud stated the purpose of life to be *lieben und arbeiten* (love and work), and Fine's life work now was *The Fine Theory,* a modern attempt to link biology and psychology. Based on his theory, he followed a high-calcium diet, jogged compulsively, and analyzed. He faced the mirror, zeroing in on his lips: the upper, a definitive line, the lower—the unconscious?—a plump, pink, devil-may-care curl. The Fine nose still seemed a rudely displaced Diasporic "J," plodding along against the flow of the face. And yet I have worked through my nose: in some scents—oops!—great slip!—my analysis was a seven-year nose job. And

a fruitful one, at that! He fondled his neat beard—grown when
he'd joined the Institute—trimmed in the image of S. Freud.

Fine washed, peed, washed, shaved, brushed teeth, hair, and
then, strangely, felt an urge to move his bowels. He sat, praying
for peace with his rear end, associating: why do we take care of
the earliest stages of development—oral, anal—in the earliest
stages of the day? Today, clearly, anal is ascendant. Fantasy: Stephanie, three days per week at work in Washington, D.C., is having an affair with a large black man with a large purple penis, a
Washington Redskin. Wiping, flushing, washing, ready to face
her, he hid his penis with his palm and entered, genital stage left.

Stephanie stood in her nightgown in front of the lightening
window. The dawn, reddish gold, came through in soft ellipses
and sharp brighter wedges. From this high perch, Fine could see
across the harbor to Boston. Putting her hair up into an all-busi-
ness bun; her breasts, pulled high, were filmed, sharply outlined,
elongated.

"Mangoes," he whispered.

From analysis, Fine now understood his fixation: head on
mother's breast, feeling her breathing—in . . . out . . . rise
. . . fall—the most comforting feeling in the world. Aha! Another reason I'm happy: the planet has just tilted into open season
on my obsession.

At thirty-two, Stephanie was in top physical shape. She worked
out every day: first, a series of balletic stretches and her morning
five-mile run; then, at lunch, the Cosmos Gym in Boston, or the
Washington version of same. Naturally athletic, for the past two
years she'd been into bodybuilding, and was at the stage where
the soft rounded feminine was being edged by the "cuts," the slip
of the biceps in under the deltoids, the pecs shaping the breasts,
the lats echoing through her back like ripples as she brushed her
hair and looked out the window across the water. She stood
spread, statuesque. As she turned, he saw the soft mound of
tummy and associated:

A baby should be nesting in there, yes. The energy stirring in
spring. A baby. And, surprised, he whispered:

"Tomato!"

"Sorry, Fine," she said, seeing him in the mirror, "I'm in hang-
over-city—but as they say: *No pain, no gain,* eh?"

Her sheer silk added mystery. How right Freud was—the fantasy *is* more erotic than the real. In the puzzle of the world, to find an interlocking piece? In the fifth year of analysis, he'd discovered them to be the perfect match: obsessive to hysteric. The shape of his wife took his breath away. As she turned toward him, he thought: how beautiful she is! He tried to recall the last time his lips had been on her breasts, the last time that husband and wife had done the quintessentially human act, making love. His eyes settled on her chilled hard nipples. The tension was high.

Steph turned, and said, "Well!—look at the little red soldier, at attention in that cute curly hair! C'mon—just a touch, eh?"

Warily, Fine moved closer, and said: "Where?"

"Wherever you want."

Slowly, he raised his hand. His impulse was to touch one nipple and he got halfway there before he understood that this would be "acting out" and so he moved to touch her defective lip, until he understood that this would be "reaction formation" against his impulse. Fruits spun like in a slot machine, and he stopped. She reached out, put her palm on his cheek, drew him gently toward her, but just as they were about to touch, he, startled, moved away.

"What's wrong now?!"

Fine had realized that they were standing in front of the other window in that corner of the room, the floor-to-ceiling window that faced Jefferson House, where he was the psychiatrist-in-charge, where all of his inpatients lived. He'd had the suspicion, for many months, that they'd been peering in. "They can see us, Stephanie!"

"How exciting!" she said. "Take a risk!"

"It's never enough—"

"Used to be more than—"

"Later," said Fine, heading toward the closet for his pin-striped suit. He transferred the hopper to his shirt pocket.

"Pshhhhh," said Steph, watching his penis deflate, "the flesh is willing but the spirit is analyzed."

"There's no time now."

"There might never be another 'now,' Fine, ever! My flight tonight might crash! I've had such a premonition, all weekend long! Why wait, if you know you're going to die!"

"Freud says that the thing that separates man from animals is 'the procrastinating mechanism of thought.' "

"Oh boy! If Six o'clock only knew! She thinks you and I are making wild, passionate love, right now—she imagines *we* do what you imagine doing with *her!* What a scene: all across America neurotics are having fantasies about what their shrinks are *really* like, totally unaware that they're the same compressed nebbishes that sit behind them grunting and yawning, at seventy-five a shot!"

"Hmm," said Fine, flashing on Semrad, teacher of Vergessen, " 'we analysts are just messes, trying to help bigger messes.' "

"I wish you'd say something just from you, to me. Not your head, but some simple message, from your heart? Like you used to?"

"Yes!" he said, delighted at her softening. "Read *The Fine Theory*—it's all there—the synthesis of head and heart!"

"Read it? Why read it when I have to *live* it?!"

"It's different in print. If you'd only learn to work my WANG, you'd see!" Socks and shoes in hand, he was at the door. "Great, isn't it, Fine?"

"What's that?"

"To think you're never going to die?"

Fine was startled. About a year ago her beloved father died. Is this an "anniversary reaction"? What technique to use? Try the "exploratory": "Yes, and what was the date of your father's death?"

"What?!" she said, shocked, her face sagging with hurt. "Please, Fine, don't drag him into this, okay?"

"I wish you'd get yourself into analysis," he said. "Fast!" She blinked, laughed, reached for her Nikes, shaking her head.

"Married to you, Fine, I feel like I already am."

"What an incredible wish!—to have me as your analyst?! Gosh, look at the time—see you at breakfast, hon, okay?"

"Fine," she answered, offering the setup for the punch.

"Yes?" he asked, not catching it. Then, from her silence, he did, but too late: his response—"Stephanie"—bounced aimlessly around the bedroom, and then forlornly out into the hallway, and Fine, feeling attacked and strangely gloomy—her "never going to die" still reverberated deep down, like a night terror sensed dimly in daylight—stumbled barefoot down the stairs and out the front door into the innocent and reliable air.

Although it was chill, it was spring. The season had flowed

north at the rate of fifteen miles and one hundred vertical feet per day. It would reach the summit of Mount Washington at the same time it would reach Labrador. The season of procreation and suicide. May had been proclaimed "Mental Hygiene Month" in the Commonwealth of Massachusetts. The state fish was the cod and the state drink cranberry juice. Fine sat on the front stoop of the stately brick Greek Revival house that he lived in rent free, on the grounds of Stow-on-Wold, and put on his socks and shoes. He owned only black socks, so he never had to worry about mismatching. The huge copper beech in the front yard, five feet across the elephant-skin gray trunk, all gnarled and solid and rising in a river of limbs two hundred feet in the air, was just fattening into bud, for the season, that year, was late. Fine watched a thin squirrel flow downlimb to land, scrabbling in the hard ground for a nut, and said: "Ovary." A robin red-breast bent an ear to a fantasied worm. The cold dawn seemed sinister. In New England, May was the cruelest month, with suicides cresting in spring. The peaks of suffering come at the peaks of renewal, Fine thought, the marginal ones, fearing rebirth more than demise, pine away. The pineal: in spring the fuller spectrum of sunlight hits the pineal gland in the center of the skull, the absorption of calcium goes up and there it is: spring fever! Calcium the rockbottom of everything!

Despite the tinge of warmth in the cold, Fine shivered. The rough winter was barely over, there were residual gravelike mounds of snow, he could see his breath. He walked down the path, opened the gate, closed it behind, and took in the vista: to the northwest across the bay, the City of Boston was catching the rouge dawn light. The buildings preened—a row of gray ladies, waiting. In their years in Boston, Steph and Fine had seen the dull skyline sprout—as empty of character as, say, Houston—fueled by corruption. The most racist and corrupt city in America, he thought, where blacks too don't dare walk out alone after dark. The pine and sea grape, the whippets of sumac, flowed with the brisk ocean breeze. We're in an "icehouse age," Fine knew: carbon dioxide being sucked from air into land-calcium and then washed into the sea as carbonate spheres, "ooids," forming shells, and calcite. Analyzing the chill, Fine hardly heard the cry of the lone gull perched on a branch of the wind. Prior to his analysis, this shape—the John Cage-atonal squawk coming out from the asymmetrically perfect flying machine to crackle in the spacetime topology of dawn—this would have delighted him. Not now.

For by this time Fine's inner world had separated itself off from —and blanketed—his outer.

Fine turned up the hill toward his office on the top floor of Jefferson House. He started to whistle "Some Enchanted Evening"—his father often whistled it, cutting meat—but a sharp throb behind his right eyeball, in over his temporal lobe, stopped the sound.

Another headache? Been getting a lot of headaches, lately. Why? I've terminated. I should be done with headaches already! He started to analyze this headache, but his glance at the Stow-on-Wold water tower on the hilltop brought associations: penis/pineapple. Another throb. He flashed on Fumbles. It eased. He went on.

Stow-on-Wold was four years old, a private mental hospital set on Long Island, a long thin hilly finger of land poking up into Boston Harbor from the south, at Squantum. The island was joined to the mainland by the mile-long, two-lane rusty metal Curley Bridge, named for the corrupt mayor. During the seven years of his analysis, Fine had completed his four-year residency in general psychiatry at McLean Hospital, which certified him to practice psychiatry. (He had also enrolled at The Boston Institute to become a Freudian psychoanalyst.) For the past three years he'd been on the staff at Stow. He was chief psychiatrist of one of the inpatient wards, Jefferson House. He specialized, there, in the treatment of the very sick patients (not candidates for Freudian analysis) whose psychoses often involved problems with eating disorders. Stow-on-Wold also provided Fine with a modern, fully equipped laboratory for his biological research. In his continuing effort to understand the neurophysiological basis of learning and memory, he continued to teach grasshoppers to lift their legs. Finally he seemed to be on the verge of a major breakthrough concerning the effect of calcium on this learning. He'd even begun to use his Jefferson House inpatients as human subjects, feeding them calcium, getting their informed consent. All was done kosher, here—

"Hooray hooray it's the first of May! Outdoor fucking begins today!" A tall, tanned, athletic-looking young man with blond hair stood before Fine. Name? Cooter. Diagnosis? Manic-depressive illness, manic-psychotic phase.

"Up early, Cooter, eh?" Fine asked.

"Always, doc—how they hangin'?"

"Think about that," said Fine, trying to encourage "ego functions" in his poor psychotic, and, going in the back stairway of Jefferson House, started up the three flights to his attic office. All mental illness is divided into three parts: neurosis ("us"); psychosis ("them"); character disorders (sometimes "us"/sometimes "them"). Fine entered his office, out of breath.

Every detail of his office, he knew, said something about himself. Being committed to being a "blank screen" for his analytic patients' associations, he was careful about what he kept and where he kept it in his oak-paneled sanctuary. The analyst's couch was standard issue, neutral dark-brown leather. He unrolled the roll of paper head-napkins and ripped one off and placed it perfectly in place. His fingers brushed the smooth leather and he felt pride at being one of the long line of practitioners of this most sacred art of delving into another human being's mind, with the hope of healing. No, not "hope," for the analyst must be without "hope." "Hope" is the patient's problem, not mine. Fine checked the position of the analyst's easy chair, behind and slightly to one side of the couch, out of view of the analysand. In his line of sight across the room, on the bookshelf, were the clock and the several horizontal feet (twenty-four volumes) of *The Standard Edition of the Works of Sigmund Freud* (Strachey ed.), in pale-blue paper covers. On top, two photographs: the classic Freud-at-thirty-four, all bushy beard and floppy forelock, the eyes dark, riveting, piercing; and Vergessen, his modern idol, head of TBI, an all-white albino, with pale pink eyes, plump fist supporting chubby rosy cheek, head cocked, smiling. Pop; mom.

Fine felt anxious, and, wondering where his work with his Six o'clock had left off last Friday, picked up his case notebook that contained his transcription of every session for the past year of treatment. He stopped himself: my wish to do something for my poor hysteric is *my* problem, not hers. ("The ideal analyst is without thought, memory, or desire,"—Vergessen.) Analysis is nonjudgmental, i.e., I should not have a "wish." (Never mind that last judgmental "should.") My wish is part of the well-known "Monday-morning crust." After the Saturday-Sunday break, the

analysand has a higher resistance to the analysis. And so does the
analyst. Well then, where are we in her analysis? Associate: tits.
Startled at the crudeness, he stopped. ("If it's tits, so it's tits"—
Fumbles.)

So, Fine thought, relieved, it's tits.

He went to the door. What a great thing, he thought, to be paid
to do what you love to do! What elegance, to have, as your only
tool, yourself!

The question on the leading edge of Fine's mind?

How do people change?

The answer: orthodox Freudian psychoanalysis.

Six o'clock, conditioned by her two hundred and thirty-nine
previous sessions as "Eight o'clock" (Fine had rescheduled her
last week, after he terminated with Fumbles), entered the waiting
room from the bathroom right on time, at six o'clock precisely.

7

ALTHOUGH HER NAME was Duffy Adams, Fine had nicknamed her "Dora, the Hysteric," after Freud's famous case *(Dora, an Analysis of a Case of Hysteria,* 1905). This, common practice at the Boston Institute, helped Fine keep in mind the rules for the analysis of a hysteric. She was one of his two control cases, part of his training to become an analyst. The other was his Five o'clock (P.M.): Maurice Slotnick, alias "Ratman, the Obsessive." Fine had to report each session to his supervisor at TBI, Vergessen, and so he was always wary of making analytic "mistakes." If Fine failed his hysteric, he'd have to repeat with another, adding five more years to his training; a failed obsessive meant another five-year bid. His palms were sweaty—such was the pressure to do a "perfect" session. Vergessen was said to have done seven, one in front of the two-way mirror at the Institute. V.'s mentor, the legendary Semrad, had done dozens; and the mysterious Frau Metz was rumored to do them every time out! (Though Metz was said to have said: "The truly *gemütlich* session—total silence, no analyst, no analysand—is impossible." Like the Heisenberg "uncertainty principle," Fine thought.) Fine knew that his competitiveness was his Oedipal rivalry with "The Man Behind the Cleaver," his pop, and he *accepted* this. ("In the Oedipal fight there are no winners; it's how you lose that counts"—Vergessen.)

Fine opened the door and saw his hysteric: twenty-six, rich WASP, only child, many love affairs, inappropriate marriage, no children, frigidity, appropriate divorce, remarriage, divorce, many more love affairs, worse frigidity, genital-phase arrest, meteoric rise to top job at Federal Reserve Bank of Boston, paralyzing frigidity, analysis, presently in midst of erotic transference to her analyst, Fine. He thought:

An example of the most profound aspect of human nature: unanalyzed, we continually do things that wreck our lives.

As soon as she saw him, she jumped to her feet. From the harmonic recoil of her breasts, Fine saw that once again she was braless. Honeydews. His years of training had shown him that any detail of body and/or dress was a holograph of the psyche, and, with Sherlock Holmsian precision he noted her freshly shampooed flax-blond hair, and her green eye shadow and hot-pink lipstick (Stephanie had pointed out that women who wear such makeup spend lavishly on sexy underwear). And why is "Dora," today, dressed all in black?

Without realizing it, Fine did not meet her gaze. He made no real contact with her. He hardly saw her at all.

She seemed on the verge of tears, and waved a newspaper at him, snuffling. Hysterical, from *hysterikos* (Greek), womb; the seventeenth-century theory that such symptoms were caused by a womb that casts off and wanders through the body, filling the mind with toxic vapors. She did not say hello because she knew Fine would not respond. As he followed her into the office, staring at the undulating lace edge of her panties, Fine wondered how this sniffling "loose" blond sex bomb could be the highest-ranking woman at the Federal Reserve? A jiggle, the yen plummets? A wiggle, a million Germans get nostalgic about Auschwitz? Her scent? Sex. Her flaunting her body like this, knowing I cannot respond, is sadistic! Scary! Testosterone, the only hormone that peaks in the morning, is critical at puberty in the development of spatial awareness. What good is that, Fine?! He sat, took up his pen and pad, ready to work through the frigidity hidden under all this heat. ("Hysterics suffer from reminiscences"—Freud.) Undress her mind, Fine. Listen, but not too carefully, for "selective inattention"—"listening with the third ear"—is key. What a job:

you get paid to daydream! *Rule:* the affective, or emotional, content of the *first* thing a patient says is what the whole session will be about. *Feeling* never lies. On edge, he honed in on doing an A+ session. Wouldn't it be great today if I could say nothing at all?

"Did you see this morning's paper? Oh God I'm so scared for you, Dr. Fine, did you see it, huh?"

Affective word: "scared." Follow it. She waited for a response, and in deference to the Monday-morning crust, Fine decided to give her a gift, a psychoanalytic grunt: "Umphgh?"

"Someone killed another psychiatrist—right across the bay in Boston! Shot him! Dr. Timothy Myer—did you know him? The second one murdered in two months! I'm terrified for you! If you were to die I don't know what I'd do!" She gathered herself up and, voice trembling, barely in control, said: "I'd *kill* myself! I really really would! I had the pills in my hand not an hour ago!"

What a great beginning! Beneath this silly chatter about murder (Fine *did* vaguely know the victim—an arrogant, C+ practitioner) lies that gold nugget of analysis, a "transference neurosis"! She's distorting her "real" relationship to me, her analyst, in a way consistent with the hidden neurotic conflicts of her infancy! Her fear that I be killed is the same as her wish that I be killed. ("There are no negatives in the unconscious"—Vergessen.) The task: to find out *who* these feelings she is putting onto me belong to.

"Imagine—sitting here in your office, vulnerable, anybody can walk in, you're so innocent and trusting, they pull a gun—"

Fine watched, incredulous, as she did something she hadn't done since the initial session: she turned on the couch, propped herself up on her hands, and stared at him. He found himself sighting straight down her half-unbuttoned blouse at her breasts! Oh, that uncanny knack of hysterics to sense my sensual obsession and use it to put me on the spot. Her breasts hung down, swinging, seeming to swell out against their curved topology before being pinched in by the rosy nipples. Cranshaws! Fine felt a stirring in his pants—the classic Führersitzer sign for diagnosis of hysteria! He marveled, anew, at being a tool: what the patient makes the analyst feel (if the analyst is perfectly analyzed, without his own distortions called "countertransference") is the same as what other people feel from the patient, and is, hence, the neurosis. To make these unconscious distortions conscious is analysis, cure. Hysterics cause erections; obsessives cause somnolence; schizophrenics cause the hair on the back of your neck to stand on end; depressives get you down; psychopaths get you to cash bad checks. She's using her eroticism to attack.

"Oh, Dr. Fine, it made me realize how much I love you!"

Fine looked from her breasts to her eyes, felt her hunger, and was filled with the wish to fuck the living daylights out of her. A hundred years ago Breuer had been confronted with this same situation, when Dora turned on his couch and embraced him. Scared, Breuer told Freud, who'd been through similar stuff. Breuer returned the embraces. Freud, who felt unattractive to women and couldn't believe that they wanted to fuck *him,* instead of *acting* took the incredible step of *thinking* about it. He reached the conclusion: they're mistaking me for somebody else. And psychoanalysis—the greatest tool of the century—was born. Fine was staggered that here he faced the same choices as those brave pioneers of the mind: return the embrace, repell the embrace, or make himself *meta* to the embrace and, with the patient, work it through, explore the feelings and thoughts that *are* it, and by bending the bars of the neurosis, free this poor sex-riddled female from yet another fruitless pacing around her cage.

"I really do love you!"

Eye to eye, Fine felt flummoxed, and glanced at her boobs.

"Don't you have any feeling at all when I say that?! All you can do is look down at my breasts? Answer me!"

Fine knew she had him, and, feeling guilty, riffled his head for the "correct" response. Still in the opening ten minutes, too early to interpret. Intense feeling here. ("When they talk thought, you talk feeling; when they talk feeling, you talk thought"—Reuben, expert in anal aggression, Fine's rival at TBI.) Play it safe—address the defense—the resistance—use the "what keeps you from" line: "Yes and *what keeps you from* lying back down on the couch?"

"Come off it! You're leching after me and we both know it—AHH!—what's *that?*" Fine, perfect analyst, never moved, as she pointed at his heart. "Something's in your pocket, something's moving around in your pocket! Icky! What is it?"

"You have the fantasy that something's moving in my pocket?"

"It really is—look! Ucky!"

"And tell me about this fantasy, hmm?"

"It's no fantasy, it's real. It actually *is!*"

"Yes, and what are your thoughts about this 'is,' hmm?"

"Oh God! You make me so mad—I could kill!"

Fantastic! This tawdry murder, even if real—it might be her fantasy or joke—is providing terrific material for the session.

"Look—I don't mind that you're weird and inhuman—I don't even mind that you stare at my boobs—but I can't stand your staring in secret like a Peeping Tom. At least have the decency to admit it!"

Inwardly wincing, Fine tried hard to keep his face a blank screen for her projections. How do they do it? How do these hysterics intuit their analyst's weaknesses, every damn time! She's right. I should admit it. She's making me feel like a rapist, like I'm totally incompetent to deal with her, either as an analyst or as a man. She's as demanding as my wife! Fine had an urge to tell her all this, and with the urge, felt strangely closer to her, more *with* her. Tell her. But no. *My* feelings have no place in the analysis. Trapped by her intense gaze, Fine shifted his own to the photo of Freud. Rumor had it Freud couldn't stand eye contact with patients (in a Ferenczi letter he'd called patients *gesindel:* "rabble"), and had sought out couch-and-chair. Fine glanced next at the photo of Vergessen, and, desperately merging two famous techniques—the "counterprojective" and the "empathic"—mimicked the earnest tone of the great V.: "Yes, and *how hard it must be* for you to have these strong feelings for me. These erotic feelings—these *sexual* feelings, hmm?"

"What?!" she said, startled. "Yes, perhaps it is . . ."

Fine knew from her silence that he'd hit home. This was the story of her life. She did this with everybody. Under control again, he mimicked V.: *"Tell* me about these feelings, hmm?"

"OK, Dr. Fine, OK. . . ." and she rolled back on her back and said "Breasts—I have the fantasy of your touching my breasts. Drives me crazy. I see you reaching from where you're sitting and putting your long thin fingers on my shoulder, my neck . . ."

What a great case! Long thin fingers?! Mine are short and fat! Fine, relieved, now knew he could let her go on associating until about the twenty-five-minute mark, at which time he would enquire as to *who*—mom, pop, this Uncle Savage we'd heard so much about who'd often locked her up with him in the maid's closet—these long thin fingers belonged to, on the little girl's buds, the hairless musky pudendum. And she thought that this *murder* was the issue, imagine that?! How cleverly V. had first introduced me to transference:

"You have a date with Marilyn Monroe. What comes to mind?"

"I better wear my gabardine coat."

Smiling, the sly albino: "Why your *gabardine* coat?"

Sheepishly, Fine: "My *mom* wears gabardine coats!"

"That's transference."

The implications, Fine thought, are staggering. We distort all relationships, we are always treating the other like mom, pop, or Uncle Savage. We paint every person with the colors of our childhood. A great gap exists between self and other, and all closeness is a mere shouting across that gap. One never is "as I really am." Stephanie does not believe this, but thinks that we can get closer, and demands this from me. Her resistance to getting analyzed is itself a neurotic defense, in need of analysis. If patients only knew: therapy is not the telling of the story, but the analysis of the *resistance* to the telling and the *transference* distortion by the teller of the told. Not past but present—analysis is in the here and now.

For Fine, transference was a double distortion, for he had the extraordinary fate of being a man often mistaken for other men.

"—your penis. With the tip of my tongue I'm licking the soft skin underneath, then I run my tongue up to the top—it's like a cap on a mushroom, or a hot-pink rosebud—"

Helluva profession: seventy-five an hour to listen to a gorgeous blonde talk about sucking your Weimar—oops!—weiner? Most powerful tool of the century. Why can't my wife do that? Our oral sex has stopped. How lucky I am to have found psychiatry!

Yet it had not been easy. Fine's first year with Fumbles had been an unhappy, stressful time. His whole world had come tumbling down around his ears. It had also been the first year of his psychiatry residency, when he'd done six months of internal medicine in a hospital—frightening and disgusting. In his psychiatry training, he'd felt totally incompetent. While everyone regresses in analysis, Fine, as usual, had done it more and deeper, and after a few months had turned into a bawling infant on Fumbles's

couch. He was unsure of everything! Totally lost, he missed Stephanie terribly. She'd gone to Paris, and Fine couldn't stand it.
He wrote voluminous passionate letters, made long sobbing calls
across time zones waking her in the middle of the night. His
paranoia, inflamed by his analysis, raged—he was sure she was
having an affair. He begged her to come back. After all she was
his wife! She, enjoying her freedom, resisted. Fine said to Fumbles: "I've got to fly over to see her!"

"If you got to fly, so fly," said Fumbles.

So Fine flew.

She'd never seen him so vulnerable. He, crying out for help,
touched her soul. He stirred up old, caring, almost maternal juices
in her. He needed her, desperately. He would kill himself! He
wimpered and pleaded with her for a whole weekend, and then, so
as not to miss his Monday morning session with Fumbles, left.

She came. She gave up her job in her father's business, came
back to Boston, moved in with Fine, and, through contacts she'd
made through John in Southie, got a job in politics, working for
the senator, first in "cultural affairs," and then, in fitness. And
Fine, comforted, continued his analysis and his residency. With
her support, he righted himself, and soon began to enjoy the challenge of learning to become a psychiatrist. He came to think that
in his neurosis lay a real gift: an acute sensitivity to the mental
state of others. With Fumbles he conceptualized his hyperacute
attention as a healthy side of his lifelong paranoia—he thought
himself one of a whole generation of Jews propelled into psychiatry by bigotry. Having been on guard against people, he now was
rooted in people. When he joined the Institute, he felt *at home.*
And he discovered, too, the power of therapy: contrary to public
impression, as a psychiatrist you really could cure. Most diseases
of the body—lung, heart, liver, kidney—have no cure; doctors
palliate. But as a psychiatrist he found he could lock into a person's life at a crucial moment, and tip the balance in a life-saving
way. Out on a ledge? We bring you back! Through therapy armed
with insight, you may never go out on the ledge again! Most
patients are so psychologically unaware, even a simple insight can
bring enormous change—like saying: *"Think* about what you
feel." The greatest. And the greatest of the greatest? Analysis. In-
depth five times a week for years, bringing about true change of
personality. Fine felt exuberant, full of that zest for life that had

been his salvation. The only real problem he'd encountered was not to *show* his "zest." As Vergessen asked: "Zest? What place does 'zest' have in the work?" It was years before Fine analyzed out his "zest" as his own neurotic need, and stifled it. It came from his—

"—*mother?*"

Silence. Uh oh. Trouble. Fine knew that this was the end of a question, and, wondering if it demanded a response, checked the clock. The twenty-eight-minute mark? Perfect time for an interpretation, but his attention had floated too far off! Damn—the session is going so well—I've said almost *nothing!* One of my best sessions ever! He tried another grunt—"Rghmphgph"—but the silence continued, and the tension mounted. He felt himself *blocking!* What to say?! ("When you don't know what to say, say '*Tell* me about it'—'it' being the last word heard"—Vergessen.)

"Mm, yes, and *tell* me about . . . your mother?"

"OK," said Six o'clock, relieved. "Her long thin fingers, with their perfectly manicured nails . . ."

The fingertips on the breasts are mom's?! She is treating *me* as if I were her mother? And all the others—lovers, enemies, pop, Uncle Savage, even her own mom—as if they were her mom! In *The Fine Theory: Biology and Psychology: Resynthesis,* Fine was trying to join body and mind in a general theory of being. Now he keyed on *Part II: Psychology:* Freud had been expert in genital-Oedipal struggles (father); since his death, others had looked earlier in development, at pre-genital-Oedipal (mother). Freud saw men and women as two sides of the same coin. The thinking was symmetric, linear. Fine saw himself making the twentieth-century leap that Einstein had made in physics: he was bringing nonlinear, relative thinking to the study of human development. Rather than men and women being two sides of the same coin, they were two different currencies. Fine had written in *Anal. J.:* "Relationships are relative. All fetuses start off female. In the womb, in a great military rush of testosterone, half split off as male. Thus, the first asymmetry: men *separate from,* warring; women *stay with,* relating." The key, Fine realized, was "empathy": the ability to put yourself in another person's shoes, feelingly. Fine had data that the capacity for empathy is qualitatively different in women and men (female newborns respond more than males to other babies' cries of distress). After all, who ever heard of *"men's* intuition"?

Of a *"matriot"*? Yes, when testosterone kicks in, empathy gets kicked out.

Thus Freud's most famous question, stuck in the side of the century: *"Was will das Weib?"* ("What do women want?"). Fine saw this as Freud's admission that, given his limited empathic skills, the female was beyond him. Hadn't he called women's psychology "the dark continent"? Yet that question is easy, far easier than asking *"Was will der Mann?"* What *do* men want, anyway? Hard to say. Women are so different from men that a qualitatively new theory, centered on empathy, is needed. The empathy-schism lay at the heart of the failure of male-female relationships, of the human sacrifice called "marriage." Women want "intimacy"; men see this as "demand"; men want, say, "expression"; women see this as "distance." All of this in the name of love. Yet with two such disparate feeling-concepts of "love," what chance do "relationships" have? One needed to find the missing link between biology and psycholo—

"—so why in the world can't I make it with men? Every time I get involved, I get terrified! Because of my body, my sexiness, I'm pursued everywhere, these men try to meet me—the way they do it is so comical!—I meet someone, they seem fine—oops—"

"Umph."

"—we talk, we get to know one another, I warn them that I'm a handful, that I have to feel *related* in order to go down—to go further in the relationship I mean, and they say okay, and we relate—I only choose nice warm men, inept warm men, actually, like Woody Allen and you—I mean like you only warmer—"

Fine, impaled, grunted louder: "Umph!"

"—and then, finally, we get into a room, a room with a bed, into a bed, they start to put their hands on my breasts, and there I go—Miss Eskimo of the Back Bay! It happened again over the weekend! I can't stand it! I don't want to be frigid, I want to really make love! No matter how hot I get at the tenderness, I get ice cold at the touch! I hate myself for it! And I hate my mother! Hate hate hate!—" She burst into tears, sobbing.

What a great case! Fine thought. ("WASPs are God's Frozen People"—Dr. Pelvin, chief of Stow-on-Wold.) As with an Eskimo and snow, so with an analyst and tears—twenty different kinds. These? "Self-hate." We love to see tears, for it means we've ripped through the defenses and have gotten a straight shot at the affect.

Dr. Leon Bergeneiss, the ranking Jungian-Freudian at TBI, often claimed, with pride: "I have never failed to make a female patient cry." Fine, feeling happy, let her cry on. Her tears are proof, he thought: she can't hate mom without hating herself. Women are connected/men are separate. She is opened up—zap her now! A glance at the clock—exactly the "correct" time! Here comes the cruncher—the single Fine interpretation.

"Umghrgch!" Fine cleared his throat. She stopped crying.

In an empathic tone: "You are searching for a good mother in me, in men. But when they touch your breasts, you feel your own bad mother's fingers, and your 'relational-self' is transformed. You relate to all of us as your own bad mother. And how could you help, then, but freeze, hmmm?" Not bad. Wordy, even prolix, not surgical like Vergessen, not colloquial like Semrad, and certainly not the mythical "golden bullets" of Frau Metz. Yet without the sadism of Bergeneiss or "Crusher" Gold, the TBI giant whose hobby was pro wrestling. The "correct interpretation," yes. Let's see what she does.

The clock moved. Six o'clock did not. She lay there, weeping softly, shoulders shaking, not bothering to search her purse for a hankie. Fine, in the notorious debate at the Institute on "whether or not it is the responsibility of the analyst to provide Kleenex," had come down firmly on the side of orthodoxy, and there were to be found no Kleenex in his office. Keenly, Fine analyzed these tears: "grief, mourning." He saw clearly that in the session her tears had gone from (A) hysterical-manipulative through (B) infantile-regressed to (C) mature-adult. Just as they were supposed to! He watched her shoulders shaking, heard her sobs, saw her wet cheeks and reddening nose and congratulated himself: a virtually perfect session! Fine said: "It's time for us to stop."

Good analysand that she was, she got up, went to the door. He arose and walked halfway across the room behind her, once again admiring her valentine of buns, slightly a-swish, but, somehow, now, less provocative and sadistic. She opened the inner door, turned to him, and said: "Thank you."

"You're welcome good night."

"What?!" she said, shocked to have gotten a response after the session was technically "over." This had never happened before, and she looked at him, amazement in her eyes.

Oh no! Fine thought. Me and my courtesy! After a session like this, to ruin it with a "doorknob" comment?! One of the dumbest mistakes in the book! How could I do this? She's looking straight at me, like she expects something. What now? Panic! ("In panics, cough"—Vergessen.) Fine coughed.

"Why Dr. Fine, you're blushing!"

Fine, in a total curfuffle, coughed harder.

"Maybe they were wrong to laugh at you! You're human, after all, honey—ciao!"

Fine watched her instantly transform herself back into her hysterical mode—the jiggle, the wiggle, the "honey," the "ciao"!—and wondered again who the "they" are who "laugh" at him. As if she were in cahoots with my wife. Six o'clock finally left.

Shattered, Fine slumped down onto the couch. Associate. I can't take endings: as a boy saying nighty-night to my dear mother, I felt such heights of love for her that as she left, my fear spiraled terribly, down the steep slope of sleep. Oh! This'll set us back months! How can I face Vergessen in supervision? In an effort to firm himself up, Fine decided to suck the first Finestone of the day. He went to his desk, opened the small inlaid-cedar box he'd bought in Marrakech. Within were several chalky-white stones the size of prunes, similar to the stones sold in flower shops to put around potted plants. Finestones. He and his research assistant, the sinewy Ms. Ando, had perfected the process of polishing the rough stones to a milky-smooth surface. Finestones were the practical application of *Fine Theory, Part I: Biology.* They were high in calcium. Calcium, with two positive charges, attracts negative-charged things, neutralizing negativity, forming links, binding, firming up. He had high hopes for marketing them, to reach vast segments of America. Fine put one into his mouth.

Plop. Suck.

Soon he felt firmer. He went downstairs, bracing for his wife, homing to breakfast. On the stoop lay the folded *Boston Globe:*

PSYCHIATRIST SLAIN IN OF
SECOND IN PAST TWO MO

Fine was shocked, feeling that same sick, "it can't be so!" revulsion he'd gone through with awful regularity over the last twenty years, from John Kennedy through John Lennon. So Six o'clock was accurate after all. Why would anyone want to kill a psychiatrist? He sighed, resigned. The world is going to hell. Statistics show that modern-day America is shifting, diagnostically, toward more severe psychopathology. While the percentage of psychotics stays the same (across culture and throughout history, 1 percent of the population is always schizophrenic), in the past decades in the USA the percentage of character disorders (borderlines, narcissists, psychopathic killers, drug addicts, etc.) has increased, neurotics declining proportionately. The diagnostic spectrum, like a child's toy of steel-balls-in-clown's-eyeballs, has tilted, and tilted back, bunching the sickies in the middle. There's a shortage of healthy neurotics for analysis. Desperate for cases, some analysts are advertising—even hooking neurotics in Harvard Square. I'm lucky. Happiness is having two healthy neurotics.

Fine thought the headline, somehow, too lurid. To cheer himself, he began whistling his father's favorite tune, "Some Enchanted Evening." He went into the kitchen and put the paper, like a joint of *trayf* meat, on the table for his wife. His headache abated, a bit, and he remembered that he'd forgotten something, but for the life of him could not recall, now, what.

8

FINE LONGED FOR a world of restraint. Upon entering the Institute, he'd been relieved to discover that Freud's famous line— "Times change, but the meaning of the unconscious is immortal" —had freed all candidates like himself from the guilt of not attending to "the news." He'd come down firmly against the drivel for the lumpen on TV, and had no car radio. He'd garnered many fruitful associations while driving. Fine read no newspapers. He assimilated news from patients, staff, and wife. Today's headline sufficed: for the second time in the past two months, a psychiatrist had been shot dead.

Fine, preparing his usual high-calcium, high-tryptophan breakfast of herring, tofu, and a dolomite cocktail (a mixture of magnesium and calcium, used for centuries by Eastern spiritualists on fasts), thought about the murders. Each victim, a male in his mid-thirties—had been found in his office. David Wholer, the first victim, was a married father of two, an expert on bisexuality (and, the gossip was, rumored to be bisexual). He'd been found on Sunday April second by a male "friend," slumped over his desk in his office in Coolidge Corner, Brookline, just past the Boston city line. He also saw patients in his home-office in Newton, five miles west, but had gone into town that particular Sunday on the spur of the moment, for an emergency session. No name had been written down in his appointment book. Money and credit cards had not been taken, and so robbery was not a motive. Fine glanced at the paper. Below the fold a photo caught his eye: a smiling, boyish-looking man, arm around wife and son, and testimonials—"a truly dedicated physician," etc. This was the second victim, Dr. Timothy Myer, an expert on gender. Fine had seen him around the Institute—his smooth cheeks fostered rumors that he was a secret transvestite, into electrolysis and estrogen, prepping for sex change. He'd been in his office on Sunday night, and the security guard had found him sprawled on the carpet in his ferny, exposed-brick office on Lewis Wharf, overlooking Boston Harbor, directly across from Stow-on-Wold. Again, no name appeared in his damask rose-colored log—another unscheduled, emergency session. He too had not been robbed.

Except of his life, Fine thought, sighing. Unbelievable. Every time he snuck a glance out into the "real" world, his worst fantasies proved an underestimate. One such murder could be chance, but two is sick design. There was no getting around it: someone was murdering psychiatrists.

Stephanie returned from her five-mile loop around the island, all flushed and beaming, and Fine listened hard for the affective content of the first thing she was to say.

"Hey, Fine, I saw your patient come and go—" she paused to catch her breath, check her pulse "—do you know she stashes her bra in her handbag, and puts it back on after the session?"

"What?" Fine blurted out.

"That's right. Those jiggly titties are exclusively for you. Know what it's like to carry those boobs around loose? Hey, it hurts! Beside, with her buns, that frontal bounce is overkill. How in the world did she ever discover that your thing is tits?"

Wobbly from this diclosure and from Stephanie's intrusion into the sacred grove of analysis, Fine dug deeper for the affect: jealous of my patient. She is competing with the other woman for the man's love. Little girl with mom for pop. The Oedipal—more accurately, the Electral—competition of the hysteric.

"And on the run, I remembered two new quickies!"

Oh no, Fine thought, not jokes. "Umphg?"

"What's the difference between a Jew and a canoe?"

Fine had grown to hate shtick jokes, and she knew it. The

affect? ("People are either sad, mad, or glad—all else is a defense" —Semrad.) Stephanie was "mad." My rejection of her "cuddle" earlier today. Use a neutral tone: "Tell me the difference, hmm?"

"A canoe tips."

Fine drew a blank. "I don't get it."

"You're joking!"

"No. I see a canoe tipping over, in a stream. But what's that got to do with Jews? 'Stream' of consciousness or something?"

"Oh boy!" She shook her head in disbelief. "Here's an easy one." Slowly, as if to a moron, she said: *"Why do Jews have big noses?"*

"Yes, and let's look at the dynamics of this, Stephanie?"

"What 'dynamics'?—I'm practicing for my act."

Fine groaned. Stephanie had been getting bored with her job as expert on fitness. She was talking more and more about her dream of becoming a stand-up comic. Fine, through his own analysis, knew that this came from her identification with her Yiddish-theater grandpa Al and her joke-cracking father. He usually humored her in this, but not today: the vulgar tide of these Joan Rivers must be stemmed. "Your jokes are a reflection of your hostility to me."

"They've got nothing to do with you, they're just jokes."

"Nothing is 'just' anything. Jokes, more than anything, are not just nothing, but something, if not everything. Read Freud: *Jokes and Their Relation to the Unconscious* (1905). The classic."

"Great sense of humor, Freud. All those great German comedies, like *Faust."*

"Freud was Austrian, not German."

"Name a great Austrian comedy, I dare you."

Unable to name even a mediocre Austrian comedy, Fine said: "Freud cracked jokes in that monograph. Here's a famous one: 'A wife is like an umbrella; sooner or later, one takes a cab.' "

"I don't get it."

"You're joking! Freud dicovered that jokes are an expression of hidden aggression—repressed, disguised, and expressed in a way that is acceptable. Jokes result in the release of libidinal energy in the phenomenon of laughter."

Stephanie, making her own high-carbohydrate breakfast, mumbled: "So what's wrong with being funny?"

" 'Funny' means something else—"

" 'Funny' should mean something else—"

" 'Funny' is neurotic—"

"So what?"

"So your task is to explore your feelings toward me that drive you impulsively to lay these jokes on me, every morning."

"I tried to lay a lay on you this morning, remember? Making love with your wife? What normal couples do and we don't anymore?"

"That's the biggest myth around."

"What?"

"Marital sex. Married couples don't have sex much anymore. The surveys are all distortions. *Playboy,* TV, movies—they make us think we *should* be having sex, and that others *are,* but in the sanctity of my office I hear the truth: not much sex out there anymore, no. Even nonmarital sex is mostly hype, 'specially with the need for trust inherent in herpes, AIDS. For solid psychodynamic reasons—men's wives have the same last name as men's mothers: the 'Madonna/Whore' syndrome—husbands rarely have sex with wives."

Stephanie stared at him, lip fallen in disappointment. She said, softly: "I didn't say 'sex,' Fine, I said 'making love.' "

Hurt, he hid it. "You imagine you're angry at me—"

"I *am* angry at you, Fine!"

"Tell me about it, Stephanie."

"Stop acting like my mother!"

Another mother-transference to me. "Your *mother?* Hmm?"

"This marriage is in trouble!"

Fine gasped. He felt like he'd been punched in the gut. Real pain spread, and real terror—a sinking falling feeling—and he used all his skill to quash it. "An interesting fantasy, Stephanie."

"It's not a fantasy, it's reality!"

Fine flashed on a famous V. quote: " 'Reality's a crutch!' "

"Help!"

Use a "clarifier": "There is no reality, there is only the individual perception of experience. Your anger at me is your anger at your mother and your job. Get onto the couch, work it through."

"After what analysis did to you? Are you kidding?"

Use the "interrogative": "Yes, and what did it 'do to me'?"

"They analyzed out the Fine I loved! You used to be funny, lively, daring! Now you're so wooden—every response is like there's a two-second tape delay, censoring. Why are analysts so weird?"

"Only the ignorant say we are weird—"

"*Everybody* says so! Your wives, fathers, mothers—even your friends, even your former best friend John James—he thinks so too!"

"How do you know that?"

"I talked to him yesterday, about his party tonight."

"Are you going to go?"

"I dunno. The only ones who *don't* think analysts are weird are other analysts! There's nothing spontaneous left! That party last night?—a dozen Freud lookalikes talking about money as if it *really were* shit?! I don't get it, Fine: to be accepted at the Institute is a crowning achievement—you all go in there the smartest, highest achieving—and you come out like shells sucked dry! Each of you tiptoeing through your life scared to death of your unconscious, like it's some monster, nesting down there, waiting to attack! Was there ever a man *less* at peace with himself than Sigmund Freud?"

As Fine waited out the storm, he had a worrisome diagnostic impression: the intensity of her rage suggests that her developmental arrest is pre-Oedipal; what if she's not a hysterical neurotic, but a borderline character?! My wife a sickee?! Worrisome.

In a softer tone, Stephanie said: "I'm scared, Fine. Your patients are more real to you than I am. You feel more for them than for me. To them, you're God; to me, you're just you, warts and all."

Fascinating fantasy, Fine thought: that I have warts.

"I really think that sitting there with your patients for all those hours, listening and not being allowed to say what you really feel, is a *very unnatural act*. They pour out their hearts and you say *nothing?!* Human beings are not built that way. To do what you do puts a spin on your soul, Fine, and I'm scared to death that it's killed off our love, that it's going to be the end of us."

Rocked back on his heels again, Fine steadied himself. "I love you, Stephanie. My analysis has helped me to love you fully."

"Oh Fine, the worst part is that you *did* love me—you loved me so damn passionately, you showed me such attention, every time I saw you my heart spun around and I felt a warm rush all through me! God, the letters you wrote me when I was in Paris!

Passion and invention and dirty jokes and puns and mathematical equations to spell out love—I've been looking back at them lately, Fine—you wouldn't recognize them!—all all all in the service of love!"

"I now love you maturely, with an age-appropriate love. We're almost mid-thirties. We must face having a baby. I am ready."

"I'm not."

"Yes, and tell me why not?"

"Because you're not ready to be a father! To have a child we have to provide an environment of love, of closeness. With the distance between us now, it would be impossible. Oh, Fine, I'm more lonely when I'm with you, now, than I am when I'm alone!" She stared at him, as if, he thought, assessing a chop. "The weirdest kids I know are the kids of analysts—isn't there even a syndrome, now?"

"The 'analyst's child' syndrome, yes."

"I can't bring a child into this. We can barely talk to each other anymore—we're on the verge of splitting up!"

"To split up now is to act out," Fine said. "If you are fully analyzed and still think it makes sense to separate, I will accept it. We will be acting through understanding, together. I have confidence that this will not happen, if you get yourself to a top-notch analyst and work through your neurosis—"

"Like you? You want me to see the world as you do? Pricks as bananas, twats as tacos, and tits as mangoes, kiwi fruits, and ten different kinds of melon?! At the aquarium, do you see fish? At the funhouse, do you have fun? Making love?—*fruit salad!* And you think the problem with this marriage is *my* neurosis?! No, Fine, you've hooked me on that one for the last time. Tomorrow in New York, maybe I *will* try stand-up comedy, who knows?"

"One would hope you'd get yourself analyzed, first."

She saw the *Globe,* and her face twisted in horror. "Oh no. Did you see this?" He nodded. "Did you know him?"

"Had met him at the Institute, that's all."

"There's analysis for you—you guys sit in your offices, analyzing like crazy, but what do you actually *do?* You can't even protect one of your own from a killer! You're hardly able to tell one nut case from another! All these sickos have therapists these days, and does it help? And after the crime, they march you into court

—one for the prosecution, one for the defense, both claiming you're right—and parade you around like freaks!"

"Yes, *The Fine Theory* calls this the 'disjunctive age'—the quick cut, the pull of the trigger, the switch of the channel. We're seeing a dissolution of the superego—conscience—of barbaric scale!"

"Why don't you *do* something!?"

"Analysis doesn't *do* things, analysis eases neurotic pain. You're talking *very sick people.* No one in America wants to face the data on just how sick these sick people are! If it takes intensive psychoanalysis with motivated, quite healthy people to bring about character change, how can you expect to alter anything in a killer? You can't *re*habilitate what was never habilitated in the first place! This is the land of opportunity—hope's way too high here!"

"Then what the hell *are* you doing? Analyzing the healthy? Analyzing analysts so they can analyze analysts? *Do* something!"

"Do poets do things?" She nodded. "Well, Freud was a poet." She seemed to appreciate this. "And Finestones do things: the data from my hoppers and inpatients suggest that calcium may just work! The world's coming apart; people are coming apart; the synaptic junctures between nerve cell membranes—all coming apart. But calcium, with two positive charges, attracts two negatively charged molecules, and bridges the gaps! It binds up shattered neurons, brains, people—the world! Calcium overcomes entropy—maybe *that's* the biological basis of empathy: fight entropy with empathy!" Fine recalled what he'd forgotten: the grasshopper in his shirt pocket. Excitedly he envisioned the upcoming week of research.

After a while she said: "Tell me, Fine, what are you feeling about us? I need to get in touch with you before I leave."

Fine was full of feeling for his work, and for his internal world, but was startled to find that he did not know what he was feeling for her, his wife. The harder he tried, the more he did not know. Damn, he thought, I'm *blocking!* "What do you *think* I'm feeling?"

"I'm not your patient, schmucko, I'm your wife! Just tell me, before I go, where you are with me, okay?"

More blank for her pressure, Fine said: "Don't pressure me."

"God, I get so crazy when I feel you're treating me like your mother!"

"Am not," said Fine, coldly.

"Wait—let's not go down this path again—it's so *old:* I ask, you see it as an attack rather than an invitation, you retreat; I ask again, you withdraw; I feel cut off and frantic, you get comatose and analyze—please, not now—just tell me, simply—I mean with me now, about us—what you *feel?*"

The word hung on a hook in the air, dropped, balanced, tilted, fell. Fine sensed, in his wife, the same neediness he'd just sensed in his hysteric. Yet without the luxury of analyzing it, he felt paralyzed. Her asking seemed a demand, and he could sense, in his silence, a chill and dead hollowness. He heard her, knew she cared, and wanted to respond—but could not. Had he terminated Fumbles prematurely? No, the problem is not me, but her—her neurotic hunger. Distracted by cries of birds, Fine glanced away, looking out the window at the gulls diving for the garbage thrown from the Hull-Boston commuter ferry. ("No one can get an erection on demand"—Leon Bergeneiss.) He felt locked into silence.

"You really don't know how to relate, do you, Fine?"

"No," he said, relieved, "I don't. Men don't have the capacity for empathy that women do. Basic biological difference."

"You're saying men don't know how to relate?"

"Not nearly so well as women."

"How do you know that?"

"I'm expert on empathy—"

"Ha! Haha!" She exploded with laughter. "You? You're the least empathic person I know!"

"Yes," he said, happily. "That's why I'm expert—I can be totally objective about it."

"Oh boy! And you're saying men can't *learn* to relate?"

"Good question. Empathy's strongly biological—you can't alter it much. Men can learn a little, but male/female differences remain enormous. Men and women are like two different species. Men like men, and women like women. Given your empathic nature, it's amazing that *all* women aren't lesbians. The best marriages are with the least machismo males. We—men and women —have to accept it."

"That's a cop-out, Fine! Some men have empathy, believe me, I know." Fine felt a twinge of jealousy. "Men find a way to relate, when they see that their lives depend on it."

Fine felt a light bulb click on: men can *learn* to relate? She

knows an empathic male? Tempted to ask for his name, Fine
knew this would seem even less involved in this interaction, and
held back. He said: "I doubt it."

As if in eulogy over a body, she said: "Amazing—you—all you
analysts—you're supposed to be the most open to garden-variety
human feeling, and you're the least. I hate to say it, Fine, but
you're becoming a totally *vicarious* man. There's no attempt at
relationship anymore, with your patients, with your wife, no attempt at response, it's all self. You hardly respond at all."

"The reason we don't respond is that we don't want to contaminate the data with ourselves."

"And the patients lie there imagining you're wonderful!"

"In their imagining is their cure."

"There's just no genuine, free, happiness left, is there?"

"Freud said: 'Much will be gained if we succeed in transform-
ing your hysterical misery into common unhappiness.'"

"You're joking!"

"In the post-Holocaust era, quite a profound thing to say."

Stephanie got up to leave. "Well, Fine, it's not enough. Not
enough for me, not enough for us. I didn't bargain for this, for the
young man I fell in love with turning into this."

Hurt, he shot back: "And I didn't bargain for the woman I
married having a job that sends her all over the country and
leaves me alone three days and nights every week!"

"Well!" she said, eyes lighting up. "There *is* someone alive in
there after all! Is that where you are? Huh?"

Fine thought then that their fighting was a way of dealing with
the pain of another weekly separation. But that too was an old
argument, she answering his protests by saying it was a "totally
modern marriage." She turned away. But as she went toward the
door and the loss became imminent, the vacuum of feeling was
punctured by sadness and guilt, instantaneously filling, and a
great Whoosh! from his deadened heart knocked over his analytic
constructs and carried them along like a flood does houses and
cars and chicken coops with dogs on top, and he blurted out:
"Hey—wait!" She turned; he felt, from her, a plea. The balance,
tipped precariously, started to ease back. "I really do love you,
kid."

"Yeah." Eyes glistening from his use of their old love word—
which he'd picked up from her father's using it with her—she

said: "Yeah, kid, me too." She blushed, her skin rosy. "I'm scared, Fine, I've got a premonition something bad's about to happen."

"These murders? I don't take patients like that." She asked how he knew it was a patient. "Clearly a psychotic transference to a therapist."

"To *two* therapists? And if it were a patient, wouldn't the cops have found the killer through the appointment books?"

"Good points. Anyway, the man's very sick—probably a paranoid schiz."

"Why a man?"

"Statistically, 90 percent of murderers are. Of the 10 percent who are women, most are psychotic mothers murdering their babies."

"Four weeks apart—it almost sounds menstrual."

"Fascinating. And Freud thought women had *weaker* superegos. *You* should be the killers, not us. How 'bout a last hug?"

His nose snuggled into her neck, her cheek on his temple. Feeling safe, Fine thought: How many years I've loved her!

"Oh, hey, Fine, listen—" she said, releasing him, wiping tears from her eyes, "it's because air's free."

"What's that?"

"That's why."

"That's why *what?*" he asked.

"That's why Jews have big noses."

"Because air's free?"

"You got it."

"Ha!" Fine was surprised at how hard he laughed. "Haha!"

"There's hope!" She turned to go. He felt the emptiness seeping back in, and blurted out:

"Will you be at John James's birthday party tonight?"

"Can't. I've got a meeting in DC."

"But it's his thirtieth!"

She stared, quizzically. "You're such an innocent, Fine."

"I am?" asked Fine. "How?"

"See?" She chuckled—an old, reassuring sound. "And you're getting so kinky—sucking rocks and all? Turning into someone my friends are scared to even say hello to. Yeah, you're becoming a man we all love to hate."

He chuckled, too. "Ah, 'love,' 'hate,' what the hell's the difference? Deep down, it's all *cathexis.*"

* * *

Later, on his way to the lab, Fine thought: she thinks my former best friend John James doesn't like me anymore? Funny, I thought he still did. And she thinks men can *learn* to relate?! If only it were so. A way out of the trap of biological determinism, Freud's "anatomy is destiny." A hope for mankind. She's the greatest! Get to work, Fine, right away!

There was one problem with Fine's having "analyzed out" his paranoia: he was now quite slow—ploddingly slow—to suspect.

9

ANALYSTS LOVE ROUTINE, and in this regard Fine was no different from others. He spent the morning as usual.

First he stopped in at his neurophysiological laboratory, and was greeted by Ms. Ando, a Japanese immigrant with silky ink-black hair and an oblate torqued face that was just the right juxtaposition of shape to fill Fine with a sense of her beauty. At scientific meetings he'd heard of her skill in placing microelectrodes in single sea-slug nerve cells, and a year ago had imported her to try his grasshoppers. Now she easily impaled single hopper neurons, and recorded their electrical activity. Usually she was matter of fact, but today she was excited: *"Hai!* Over weekend I ran data from repeat experiments. Factor analysis showed that the electrical potentials in 'smart' hoppers really are stronger than what we see from 'normal' control. I think we got it!"

"Calcium boosts the excitatory post-synaptic potentials?" She nodded. Fine felt a chill in his spine. After ten years' work he was proving that calcium not only made grasshoppers learn to lift their legs faster and retain the learning better, but now he was identifying electrical learning in a single nerve cell 'causing' the behavioral change. Yet he had to be *sure.* "Not so fast. Let's repeat it."

"Again?!" He nodded. "Okay. Do a smart hopper for me, okay?"

"Okay. I found this one in my bed this morning, imagine?" Ms. Ando was meticulous, queasy about doing gross surgery on the grasshoppers. She turned away. Fine took the smart hopper from his shirt pocket, picked up a small scissors, wedged the point between the thoracic carapace and the fantically wriggling mandibles, and cut off its head. He handed the kicking body to Ms. Ando, who pinned it upside down to her corkboard, humming. As he turned to go, Fine noticed that the head had fallen upright on the lab bench. The antennae were still waving, the mandibles at work. He felt a twinge of guilt, but analyzed it out: castration anxiety. Anthropomorphosis has no place in scientific inquiry. Not like it's a chimp, or even a dog or cat. It's only an invertebrate. As he left the lab he still felt chilled, thrilled at, finally, finding order in nature.

Next Fine met with his cheerful secretary, Mrs. Neiderman—a large, light-blond–haired fiftyish woman with an open, kind face and eyes that always looked straight at you—to go over his schedule for the week. "Oh Dr. Fine," she said, "that woman's crazy about you! I really think you're helping her." Fine knew that Six o'clock often talked to her after the session. Neiderman often overstepped her role, telling his patients details about him. At first he'd been annoyed; now he accepted it: no matter what went on outside the office, inside it was all transference. "You're a terrific therapist."

"Therapy goes on in privacy—no one knows who's good or—"

"I do." He asked how. "The bad ones charge the most."

He then chaired hall meeting for his inpatients at Jefferson House. In the meeting—as with Ando and Neiderman—there was much affect about the latest murder. He responded analytically: listening for "murderous" latent content, exploring, interpreting. His psychotic patients were wild. Since they lacked the intact ego functions to use his analytic method, he provided "reality testing" for them. During the meeting he told Eli, his insane Jew: "No, that's not a storm trooper, that's a male social worker." And to his manic, Cooter: "When the President calls Russia 'an evil empire,' that doesn't make you Luke Skywalker, no." Fine enjoyed doing this, being reality for those he thought of, warmly, as his "children." Although they seemed vulnerable, he didn't have to

worry about what he said to them. Think they're fragile? Just try
and change 'em.

Fine went through the morning consulting on other cases, and
in mid-afternoon found himself sitting under the green-and-white-
striped tent that had been erected on the fairway of the eighth
hole—a flat, easy par three—of the Stow-on-Wold championship
links.

"Hey you mutha," said his manic, Cooter, nudging him in the
ribs, "whut a day for Stow-on-Wold! Kills you, don't it?"

And it was. Even the greatest private mental hospital in the
country, McLean, five miles away in Belmont, had never managed
this. The President's wife had come to Stow-on-Wold, to inaugu-
rate a new program: a pilot study to admit three of the poor
mentally ill to mix with the mentally ill rich. Standing up onstage
directly behind the First Lady were the three guinea pigs. The
small wiry Eastern European man had landed in New York three
decades before with no knowledge of English, a fear of dogs that
led him to attack them, and a bad sense of direction; the brooding,
sultry Italian woman had been found spread naked on a crucifix
of runway lights at Logan, signaling the planes on in; the huge
black man had started out from North Carolina to make his fortune, and, ending up in the wrong Boston neighborhood, had been
beaten to within an inch of his life. For the past twenty-five years,
they'd been institutionalized at Danvers State Hospital. For a
quarter of a century they had been provided with food, clothing,
shelter, TV, and that almost-nonexistent commodity in modern
culture, friends who stayed in the same place for long periods of
time. They had been quite happy. And then, a year ago, as the
guilty passion for "freeing the mentally ill" had matched the po-
litical expediency for doing so, they were wrenched cruelly from
their home, de-institutionalized. Placed in foster homes in ethni-
cally appropriate neighborhoods in Boston, fed macaroni and
cheese thrice daily by foster families who charged the commonwealth a fortune for it, they'd been abandoned. There is a limit to
subsidized love. Soon they and other state hospital alumni filled
gutters and doorways of most American cities. Somehow the head
of Stow, Dr. Edward Pelvin, had persuaded the President of the
United States to fund this pilot study, where the public-sector
poor would be taken care of by the private-sector rich. And so,
de-de-institutionalized, they were coming to Stow, to Jefferson

House, Fine's ward. What treatment can I provide? Give them drugs, keep them safe, that's about it. He sighed. No challenges to the intellect here. None of the simple elegance of psychoanalysis.

"Here it is Mental Hygiene Month and I'm glad to be here," said the First Lady. Her smile seemed stuck. Fine's mind, never highly absorbent to platitudes, leaked. This whole thing is such a repetition. The history of the insane is one big circle: (1) acceptance: the "town fools," valued as such: jesters, shamans, priests, knights-errant; (2) ostracism: in the Middle Ages, the notorious "Ship of Fools," sailing forever along the normal coasts; (3) cages: "Lock 'em up away from us!" (Bedlam in London; *L'Hôpital Général* in Paris, seventeenth century); (4) the first revolution in psychiatry: "moral treatment," begun by the Quakers, England, 1813; in America, state asylums set outside cities, on farmland— "Lock 'em up away from us!"—peak population at Danvers, 23,450; (5) the second revolution in psychiatry: the "talking cure," courtesy of S. Freud, circa 1900—later found to be of no use for psychosis; (6) the third revolution: psychotropic medications, the "chemical straitjackets," emptying out state hospitals in the fifties. And now? "Lock 'em up away from us!" We even repeat intra-psychic history—the neuroses of child—

"Help!" screamed the First Lady, turning red, as if having a fit. "Help!" The Secret Service drew guns, shielding her, scanning the tent. Many psychiatrists hit the deck, a few drew guns of their own. The shared fantasy—the killer had come to Stow!

But no. It turned out to be merely an unfortunate accident, ending the ceremony on a sour note: the huge black man standing in back of the First Lady, full of unfamiliar afternoon wine, had unzipped his fly and urinated upon her. They whisked her away. Fine and the others were led down the seventh fairway—a tough dogleg around the Hartnett House for Psychopaths—toward the Schaffran Lawn Tennis Pavilion, for the press photos.

"Visigoths!" said Mr. Jefferson, pointing to the large black man lumbering down number seven like a caddy who'd lost his bag. Fine chuckled, for this white-haired middle-aged man was his favorite chronic schizophrenic. What a story! Mr. Jefferson was a sailor. Asked about himself, he smiled and said: "Boats!" Growing up in the coastal town of South Duxbury, he sailed boats, raced sailboats. He and his female cousin competed, until she won. He began to act "strange." When father asked him what he

loved about boats, Master Jefferson said: "The sails talked to me."
All thought this a wonderful metaphor until they realized: he
thought the sails *talked* to him! Following a period of torture and
ritual murder of small furry animals, he came into a period of
naval masturbation, up and down in boats, waves whispering
dirty words. He was caught with his cousin in the wrong state:
erect. They sent him to the "best" hospital, McLean (The
Brahmins used to brag: "A son at Harvard, a father buried in the
Mount Auburn, and a mad cousin out at McLean"). He stayed
only eight years, and, against his family's wishes, left, entered and
then left several other ritzy mental hospitals. He claimed he
needed to be near water, to sail. Stow-on-Wold opened. The family donated three million for Jefferson House. Mr. Jefferson
agreed to "harbor at Stow," pleased with the deep-water port at
the end of the stone jetty arm, down the long-lawned hill from
Jefferson House. He found "the tides and winds familial." He
sailed every day. Regressed to boyhood and thoroughly happy,
he'd become everyone's favorite madman. His dream was to guide
the family tall ship, the 'rigger *Thomas,* in full sail and with all
majesty, from its berth in Duxbury north to Stow harbor. He said:
"Large negro, no, er, yes!"

Fine asked him: "How *can* one sail against the wind?"

"Vectors!" he answered, laughing delightedly.

"Did you know that Einstein, who loved to sail, never got the
hang of it? Off Rhode Island, the wind would blow him out until
he ran aground, and they'd have to come get him and sail him
back."

"Couldn't fathom vectors!" said Mr. Jefferson, excitedly.

Fine stood with his chronics on the grass center court. Looking
over the psychiatrists, each head of a ward, he made a remarkable
discovery: psychiatrists specialize in their defects.

Pelvin, a psychopath, specialized in the treatment of psychopaths. Seeing everyone as a psychopath, he'd formalized this in
the "automative theory": the car you drive is, in every respect—
make, year, color, condition, extras, position of dents, driving
habits—the person you are. Fat people drive fat cars; thin, thin.
The typical Pelvin interpretation: "You feel your brakes are going,
your front end's crooked, and you're leaking oil? Tell me about it,
hm?" For this he charged the highest fees in the city, if not the
world. The President's wife he'd introduced as the "Cadillac of

First Ladies." The expert in schizophrenia, a closet schizophrenic, treated same, and so on with the experts in narcissism, border-lines, children, adolescents, sex, perversion, drugs, money, behav-ior, psychopharmacology, mania, and depression. The expert in depression, depressed and suicidal, had an affinity for depressed and suicidal patients—they made him feel less alone. His own moroseness affected his patients adversely, and they were forever killing themselves.

The press crowded the manicured court, and the spectators filled the seats. Across the net Mr. Jefferson faced the new poor black man. Neither had had a game of tennis for quite some time: the former, for over twenty years; the latter, forever. Dr. Edward Pelvin placed the Prince racket in a delicate white hand, and the governor placed its twin in a massive black one, black-and-tan fingers as wrinkled as extra vecchio cigars. Told to smile, they did. Flashbulbs captured them, each the negative of the other. TV, too. And then the dabblers left, and Fine was left alone with them. The pilot study had begun.

On one side of the net, the rich old-timers of Jefferson House; on the other, the three chronic poor mad poor. At the net, as ball boy, Fine. He waited. The tension mounted. He could almost *see* the hallucinations and delusions and crazy associations. Finally the wiry little Eastern European, née Sczyncko, shouted out, inappropriately loudly, like the bark of a dog: "Stinko!"

"Welcome Stinko," Fine said, "and let's welcome the others."

"Noblesse oblige, yes, err, no!" said Mr. Jefferson, and sailed his Flaubert of a hand across the net to his opponent. "My name is Jefferson, sir, yes."

"Jefferson?" asked the black, mashing the hand, "Me too!"

"Jefferson?" asked Mr. Jefferson, withdrawing, "You too?!"

"Jefferson?!" cried the others, wondering if this too were a hal-lucination. "JeffersonjeffersonJEFFERsonjefferSON—*JEFFER-SON?!*"

Fine felt their panic. Each of them suffers from an early devel-opmental arrest, failing to take the infant's step of finding the edge between self and other. Total empathy—inside each other's skins, feelingly. This Jeffersonian mirroring must be terrifying for them, they must feel "fused." Fine tried to explain, but their paranoia, building higher, would have none of it. Each group retreated, mumbling, suspicious. The potential for violence was high. Fine reached into his pocket, and came up with a palmful of chalky-white stones.

"I think this is a good time to introduce our new arrivals to Finestones. Come and get it!" His old rich patients, delighted to be given an extra dose of calcium, rushed the net.

Plop. Suck.

The newcomers came.

Plop. Suck.

Sighing, Fine thought again of how America, his dear country still so frayed by the assassinations, Vietnam, Watergate, and the Ford pardon of Nixon (psychodynamically the worst, for it deprived us of the chance to mourn the death of integrity—"The only way to forget is to remember"—Semrad), refused to face up to mental illness. How hard for this restless nation of evangelists to accept the profound sickness of the sick.

The sucks broke the tension. Slurps, gurgles, and burps mixed with noisy chatter, even glee.

Eli the Hassid was talking with Stinko, "also Jewish." Eli introduced Stinko to his white giant poodle, unaware that Stinko hated dogs. "What?" said Stinko, crouching. "Any dog, I'm not afraid, I chust take heem back of hees neg and *keel* him!"

"But this is a Jewish dog," said Eli, "circumcised."

"Smartest dawg in the world, you mutha," said Cooter, "French poodle. Lafite Rothschild. We call 'im Lafite."

Before Fine left, he listened in on the animated conversation of the two Jeffersons:

"Yes, yes," said Mr. Jefferson, white, "they place you in a tub of water and tie you down and douse you up and down with water from nozzles, you almost drown, no?"

"Yes suh! Wet as a catfish in a pond! Wet sheets, too!"

"And the worst treatment were the enemas—"

"Enemas! Yow! Those was the baddest things!"

"High colonic irrigations! Why did they do that, Dr. Fine?"

The two had found common ground: the past thirty years of "in vogue" treatment to which each had been subjected. The insanity of the treatment of insanity, the treaters' need to *get in there and do something, anything!* Anything other than accept being powerless and in the dark. Insulin shock, hydrotherapy, purges, force feeding, lobotomy, a rainbow of drugs that would have mesmerized fifty years of elephants—oh you poor poor Jeffersons!

"Stuck that tube right up my direcshum hole!"

"Why did they do it, Dr. Fine?" The white-clad elder statesman turned to Fine, his eyes innocent and trusting. "And why, if the high colonic irrigations worked, were they stopped?"

Relieved that he could be frank—they lived in a continuous curvature of fantasy-reality, mental hyperspace, needing Fine to carve "real" edges (the opposite of his neurotics' needs)—he said, "Your docs were shooting in the dark; going not on science, but faith."

"Faith?" said the black. "Yeah! I got Jesus Christ *in me!*"

Crazy, Fine thought, as he moved to Eve his anorexic and Fat Sadie, who were talking to the new woman, Mary, as she swung a crucifix before her crotch. Eve, having been in therapy since the pubertal onset of her anorexia, was furious at doctors. She said: "I think it's okay that patients are killing doctors. It makes a nice change from doctors killing patients." For months Eve had gone on passes to her apartment on Louisberg Square. Her rage came from her upset at the latest brutal murder. "That creep Myer probably got just what was coming to him. A patient-fucker I bet he was too!"

"The poor wife," said Mary, bumping and grinding, "how long was he in her bed? Cocks and cunts are Christian, in the sacred convent of marriage. The one place that still is herpes free—"

"Herpes *frei?!*" asked Stinko, excitedly, "Who, where, why?!"

"Fish fry?" asked Fat Sadie, and, rubbing her hand on Stinko: "Is this called sexual intercoursing and having smelts?"

Fine walked up the hill to Jefferson House, climbed the stairs to his office. From the balcony, he scanned the dazzling shape of late afternoon, partly overcast, still chill, shafts of sunlight zapping through the shadowed cutout skyline, splashing off the roiling ocean, straight on into his eyes, as if coded letters meant only for him. He wondered if he could go mad. He looked down at the group. The two Jeffersons were gesturing animatedly across the net. Long-lost relatives, reunited at last. Impossible. And yet, with Thomas the great *schtupper* of slaves, could be. The poor; the rich; love. Love at first sight is easy. Look at Stephanie and me. It's when the blush of novelty fades and the person shines through that love gets tough. The only true love is between two perfectly analyzed human beings.

Fine looked at his watch, realizing Three o'clock was due. He conceived the thought: each Jefferson has what each lacks; together, they make up one complete human being: "The Jefferson."

10

FINE HAD A small lucrative private practice. These patients did not lie down on the couch for analysis, but were seen face to face, using Freudian techniques. Mostly outpatients, they were seen once or twice a week. With referrals harder to find in the recession, Fine used the "old boy" network—the elite Boston Institute, Stow—and had a full practice. Like his father, Fine worried about money. With an hourly wage, psychiatrists made less than any other doctors. At three the phone rang. A woman cried out: "I'm going to *kill* myself!"

"Where are you?" Fine asked.

"Click."

Relieved, Fine rushed to the gym to see Mardell. The call was from Joy, a borderline woman who'd made a suicide attempt (car-garage-monoxide) a year ago (saved by the new emission controls). Having gone through hell trying to save her, he'd had trouble working through his anger at her. Perhaps sensing this, being too vengeful to face him, she'd quit. He'd felt relief. Thank God "bad" borderlines like her were not candidates for analysis. No acting out allowed. But then she started calling, Mondays at three. Fine kept answering, keeping her alive. He billed full fee; she paid.

At three he'd also scheduled Mardell Jones. Black, six-nine, two-sixty, paroled from the Cleveland Cavaliers, Mardell was warming up, taking alley-oop passes for dunks from the mental health worker. Mardell, admitted to the drug unit that day, was still high on cocaine. He'd just made two million as a silent partner in a marijuana deal. Wired, Mardell challenged Fine to a game of H-O-R-S-E. Fine accepted, for the sake of the "therapeutic alliance." ("The purpose of the first interview is to have a second interview"—Havens.) Mardell spotted Fine H-O-R-S. "Go 'head, baby," said Mardell, all silvery in his Cav warmups, "if'n you make one shot and I miss—I get 'E'—you win a grand." His pass hit Fine in the gut; Mardell laughed.

Fascinating case, Fine thought, bouncing the ball. Diagnosis?: antisocial character. Drugs + impulsive character = violence. Such a man could kill. The name of the game was still F-R-E-U-D: "ball," "basket," "H-O-R-S-E"—all meant something else—

"Put that fuckin' ball in the hole, baby!" yelled Mardell.

Fine smiled: clearly a referent to the "primal scene." Fine rolled up his sleeves, went to the top of the key, took aim, and let fly. The ball bounced hard off the rim. Mardell howled, started dunking and whirling, and had soon beaten Fine to a pulp. He asked Fine about the latest murder. "Hey man, you want me to drop a dime?" Fine asked what he meant. "Phone call. Find who done it. Easy."

Fine declined. As Fine departed, Mardell, like athletes caught in the TV camera, stuck up his index finger, waved, and said: "Hi Mom!" Fine was delighted: confirmation of a basic aspect of *Fine Theory:* father is but a shadow over mother. Out loud he said:

"Show me a man, I'll tell you about his mother."

Remarkable, Fine thought, going to his office, no matter who the patient, no matter how sick or culturally foreign, in treatment you grow to like them. We'll soon find unconscious forces that drive him to drugs, to do these things that make his life a living hell. Look hard at someone, you always see mom and pop waving back at you.

Four o'clock, too, Fine thought fascinating. Sylvia Green was a cute, short, trim brunette with an aquiline nose and a glass eye. Knowing that any severe handicap *is* the person, knowing that no loss ever happens by chance, from the start Fine had been curious about it. Diagnosis?: garden-variety neurotic same as everyone. She did volunteer work at the Aquarium (Fine's association: fish!), and had come into therapy recently. Fine always had trouble announcing his fee. An obsessive, he knew this was an anal conflict ("Fee = feces"—Pelvin). He'd barely been able to get the words out of his mouth: "Seventy-five dollars—" (he always heard his wife's joking echo: "—and a choice of two vegetables"). Money was no object; Fine regretted not asking more. A fillip on the case was the first encounter in the waiting room, several weeks ago. She'd gasped, stared, and cried out:

"Stuart? My dear Stuart? It's actually *you?"*

Fine had sighed, realizing it was happening to him again. Not wishing to contaminate the data, he'd *not* revealed to her that Stuart was not his name. He'd handled it in orthodox manner: grasping her hand firmly and saying: "Hello. I am Dr. Fine. Come in."

Fine had the strange fortune of being a man mistaken for other men. Across continents, over years, people were always leaping up in crowded restaurants or rushing across heavily trafficked streets, shouting out to him "Danny!" or "Rick!" or "Sig!" or "Ali!" or "Bobby!" or "Jonathan!"—or even "Rose!" (a mistaken last name?) or (!) "Barb!"—only to find, at the instant of the arms being thrown around in greeting, that he was none of these, but merely "Fine." Haunted by this and puzzled by this, he could not figure whether it meant that his appearance was extremely common or extremely rare. Like the question of whether—given the infinitely large universe on one hand and the infinitely small chance of right combination for "human being" on the other— there was extraterrestrial life. And where were all the others, mistaken for him? He'd never seen any! It happened to him, on average, once a month. But this time was different: it was the first time the last name had been the same, and never before had it happened with a patient. He hoped that from treating Sylvia he might understand this better. One of the joys of this elegant profession, Fine thought, is that you learn everything about everything.

Sylvia had grown up in Tuscaloosa, Alabama. Apparently she mistook him for a high school sweetheart, "the only Yankee in our class—and Jewish besides. And you really did it—became a doctor—good for you!" The years had taken their toll, the goatee made him look "harsher," but underneath she claimed to see "the

same ole Stu!" She noticed he wore no wedding band, assumed he
was single. Relieved, she reminisced about their high school romance. Girlishly, she'd flirted with him, her "real" eye, a light
green, intermittently flecking with black. Her smile, though pleasant enough, seemed tight from disuse.

Fine had not corrected her impression he was unmarried. He
wore no ring for that precise reason: to be a blank screen for his
patients' projections. Her associations were sensuous yet innocent
—often about her passion, horses—suffused with the bittersweet
taste of nostalgia. The initial transference had been "Fine as a
boyfriend," a surface metamorphosis of deeper feeling. He'd yet
to find out which primary object—mom, pop—this "boyfriend"
material was a screen-memory for. The same age as Fine, she too
yearned to have a child. She'd had previous therapists, but
claimed this the best "fit" ever. Now, sadly, she was talking about
the latest murder: "The world sucks! Why live? It makes me feel
like killing myself!"

Great case! Fine thought, happily. He went through the "suicide inventory," and as he asked the routine questions, recalled
how upset he'd been the first time a patient of his had threatened
suicide: shocked, he'd panicked, gone past the end of the session,
even, that night, called her up! Incredible! How different I am
now: having analyzed my being so emotional, having realized
from the Institute that *my* feelings have no business in the sessions
—I never get emotional at work. I am now in a terrific position:
the most heartrending human drama, the most severe and brutal
affect, I am able to sit with it and feel nothing, nothing at all. I
can think clearly and be of use. The secret to assessing suicide
potential, he knew, was specificity, and he asked the usual questions—"Do you have a specific plan?"; "Weapons, pills?" etc.—
assigned the weighted numbers, added up the total and concluded
that suicide was highly unlikely. Thanking him, she left.

Now Fine sat looking over the salt-and-pepper Isro-Afro of Maurice Slotnick, AKA Ratman, the Obsessive. This was his second
analytic control case. Yawning, Fine looked at the clock: 5:38.
Almost time for the one interpretation of the session. The main
task of the analyst with an obsessive neurotic is to fight the incredible boredom. ("If *you* feel bored, it means *they* are angry"—
Crusher Gold.) Fine had tried every technique to break the bore-

dom, for the first several years keying on the analysis of Ratman's dreams. The dreams turned out to be as boring as the reality—so deep did the Rat's fear of letting go go. Tough case to crack, Fine thought, "anal-stage rage." He shifted in his seat, wincing—before Five o'clock he'd gotten up to stretch and had slipped on something in the carpet—a cat's eye marble of all things!—and had fallen flat on his back, *thump!* Why a marble? The cleaning lady's kid? And then Five o'clock had gotten off to a rocky start when Ratman had said: "—my middle name."

Caught unaware, Fine had repeated: "Your middle name?"

"Raskolnikov," said Ratman.

"Raskolnikov is your middle name?" Fine asked.

"No, no—that was just the first thing that came to mind."

Ratman was a Jewish writer who'd come to Fine six years previously with a chief complaint of writer's block. Fine knew this was a mere symptom of the obsessive neurosis. Ratman had been chosen by TBI for Fine's control case because he hit Freud's famous case *Notes Upon a Case of Obsessional Neurosis* (1909). Obsessive, Freud was great on obsessives (was he, too, expert in his defect?). TBI was packed with obsessives, and the whole first-year seminar had been "The Obsessive." Fine had obsessives down cold.

The three hazards in the analysis of Ratman had been the boredom, the shit, and his similarity to Fine. Early on, Ratman had poked fun at Fine's nose. Fine had retaliated, analyzing that of the Rat. Ever since internship, Fine had been phobic to body fluids—Stephanie claimed to bodies as well—and the currency of the analysis of an obsessive was feces. An analyst had to learn to handle everything, however, and with V.'s help, Fine had dug in. Ratman had been terminating with Fine for the past two years, not wanting to leave anything undone as he said good-bye. The neurotic defense of the obsessive is ambivalence, and Ratman's repetitive "Yes, but . . ." to every Fine interpretation had made the work slow and dull. Fine now saw why, before his own termination with Fumbles, Stephanie had lost patience with him, mocking his "Woody Allen-itis." Incredible, Fine thought: obsessives really *do* dole out feelings like little turds. Into cleaning, obsessive husbands wipe their wives' messy countertops. To Fine, these diagnoses had always seemed male/female gender-specific; lately, the gay movement had fostered crossover. Soon, Fine mused, there'd be whole armies of stubbly anal thick-necked women, marching against smooth oral floopy-wristed men. Fine knew Ratman was a lot like himself. Given what Fine was going through, it had been difficult to analyze Ratman's crappy marital sex life: "Talk about castrating? Joann not only made me feel it was too short, but somehow, even, that it was *on backwards!*" Fine tried to get him to analyze it, but Rat, unlike Fine, acted out: divorce. He dated teenagers, began a trashy novel, *Vampire Mom.*

Another almost perfect session, Fine thought. Perhaps I won't even offer a single interpretation! Fine's analysis of Ratman had gone along in parallel with Fumbles's analysis of Fine. Fine's sizzling interpretation to Ratman at 5:40 P.M. would often be a word-for-word repetition of Fumbles's 6:40 A.M. sizzler to Fine. Their analyses were classic male Freudian, focused on father. "Writer's block," Fine learned, was the superego perched on the shoulder, cackling like a bird at an undersized nut, as in Poe's raven's "Nevermore." Scrutinized, the writer failed to do the first of the two essential creative acts, "let go." Both Fine and Rat worked the father-transference orthodoxly: from fear of castration, through hate, to love. This brought up, in Ratman more than in Fine, rage at mother. It turned out that the Jewish mother was the key to the Jewish writer. The tremendous encouragement ("Momma's boy can do *anything!*") coupled with intrusiveness ("Let momma *see* what you did!) and criticism *("Don't* talk to your mother like that!") both fed the creative urge and barred it from expression in relationship. The writer sought sanctuary in words. Ratman blocked worse that ever. His editor, furious, called Fine, demanding termination. Ratman screamed at the editor: *"Vampire Mom* isn't a book—it's shit!" The editor said: "So? People don't read *books* anymore, they read *Krantzes.* Finish, we'll make a million."

And then came the breakthrough: Fumbles asked:

"Er, and what is more wonderful than a loving *father's* hug?"

Fine asked: "A loving *mother's* hug?"

Touchdown!

Fine asked Ratman the same question, got the same association back, and there it was: two little Jewboys in love with mom! Fine resumed work on his theory, Ratman finished *Vampire Mom,* which, due out soon, looked like a best-seller. Ratman's dream—

to have his picture taken with Liz Taylor—seemed within his grasp.

In the middle of Ratman's pulpy description of sex with an El Al flight attendant, Fine said: "Hmrgh. It's time for us to stop."

A perfectly trained analysand, Rat did. Wiping off the couch with a hankie, he smiled at Fine, and turned toward the door.

Fine rose, took one step, and: "PPFFFffffuuuttTT!"

A terrible silence. Ratman turned to face Fine.

"A fart? Hey, Dr. Fine, did you fart?"

Fine tried to clench his cheeks, to stop, but: "PFFT!"

Oh no! Fine thought, panicking, feeling himself blush, what a mistake! What's wrong with me today?

"You're blushing! Hey—farts are nothing to be ashamed of, take it from an expert. Besides, doc, the loud ones don't stink! What great material for the new novel—thanks!" Fine cringed, seeing his analytic mistake spread all over the public domain, and blushed a deep crimson. Why wasn't there confidentiality for patients? "Hey, Fine, know what you are?" He paused. Fine could almost feel the anal-sadistic dart: "A hot shit! Haha!" He left.

Mortified, realizing he'd again spoiled an almost perfect session and that this would set back their work many weeks—if not months—Fine tried to analyze what was wrong: the upset with Stephanie this morning? The pickled herring at lunch? While flatulence can be an important and useful analytic "body sound" during a session (cf. article in last month's *Anal. J.*), it's a big mistake to let fly right at the end, not giving the analysand a chance to work it through. What's going on? Two control cases, two mistakes? I'll get roasted by Vergessen in supervision! Fine tried to associate.

Pheoo! What a stench! Must have been the fish.

What to make of his parting shot, the sadism in it? He is regressing under the stress of saying good-bye. May take another year to work it through. Oh God what if I fail the Obsessive, and have to repeat with another seven-year-long boring control case!? Wait—even *I* regressed, with Fumbles, at the end. Even knowing the rules, in my last session I had the overpowering wish to hug him! We of course settled for the orthodox shake of hand. His was surprisingly delicate, given his footballing.

Fine noticed that Ratman had left his new leather jacket on the floor behind the door. Psychodynamically, it was part of Ratman, and Fine, reluctant to touch it, associated: dead body.

Holy cow! Of all my patients, only Ratman never mentioned today's murder! Given his cruel father and his own murderous anal rage, it must have been too painful. On a deep level, it expresses his wish to kill *me!* He's not ready to terminate at all— maybe I wasn't either? Witness his harsh laughter at my poor importunate fart.

Fine was a creature of habit, and now his workday was over. With the exception of the Vergessen Monday-night seminar at the Institute, at eight. He glanced at his appointment book. He'd RSVP'd to John James's birthday party in South Boston. Wrapping his rumpled ego around him like a tattered cape, Fine jolted downstairs, stomach queasy, headache banging, to his car.

11

WITH ALL THE trepidation of a jungle missionary, and yet with all the confidence of a fully analyzed one, Fine drove his black diesel Mercedes up L Street into Southie. As he passed the massive pink-and-blue hedron on his left, the power station, a spout of steam shot up as if from a blowhole, and provided temporary comfort: the familiar shape of utility as leviathan, or, an ejaculating pear. Crossing Broadway, Fine saw the signs of the natives, and felt a queasy slosh: free-floating anxiety. Carved on a sorrowful brick wall were two slogans, scars of forced busing, in brash, indestructible day-glo:

> GOD MADE THE IRISH NUMBER 1!
> NIGGER GO HOME!

Fine associated: projection. How hard to *own* self-hate, how easy to find the object out there in the world to project hatred upon. How easy to destroy, how hard to create. Fine sighed at the wasted expense of spirit. All wars are religious; inner peace alone brings world peace. The only peacekeeper is empathy: putting yourself in the other guy's shoes, feelingly. My wife has remarkable empathic skills. She sees the world with the eyes of the deaf,

the touch of the blind, feelingly. He loved her for this; and he
loved her for having loved her for so long.

Fine drove past the Bellevue Bar, still owned by John's Uncle, a
decrepit rectangle with wire grills over the opaque windows, a
neon Schlitz next to a hand-lettered Light Lunch. As John always
said: "A lunch so light you 'ad to *pour* it!"

Fine hadn't seen John in over a year. He'd worked at the Abbey
Theatre in Dublin for four or five years, with time in London as
well. Never one to keep in touch, John had let things lapse—not
coming home, not answering their letters, unreachable by phone.
They'd get Christmas cards from him, from Ireland, England—
once from Hong Kong—last year from San Francisco. The cards
were line drawings of John in various costumes—comic poses
poking fun at his looks: large head, woman's lips, gangly body.
Rarely was there a personal note. He'd been back in Boston a few
times, and the last meeting of the threesome had been awkward,
tense. He'd seemed to Fine flamboyant, aloof, false; and, beneath
it all, sad, desperate, enraged. And drunk. Fine recalled it now:
murderously drunk, John, only half in jest, had picked Fine up in
the air, shouting:

"Kill all the shrinkers!"

Every time Fine had seen John since college his friend had been
drunk, hiding any and all details of his personal life. Try as Fine
might, the person remained buried under six years of stories, esca-
pades, shows. He'd shut them both out, totally. And so, when
they received the line drawing of John as Father Time, inviting
them both to a thirtieth birthday bash in Southie, Fine was surprised, but pleased. This, clearly, was a more mature attempt to
strike up the old friendship. The note read: "Back in Sout'ie fer
good. Love to see ya both! Fer Jayzez sake—come!—JJMO'DJr."

Fine, while disappointed that Stephanie decided not to come,
understood: being a woman, her attachment to John had been so
strong that it was too painful to be with him *un*attached; i.e., his
narcissism cut her to the bone. Understanding this, Fine could
accept it, and her. As he was about to *accept* his old pal John.

Fine came to the sea at Carson Beach. The dusk was chill. A
grease-stained brown paper bag blew into the oily water, bobbing
restlessly. Ahead, on a yellow brick building, a baby-blue scal-
loped sign read: THE JAMES MICHAEL CURLEY RECREATION CEN-
TER, known as the "L Street Rec." Above the men and boys'

entrance was the motto: "Cleanliness is next to Godliness."
Above the other gender: "Let health my nerves and finer fibers
brace." Curley was the only mayor ever to get reelected from a
federal jail cell. Despite the current federal investigation into
mayoral fraud—*The Globe* reported allegations of the use of his
wife's birthday party to launder money—the current mayor was
odds on to repeat. Fine's gaze swung down the beach to the
bombed-out housing project for blacks on Columbia Point, and,
nearby, the dark obelisk on the tip, the JFK Library. Only tourists, unaware of the danger, made the trip through the ghetto to
the library.

Fine parked, locked, walked away, then back to repeat his lock
check, and then on toward the two-turreted three-decker rust-
colored wooden house. A burgundy Rolls-Royce, as sleek as a big
cat, was parked in front, drawing a crowd. Fine hadn't been chez
O'Day for years, and took a minute to analyze it, from the sham-
rocks on the curtains in the top-floor windows (John's room),
through the balconies on the second floor (the preserve of mother
and three older sisters), down to the small front yard (dog) where
the Virgin stood in her all-weather protective cowl, always bringing the association: cobra. Key to the Irish?: mother. Attend,
Fine, there's data, here. He went up the stoop steps, straightened
tie and vest. Tense about seeing his lost friend again, he pointed
his finger at the doorbell.

As if by magic, the door opened and he was pushed to the side
by several big lunky men, drunkenly singing the last verse:

"—habby birthday too yoooo!"

The party was noisy, boozy, and chaotic. Fine was pushed to a
side wall, then in toward the center. To be in a tight space with so
many floridly unanalyzed Celts made him anxious. Associate:
sock hop at Mt. Carmel Church in Columbia, age twelve, when a
cretinous Gorman put a cigarette out on the back of my neck.
Fine searched for John.

He was in the center of the room, kissing women serially on the
lips. Some kind of native ritual, Fine thought, analyzing John's
wild joy as acting—a defense against the empty self deep within.

Fine saw little value in "face value." He'd taken Freud's "every
symptom is multidetermined" and used it to shut out the obvious.
Nothing meant merely what it meant anymore. The man who

now saw a thick penis in every pineapple also saw, in sheer joy, vast despair.

Katey, O'Day's mother, sharp-featured black-eyed born-in-Ireland, greeted Fine coolly, staring at his expensive suit. Realizing that he'd seen only polyesters, double-knits, and sweaters, Fine felt overdressed. He and Stephanie had always been treated with suspicion by this hypervigilant woman, who fantasized they'd "ruined my son at Harvard." She made polite hostile conversation. Filled with primary-process dream images, he squirmed.

And suddenly he was face to face with John.

"Fine!"

"Hello John Ja—" Fine was enveloped in a giant hug. Ears muffed, Fine recalled that he always forgot how *big* his friend was. He was surprised at the feeling rushing through him, making him tingle—love for his old pal! He came out of the hug with high hopes. Yet looking into John's eyes he was startled by their blankness—two light blue disks, icy barriers to whatever lay behind; cold, calculating; *old?!*

"Grand, just grand! Glad you could come!"

"Happy birthday, John James. Seeing you again, I feel so—"

"Where's Steph?"

"She couldn't make—"

"Too bad, but I'll see her—I'm livin' here, now, again—just grand—izzat Tim?!—grand!" And he was gone, hugging this Tim.

Fine felt slighted, hurt, angry. "Grand just grand" indeed! In his eyes I hardly exist. Like Narcissus at the pool, John made me feel like the pool: I exist only to reflect him. Always a watery gap between self and other. Poor guy—homeless, lonely, insomniac in the midst of dreamers. Fine tried to go, but found himself with Nora Riley, a warm, down-to-earth, Fine-sized woman who owned the Rolls. Finding out Fine's occupation, she said the first victim had lived near her, in Newton. Fine asked what he was like.

"*Weird!* Must be terrible, to know someone's after you."

"Me?!" said Fine, startled. "Why would anyone be after me?"

"Why were they after the two others?"

The party was ending. A slobbering ugly drunk named Tim was screaming a toast: "Southie boy makes good!" Katey, her daughters, and her pal Mrs. Curley were off to the Callahan Tunnel, the main artery into Boston. Having voted for tax cuts, they were now protesting the effects—layoffs. Katey unfurled a banner: HONK IF YOU HATE KEVIN! Katey asked John what he thought of it. "It's great, muther, if you're the kind of person who loves to hate!" As John led the party out, Fine tried to say good-bye, but John would hear none of it: "C'mon, you've got time for a few glasses at the Bellevue, surely!" He threw one arm around Fine, the other around Nora, walking them out to the street. Nora broke away to the wine-colored Rolls.

"No," she said, "I won't go to the bar. I don't believe a lady should, you see?" John hugged her and kissed her hard, a swash-buckler, saying "Grand, just grand—see you tomorrow, Nor!" And she shot back: "Easy on the booze then, ya big dope, you hear?" He laughed, a great guffaw followed by an insucking chor-tle, and, watching the chauffeur hold and close her door, repeated the act on the chauffeur's own door. "Repetition," said John to Fine, winking, "the secret of life!" He slapped the red roof; the cat of a car purred off.

They walked toward L Street, John with his arm around Fine's shoulder. They passed a black marble statue of a priest behind a boy, hand on his shoulder, and John, fervent believer and staunch anti-Catholic, cracked a joke about the boy's backside ("South End") being at the father's groin level, and Fine, feeling John's hand squeeze his shoulder, flushed with homosexual panic. ("If you feel gay fear, so feel gay fear"—Fumbles.) So Fine felt gay fear, and calmed. "Well, John James, thirty now, eh? Big birth-day, isn't it?"

"Feels grand so far. If I can just keep the right level of booze in me body, it might not be so bad. God—remember when you gave me that Freud thing—*Zur Onanism!*—was that funny or what?"

"A lot of truth in that paper, yes," said Fine. John stared at him. Fine decided to give him a gift, the chance to mourn his twenties, and said: "Yes, starting life's fourth decade is hard."

"Fourth?" said O'Day, shocked, doing a stage-lean against a doorway, clutching his heart. "Christ, man, I never thought a' that! Give a poor drunk Irishman a break, cantcha? Fourth is scary!"

"Yes, and tell me about feeling 'scared'?"

"Come on, Fine, don't play headshrinker tonight! It's me *birth-*day, okay?!" Fine asked why he was back in Boston. "I'm the lead actor with the Shakespeare Company—a ratty group—I'm savin' 'em!" He plowed on into the Bellevue, Fine paddling in his wake.

If Fine had felt an outsider in the house, he felt doubly so in the bar. It was seedy and dark, suffused with the sickly-sour smell of beer, dirt, and urine. At first, in college, Fine and Stephanie had both loved it. Now, for Fine, it brought back, live and off color, memories of his adolescence—the brutal anti-Semitic words and acts that had crushed his quest for harmony. The denizens of the bar greeted John warmly. Again Fine found himself pushed to the side, perched like a heavy bird on a ripped barstool. Fine did not drink, and as the orders were placed, he stared at the photos resting against the mirror behind the bottles: three-year-old John and his da—a less graceful, more unhealthy-looking replica; six-year-old John and his da and a Boston Bruin and an autograph; high school John without his da with a sports trophy. Having gone to Harvard on a full scholarship, John was God to these barflies. Sonny McDonough, a famous old Boston pol, had died recently, and Fine stared at his *Globe* obituary. Encircled in red was his quote: "The worst thing in politics is gettin' the envelope with four hundred dollars in it—you don't know if the guy took one or six."

The only thing worse than dishonesty, Fine thought, is to glamourize it. A Celtics basketball game was on TV, and the "nigger" jokes were flying. Fine overheard The Uncle ribbing O'Day about the Rolls. John had been dating Nora—discovered by Katey—for a month. Nora, a widowed mother of two, was "lace-curtain" Irish, rich from a first husband. The metaphor, Fine noted, was fruits: "A plum!"

"A fookin' plum!" said The Uncle, sitting down heavily across the bar from Fine. "Marry that woman Nora, our big faggot there could stay pissed the rest of his natural life, couldn't he?"

Fine used the "repetitive": "Could he?" On one hand, he was relieved once again to be in a dyad, a form he had down cold; on the other hand, he was startled at the primary process—the homosexual, heterosexual, and urological themes—flowing confluently straight out from the sewer of The Uncle's unconscious, his id.

"Who said he couldn't?" said The Uncle, indignantly.

"Who do you *think* said he couldn't?" asked Fine.

"Why I dunno," said The Uncle, breath warm and gummy, "who?"

Fine in the interest of hygiene looked away. Feeling, strangely, as if he were talking to another analyst, said: "And what are your *thoughts* about who?"

"Nora has hands like sledgehammers and an arm that could break a man's neck! That's the only t'rouble, that there, isn't it?"

"Think so?" asked Fine.

"Bet your ass I do!" said The Uncle, and, looking closely at Fine, said: "Jesus—that's it—I almost forgot—you're a shrink! That's why you talk so foonylike, right?" Unwilling to inflame the transference further, Fine fell silent. The Uncle began talking about the murder, and Fine felt irritated at again being dragged into his version of reality. "Yer man O'Herlihey just left, the police detective on the case. C'mere, c'mere—" The Uncle leaned over the bar and pulled Fine closer by the lapels. "The victims each 'ave been shot at close range, twice—one bullet right in the face and—" he stopped, winced, gulped, "—the second one, where do you t'ink?" Fine asked where. The Uncle whispered, gleefully: "In the knackers!"

" 'Knackers'?" asked Fine. "What are they?"

"The balls, man, the fookin' balls! Turns their balls to mush. You t'ink for a minute that that don't hurt?! Get a pain in your nuts that'ud castrate a bull, just t'inkin' it, don't you?" Fine was about to suggest that it couldn't hurt if the brain were dead, but The Uncle continued: "They know it's the same gun what killed the two of 'em—a mass murtherer! 'Course O'Herlihey says you got nuthin' till you got a motive, but I dunno, I t'ink it's just some nutbag myself. But I wonder how the murtherer does it so neat-like, gets in so close for the kill, you get me?"

Tired of this man, Fine nodded, looked away.

"Hey, I'm talkin' to ya," said The Uncle, dragging him back. "I'm tryin' to save ya, pal—you better hope he ain't after you!"

"And why would he be after me?"

"Why was 'e after the two other assholes, tell me that one, will you, doc? They ain't found nuthin' in common, yet."

"What are your *thoughts* about why?"

"Christ but you're hard to talk to!" said The Uncle, slamming a fist on the bar. "Ah, maybe you're right not to be scared—God's will, no choice, you go when your number is up. The t'ing is, is that they say their balls was turned to fookin' liver! A faggot—a fruit—they think mebbe. When they find that fruitcake, they'll fry him but good! Thank God for the death penalty, yeah!"

Fine said: "The killer isn't to *blame,* but, rather, insane."

"Yeah?" said The Uncle, testily, "who says?"

"Anyone who murders two psychiatrists in cold blood is obviously insane," said Fine. "Not guilty by reason of insanity—NGRI—like Christ, my friend, NGRI, like Christ."

"Christ? Leave Christ outa this!"

"Sorry." Fine wondered what was wrong with him today—everything was just out of sync. "Not guilty all the same—"

"Guilty as hell!" said The Uncle, getting red. "He knows what he's doin', you can be sure of that!"

"So you think the murderer has a choice?"

"A course he has! Like the one who shot the President—"

"You actually believe," Fine asked, voice rising, "that the killer *chooses* to be a killer?"

"They get their kicks from it—you should know that—"

"No, no—as you yourself put it: 'God's will, no choice—' "

"That's different, that's God—an act a' God!"

"Yes," said Fine, *"your* God. You can't have it both ways—"

"Who says I can't? Wait'll it happens to someone you care about, pal, or, even, to you yourself!"

"I care about everyone," said Fine. And then, calmly, as if he were a great sage come to enlighten the heathen: "No, my friend, the murderer has as little choice as you or I. 'Choice,' 'chance'—what's the difference? Deep down, it's all *libido.*"

"Get off! You know, Fine, sometimes I start t'inkin' that your elevator don't go all the way up!"

"Is it by choice that in a basketball league where 80 percent of the players are black, the Celtics field six white players at once?"

"Six! Didja hear that, Johnny?!" John turned, saw how angry The Uncle was, came toward them. "Six, asshole, is hockey!"

"When's the last time you saw a black playing Celtics hockey? As one psychiatrist said: 'We're all more human than otherwise.' "

"What's that?" said The Uncle, fuming, rounding the corner of the bar to get at Fine. "More of your Jewish headshrinker talk?"

"An Irish-American," said Fine, "Harry Stack Sullivan."

John had grabbed Fine and was pushing him out the door.

"Get outa my bar, you fookin' Hahvid weenie!"

"You have no choice but to hate me," yelled Fine back over his shoulder, "blame has no place in the post-Freudian world, and—"

"Out!"

They stood out on L Street, looking up toward the Rec, where the old men were huddled on the old benches, talking. Uncomfortable with each other, neither knew what to say. Fine maintained analytic silence, preparing to key on John's very first affective word. In a false brogue John said: "A quare people, the Irish —mad altogether."

Noting the homosexual "quare," Fine keyed on "mad": "Yes, and tell your Uncle he's not 'mad,' just caught in the swamp of his projections, and that he's a fine candidate for analysis." John's laugh exploded—why, Fine wondered, are both he and Steph blasting me this way? "It may not seem so to you, John, but in his very fear is his hope—if he could learn to 'own' his projected rage, he's well on his way to mental health. And he meets all but one of the criteria for analysis—IQ, insight, income; I query only motivation."

John stared at him, about to laugh. "This is a joke, right?"

"No. The Institute is always looking for controls. He'd be a fascinating case. Remember: 'All the world's an analysis, and all the men and women merely patients.' "

"Grand, grand," said John, falsely. "Write him a letter, why doncha—oh, hey—you still write those weird crazy letters, do you? Remember that one we wrote to the Pope? Wish I had a copy—who has 'em—you, Steph—I could get up a review—'Letters'—"

"No."

"No, what?"

"No, I don't write letters anymore."

"But you were grand at it—we all were! Why the fook not?"

"I learned in my analysis that my letter writing was immature and grandiose—an attempt to relate to the 'Father.' "

"God?"

"God!"

"The 'Father'—we never wrote to God, did we?"

"What are your thoughts about if we did?"

John fell silent, seemed itchy to get away. "Too bad Steph couldn't come. Feels like something's missing, doesn't it?"

Fine associated: castration anxiety, and said: "Does it?"

"But we never could count on her to show up, could we?"

"Wish she'd get herself into analysis," said Fine.

"Huh?" said John, and then, wide-eyed in disbelief, turned away from Fine's insistent stare, took a deep breath and said: "Grand to see ya, Fine. I'd best go back, see if I can patch things up."

"Good-bye, John," said Fine, stiffly, holding out his hand.

"Cheerio!" said John, taking it.

"Happy birthday."

"Let's get together again soon. Give Steph my love."

Fine walked off. At the corner he looked back, and saw John standing, puffing on a cigarette. Strange, he never smoked before. He's become expert in "celebrity," now, filled with false sincerity, making everyone feel "grand" in his presence, as if life were nothing but a postshow dressing room. Same as at college. Yet while this wunderkind blitzkreig was acceptable on the playground of Harvard, at thirty it was worrisome: he'd grown worse, a "character." Fine reluctantly made the diagnosis: character disorder; "as if" personality; with no solid self, repeatedly and chameleonlike, he invents a self, performs a self over and over again. An actor, even in real life he acts "as if" he were O'Day. Yet he's lucky: his psychopathology matches his profession. Only in rare dark nights of the soul, critics asleep, does he feel the hole where the self should be. Amazing—the more you find out about people, the *more* sense they make.

"And she thinks *I'm* innocent?" Fine said, out loud. "The as if personality is innocence itself! Yet I *accept* him, yes."

Again he felt cold, and shivered. All the way into Boston he had the lurid fantasy that he was being followed. Having discredited as too simplistic the idea of "things as they actually are," Fine did not bother to check out the reality. Rather, he soon thought he'd analyzed it right out: "followed" was his wish that his friend had followed him in a mature path to mental health; also his wish that his wife had followed him in readiness to have a child. So much, Fine thought, for the fantasy "being followed." Child's play.

If he had bothered to look, he would have seen that he was being followed by a beat-up Ford, two cars behind.

12

WHISTLING "Some Enchanted Evening," Fine repeated his last compulsive car-lock check, walked across Exeter Street, and turned right-angle-left down Commonwealth Avenue toward The Boston Institute. The Back Bay was a filled-in swamp, the only orderly laid-out part of Boston. Stephanie was fond of saying that while Boston was built on swamp, New York was built on bedrock. In an effort to match the classy "I Love New York," Boston had held a slogan contest, picking a clunker: "Boston: Bright from the Start." Steph coined "How 'bout Boston!"—too late. Clever woman, mused Fine. The evening light bathed the rows of magnolias, whose buds—clenched like babies' fists against the unseasonal chill, pale white and pink on the weathered brownstone —were waiting to open into blossom, into bloom.

Fine crossed to the grassy promenade running down the center of the grand boulevard, and marched royally along. He'd given the latest draft of his theory to the only woman in his class, his only ally, Dr. Georgina Pintzer. He hoped she'd read it. From Fumbles he knew that, given the emotional land mines of the family Fine, he'd tried to sweep a way clear with similar achievements. He'd brought home countless trophies of the intellect; now he understood that he was still awaiting a response. Yet understanding, he'd *accepted:* no response would ever come. His own father had abdicated the realm of the intellect for that of the meats, and so Fine had reigned as father to himself. Thus tonight's regal walk: *Fine Rex.*

Ahead, walking with head down and hands clasped behind back as Freud himself was said to have walked, was Fine's greatest rival, Dr. Ronald Reuben. Reuben, a tight, orthodox candidate, tolerated little deviation from Freud—yes!—Reuben's specialty was also his defect, for he was expert in Oedipal, i.e., father. Being in the eighth year of his training analysis, he claimed to have worked through his fear of aggression, and yet, fearful of not being aggressive enough, had become the most aggressive candidate at TBI. Fine knew that Reuben hated him because Fine was expert in empathy, i.e., the mother. Reuben, locked into symmetrical, either/or thought, viewed Fine's new "relative" concepts as "garbage." Yet Reuben, using a hard-knuckled Freudian technique, was unable to keep his patients in treatment with him. Time after time he'd hit them with the "correct" interpretation, and they'd terminate, or go mad, or kill themselves. TBI kept finding him fresh analytic cases.

Like prize fighters, Reuben and Fine were matched as "discussors" in the Vergessen seminar, six Monday-night sessions. The first, a week ago, had been "The Breast—Saying Hello." Fine, showing his expertise, had won round one. Tonight was: "Transference—Beyond the Pleasure Principle." The final four: "The Anus"; "The Penis/Oedipus"; "Countertransference"; "Termination—Saying Good-bye."

Reuben made a quick about-face. He was checking out his stash of cigars. Fine found himself looking straight up into his enemy's eyes. Reuben was the winner of the "Freud-at-thirty-four" lookalike contest. Stern and tall, Reuben looked down on Fine, layering the air with analytic silence. If sadism could talk, Fine thought, this would be it. Realizing that he had forgotten his own cigars, Fine blurted out: "Can I borrow one of your cigars, Reuben?"

Just about falling over at this incredible request, Reuben offered an interpretation: "Think about that, Doctor Fine."

"Oh, come on—I forgot my own."

Silence. Then: *"Think* about it."

"Oh, go to hell."

"Anger, Dr. Fine. Premature termination. Get back on the couch. Work it through, you won't have to act it out."

Hurt, Fine blurted: "Up your ass, Reuben, up yours!"

"You're *psychotic!*" Reuben turned away to cross Commonwealth Avenue.

"Hey, you asshole," Fine shouted after him, "I wish you'd just *drop dead!*" Shaking with rage, ashamed of losing control, Fine sat on a wooden bench and tried to analyze out this burst of emotion. What's wrong with me today?! "Premature" is the worst adjective in analysis: "termination," "interpretation," "ejaculation"—in descending order of importance, all mistakes! I fail to *accept* him. Why?

Fine's headache pounded. His world blurred. He sensed dimly the stares of joggers, two kids, chilled lovers, a woman standing nearby, who, when he glanced at her, turned quickly away.

And Stephanie thinks *I'm* bad?! How does this jerk get to me? He's a plodder; I fly. All my life I've been hated for my creative leaps, why should it stop here? And his height. His main weapon is his height. *The Fine Theory* suggests this as a crucial reason for discrimination against women: they're shorter. Even for Reuben, Reuben seemed tight, anal. Is that it?—he only *thinks* he's made it to the Oedipal—he's still stuck in the anal? The rumor was that Reuben, his sadism too vile, might be failing his analysis. He was on the verge of being sent to an even taller, more sadistic training analyst, Crusher Gold. The Crusher had never failed to crack a case. An eight-year setback! Reuben was caught in a usual bind of his training analysis: on one hand, "Say whatever comes to mind"; on the other hand, "Whatever you say can be used against you." Rage being forbidden, rage was rife. Anger was viewed as the one true malignancy of the mind. Creativity was not far behind.

Fine climbed the stairs to the Institute, whispered the night's password—"Anna Freud"—was buzzed in. Up in the oak-paneled seminar room, he sat in his usual seat, tense. Everyone, tonight, looked tense. Perhaps it was because of Janet Malcolm's book, *The Impossible Profession,* revealing so much about New York analysts? And yet, Fine thought, give her credit: it was the best work on transference since Freud. No one said hello.

" 'Why do we repeat painful experience?' "

Professor Sean Vergessen, quoting the theme of Freud's *Beyond*

the Pleasure Principle (1920), was introducing the topic: transference. Fine thought: the most profound question! Over and over,
people do things that are bad for them! They quit perfect jobs;
they marry perfectly wrong women; those beaten as children later
seek out brutes; they elect leaders who will nuke 'em—they're all
like the acrophobe who becomes a bridge painter! Why? Who kills
herself?—Marilyn Monroe! *Why?!* What a deep, exquisite query!
   Many of Fine's eleven classmates were smoking cigars, even
Georgina. Through the haze Vergessen, although albino, appeared
to have some color in his cheeks. Always the analyst, he never
seemed the analyst, but merely, like his own remarkable teacher,
Semrad, "a good ole farmboy from Iowa." Several of Fine's col-
leagues mimicked V.: the famous posture (leaning chubby white
cheek on chubby white fist), the famous accent (a twanging mix of
Warsaws—Poland and Missouri), the famous laugh ("When
trapped, laugh!"), the famous attire (rumpled; outdoors, every
inch of skin protected from the sun), and the famous analytic
stance (Freud's "evenly suspended attention"). One candidate was
said even to have powdered his face! With Semrad dead, Vergessen was now on the penultimate rung of the ladder of couches.
Frau Metz, age-dessicated yet said to be razor sharp, was the
titular head. The ladder consisted of analyst-supervisor dyads.
Vergessen supervised the supervisors who supervised the supervisors. Fine likened him to the bell on the top of the "ring-the-bell-
with-the-sledgehammer" contest at a carnival: In a panic-attack, a
female patient might say to a medical student-therapist: "My husband Ralph wants me to *blow* him—I'm flipping out!—what
should I do?" Panicked, blushing, the medical student ends the
session, rushes to his supervisor, a psychiatric resident, who, hearing this and blushing, ends the supervisory session early and
rushes out to his own therapist who, hearing about the oral sex,
blushes and, later that day at his analyst's, associates to fellatio,
which his analyst interprets as sadism and, ending the session on
time, goes to his own training analyst, Vergessen, associating to
his own oral libidinal urges. No one is *sure* how to handle this
crisis; all await V.'s "correct" interpretation that will relieve the
turmoil that this "bad" patient has caused and that will keep her
from either blowing her husband or flipping out. Vergessen, who
often breaks the boredom of his strange work by singing, bursts
into song:

"You only hurt the one you love, the one who really cares."

That's it! Back down it goes in a daisy chain of therapist-patient links; a week later out of nowhere the med student bursts into song: "You only hurt the one you love, the one who really cares."

And the patient, startled that he sounds so *sure,* forms a therapeutic alliance—fantasizing med student while reaming husband Ralph, and everyone can breathe easy a little while longer.

Sitting with patients *was* scary at first, Fine thought. You don't know the "correct" thing to say, and your natural human responses—unanalyzed distortions—get in the way of the work. In the interpretative chain, strict confidentiality being the rule, wild gossip was the result. Silent during therapy, analysts blabbed outside. Hearing all, Vergessen could influence all. His singing interpretations rang out all across New England, the Northeast Corridor, all America, the world. Some said his famous analytic pearl —"Reality's a crutch!"—was not a carefully thought-out construct at all, but rather a cry of pain from a time on crutches after a skiing accident. And now those same words fill issues of commentary in *Anal. Quart.!*

> *"Janseit der Lust Prinzips,* 1920: In the theory of psychoanalysis we have no hesitation in assuming that the course taken by mental events is automatically regulated by the pleasure principle. . . . The mental apparatus endeavours to keep the quantity of excitement in it as low as possible."

The presentor was Dr. Pete Gross, a decent, bald, hefty man who'd left a promising career in pathology for analysis. His morbid side had found an outlet in work with the dying. Straightfaced, he'd once said to Fine: "Dying is the only truly time-limited psychotherapy." How fitting, Fine thought, that this solid, plodding fellow is reading this. What has happened to Freud's spirit? Isolated and iconoclastic, Freud had started it all as a rebel against rigid *fin de siècle* Vienna. Hitler had helped, making the usual mistake of despots about Jews: getting rid of them. Hundreds of European analysts came to America. Each gangplank lowered onto Ellis Island was like a new flow of creative energy for a grand endeavor, the golden age of psychoanalysis! Had there ever been a more concentrated decamping of ideas? These ragged refugees had been the true explorers of the mind! But then something funny happened: the next generation got scared, devolved into safe cautious orthodoxy. It was common knowledge that if Freud himself applied to the Institute, he'd never be accepted. Troubled, Fine realized that no genius had ever flourished within an institution. Contemporaries had called Einstein "retarded"; Freud "sick." It was pure Marx: "Any club that'd have me as a member, I wouldn't want to join." And so American institutes had gone from being the most daring to the most timid, the most compassionate to the most cool, the most permissive to the most judgmental. The candidate was taught to be *like* the teacher. Formalization of genius had done away with creative doubt. The Institute existed to disburse the final merit badge: "psychoanalyst."

Gross finished: "And so, as Freud says, we are constantly repeating the painful, traumatic, and fixated events of childhood. We treat others only as objects of transference." He sat down.

Nothing more boring than a zealot, Fine thought. If Stephanie only knew: here at the Institute, *I* am viewed as a rebel.

Vergessen said: "But, if it doesn't give us pleasure, *why?*"

This was the cue for silent association. Fine did:

Child. Playing. I want a child. Pleasure. Georgina has big suckable tits. Expensive see-through blouse. She leans back, stretching! Sees my stare, blushes, smiles. Each nipple like fingerprint or snowflake, unique. With the parasympathetic buzz: bing cherries. From day one she flirted. Last week, at "The Breast," I fantasized that she, at V.'s question—"What's it *like* to have breasts?"— would unbutton her blouse, unhook her bra, and sit the seminar out naked. Publishable! Analytic history in the making! On a par with Freud's failure to find a public urinal at Coney Island, his painful prostate ruining his trip to the fun house with Jung, 1909. With that cigar she's a blue angel. Ah breasts!

"—because we are *stupid!*" Georgina was saying, indignantly.

"What?" said Reuben, startled.

"We repeat painful experience because we are *stupid.*" She looked to Fine for support. Fine—thinking I'd die for those knockers!—said: " 'Stupid' is just another way of saying 'blinded by transference distortions,' right Georgina?"

Reuben got up and, as codiscussor, made some solid points about the paper. Ending, he turned to Fine: "Freud is quite clear: two principles: life instinct, from *Eros,* pleasure, sex; death instinct, from *Thanatos,* unpleasure, death. *Eros* binds; *Thanatos* splits. The 'repetition compulsion' is a biological drive toward merging with the dead. Birth starts it; death ends it. Death in life. As simple as arrows going both ways in chemical equilibrium, as time going forward and backward, all at once. Yes, and in developmental terms, we repeat to *do* and *undo*—to get it right."

Fine rose, and began his reply: "Modern physics has shown that time does not go backward. Freud was caught up in nineteenth-century Hegelian dualism. How could he help trying to tie things up neatly, in dichotomies, two by two? He turns metaphor into instinct. The death instinct? Remember: he's just lived through the Great War."

"Dualism's the strongest force in nature," Reuben cried out. "When Newton wrote: 'All action has an equal and opposite reaction,' the whole world sighed: 'Ahhh!' why? It made deep libidinal sense."

"Male sense," said Fine. "Newton was sweet, but, as Einstein showed, wrong. Even our two hemispheres are not symmetrical, but nonlinear, more like two symphonies than two harmonics. Read my monograph. There, based on new biological and neonatal data, I make two new basic assumptions: A) a core *asymmetry* of male/female body, mind, and development; B) a newborn's basic state of *relation,* not narcissism. Studies show a baby is not a closed-off, isolated self-lump, but a feeling, thinking, actively relating being."

This contrasted with Freud; the room filled with objections.

"Thus the asymmetry in male/female relationships, the epidemic of failed marriages. Right here in Boston, women are making new developmental theory: Gilligan on sex differences in moral development: on the playground in disputes, boys fight it out, but girls end the game rather than threaten the relationship; Surrey and Baker Miller on 'Subject Relations, a Theory of the Relational Self': for women, as opposed to men, self is enhanced, not threatened, by intimate relationships (as opposed to classic theory, where growth means *dis*connecting from early relationships to form a separate, firm sense of self). Freud decried women's self-sacrifice as 'moral masochism'; yet call it 'nurturance,' it becomes a great gift to civilization! I'm using this Boston Group's work to look at the male side. Not *self*-development, but *self-in-relation* development. Like Reimann's creation, from Euclidian geometry, of higher-dimension topology, leading to Einstein's use of Reimann-space to generalize special relativity to a theory of quantum gravity." He'd lost them. "We should invite these women here to speak to us." Murmurs of protest—none of the women were Boston-bred analysts. "Anyway, while I agree that Eros binds—perhaps aided by calcium—there's no need or evidence for Thanatos."

"Oh yes?" said Reuban's ally, a Jungo-Freudian named Leon Bergeneiss, a man with black bushy hair and a terribly pocked face, expert in sadism and paranoia. "What about masochism, hmm?"

The codiscussors began going at each other. Reuben attacked: "Freud himself used invertebrates to prove his point: 'The instinctual forces that seek to conduct life into death may also be operating in *protozoa* from the first.'" Reuben leaned back, puffed. "I assume it applies to your roaches, Dr. Fine, your *Küchenschabe?*"

"*Grashüpfer,*" Fine said testily. "And *Heuschreke*—locusts."

Reuben quoted again: "'The greatest pleasure attainable by us, the sexual act, is associated with a momentary extinction of a highly intensified excitation.' Freud is clear: orgasm = death. We repeat childhood trauma 'cause we follow an instinct toward death!"

Fine taunted: "There's no evidence for repetition compulsion as biological drive. As a scientist, I don't believe it exists."

"What?" said Reuben, sitting up as if shot. "You *don't?*"

"Nope. Life is unfair. There's no perfectibility, no march of progress. Are we biologically bound to repeat pain? No. New data show that the first six years are not carved in stone—female moral development explodes at puberty, drug addicts burn out and become real-estate tycoons, juvenile delinquents are now esteemed Boston pols. Some of us are more crippled than others in childhood, but we all grow up—some faster, more completely, some more slowly. Faster, I think, with a high blood level of calcium." Fine took out a Finestone. The biological part of Fine's work was highly suspect at the Institute. And yet, since no one yet knew whether Fine was a genius or an idiot, few risked openly criticizing him on his rocks.

Plop. Suck.

For Reuben, this was the final straw. He was speechless with fury. Leon leaped in: "Jung would never agree with that, never!"

"Jung! In '34, a year after Hitler came to power, Jung said: 'The Aryan unconsciousness has a higher potential than the Jewish—' "

"Jung was caught in bad historical *anima,*" said Dr. Solarz, a childlike expert in narcissism, "but like Brecht he had that certain German *Putsch*—I mean *Punsch!*" He laughed, barking like a dachshund.

"The only true history," said Fine, "is a history of mind."

"If you forget history you'll *repeat* it!" said Georgina.

"We must listen to the women!" Fine said, excitedly, thinking how much more he liked women than men, and how much more wisdom he felt there was, nestled deep down in the lap of the minds of the more empathic, accepting, gender. "A mother's relation to her daughter is qualitatively different from her relation to her son. Freud, trapped in a society of fathers, knew he'd failed to grasp mothers—"

"Yeah?" said Reuben, challenging. "What about all the new data on the importance of fathers in childrearing?"

Fine's headache throbbed. In pain, as if trapped underground in a tunnel, barely in control, he cried out: *"Pop's a poor second!"* Then, like a footballer on TV sticking up his index finger (The "Hi Mom!" syndrome) he said: *"Mom's number one!"*

"You're psychotic!" said Reuben, veins in his neck bulging. "Angry, incompletely analyzed, and psychotic!"

Fine, head blasting, saw red: "Drop dead!"

"See?—*Thanatos!*" Reuben said, standing, glaring down at Fine. "Oedipal! Still into showing off the size of your penis!"

"Better than showing off the size of your anus! Get ready for a second analysis, Reuben—get set for Crusher Gold!"

"Better a good second analysis than a fumbled first!"

Fine exploded. With a wild cry, he lunged at the taller man's crotch. He never got there. Fuzzily, he felt strong arms grasp him, firmly, and pull him back into—what?—fragrant soft silk? Smooth pink flesh against his cheek? Georgina! He went limp against her breast, panting, raging, and, before Vergessen, ashamed.

V. never broke his psychoanalytic calm. Grandfather to this nest of sons seeking fathers, he said: "It's time for us to stop."

Fine watched his idol lift his bulging white cheek off his lily-white fist. The indentation remained pink, fading. V. rose slowly, and, grinning at his boys, rolled out the door in silence, leaving behind a roomful of fantasies: guilt, shame, vengeance. Fine was terrified that in his upcoming supervision with Vergessen, the silence would be damning, hostile, inquisitory. No one said goodbye.

In silence the candidates filed out. Reuben glared at Fine. Georgina took Fine's hand and walked with him. Fine ran the fingers of his mind over himself, patting down odd edges, pushing the furniture back into place. Shaking with rage, he thought: I wish Stephanie could have seen that. She thinks I'm too controlled, that I've lost my spark, my daring. With her, yes. I *feel* daring with her, but can't *show* it. Because of her, or me? Maybe I just dare here, in this ghetto of Freudian Jews. Out in the world, I feel timid again.

"I really *cathected* to you!" Georgina said, as they walked a respectful distance behind the lockstepping Reuben and Leon. "The world is anything but Newtonian, anymore. And to link it with the female I think is very clever." She paused, and went on: "I read the draft of your monograph, and I think it's absolutely brilliant."

"You do?" said Fine, lighting up with pleasure.

"Yes! I want to talk to you about it."

"When?" Fine asked, whipping out his appointment book.

"How 'bout now?" she asked, a lilt in her voice.

"Now?" Fine was startled at her rashness. Rarely, now, was there time for spontaneous *now*. He looked at 'George' as if for the first time: same height as me, short hair streaked with gold, chubby, brightly madeup face—what inviting dark maternal eyes! —and a frankly *zaftig* body. Not pretty, but attracting. Scent? Sweat-laced Chanel. Transference? Mom. Was this a proposition? He'd never yet been unfaithful to Stephanie. Gulp. "I mean, *now?!*"

"What I'd really love to do is go out to Stow with you—right now—and see your grasshoppers. The high-calcium smart ones. Do they really learn to lift their legs?"

"You bet your tits!" said Fine. Mortified, he blushed, and said "Oh! I mean—"

"What a terrific association!" said Georgina, laughing.

"Think so?" said Fine. She nodded, and Fine felt that this was not a seduction, but a scientific inquiry, kind of a site-visit. Besides, who knows where Stephanie is now? Perhaps with a Green Bay Packer! After our fight this morning, she, unanalyzed, might well act out, even sexually. And big George and I will only be looking at my hoppers, right? "Let's go!" said Fine. She took his hand and squeezed it. Associating: "Peaches," he squeezed hers back.

As they turned right-angle-right off Commonwealth and walked across Exeter toward Marlborough, they passed an alley running parallel to Commonwealth. Fine looked down it, to the parking lot in back of the Institute. He saw the tall awkward form of Reuben, alone, at his car, a new scarlet Buick. Somehow Reuben had managed to get a numbered parking slot in the TBI lot. He fiddled with the lock, and opened the car door. The light from the car interior shined on his face. He was about to get in, and then looked up, as if sighting Fine and Georgina. They couldn't tell whether he was grinning or grimacing, shouting or associating. A wind whipped up, chill, and Georgina huddled against Fine for warmth, her flimsy blouse no protection against the strangely chill May night. A car backfired twice down the alley, and Fine, edgy, fantasizing gunshots, jumped. Reuben vanished from their sight. The car door eased closed, the light fading at the midpoint of the swing. Whether from his murderous rage at Reuben or from the damp night air or from his anticipation of Georgina's body, Fine shivered. He had a strong sense that something was wrong there, down in the alley. He said to Georgina:

"Let's go down there—" and started to move.

"Why?"

"Something's wrong."

"What do you mean?"

"I dunno—I just feel it—"

"Oh, you," she said, snuggling close, "always so paranoid!"

"Paranoid!" Fine was startled. "Hm." ("If you're paranoid, so be paranoid"—Fumbles.) So I'm paranoid, Fine thought, sighing. "Right. I've had enough of that jerk to last me a lifetime!"

"Each life is a creation," said Georgina. "No?"

"Yes," said Fine, "but sometimes you wonder."

As they drove back out to Stow, Fine, excited at having an appreciative audience, chattered on about the psychological part of his theory. He mentioned the three main events in women's lives—birth, giving birth, death—and how different they were from the three in men's—birth, switching gender identification from mother to father, death. "Oh yeah!" said Georgina, and produced a bottle of George Dickel Sippin' Whiskey. Fine talked on. By the time they were clanking over the Curley Bridge between Squantum Neck and Long Island, Georgina was snuggling close, saying: "Right on! Have a drink! Let's go for it!" Fine, true to his theory, moved away, refused.

As they parked outside Fine's house, he felt proud of the synthetic, almost feminine, quality of his mind, and overjoyed to have a sympathetic analytic listener. He realized how much under attack he felt from his wife, how unloved! Cracking those jokes about psychoanalysis *hurts!* "Yes," Fine said, walking Georgina to his lab, "Freud's greatest *and* worst moments are in *Beyond the P.P.*"

"I really *am* cathected to you!" she said, snuggling as their steps matched, crunching the gravel of the driveway. "Come on, big boy, it's great stuff—have a nip."

So Fine took the Dickel bottle, sensing that the bourbon was a vestige of her being a tomboy, and drank deeply. The whiskey burned his throat, but he swallowed it, hard. He put his arm around her. Her breast felt enormous compared to his wife's. She kissed him. Her lips seemed enormous, her tongue soft. Her hand at Fine's cheek smelled of her sex. Her other hand rubbed fondly at Fine's pants, bringing an erection to bloom. Fine felt tense.

"Here's the lab," Fine said, and flicked the switch. The light glinted off a million dollars worth of neurophysiological instrumentation, courtesy of the president's wife's wish to "cure" the mentally ill. Georgina was impressed. In the limelight, Fine talked biology. Historically, no one yet had been able to link body and mind. Calcium, a bivalent cation, attracts two negative charges, hugging them to it tightly. Just as Freud's "energy of libido" theory started as a "concept" but made the jump from metaphor to "reality," Fine thought that a real substance, calcium, that links molecules in actuality, could become a metaphor for sociological cure. In this society, many people felt that if there was pain, there could, with a quick disjunctive and often violent act, be pleasure. Finestones would raise calcium levels in brains, firm up fractured parts into wholes, join synapses, bind aggression, form links. "Bees, termites, ants—maybe grasshoppers too—are social insects: the group *enlarges* the individual. Like, at their best, women: relationship *enhances* the self, and is the greater good. Being in the world means being part of a larger whole. Could a mother push the nuclear button?"

"Hell, no! You can really teach a hopper to lift its leg?"

"You bet," said Fine, and quoted the classic experiment, by Hoyle. "You suspend the hopper in the air, and every time one leg lowers, you shock it. The leg on the other side serves as a control. The shocked leg learns to stay up; the unshocked does not. And listen to this!" Fine paused, dramatically. "If you cut off the head, the rest of the hopper still learns; if you cut off all but the meta-thoracic ganglion—the bunch of nerve cells that control the two legs—it will *still* learn. Which means that the learning is taking place inside a few nerve cells—watch!"

Fine showed Georgina a prep: a little round ball of grasshopper tissue—a grasshopper from the waist down—was suspended in air. Both legs were down. Fine flicked a switch, a bell rang, a shock buzzed, and one leg went up. And stayed up, cocked like a dog at a tree. Excitedly, Fine said: "A single nerve cell learns, and remembers. And I've found it! The biological basis of learning!"

"And calcium makes that single nerve cell learn faster?"

"And better! Each calcium ion, under the influence of membrane current at a juncture of nerve cells, grabs two proteins and shapes the membrane differently; current flow in the net is altered."

"Like new links in 'cat's cradle'? Or like hugs?"

"Yes! Calcium's the greatest, for hugs!" Putting his arm around her, feeling a little lightheaded from the bourbon, Fine led her to a cage full of intact grasshoppers. Insect eyes stared at the two humans. "See how the hoppers have separated themselves into two groups? The high-calcium diet ones are here—see how they've come together, facing off against the others, watching? It's almost as if they're having *thoughts!*" Flashing on Roentgen and the role of serendipity in discovery, believing that the Nobel was possible for him, Fine lifted a smart hopper, and half-expected to cry out, "Eureka—penicillin!" and see the ghostly X-ray of a key underneath. He asked himself: could this incredible creature, unchanged from prehuman times, transmit, to me, a thought? No. How old and yet how transient. Fine held it close to his eye. Human tried to empathize with hopper. Failing, he tried to unravel the secrets encoded in the hall of mirrors, the hopper's compound eye. A male, the insect let out a happy chirp. "See?"

"Wow!"

"How much they could teach us!"

"Like porpoises!"

"Dolphins! Exactly!" said Fine, glad to be so easily understood. Even Georgina, one of the least empathic women, had gallons of empathy, compared to most men. "Freud, at our age, was also searching for a grand synthesis—he looked into the thyroid—perhaps even the parathyroid, and calcium itself! And then, with Fleiss, up the nose! Nasal eroticism!"

"Awesome!" said Georgina.

"Have you ever seen such great legs?" said Fine, peering cheek to cheek with her, at his insect. "If I had 'em, I could fly!"

"Let's see your legs, then, honey!" she said, and, at first playfully, but then more and more excitedly, started to grab at Fine. He, at first playfully and then more and more fearfully—for the sake of his marriage—tussled with her.

"No," Fine said, "please, don't! What about love?"

"Love?" Georgina snorted. "Love is romantic software."

And, somehow, there amid the bunsen burners, rat decapitators, and ultracentrifuge, surrounded by grasshoppers smart and dumb, off came her blouse, and then her big bra and there she was, breasts bigger than ever—enormous fruity souffle-ey things —all floppy, nipples two huge dried apricots. Fine got aroused. Georgina, with firm surgical touch, unlatched his buckle and unzipped his pants, and with a clinical flip uncoiled his schlong. Fine watched it spring up, unencumbered, and whispered: "Cucumber."

"Ooooh, look!" said Georgina. "A redhead! Wow!"

"Yow!" yelled Fine, feeling her cold hand. He was muffled by her sticking a tit in his mouth as she worked his penis not any too gently and differently from his wife—at the thought Fine flopped, but, analyzing out the superego remnant and aided and abetted by his colleague's warming hand, he maypoled back up—and then off came her skirt and he felt the soft silk of her panties a billowing sail before her pubic hair and then those were off too and, just about ready to blast off himself with the thrill of it all, Fine nudged his finger into her vaginal orifice and was shocked: cool and dry. Thinking she must be anxious, he caressed her, softly, and then gave a gentle push and—"Yeoww! Ow!" She was screaming.

"Shhh!" Fine clapped his hand over her mouth, fearful of Mr. Royce of Stow Security. Scared, Fine fumbled through his associations and, startled, recalled Georgina was expert in *vaginismus!* Oh. In her palm, he went limp, a dead fish.

"I . . . I'm sorry, Fine. I thought that with you it might be different. Because of my strong cathexis to you, you know?"

"Uh huh." Fine wished she'd let go. "Let's talk about it."

And so they did, conducting a sort of microanalysis. Starting with the conflict between, on the one hand, her large breasts, on the other, her "wish-you-were-a-boy" name, Fine analyzed her trauma at being a tomboy. Georgina, in turn, heard out Fine on the *Sturm und Drang* of his marriage. Working through, they drew closer. Fine was much moved: how easy it is to relate to another almost fully analyzed human being! Georgina coined a metaphor for their new friendship: "sharing a foxhole." Feeling warm and good, they parted at 3:00 A.M., sealing their relationship with a sibling-kiss.

Fine, climbing upstairs to bed, felt relieved that he had not betrayed his wife. He was worried about getting only two hours' sleep before facing his torrid hysteric, the erotic transference inflamed by his doorknob comment. He yawned, feeling how much he loved her, his wife, and, alone, indulged in an out-loud association:

"Why do I love her? Ah—the easement of feet from the lot of socks. Must buy our own house. I love her because she has silky breasts more firm than Georgina's. Because she always asks me questions in what she calls the 'scienterrific' category that I always answer. Because she makes me see the limits of my seeing and the emptiness of my vision when it gets small. Because she is intuitive and I am not much because she exhibits and I voy because she loves me."

And hoping for the good dream and fearing the bad and asking God why *still* his pounding headache, Fine settled into bed alone, too comfortable, without her strangling arm, to be comfortable.

We love each other because like The Jefferson together we make up one complete human being. Together we're as full of strength as was the first jay to dare stay through winter, and as full of hope as was the first robin to dare soar off toward imagined sun. Soon see her. Friday, at home, frolic at Crik, bouncy, optimistic as puppies, as pups, we'll give each other that rare gift in the totally modern marriage: time. Tell her I want to be more settled, house off the Stow grounds. Have a child. Give up this crazy frenetic separated and disjunctive life. Maybe she's pregnant? Yum.

And it isn't just me—*nobody* at the Institute paid the least attention to this latest murder. Why should we? We face the murderous fantasies of our patients every fifty minutes. It's enough, already, without the tabloid sheets of unanalyzed reality.

Fine's final association of the day? Fatherhood. In that rare and fertile hypnogogic gap between wake and sleep, he saw himself starting a whole line of crested Fines. He pointed toward the time of his wife, as chubbily expectant, as mindlessly blind, as a red nipple, rampant.

And just as unaware.

13

STEPHANIE WAS A New Yorker's New Yorker. That next afternoon, she flew in on the shuttle from Washington.

Later she was to tell me about this pivotal trip home.

Her first clear glimpse of the skyline—she saw the buildings as feisty young women rising from a crowd hidden in yellow, dusty sunlight—was a comfort. When she felt the rootlessness, the homelessness, she knew she was rooted, home. She felt so at home in the City that she saw it as a visitor would: a great hive of life, with people down there in streets tiny as insects and people up there on screens big as gods. She opened the cab window and was hit by atavistic smells—sewerage, restaurantage, dogage, flowers —and knew that her city was acknowledging spring. The cabbie cursed: "Get outa my way, you fuckin' nickle-chiselin' hack!"

"Hey," said the truck driver, "fuck you!"

Stephanie tipped him for this bravura performance, and got out. The senator was sending her on a fact-finding mission on senior citizens. In the next few days she was to make a swing through New York, Texas, and California. She was in New York to visit a senior citizens' school, which had been suggested by her Aunt Belle, her father's sister. Her widowed mother—with latest beau, named "Tray" (short for The Third)—had gone off to "Palm."

And so she waited in the empty apartment for her Aunt Belle, wondering, why with the Jews, is it always the "East"? London's East End; in the east of Paris, le Marais; Eastern Europe. Her Grandpa Al had started in Yiddish theater (as "second schlemiel") in the Lower East Side. After a brief bounce against West End Avenue, for many years they'd lived here, on the Upper East Side. What did it matter? Jews inhabit time, not place.

Since her fight with Fine the previous morning, she'd felt down. The marriage was in grave danger. She saw no way out. Was it that she feared leaving him, and being alone? Or was it that she still had hope he'd change, they'd work it out? Not a question of love, but of fear or courage. She'd been thinking of having an affair. From an early age attractive to men, growing up in New York she'd often been under assault and had become expert in saying: "No!" Connected to Fine so primitively, during their marriage she'd kept on saying "No!" to other men. The most difficult "No!" had been to John. She'd often thought that if Fine hadn't shown up in Paris—needy, vulnerable, begging—she and John would've gotten together after all.

The doorbell rang. Through the peephole she saw her Aunt Belle, and let her in. A husky, compact, and determined woman with that armor of makeup of the total New Yorker (double-omega eyebrows, bright cheek-blush, dazzling red lips), dressed for any aspect of urban-guerilla warfare, Belle greeted her favorite niece warmly. Chattering, they soon got to Fine, and John.

"You know," Belle said, "just the other day I was thinking of John—that time they stayed with me when he talked to the egg-plant, remember? Such energy, those two! Such a zest for life!"

"Fine, too? I was beginning to think I'd dreamed it."

"Sure. He's still analyzing?"

"He just stopped. They analyzed out the zest. But he still has nightmares—every night, imagine? And now I have only happy dreams. The other morning I woke up dreaming about porpoises —a whole kickline of porpoises in pink tights and tutus—"

"Oh I know," said Belle, laughing, "they *are* so sweet!"

"—and I said to Fine: 'I'd like to have married a porpoise.' And he said: 'Fascinating association, Stephanie—he calls me Steph*anie* now—I hate it!—'but where would you put the ring?' "

"I see," said Belle. "And why is it that at a certain point in life we get scared? Well, dear, when you get to my age and the phone rings less and less and you go to funerals more and more, you say to hell with being careful, and you just go ahead and live."

"I'm fighting it myself. My job stinks. My life stinks! I walk a tightrope between anxiety and boredom."

"So change."

"To what?"

"Whatever's inside you, truly. Whatever's been in there all your life—that's what you should do."

"I'm so confused. What was I like? Give me one word that tells me what I was like as a girl?"

"One word?" She paused. "Funny. You were always making us laugh, like your grandpa, like pop. Like what your father wanted, and never had. And did I tell you how beautiful you look? Really!"

"You're always in such a good mood, Belle!"

"I always feel good coming from someone *else's* funeral."

In the narrow hallway, their eyes met, and something old but known and having to do with women having lost men and being left alone together hit them both. Steph threw her arms around her dear old aunt's neck and, together, they cried. And then they went on.

They walked along the isthmus of crimson tulips on Park, and over to Fifth for the bus. Belle could afford cabs, but enjoyed the social life of the buses (a second mugging and a recalcitrant hip had soured her on taking the subway). They jolted along, noisy and stenching, Belle talking loudly. (The true New Yorker is either silent as a thief or loud as a lunatic.) In the back of the bus was an obese screamer with shopping bag, loosing a diatribe about "all the millions of earthworms squashed on the sidewalks of New York."

"Too bad Fine isn't here," said Steph, "he loves crazies."

"Oh she's not crazy, dear, that's her job."

"Her job?"

"Sure. She gets paid to scream like that in the back of this bus. City employee. Keeps her off the streets, off welfare. It's a good job, that one."

"You're joking."

"I'm not. Look!—see that man out there, hitting that building with a chair? Same thing. That's a good job, too."

"They're insane—they've been dumped from state hospitals."

"No, no, dear, they're ordinary people, just like you and me. Every Monday morning they go down to the employment office, get their week's assignment, get made up, and go to work—scream, hit buildings, lie down hollering on corners, chirp like birds—it's a new program. And they do a good job, too, don't you think? I mean they had you fooled, didn't they?"

"But why does the city pay them to annoy us?"

"Annoy? No! It makes us feel better! We see them, we say: 'I may be bad, but I'm not so bad as that poor schnook hitting that building with a chair!' There's even a psychiatrist does it—instead of golf on Wednesday afternoons—he was on Donahue."

"Unbelievable! Maybe Fine can start that in Boston! But where do they get the funding for the—"

Belle broke out laughing. "Oh boy did I fool you! Haha!"

Steph was flabbergasted. "What a hot ticket you are! No wonder you're the only one in the family who still lives here—like natural selection, New York weeds out all but hot tickets like you!"

"That's our lecture today—evolution. Wait'll you see Dr. Dandi—from Sri Lanka, used to be Ceylon—a doll! Oh, there's Lila!"

The lecture hall was filled with buzzing senior citizens. At three precisely, a slim nut-brown man with sleek black hair, a prominent scar on one cheek, and dressed in a brown khaki suit—Professor Nipak Dandi—entered. He reminded Steph of a small alert land-animal, say, a mink, or a ferret. After a warm welcome from his students, he began his lecture on "The Evolution of Mankind: Will We Be Fit to Survive?" His impeccable Oxford accent was lightened by his pronouncing the "W" like "V." He began with a diagram of the universe: "The 'Beginning' 20 billion years ago; 10 billion years the Milky Way galaxy; 5 billion years, solar system; 4.5 billion, the Earth; millions of years of slime molds and worms; 400 million years ago, cockroaches." Laughter. "Plant life enriches the atmosphere, which, miraculously, remains stable for hundreds of millions of years! And then—listen!" The old ones bent forward, turned up their hearing aids. How unlike classes at Harvard, Steph thought, where, as an ichthyologist put it: "Learn the name of one more student, you forget the name of one more fish." *"Homo sapiens sapiens,* brain capacity—1,350 cc!" Delighted noises—to have so much! Lila beamed with pride; Belle nodded, lips set in a firm congratulatory line. "And yet, not so fast," said Dr. Dandi, "for as Darwin said, we are freaks of survival. Freaks, or God's chosen? Throw of dice or grand design? Two points of view: one, it is all so freakish, it could never be by chance, but must be the creation of God; two, it is all so freakish, that it could only be by chance, a random event in the Godless cosmos. One thing is clear: we're headed for destruction. Four million years on Earth, and *this* generation will determine our fate. We must use our 1,350 cc in new ways, or die. After all, who grieves for the woolly mammoth?"

Steph looked around. The old ones sat, rapt as kids. The true life force comes from taking risks, over and over again. Our Harvard troika had had that life force, she thought, but now? Fine's lost it, I'm losing it; John James? She thought of Kierkegaard's *Crisis in the Life of an Actress,* and wondered if he, like an older actress bettering the Juliet she played at fourteen, would now be better as a young lover. She felt bad she'd said "No" to his birthday party.

"—another way to survive is extraterrestrial migration." Quoting O'Neill's *The High Frontier,* Dandi talked dreamily of space stations—perfect bubbles and hubbed wheels, lushly vegetated. "Imagine, sex without gravity? Yet true survival is that of the spirit, of awareness. Next week, my guest will be my friend the exiled Tibetan lama. Thank you." Applause. Steph looked at her watch: he'd spoken for forty-five minutes and he had covered everything!

Question: "What was before the big bang?"

Answer: "No one knows, but astronomical evidence suggests that the universe expands, contracts to a big bang, expands, contracts. Some see this in purely scientific terms. I see it as—" (dramatic pause) "—the breathing of God." Oohs! and Ahhs!

Belle and Lila introduced Steph to Dr. Dandi, and then marched off to another lecture, "Following the Paths of Marxist Upheaval," a preparation for their upcoming trip to Central America.

Dr. Dandi, alone with her, started giving evidence of the usual earthly concerns, first looking deeply into the eyes, then staring intensely at her cleavage. Why are men turned on by *parts* of women? He asked if she were interested in getting together that night. More vehemently than she'd wished to, she blurted out: "No!"

Chuckling, he said: "Well then I shall dog you, like the ends of the earth." He gave her his card, and they parted.

Free for the rest of the day, Steph walked around downtown, aimlessly. Weakened by the strength in the old ones, she felt lonely—the deep privileged loneliness of an only child. (For years she thought people were saying to her: "Poor you, you're a *lonely* child.") Her city seemed to turn on her, shutting its doors, leaving children outside on streets lined with danger and depravity. She found herself on a cross street in the flower district, the west twenties, warehouses looming tall, no one around, and knew, instinctively, that it was a dangerous place and time. The sun was low, the air chill. There was a man sauntering toward her. She wondered if this would be it—the demand for cash or sex her defiance his shiv or gun severing her from this life and even from that of sex without gravity. She felt caught, caged, crumpled down into the recesses of the city with the usual detritus—food, mulched excreta, lost addresses and fragments of great beat poems. She was afraid. He'd seen her, was coming closer. She got to a pay phone, picked up the receiver. And put it down. She was through being scared. He came up to her, she faced him. He met her eyes, must have sensed her fury, smirked, passed by. She shook with fear, and felt an urgent need to talk to Fine. His one stellar quality, still, was his reliability. She called; the phone rang.

"Please, Fine," she said, "be there!"

"*Click* . . . this is the sound of the playback of the tape recording of the voice of Dr. Fine—"

She waited for the *beep,* and said: "Fuck you Fine! Steffy."

We who are not afraid to die survive. The mugger reads fear in the gait of the victim (too fast, too slow); the prey knows the hunter in a deep intuitive way.

Stephanie sat in a cafe with a cup of coffee, reading the *Village Voice.* She looked over the announcements of the city's comedy clubs, and saw that "Open Mike Night" at Catch a Rising Star was that very night. Could she do it? She said, to no one: "No."

And suddenly, spread out before her mind's eye as if a veil had been lifted, she had a vision: the last time she saw her father:

In spring almost two years before, she'd driven him to Kennedy Airport for his night flight to Paris. They, as always, had talked about life in general, and then, her life. And he'd said to her: "There's something missing, Steffy."

"No fooling. But what?"

"Remember last winter, when you visited us in Florida?"

She and Fine had arrived for a week on Siesta Key. After a day at Lido Beach (at Fine's insistence, the topless part), they'd rejoined her parents at a restaurant called the Columbia, in St. Armand's Circle. The floor show was novice comics, Open Mike Night for any and all comers. Her father had wanted her to try; her mother had not; Fine, sunburnt and irritable, had analyzed.

"And remember what you said, Steffy?" her father asked.

"I said 'No.' "

"You said 'No.' " They were sitting in the departure area. "Listen: I met a man once, who'd found out he had a rare and fatal disease. He had no disability at the time, and he didn't know how long he had left. He decided to take a last trip around the world, and he decided that on this trip, whenever he was presented with a choice, he'd say: 'Yes!' " He paused, his eyes glistening. "And I'm telling you, Steffy, that man had the most marvelous adventures, you should have heard! I've always wanted to be that man, always." His silence filled with regret. "Because he's each of us. Our disease is fear. That's what's missing in you. And me. In us all. The daring, come what may, to say 'Yes!' 'Cause life's too short for 'No.' "

Their hug was magical, overtight, both crying. He left. A few hours later, miles above dark water en route to the City of Light, the sloppily designed cargo door blew out and he was dead.

Sitting in the shabby cafe, tears came to her eyes. Ordinarily she would have wept, and fallen, and walked out defeated—even taking slight pleasure in her melancholy. Not now. She felt, just then, a strange new resolve. As if she were being filled out with earth, she felt in her gut—her bowels—solid, *sure*. And so, anchored to herself as she'd never felt before, she spoke, hissing out the final word:

"From now on, I am saying *'Yes.'* "

She phoned Professor Nipak Dandi and startled him by saying

"Yes, yes I'd love to see you tonight meet me in an hour at a place called Catch a Rising Star on First Avenue and 77th, yes!"

She sat with the natty Nipak, drinking bourbon with beer chasers, as, one after the other, the raw and aspiring stand-up comics did their five-minute bits. She was last. She rolled up to the mike and all tanked up and feeling blurry and free, said:

"Hi, I'm Goldie. How'm I doin' so far? What was the first Jewish settlement in America? Ten percent." One chuckle. She took her hair down and made a funny face, and then out of nowhere came: "New York is funny, isn't it? Whenever you're on a bus, there's always some fat lady with a shopping bag, screaming, in the back, right?" She mimed it. Laughter. "And you know, sometimes, on the street, you see a guy looking up at a building and chirping like a bird?" She mimed it. They knew. They laughed. "Or lying down on a corner, hollering?" She lay down hollering. Big laugh. "Well, today I saw the limit: a guy is standing there, hitting Rockefeller Center with a chair, okay? Now listen: you think they're crazy, right?" Right. "Well, I got news for you—they ain't crazy, that's their jobs!" What, jobs? "Sure, you see, every Monday morning, they go down to City Hall . . ."

And off she flew, high as a kite, using Belle and Grandpa Al and poking fun at Fine the Analyst and Nipak the Cosmologist and using quasi-feminist and ethno-erotic jokes and put-downs that she'd been using in front of the great audience of New Yorkers all her life. It might have been a disaster except for the fact that her spirit, alight, lit up the others with that special electricity that comes only through live human contact, and, hearing their laughter she said to herself: *It's working! I'm funny! Whoopee!*

She stayed up at the mike till she closed the place down, ending with the theme song from her cabaret with John: "Carry me back to old Manhattan, that's where my heart belongs . . ."

Afterward, thrilled, congratulated, surrounded by the hangers-on, she felt great. The manager said: "Dynamite! An original, just like Joan Rivers!" and invited her back whenever she wanted. A hideously ugly, oily haired talent agent named Howard Rosensdork said: "Beautiful! Only one problem." She asked what. "Too pretty. People won't laugh at a pretty girl. Like they say: 'Show me a funny woman, I'll show you a man.'" Steph gave him the finger. He laughed, and said: "I love it! I take it all back—I'd *kill* to handle you! Let's take lunch!" They all called her "Goldie." Exhilarated, she floated out into the 2:00 A.M. crispness of the Upper East Side, feeling, finally, that she *owned* a small piece of the City. The limos outside the singles' bars, reflecting the neon and all reflected once again in the damp streets, seemed to be there only for her.

She walked drunkenly down the city streets, bumping into Dandi who, she thought, was sticking around to give it the old cosmic try to get into her pandies. She turned to him and cried: "Put me in a taxi pummeeinnatagzi!" He put her in a taxi. Outside her building she looked up at the sky and screamed like a paid loony:

"New York I love ya!"

Dandi, trying to hang loose, asked: "And why?"

"Vhy?" she said, mimicking him, "because this city has seen *everything!"* She hugged him, and then, glancing down at his crotch, said: "Hey, lookit: *homo erectus!"*

Embarrassed in front of the doorman, Nipak said: "Shhh!"

"Hey, fella, you sure you ain't just lookin for the Big Bang? Ha!" He looked as if he would flee, and so she threw her arms around him and kissed him full on the pulpy lips. "Watcha say, Neep, wanna go to bed?"

"Bed?!"

"Yes!"

"What?!"

"Sex without gravity, yes!"

"No, wait, but I—" he seemed frightened, edged away. "That was not meant to be reality."

"Reality's a crutch!"

"There is a busy schedule tomorrow—"

She mimed him: "And must vee *shhed-dule* dee love?"

"—a remarkable woman and I shall call you, no?" Overwhelmed, he nipped off along the avenue as if his nut-brown pants were on fire, waved limply from the corner, and orbited off, home.

Amazing, she thought, undressing, banging against walls, tugging at pantyhose, the freedom and power of saying "Yes!" She slid into bed and replayed her comedy routine, and realized she'd glimpsed the receding edge of a dream and reached out for it and had found, in her hand, not nothing but something, a nugget of hope that portended, at least, her survival. I *am* funny! Imagine that?

"Daddy dear dead daddy you'd've been laughin at me tonight!"

Goldie?! Where'd she come from? On the weekend at the Fine *briss* I'll make a clean breast of it to him. Maybe quit my job. No more wooden men, senator husband or otherwise.

Dressed in the colors of change, like a kid comforted by its own voice, she let laughter lift her higher, up past the sour-breathed despair that had dragged her down the day. She lifted toward night, toward peaceful moons, toward slow and silent spinning planets with rings and rings—the closer you look the more rings there are—toward stars, toward galaxies, toward unimaginable endings of unending universes imagined and not, toward dreams of sea creatures, toward porpoises whose mouths are fixed in smile. And John. Rare day, this one, when a life, asked a question, answers back.

She picked up the phone, dialed. Same tape. At the *beep* she said: "Fugg-you-Fine! Goldie!"

14

"DEAD?!" Fine cried out, incredulous.

Mrs. Neiderman, gulping, nodded. Ms. Ando shook her head.

"But how—why—how could Reuben be dead?"

Early that next morning, a jogger had found Reuben's body in the front seat of the Buick. Fine's gut wrenched—he'd been murdered right before his eyes! Stunned, he felt a chill in his head, as if his brain had turned to dry ice. The chill spread down, numbing him through and through. He had a terrible thought: if only I'd followed my hunch, gone down the alley—maybe he'd still be alive today? What kind of asshole am I, anyway? And, worst of all: I fought with him, just before? I actually wished him dead? Oh, shit!

Georgina called, frantic. They went together to the police.

The Boston Homicide division, as usual, was checking out all "enemies of the victim," and in fact had already heard about Fine's fight with Reuben at the Institute. They interviewed Georgina and Fine separately. The interrogation started off routinely. Yet as they went on, Fine's analytic style—answering a question with a question—first puzzled them, then infuriated them, and, finally, made them believe that Fine had something to hide. They brought in Fine's old acquaintance, Detective O'Herlihey, who, after a few rounds of this question-handball, said: "Look, Fine, you better come clean."

"Yes, and what are your thoughts about 'come clean,' hmm?"

O'Herlihey said: "Our t'ought is this: *you* killed him."

"Umphgh!" said Fine, understanding at last.

"Unless you can come up with an alibi, we're bookin' you!"

Georgina's corroborating testimony cleared them both as suspects. They became sole witnesses. They told all they knew: the startled look, the shots, the slow darkening of the interior. They were dismissed with a warning: "Be careful. You two could be next."

"Next?" asked Fine. "And what are your thoughts about—"

"Out!"

Georgina, shaken, insisted Fine buy her a drink. Dazed, they searched for a bar. It being Boston, there was one right next door. Soon one of the cops came in, and, breaking confidentiality (just like the Institute! Fine thought), told them the details: Reuben had been found spread-eagled across the seat of his Buick, one leg still out the door, the other stretched to the accelerator. He'd been murdered in cold blood, shot twice at close range, with deadly accuracy. There was one top-secret clue, a link in all the murders, a bizarre mutilation of the body kept from the press, even from the cops—a so-called "key" that only the killer would know—and no other witnesses. The MO was identical to the two others; the murders were the work of a meticulous, vengeful pro.

Psychiatrists were scared. At Stow, tremendous precautions were being taken, under the direction of Mr. Royce, Security. At the Institute, they employed their analytic expertise to work through the brutal murder of one of their own. Familiar with death (suicide in psychiatrists peaked high, just below dentists), they marched through the familiar ritual: funeral, condolence call, plan to talk about it at the next Vergessen seminar. The Institute secretaries brought up concerns about their "security"—analyzed out as "dependency needs"—and only when they threatened to walk out were they allowed to do "whatever you need to feel safe."

And yet, to many, the latest murder came as a kind of macabre relief. The usual six months of Boston winter was one thing, but the overdue delivery of spring was another, and humans, biological clocks awry, were reacting to the repetitive dull cold and pre-cipitous delay with irritation. All across the country, the weather had been bizarre. Something big was out of whack. A sense of dread was hanging heavy in the air. Like birds before storms, humans quieted.

As if to mirror the deceit of the season, the recent revelation of corruption had been extraordinary. For many years, graft had been taken for granted, but in the wake of the election of an honest man as governor, a commission had investigated the award of state building contracts: the reason that buildings were falling down on people and concrete panels in bridges were falling into the water and roads were the worst in the country despite the highest road taxes was that yes, citizens, the contractor had laced the concrete with extra sand, and no, citizens, the bridge architect had not gone to architecture school after all! Over the past ten years it had cost each taxpayer about three grand in payoffs, kick-backs, and bribes. The march of crooks across the headlines had been sobering, and the FBI videotapes of the double-knit bagmen talking like real crooks they'd seen on TV was easy viewing. A major extortionist, turned state's evidence, said: "The state was for sale. But when 'Duke' got in, the payoffs stopped dead." So the citizens threw this honest Duke out of office, electing a tradi-tional pol. Corruption ran rifer; payoffs began anew. The major extortionist said: "The people got just what they deserved." But the governor was in trouble: probed, a tax official had hanged himself. Somehow, the image of a devoted family man found by his wife dangling from the rafters was ugly. The governor's slogan —"Make It in Massachusetts"—was a constant ironic reminder of the sleaze. The governor's days were numbered.

The mayor's, too. In angry reaction to the citizens' vote for tax ceilings, the mayor had cut back on police and firemen. An hon-est, smart, aggressive U.S. Attorney (Yankee) was chasing the mayor (Irish) on municipal corruption. Several machine captains, jailed for extortion, bribery, and tax evasion, were about to squeal. A ward boss in Southie had had his lucrative disability pension revoked—the "accident" revealed to be a "crash" of a van going three MPH into a van driven by the future-disabled man's brother. Hence a recent *Globe:* CITY DEMANDS PENSIONERS PROVE THEY ARE ALIVE.

Angry, sick, and tired of the whole wintry mess, people sought relief. Many found it in the murder of yet another shrink.

The stories were written with verve and spark. TV—"the electronic straitjacket" (Fine)—turned the real death into easy viewing. Many residents of Boston disdained psychiatrists. Caricatured in the press, passive to the extreme, mostly Jewish, their technique mistaken for snobbery, analysts were an easy focus for mob anger. Citizens hungered for details. As the gruesome news walked across Boston, it metamorphosed to a chilling joy. Much like a good therapist, it lightened the burden of the fed-up, the depressed.

All the rest of the week, as the gray chill May days passed one after another as joyless as early November, Fine thought himself struggling to come to terms with Reuben's death. Wednesday morning with Neiderman and Ando, when they brought up the murder, he ended up pontificating: "The times have come unglued. The national defenses have grown primitive: projection, introjection. No one *owns* feeling, anymore. Too much hype, too much hope. Is it chance that our national comic is a laughing shadow who took the stage name 'Hope'? Did you know he's insomniac, calls up friends at 3:00 A.M., pops a one-liner, waits for a laugh, and hangs up?"

"Why the lecture?" asked Neiderman, puzzled. Fine stared at her, surprised—he thought his words had been in the service of mourning. "Besides," she said, indignantly, "there's no need to knock Bob Hope. He's brought a lot of joy to a lot of families."

"Ah, families," Fine said, sighing, as if "families" had been murdered. "Why do families watch so much TV? Because TV families *don't.*" Fine noticed their perplexed looks, and tried to explain: "TV is the greatest historical disjuncture. There's a stampede away from the personal. In movies, robots and extraterrestrials are more real than humans. Yet trying to recover loss of the personal is like trying to forget electricity, or the whe—"

"Dr. Fine," said Ms. Ando, pointedly, "don't you feel bad?"

"Bad?" He assessed. "Numb. Stage one of grief is numbness: psychodynamically, a wrenching away from the omnipotent mother."

"Why in the world," said Neiderman, reddening in irritation, patting her blond hair, "do all you analysts blame your mothers?"

"What?" Fine was startled. "Not I. Why, I love my mom, yes."

Fine failed to notice how, at this, they rolled their eyes.

Later that day, Fine thought that numbness was giving way to stages two and three, anger and guilt. He laid himself down on his couch for a self-analysis: guilt comes from my fantasy that my murderous rage at Reuben had somehow provoked his murder. Yet guilt is a hot potato—whoever holds it gets burned. Fine's anxiety grew, and he thought of calling Fumbles. A post-termination session? Unheard of! ("If you're on your own, so you're on your own"—Fumbles.) So Fine was on his own. He felt a twinge of pride.

Fine became more tense. His headaches worsened. He had a vague sense of doom, as if he might, in a flash, lose control, as he had at the seminar. He dug into Freud, *Mourning and Melancholia* (1917), repeating out loud, like a verbal charm, his favorite line: "The shadow of the lost object falls across the ego." This meant that if there were mixed feelings about the dead—especially anger—the death could not be integrated in the normal process of mourning, but would produce a deep, pathological "melancholy" (depression). He worked on his anger. By Thursday morning, Fine thought he'd pretty much analyzed out his feelings about the murder.

Poor Fine! Prior to his analysis, Fine more or less knew what he was feeling. Now, without knowing it, Fine was quite confused about the difference between a "feeling" and a "thought." And so while he thought he was having these feelings about the death of his rival, actually he felt almost nothing, nothing at all.

And at the interface of fantasy and reality, Fine tried to manage his fear of being in danger. While he admitted that these murders were real-life events and cause for concern, he thought his fear a mere vestige of his neurosis. The feeling "they are out to get me" was familiar, perfectly analyzed. He thought himself in no danger in reality. He knew of no real enemies, and no one—except his patients in their transferences—was angry at him. He went on with his life as best he could: doing research, trying to calm his Jefferson House inpatients (their psychoses inflamed by the murders), seeing his private patients, and working through his two incredible mistakes in his analytic control cases—the doorknob "You're welcome good night" and the profligate fart, in Six and Five o'clock, respectively.

In his supervisory session with Vergessen on Thursday afternoon, Fine began with Ratman. He decided to hide his mistake. After listening awhile, V. read from a volume of Freud:

> *"Das Unbehagen in der Kultur,* 1930: The existence of the social factor that is responsible for the further transformation of anal erotism is attested by the circumstance that, in spite of all man's developmental advances, he scarcely finds the smell of *his own* excreta repulsive, but only that of other people's. Thus a person who is not clean—who does not hide his excreta—is offending other people . . . It would be incomprehensible, too that man should use the name of his most faithful friend in the animal world—the dog—as a term of abuse if that creature had not incurred his contempt through two characteristics: that it is an animal whose dominant sense is that of smell and one that has no horror of excrement, and that it is not ashamed of its sexual functions."

V. stared at him, smiling. Fine was incredulous: from the passage, it was clear that V. had, somehow, picked up the clues in the process notes of the session, sensing that Fine had ended it with a fart! He *knew!* Staggered by V.'s intuitive brilliance, Fine confessed his fart. To his surprise, V. told a joke, which ended:

". . . and so Tausk turned to Freud said: 'You farted before Lou Andreas-Salome!' And Freud said: 'Ah, and was it her turn?' "

Fine laughed hard, as did V. Composing himself, Fine also told V. about his doorknobber. V. said, only: "So what?"

At first, Fine heard this as *acceptance.* Alone in his car later, however, as he turned it on the spindle of his paranoia, he saw in this "what" a rejection, a call to analyze it more deeply. And somehow, feeding into his suspicion, Fine had the weird feeling from a look in V.'s eyes that through the grapevine of patient-therapist dyads, V. had heard, and was musing on, *vaginismus.*

All through the stressful week, Fine missed Stephanie. Alone in bed night after night, he thought: she's never here when I need her! It's her narcissistic mother, lying there unanalyzed in her, yes. His only contact with her had been through two messages on his answering machine, on Tuesday night/Wednesday morning:

First: (clear voice, sounding sober and angry) "Fuck you Fine!
Steffy." (Strange, her using her father's girlhood nickname for her
—Steffy; a clear regression—she must be under stress.)

Second: (slurred voice, sounding angry and drunk) "Fugg-you-
Fine! Goldie!"

" 'Goldie'?!" Fine said out loud. "What could this mean?"

After meticulous, close-to-the-bone analytic work, he thought
he had it—it could mean only one thing: she loved him!

15

AND SO ON Friday afternoon at the train station on the banks of the Hudson in Columbia, waiting for the delayed New York City train, Fine felt both love and anxiety. Far off to the south, under the Rip Van Winkle Bridge where he'd worked summers as a toll collector, the train had stopped dead in its tracks. Fine stared at a rusted crane and hook, a rotting boxcar, geriatric rails. Here, on Front Street, Nose Cohen's father had tried to kill himself by jumping into the mighty Hudson. As it was only knee-deep, he survived to be taken to the State Facility for Mental Hygiene, a few miles out of town, for a long, high-voltage stay.

Fine walked up Promenade Hill to the park—honoring a patroon—overlooking the Hudson. How small it all looked now! How huge it once had been! He leaned on the iron railings, as he'd done intermittently for thirty years, staring across at Athens and beyond, the Catskills. Half a block up the street was the synagogue, scene of Fine's first memory: sitting on his mother's lap in the balcony, staring down at the flickering-red Eternal Light, crying in pain at the sensory chaos. Years later, as a kid on the fast day Yom Kippur, knee-level in the forest of hungry *dovenning* Jews, he'd signal to his pal Nose—*now!*—they'd run out, down the stone steps, down the street in squeaky new shoes and too-tight tie, up the slope to this vista, this comforting breezy shape of river and mountain, always sweetly summer or crisply fall. The Hudson seemed so close, but year after year, no one could reach it with a stone, until one year, with Fine calculating the trajectory, Nose did it! Soon thereafter, through Stephanie's prompting, Fine became basketball manager and joined the human race. He walked back down to the station.

The train curled around the last curve, tipping precariously, and Fine had the fantasy that it would fall. A few passengers got off, and then nothing. Finally, there she was! "Stephanie!"

"Call me Goldie," she said.

" 'Goldie?!' "

"Fine!"

He tried to suppress his puzzlement and his disappointment at her seeming so cool, and said: "Shall we go to our Crik?"

"Yes!"

In May of every year since their first, they'd gone back to Kinderhook Crik. They drove up Columbia's decaying main street and then out past the vibrant shopping malls, through the vistas of the North Claverack hills, the public bandstand at the cesspool at Ghent, the Greek revival mansions in Chatham, and then into the real country all chilled budding green and early yellow—cows, barns, pungent, rich. It was still cool, but clearer. Stephanie snuggled into Fine's hip, singing along with the country-and-western station blaring down from what Fine had always thought of as the metropolis to the north, Albany. Fine told her about Reuben being murdered. She was shocked and concerned. They turned down the horse-fenced dirt road past the Shaker Museum in Old Chatham, creeping up on an old Merc with a bumper sticker: HONK IF YOU ARE JESUS. Stephanie honked, the driver looked up, swerved to avoid a little girl on a horse, and, behind Fine, a beat-up Ford skidded to a stop. Surprised at there being three cars in a row on an isolated country road, Fine said: "I think that Ford followed me over on the pike."

"Really?" said Stephanie.

"A real paranoid fantasy—I've had them continuously since Reuben was killed. And nightmares? Worse than ever! I guess I haven't worked through the death."

"But you hated him, Fine."

"Yes! That's why!" He thumbnailed mourning/melancholia.

"Well, I can see why you'd be upset about these deaths, Fine, but there's one good thing about them."

"What's that?"

"They're making the world safe for patients."

Sick joke, Fine thought, and hostile. His paranoia growing, he drove on, glancing in the rear-view mirror at the Ford. Fine analyzed the car in terms of Pelvin's automotive theory—old model, two-door, green, rusted and banged up, no bumper stickers—and, seeing the driver's psyche as "banged up" and "rusted," felt even more scared. "Suppose when we stop, he stops too? What then?"

"Are you *really* worried?"

Fine quashed the analytic response and said: "Yes."

Stephanie turned around, looked, said: "No sweat, Fine, it's a woman—oh damn—look! There's a log blocking our road!"

"I'm ambivalent about stopping!"

"Well, then don't—keep driving—"

Fine slowed, stopped. Time stood still. They watched the Ford ease up, seem to pause, and creep past, the woman hardly glancing at them. The car had Massachusetts plates. Fine watched it bounce over the rise and disappear, and tried to calm himself.

The newly painted sign read: NO TRESPASSING. Fine held back, fantasizing the headline: BUMPKIN BAGS BOSTON ANALYST, WIFE —DISREGARDED SIGN.

"Maybe we shouldn't trespass—it's a risk."

"Oh come on," she said, pulling him along like a reluctant child, "risk is the motor of love."

They stopped at the top of the ravine. Fine thought of this return to their special place as a repetition, and hoped it might be, this time, a renewal. To him it looked much the same: the stone ruins of the piling of the missing bridge, a reminder of purpose and neglect; the stream flowing with a hard full rush down from the hills on the right, pooling under the fantasied bridge, curving sharply off through the chasm to the left. They squeezed each other's hands and walked down the alley of bare-limbed trees and short-branched saplings, the soggy trail that once was a road, to a clearing under the pines at the water's edge where they found the expected charred remains of a campfire, beer cans, and the Clorox bottle.

As usual, they parted. Stephanie stayed on the bank; Fine took

off his shoes and socks and waded out into the middle. The icy
water froze his ankles. "Ow! Water's *cold!*—I'm crying!"

"Yeah," said Stephanie, "it's cryogenic."

Fine chuckled at their old pun, happy she was in a joking
mood, and, ankles numbing, slipped across the smooth bottom-
stones to a perch on a dry rock in the middle. He sat, awhile,
easing down to a sort of peace. He watched the water fill and flow
in little pools, creating for a time microworlds of tiny plants and
animals, born in flood, dead in ebb. He looked upstream into the
sun toward the bend, and saw the water sparkling white, shining,
a shivering of glass beads on a tilting mirror. Turning his head, he
looked down away from the sun into shadow, and saw the water
turn dark blue, pooling between the two granite ramparts. And
then the living thread rubbled off toward a center of great gravity,
down, a flipping fish of water seeking a spawning ground. Years
ago, here, Fine thought, Stephanie opened me up. The can-opener
theory of love. Like analysis, I let down my defenses, and in came
the liquid bubble and suck of love. Who can forget the wet? How
timid I'd been when she first took off all her clothes here, one
misty summer afternoon heavy with ions after a shattering thun-
derstorm. How lovely she was! I'd shivered with expectation;
she'd held me so close! His eyes filled with tears, and he turned to
look at her, sitting under the trees on the rocks. Our separate
perches are a metaphor for our marriage, and yet, sure of the
depth of our love, I feel happy. He got up and rejoined her again,
sitting on the rocks, rubbing his feet, now white with cold.

"Here you taught me love," he said.

"And you taught me discipline," she said, sounding sad. "You
said: 'A little discipline is required.' "

A common redwing *(Turdus musicus,* Fine mused) cried out
once, tightly. The sour scent of skunk cabbage fueled their remembrance. "Ah life, life," Fine said, "it's like stuffing a fat lady
into a tight bathing suit—you get one part in, another part pops
back out."

"We can't go back, Fine, no way."

"No, we've got to move on, grow. I want to buy a house, off
Stow grounds, as you said: '*Do* something.' "

"You're so innocent, Fine—you still believe that for you, anything's possible, that you can change, don't you?" He nodded.
Her voice somber, almost ominous, she said: "Men change when

they find out that others care; women change when they find out that others don't. We've got to keep challenging each other, Fine, like we always have, over and over again—otherwise—"

"Exactly! I want to have a baby! Children are a way of moving on!" The fantasy floated up of a Fine little boy, playing in the water. He sensed her stiffen. "I really do love you, Stephanie."

"Goldie. Call me Goldie."

"Who the hell is Goldie?"

"My stage name."

"What are you talking about?"

"Moving on. Listen." She told him about her debut at "Catch." She talked about how she was thinking about giving up her job for the senator and really giving stand-up comedy a try. She had to stop taking care of other people, and take care of the "funny lady" inside herself. "I'm good, Fine, I'm really good!"

Fine felt crunched by this obvious acting out. In fantasy, he watched the towheaded little boy explode. He rediagnosed his wife as that rarity: a female narcissist—like her mother! How hard to see the spouse's parents in the spouse! We're both at the age when the traits of our parents, like long-hidden roots, push up through our characters into the light. Fine felt overwhelmed, on the verge of panic, light-headed, about to lose control. He ransacked Fumbles: "If you feel overwhelmed, so feel overwhelmed."

"I'm overwhelmed!" Fine said, almost proudly. "What does this mean for our shared task of building a family, Stepha—"

"Goldie!"

"I love Stephanie—how the hell can I love Goldie?"

"Yes!"

"Huh?"

"Yes!"

"What's that supposed to mean?"

"I've decided to always say 'Yes.' "

" 'Yes'?"

"Yes! Tell you later. Let's go."

Fine felt betrayed. Perhaps, he thought, I should find another woman, in the Freud-model of chunky hausfrau to cook and clean and worship genius while mothering three kids, someone built like Georgina. Do great men need unliberated women? The grotto, suddenly, seemed dead as stone. The sun was setting, and the afternoon cooled. A cardinal swooped past in a red streak, up to a higher level, for bugs. "I don't know," Fine said, "I'll have to *think* about it, Steph—"

"Goldie."

"Goldie? How can I—"

"Yes!"

They rose, and faced each other. She held out her arms to him, and he came to her. They held each other as tenderly as they always would when at this place. "You are sweet, Fine," she said. "No matter what happens, no one will ever love you as I did, here."

"Did?!" he said. "Don't you mean *do?*"

"Yes."

They started back up from the water, their nostalgia so big and rich it seemed to spill over out of them, trickling down behind them, linking them always to this, to each other, and somehow, to death. Fine said: "*Shabbas* dinner *chez* Fine—just what you need, hm?"

"Yes!"

"Really?" said Fine, pleased. Having taken seven years of analysis to come to terms with the guilt, spite, rage, and chicken served up in the dining room directly over Fine Meats, he was amazed that, unanalyzed as she was, it could be pleasurable. "Yes, it is fun to be with my mother." He felt a surge of love for the handsomely aging, vivacious, long-suffering butcher's wife, and sighing, with admiration, said: "My wonderful, caring mother."

"Fine," said Steph, "deep down you *hate* your mother."

"*What?!*" He was shocked. "Never. Never have, never will. Talked about her completely in my analysis. Not much anger, no."

"Your analyst fumbled the ball."

"Did not," said Fine, defensively, reaching for his beard.

"If you'd had a woman analyst, maybe you'd have—"

"Common misconception," Fine said, "that gender can affect the transference. I myself am often treated as though I were female. I sometimes felt Fumbles as maternal—hateful and loving— and I worked it through. Yes," he went on proudly, "by God I've worked my mother through, I understand her now, and I *accept* her, yes."

"Oh, bullshit! You just *think* you have, Fine."

"Yes, and why are you so angry at my mother?"

"Me? Hey, sparky, I'm looking forward to dinner, know why?"

"No, why?"

"Good material! I'd *kill* for a few good 'chicken jokes'!"

They retraced their steps up the path to the top of the ravine. Puffing, they turned for a last look back. Fine fingered the smooth stone in his pocket—unknown to her, he took one away with him every time—and said: "I feel sad."

"Yeah. Me too. It's so clear, it hurts! Our whole relationship was captured in our first moment together here."

"Love at first sight?"

"Not for me."

"No?!" he said, startled, "what then?"

"I trusted you."

By the end of dinner, Fine was fuming. He couldn't get Stephanie's comment—"you *hate* your mother!"—out of his mind. In the past, Stephanie had been under suspicion in the Fine household for not appreciating the cooking. Tonight, to every offer of more food, she replied with an enthusiastic: "Yes!"

This led to a small disaster: they ran out of chicken!

"You couldn't bring me a bigger chicken?" asked Anna, tense.

"This was a big chicken," said Leo, his voice tired, sharp.

"Not as big as Mrs. Storch's chicken."

"Mrs. Storch's chicken was a tough chicken. Our chicken was a nice chicken. Ours is to hers as prime rib is to Spam!" He winked at Stephanie. "This chicken was loved."

"It was good, wasn't it, Stephanie?" Anna asked, puzzled.

"Goldie," said Stephanie, happily. "And yes."

"Good, hell," said Leo, "this chicken was fresh—it was hopping around this afternoon!" He poured some more schnapps. "So —I've got another one for you: Two Jews are stuck in a barrel, and . . ."

Fine, tired of the shtick, tuned out. Difficult for a recently terminated analysand to be back in the lap of his "primary objects." He was becoming obsessed with Steph's comment. The concept "hate-mother" marched on in his brain, enlisting memories. Despite himself, as he watched his mother join in the displaced hostility called joke telling he began seeing her as less than all-loving. She'd always related to him with bewilderment. Not very empathic, that. Always favored brother Moe. I'm fed up with her damn bewilderment! Shocked, Fine wondered if this rage meant he *had* been fumbled on mother, after all! Look—in league with his wife, his mother was kidding his father, who, oblivious to the latent sadism, was laughing! Look again—even her smile seems sharper, almost cruel! And listen—the joke she herself picked to tell:

". . . and so from the back of the theater comes a voice: 'Give him an *enema!*' And the MC says: 'But he's *dead!* An enema can't help!' *'Nu,'* says the voice, 'but an enema can't hurt!' "

Fine did not join the laughter. Anna, tipsy, told about going to see Fanny Brice at Fox's Star, and imitated her "Indian," going "whoop!" around the little dining room. Leo and Stephanie thought this hilarious. Fine, odd man out, jealous that his wife had been able to stir up happy "feeling" in what he'd always perceived as a family of "things," left. He walked past the Henry Hudson, a sleazy bar. The night was pitch-black. At the corner, he had the fantasy that he was being watched. In fear, he hurried home.

The three were still at it, huddled around the sputtering sabbath candles. Fine announced he was going to bed. Leo said he'd arranged a surprise for tomorrow night: "A reunion of the Class-D champs, the *Blau*hawks. Oh—and that nice fella Ron from NASA is stationed out at Iron Mountain—wants you to call him —he's got another stumper for you, okay?" As Fine watched, his father hugged his wife—*hard!*—and he could almost feel the Oedipal stage tremble. Then his mother hugged his wife, and the pre-Oedipal tipped, too.

"You *should* be a comic," Anna said. "You can have children anytime. I gave up my career in music to have a family." She looked at Fine. "To learn to give enemas to him." At that Fine felt a slippage, a regression back into anal-stage rage. Anna, happily bombed, took his hand: "Ever since analysis, you don't tell jokes—why?" She sighed. "Sometimes I think your Freed was *not* 100 percent!"

" 'Freed?' " Puzzled, Fine asked: "Who, mother, is 'Freed'?"

"Sigmund Freed—definitely *not* 100 percent!"

Fine saw headlines: SHRINK KILLS MOM, POP, WIFE, WITH CLEAVER—PLEADS NGRI.

"Know why? 'Cause he didn't know about real, normal people. Your wife—she does what you never learned—she *listens.* I'm sorry, my dear brilliant son, but you never learned how to really *listen!*"

He shouted: "My whole life is listening! *I listen!*"

"Oh!" said Anna, blushing, intimidated. "Sorry, dear. It's just that, sometimes you're so busy with your fantastic projects, off in another world—and such a fruitful one!—you don't seem to *hear.*"

Stephanie, barely keeping a straight face, said: "Now, Anna, it's a *terrific* job your son's got—seventy-five an hour and a choice of two vegetables!" Laughter. "And an analyst has only three rules: one: always answer a question with a question; two: never fall asleep on a patient—that means never actually *on* a patient, okay?; and three: never open the office door with your pants down."

Anna and Leo laughed hard. Dimly, through red clouds of rage Fine felt Anna kiss him wetly on the cheek. She turned to Leo, and, unlocking her long red hair and smoothing her pink-flesh-colored dress over her breasts, her hips, she asked: "Leo, are you coming?"

Fine was shocked at her flagrant, blowsy sensuality. They still *do it?!* "Soon," said Leo. "I got a real beauty in my hands!" Anna left.

Fine stared at his wife huddling with his father. Leo seemed to be staring down her blouse at her boobs. Laughter! Hugging! His voice an octave high, Fine said: "Stephanie, are you coming to bed?"

"Soon." She blushed. "I'm in the hands of a master!"

Enraged, Fine retreated up to his old room in the attic. The stuff of Jewish novels! His obsession flared. His heart pounded in his temples, sending throbs of hot metal through his brain. Oh, this headache! He lay down, trying to associate: *Blocking!*

After a while, Stephanie stumbled upstairs. The fight began.

"Making fun of me!" Fine said. "Flirting with my pop!"

"Oo—a little Oedipal jealousy, eh Fine? Sweet!"

"Not Oedipal! I worked through Oedipal!"

"Why did the Polack marry a chicken?"

"Not funny—"

"Face it: you can't stand my being funny—nihilist!"

"No I'm *not!*"

"See? Know why? 'Cause *you* used to be funny—"

"I still *am* funny—"

"Perfectly analyzed human beings are *not funny*—"

"That's not funny!"

"They analyzed out the 'funny'!"

"I was never *that* funny—"

"Yes you were! But now, what's funny you take serious, and what's serious you take serious, too—"

"Well, I've got news for you: *you're* not that funny, either!" But a burst of laughter echoed up from Fine's parents' bedroom, directly below, clear evidence that they thought her *very* funny. As Fine and Stephanie listened, there followed giggles, then the slapping of flanken, the kneading of brisket, two pupiks, a knish, and a putz—the rough-and-tumble sounds of an aging kosher butcher making love! "The primal scene!" said Fine, burying his head in a pillow. "I'm going *psychotic!* Will you get into bed and help me?"

"Yes!"

"You will?"

"Yes!"

"What the hell is it with you and this 'Yes'?"

She slipped out of her clothes, crept in under the covers, and told him. He was disappointed, and said: "Show biz? Listen, Stephanie, we didn't come all the way from Europe to sing songs."

"What? *You* didn't come from Europe at all."

"A generation ago I did."

"That's why you don't listen—you're stuck in the past—"

"I'm expert in listening!" Startled, he thought: my defect?

"You never *show* it. Your face is always a total blank."

"You're turning into a real character—"

"Great!—that's just what a stand-up comic *is!"*

"—like John James—deep character pathology, there! Get to the bottom of your need to exhibit yourself, Stephanie!"

"You actually believe there's a 'bottom' to get to?" He grunted. "Oh Fine, you're adding *insight* to injury." She giggled.

"To have a child is to give a gift—it's time."

She fell silent. And then, her voice serious, soft, she asked: "Who are you, Fine? Do I know you anymore?"

Fine felt sick inside, a dull weight falling, falling, and, desperate, said: "Our shared task, together, is to make a baby."

"But Fine—wait—that'd mean we'd have to have *sex!"*

"Despite your hostility, I'm ready when you are."

"Did you know, Fine, that some people actually *like* sex?"

They began to make love, she on top, he thinking: peel to banana.

At one point, sighing with pleasure, slurring her words, she said: "Whadda world: men shave, women bleed." Shocked by her coarseness—the obvious latent meaning: menstrual blood, episiotomies, placentas—Fine fantasied that this act of love, this very night, would conceive their child. Sobered and happy, he whispered: "Tonight's the night we make a baby?" Boozy and loose, she said:

"Oh Fine, you're so weird—you'd be a *terrible* father!"

"No problem. No problem at all."

"How's that?"

"At age thirteen, we send the kid off to analysis!"

She laughed, he joined her. They journeyed to orgasm: Fine, as usual, thinking, associating, carefully in control up to the end; Stephanie, free and easy, letting go all the way. On the edge of sleep, Fine patted her curly soft semen-slick pudendum, turned on his right side, and felt her arm lock into place around his neck ("The best feeling in the world is patting your wife's bottom and knowing it will be there tomorrow"—Semrad), and heard her say:

"Because he *had* to."

"Huh?"

"That's why the Polack married a chicken."

"Because he *had* to?"

"Yes!"

Fine associated: pregnancy. Fruitfulness. Yet hope brought fear: a murderer is loose! I must be responsible—buy life insurance, buy locks! But he felt romantic, too, more romantic than he had in years! And as he often did at such times, he saw the clean shape of the equation he'd derived describing the flow of current in the synaptic region of the single grasshopper nerve cell that learned:

$$V_{o/c, o/c}(X,L,T) = C_o \frac{e^{-T}}{T^{1/2}} \sum_{n=0}^{\infty}$$

$$\left[\exp(-(X+2nL)^2/4T + \exp(-(-X+2(n+1)L)^2/4T \right]$$

"Two Jews are in jail and—are you awake, Fine?—and . . ."

Where *V* is voltage, *o/c* is open cable, *X* is space, *L* is length, and *T* is time . . .

The next afternoon, at Moe's baby's briss, Leo, Anna, and Stephanie were hung over, irritable. Fine, the godfather, or *sandek,* held the six-day-old boy in his lap. The *mohel* prepared his knife. Fine felt tense. His mother-obsession was even stronger, taking root in a way that made him think it was resonating with deep unconscious processes—by definition, unanalyzed! Could it be that Fumbles cut me short? What an association at a circumcision! The day, May sixth, was Freud's birthday, and to calm himself Fine recited Freud's famous "recollection" of his own mother, from *Ein Kindheitserrinnerwung aus "Dichtung und Wahrheit"* (1917):

> If a man has been his mother's undisputed darling he retains throughout life the triumphant feeling, the confidence in success, which not seldom brings actual success along with it.

Suddenly, disaster struck: the mohel cut, the baby shrieked, Fine saw bright red blood spurt from the penis, and for some reason stood up. He felt something travel up from the zone of his sigmund frex—oops!—sigmoid flexure, make a quick pass through his heart and then rush up into a jarred part of his brain, toppling something there and with a soft *whoosh* everything went black.

Fine had fainted. When he came to, Stephanie was sitting beside him. "What happened?" Fine asked. She told him. "Ohh," he sighed, thinking: what great material for the couch. She said:

"You just confirmed the classic definition of a shrink."

"Oh?" asked Anna, at her elbow, "and what's that?"

"Please," said Fine, *"don't—"*

"A Jewish doctor who can't stand the sight of blood."

Things got worse. Feeling jealous of his younger brother's having the first grandchild, Fine, as he hadn't in years, got drunk. Out in the backyard for the party, immersed in his contemporaries' children, Fine was soon furious at his wife. As they talked with Moe and Nose Cohen—now fat and happy partners in Institutional Foods—Fine exploded. Like a drunken lout, he began insulting Stephanie, who insulted him back, and before he knew it they were toe to toe, cursing. And then they were shoving, and then slapping, and then, in front of all his parents' friends, slugging it out! She, the athlete, caught him on the ear, and as he went down he saw stars and heard Fumbles—"The superego is the part of the psyche dissolvable in alcohol"—but too late; he felt her knee him in the nuts and he pulled at her tits and ripped her skirt halfway down and she grabbed at his crotch and amid the wails of the kids and the shouts of the adults, Leo and Isenberg the Rim Man and Kantor in Ladies' Lingerie and Gifts pulled her off him and hustled Fine out into Kantor's rose-colored Continental convertible and roared off down Third past St. Mary's into the marshland around Mt. Marino over the Rip Van Winkle Bridge to the Catskill Golf and Country Club.

For it was Saturday afternoon, and Fine was destined to make up the fourth, for golf.

While they were all pitiful golfers, Fine was the most pitiful of all. He agreed to play only if he could carry a bottle of Myer's rum. By the sixth hole—an easy par four up to a high broad plateau and then down to a terraced green—the three others decided they'd had enough of the drunken lovesick *schnorrer,* and had left Fine chasing his duck-hooked drive while they played out on the green. Fine found his ball, hand-mashied it out onto the fairway. There, out in the open green space, he felt totally vulnerable and defenseless, imagining the murderer close by. The hairs on the back of his neck prickled—a sure sign. His breath came shallow and fast. He took out a sand wedge, for defense, looking around. Seeing nothing, he let out his rage at the little dimpled ball—thwack! A great divot came up and hit him in the nose; the ball didn't move. Thwack! The flange of the club imbedded in the sod, sending shock waves up both arms. Fine's head reverberated —thwack! thwack!—something was about to burst. He felt wind in his face, and heart sinking, realized that the "thwack!" was nearby. He looked up.

The helicopter was almost on top of him—lower, lower, ThwapthwapTHWAPthwap!—two people sat in it, one aiming a metallic object straight at him.

He screamed: "The killer!" and ran toward the green. The copter headed him off. He ran toward the tee—same thing. The woods—it tracked him like a hawk. Trapped, out of breath, Fine fell on his back, and then up on his knees, palms together in the universal supplicatory sign. He heard a crackly shot of sound—

"Fine—what the hell are you doing?"

"Don't shoot! Please!"

"It's me, Stephanie!" Thwap thwap! "—you gone banar...s?"

"Stephanie?" It's not a gun, it's a bullhorn?

"The senator called, sent the helicopter. I've got to get back to Bos—" Thwap thwap! "—want to come?"

"I can't—the basketball reunion. Don't go!"

"I can't—" Thwap thwap! "—totally modern mar—" Whoosh! The helicopter became a speck in the overcast, then nothing. The afternoon, in the wake of the perturbation, seemed deathly still. Sadly, Fine rejoined the foursome on the next tee, a tricky par three over a stream-filled gully to a tiny green. Isenberg the Rim Man cracked a low liner that somehow tracked to the middle of the putting surface. Kantor in Ladies Lingerie put an "elephant's ass" ball (high and stinky) just short. Leo, upset with his son, dubbed into the brook. Fine whiffed, then sliced into a pricker bush, then demanded a "Mulligan," a free extra shot. Isenberg and Kantor shrugged okay, but Leo said no. Fine asked why not. Leo said:

" 'Cause there ain't no Mulligans in life."

This put the Fine boys dormie, and father and son walked back to the clubhouse. In the steaming shower, naked, side by side, they talked. "I'm sorry, Pop, for ruining the briss."

"Big deal. They'll come, talk. They'll buy more meat."

"Forever. They'll talk about it forever."

"Nobody talks forever. Forget it."

Fine looked at his father's saggy body, all blubbery rolls and oily black hairs, and thought: I love this tough little guy who's always been thus—naked next to me—who's always done his best to understand his strange son and who, failing, has never given up. I am his father. "You always seem to be forgiving me for something, Pop."

"What else is a poppa for?"

They dressed, sat out on the veranda snuggled into the foothills of the Catskills, watching the clouds sail over the Hudson. They felt freshened, as all duffers feel, after. The hacker's goal—the cold beer on the hot day—had been attained. "She's crazy!"

"So?" said Leo. "So are you."

"But I want to have kids and she doesn't."

"She will. Lotsa time for kids. You'll have kids plenty."

Fine looked into the sorrowful eyes forced to live in the jolly
face, and felt a special love. His own eyes got wet, his nose
squirmed under a tickling flow he felt ashamed of. He twitched,
snorted, tried to hold back, but the tears gushed out. He put his
arm around his pop and hugged him, and his pop, smiling,
hugged him back. His cheek still feels like the plump backside of a
plucked chicken, the cheek of my childhood. Happy and
ashamed, they looked away, two sad clowns together, rings apart.
I feel so close to my dad!

"Sometimes you're up, sometimes you're down;
"When you play against the Blue-Hawks you're upside down!"

After many such cheers, the starting five and the manager,
wiped out on beer and pot, called it a night. Fine and Roosevelt
the black center—who no longer could've won a beauty contest in
Senegal or anywhere else—wandered down Spook Rock Road. A
stream splashed along beside them. A cloudy, dark night.

"Man, I was sumthin', once, wasn't I?" Roosevelt asked.

"The best. I thought at Texas Western you'd be all-American."

"Hey, I was bad! But I lost it."

Fine felt the pathos of this—the lost chance in life—and
thought of his own lost hope, and blurted out: "I wanna have a
baby!"

"Tell you one thing about kids, man—I got six—if'n you plant
it, you gotta watch it grow." Roosevelt ambled off, away.

Fine sat, staring at Spook Rock, a huge granite chunk sitting in
the middle of the brook. The granite was unlike any other for
miles around, and the legend, Fine knew, was that it had
squashed an unfaithful lover or an ungrateful mother or an un-
gainly glover—something. Alone in this eerie place, again he had
a palpable sense of being watched and turned here and there,
trying to pierce the inky darkness, shivering with fear.

Damn, this headache's unbearable! Worse than ever! Like two
thugs fighting it out under my zygomatic arch. Always on the
right—I can almost see the defective artery straining, about to
burst. If I were to die right now—think of all I've missed! On his

knees, he said: "Please, Big Guy, don't let me die before I learn to love her."

Fine had a premonition: if he stood up, the vessel would blow, he would die. He analyzed it out: paranoid fantasy. Yet, as if made of glass, gingerly he rose. There was a loud explosion:

"Mrrrooom!"

He jumped back, noting that, jumping back, he was alive.

"Mrrrooom!" A lost cow lowed from the bank of the stream.

Fine sighed with relief. Bent to the right by the hot poker of pain in his head, he walked down the dark empty road toward home. A soiled night, and yet, somehow, cleansing. She's right: we can't go back. She'd opened me up, reached in, held my heart in her hands, blown on it to warm it, set it going again. Under the spell of these old, known, mysterious shapes, Fine's love for her surged up. Separated from her, he felt empty, and prayed that the President wouldn't push the nuke button till he was with her again. He recalled all the near car crashes he'd had, saved only by chance. How close I've come to losing her! No harm done. Still here. There's still time. I will risk, grow, open, join her on our path, the two of us together.

And then all at once before his eyes the events of the weekend ballooned out and realigned, forming a new arm of *Fine Theory!* Standing stock-still, lest motion smash the harmonic, he cried out:

"Insight!"

He watched a black shade ease up in the east. Across the horizon, russet light ran in under. Earth. Sunday dawn.

Fine could hardly wait to tell Stephanie what he—so imprisoned by his theory—thought of as vital, restorative news.

16

At just about the same time, in Boston, Stephanie was meeting John.

Later, she told me the details.

It being an election year, the senator had flown her back to Boston to cover a cultural event at the Shakespeare Company, "The All-Night Bard": three plays—*Hamlet;* a new comedy called *Courtenay's Gym;* and *The Taming of the Shrew*—presented one after the other, ending at dawn. From the first, the actor playing Hamlet seemed familiar. And yet he was quintessentially Hamlet: not a person acting a character, but the character being the person. And then, when he spoke—"Seems, madam? Nay, it is. I know not seems"—she knew: John! She felt herself go pale, begin to tremble. The past blurred into the present, like a cloud-edge into the sky. She saw, in his performance, both the spirit of ten years ago and the professional veneer he'd laid on since. A delicious feeling came over her—watching him while he was unaware, filling with expectation, in full control of the revelation—and she studied him as if he were a found artifact, a relic. She let herself go, riding waves of feeling and fantasy, caught in something beyond choice, as beyond right and wrong as a dream. The last time she'd seen him was over a year ago, in the Bellevue, with Fine. This was the first time since Harvard she'd seen him onstage, and—she was startled—the first time she'd seen him alone. She chuckled: alone with three hundred others.

She watched him repeat his two Harvard roles—(and, in the new comedy, the role of the owner of a man's gym opening up to women)—ending with Petruccio in *Shrew*. As dawn broke, she repeated with the current Kate the lines she'd said opposite him, ten years ago, as his first Kate, whispering:

> "But now I see our lances are but straws,
> Our strength as weak, our weakness past compare,
> That seeming to be most which we indeed least are."

Shakespeare—she and John shared the feeling—knew everything! The singularity in nature! In the history of the world it had only happened once, as if the man, beyond awareness, had been on assignment from God, or even, vice versa. Repeating "Kate," she felt her love for John surge up. The play ended, to much applause. The audience was invited onstage to join the performers. She got to her feet and took a few steps toward him, and then, realizing for the first time just how much hung in the balance of this simple movement—what if she just walked away?!—she hesitated. She thought: No, I better not. That did it. She said out loud: "Yes!"

Onstage, he was, as always in the past, the center of a disk of adulation. She waited on the edge.

Their eyes met. The old current flowed through her to him, and back, and back again, wrapping them, pulling them, together.

"Steph?!"

"Yes!"

"Jesus! Grand!" Throwing open his arms: "C'mere!"

His admirers turned toward her, opening an aisle to him. Mustering her lost dramatic flair she rushed—flew!—into his arms. Engulfed, she thought: how *big* he is compared to Fine! Feeling his arms around her, she lay still and let her fear flow out, in tears, the world all soft and fuzzy, muffled by his hug: endless, yet when he let go, too soon ended. Unmuffled, the world banged in, awkward, shibbolethed, hard. John introduced her to a small, stolid woman—in a *real* ocelot jacket?!—at his side: "Nora, Steph; Steph, Nora."

Steph knew that the woman sensed the electricity in the air. In a voice barely under control, a voice more cool for the heat beneath it, Nora said: "I'm going home—"

John said: "There's no need—"

"Hush. Don't make it worse than it is—"

"I haven't seen Steph for ages—"

"I expect you'll find your own way home?" and she was gone. And so they escaped. Their looks, touches, said everything.

"Your place or mine?" Steph asked.

"Mine is my mother's."

"Still? Won't you ever grow up?"

"Christ I hope not! And what about our dear little constipate, Fine? Won't Fine of the fine mind mind?"

"He's away. Won't be back till late tonight. C'mon."

They walked out into the fresh morning hand in hand, as excited as two little kids doing something bad. They came to her old purple Jag. "Same car!" John said.

"Except for the miles, yeah."

"Still talk to it?"

"Hey, you *got* to!" She hugged him: "John James!"

He stiffened. "Don't call me that anymore, okay?"

"Why not?"

"It's a kid's name, an old name—let's keep it new—"

"No repetitions?"

"No repetitions!"

"Except that one," she said. "I'll just call you John."

"Fine—" He caught himself, too late. "Uh oh, it's starting again!" They laughed. "And what can I call you that's new?"

"Goldie." He asked why. As they drove out of Boston toward Stow she told him. He loved it.

"Grand, just grand—I can see a new act: 'O'Day 'n' Goldie'—"

"*Goldie* and O'Day!"

He laughed. "So why didn't you come to my party?"

"I was afraid."

"Of me?!"

"Of this."

"Just this?"

"No," she said, softly, "of what's to come."

"Ah yes," he said, portentously, lapsing into historical-comical: "And the story is told that when Shakespeare beat Burbage to a rich admirer's bed, he was said to have said: 'Thus, William the Conquerer came before Richard the First!' "

They clanked over the Curley Bridge, stopped by the guard at the gate. Out of the low sea pine came five early risers from Jefferson House, only three of whom she knew. Cooter said: "Hooray hooray it's the seventh of May, outdoor fucking's the only way!"

"Err yes, no," said Mr. Jefferson, clad all in sailor's white, "sea men in her navel, eh?"

"Jesus told me," said a big black man, "love my neighbor."

"Sin!" said Eli the Hassid, "the anniversary of the Warsaw Ghetto uprising and where's the memorial? *Goys!*"

"Stinko!" said a one-eyed, wiry-haired man, crouching.

And the Jefferson House mascot, the poodle Lafite: "Woof!"

Steph felt a twinge of worry at being seen. She had a close relationship with Fine's patients (closer, she thought, than his). At first she'd balked at the idea of living on the grounds of a mental hospital, fearing them. But then, getting to know them, she found that no one's fear was greater than theirs, and she'd made friends. Most of Fine's chronic patients loved her.

"Who're they?" John asked.

"Them? My manager, my agent, and my fans."

They parked in front of the house, turned, looked out over the panorama. The gulls hung like ornaments on the tree of wind.

"You can almost see my house in Southie," John said.

"Let's to bed," she said, leading him inside.

And yet in the bedroom when they saw the residue of Fine— Freud, *Collected Papers*, vol. 3, four used nail files (Fine was now big on manicures), open bottles of Bufferin, Colace—they hesitated.

"Are we being very rotten to him?" she asked.

"You bet!" he said, eyes sparkling. "It's about time!"

She saw the dawn light shine softly through his blond hair, haloing it, gentling him. "I tried, John, I tried to stay away."

"You wicked girl," he said, opening his arms, "c'mere."

She went to him, riding down the wires of his light blue eyes. The eye contact sent warmth through her, suffusing down through her throat, nipples, womb, sex. His lips met hers, the touch heightening the hot wet rush. In her center, something big let go, gave out, like earth slipping. She was left bare, open, ready for anything as long as it was sensual. Nuzzling, kissing, she felt

168   SAMUEL SHEM

naughty, thrilled, dangerously safe. Comparisons to Fine flickered through—John taller, his touch—tongue on tongue, fingers on back—more delicate, even feminine. She felt him get hard, and moved her hand from the curve of his rump to his front—it was rough, bulging: "A codpiece?!"

"Look at me!" he said, pulling away. "I'm still Petruccio!"

"Never anyone else." Her words felt blurry. She was terribly aroused, flushed, wanting—*needing!* "Let's take off all our clothes!"

"Better yet—let's take off all of each other's!" He tried to unzip her dress, she tried to unlace his pants—no luck—and so he turned her around, she tried to reach around in back to get at him, and, at the silly Marx Brothers nature of it, they laughed. John got her zipper down and she stepped out of her dress and, in bra and panties, she turned to him. Posing, she said: "Well?"

"Fantastic! Grand! And—wait for it—*mine!* C'mere—"

"Nope! You gotta get naked too—hey!—"

He chased her around the room snatching at her and managing to pull down her panties and she managed to pull down his codpiece and then she tugged on his tights and out sprung his penis, and in mock shock she said: "Uncircumcised?!"

"Surprised?"

"What sweet blond curls!" she said, cupping his testicles in her palm, gently, and then—furious at Fine!—bending, slipping back his foreskin and putting her lips to his tip, kissing it, swirling it with her tongue. She felt his lips on the nape of her neck, his hand caressing the backs of her thighs—heard him say "Oh how I've ached to touch you, here!"—and his finger touched her, there. They entwined, like separated twins rejoined. Sighing, she pulled away, unhooked her bra and draped it over his head like a victory wreath. She'd always imagined he'd be just this gentle. "A little contraception is called for, I do believe?" She was steaming, furred.

"Know something?" he said. "I love you."

"Mmm." She felt like crying with happiness. "And I, you."

"For a long time."

"Yes. Me too." In the bathroom she took the 'phram, bent, put it in, saw in the mirror the russet flush of arousal dawning in her throat spreading into her chest and realized that she hadn't been so turned on—body and soul—in *years!* She opened the door to him.

Naked but for her bra as a hat, her dress as a coat, and her bulging panties—John stood on the bed, en tableau. "Guess who?" She said she had no idea. "Hint: a famous figure from our past."

"Richard Nixon?"

"Close. 'Nuther hint?" He set himself in profile, put one foot up, as if on the bow of a rowboat. He drew her dress around him from shoulder to hip, like a cloak, and shivered. "A famous American President, who, unbeknownst to history, was *Jewish!*"

"George Washington!"

Turning to her, a perplexed look on his face, in mock seriousness he said: *"Delaware? I thought they said Brooklyn!"*

And they laughed, and she joined him on the bed, tumbling, fooling around, until finally they found themselves side by side, naked and silent. The morning light played on their bodies. Illicit and too-long denied, their passion broke out. For a while, with a sweet vengeance, Steph compared him to Fine—this so much more dirty, wild, fun, free!—until thought itself cracked and died, and she let go, killed off, and, snarling and biting, came, and came.

Steph awoke to the ringing of the phone. It was light out but fading. John slept beside her. Scared, she grabbed the phone, stretched the cord to the bathroom, shut the door. "Hello?"

"Stephanie?"

"Fine? What time is it?"

"Four in the afternoon—you're in bed?"

"Napping. What's up?"

"Just wanted to tell you not to wait up for me. I'll be back late tonight. We're all going out to Pizza's, for pizza."

"Okay, bye—"

"Wait! And I had an incredible insight, too! I can't tell you over the phone but I think you will be happily surprised."

"Good."

"Except for the headaches, everything's fine!" He paused, then said: "Love you, Stephanie."

He was waiting for her response. "Umm, I'm tired."

"See you soon and don't wait up."

Later, cuddling, they talked. Whimsically, John said: "Let's run away together!"

"What a great idea!"

They fell silent again. After a while, he said: "You know something? I just realized that I mean it."

"You're joking!"

"Never been more serious in my life."

"Are you crazy? I've got a husband—"

"That's the whole point."

"Where to?"

"Wherever. 'Where' is not crucial."

"For how long?"

"What is this? I'm not a travel agent, I'm your lover. We passed it up once—let's not blow it again."

"Hold it—you know what a big thing that would be for me, to leave Fine after all this time? It's scary even to think—"

"Scarier not to."

"It's a big big deal!"

"It's over. You're fed up with him."

"Tell me about it. Fine's so negative, he'd have bad things to say about the equator!" They laughed together. "And what'll we do when we get to this 'wherever'?"

"*What*ever." He chuckled. "Who knows? I went around the world on whim—Cairo to Capetown without a dime in my pocket or a plan in my head—best thing I ever did. With your money and my good looks, all we need is talent—that's it: we'll *act!*"

"Really?"

"You bet." For the first time, he turned somber: "How can we say 'No' to this again?" She said nothing. "Let's go for it."

"Now?!"

"Why wait?"

"I can't just pick up and leave now."

"Why not?"

She said: "I need more time."

As the sun set they got dressed. In their last embrace before they went back out to her car, he cooed in her ear, a big blond dove: "You've got till five tomorrow afternoon to decide."

17

WHEN FINE GOT back to Stow late Sunday night Stephanie was asleep. His headache was so bad that even though she awoke when he came in, and asked how he was, all he could do was flop down heavily on the bed, pat her for reassurance, take off his clothes, mumble about the pain, and, groaning, go to the bathroom, take some pills, and, whimpering, crawl into bed and conk out.

Monday morning he awoke as usual at five-fifteen, headache worse: more localized in back of his right eyeball, each throb sending a spurt of molten red metal splashing against what seemed to be pretty flimsy stuff. Aspirin won't touch it. Should see a doctor. Don't have time. He dared not think the obvious: in his age group, the headache and related symptons—labile affect (highs and lows), absentmindedness, bizarre and inappropriate behavior at home and in the office—forced the statistical conclusion: brain tumor.

Stephanie was still asleep when he left. Bending slightly to the right under the incessant pounding, Fine walked gently so as not to jar his brain, into his office for Six o'clock.

A full week's hard analytic work had just about settled Dora down from his mistake, and she was back into flagrantly erotic material. As he listened, Fine's arousal slammed his pulse rate up, each beat a screamer. He took comfort in his new insight, and said virtually nothing the whole session. Ending, she said it had been one of the best sessions ever. Seventy-five dollars. When he went back to join Stephanie at breakfast, she was gone. She'd left a note: "Quit my job. When the going gets tough, the tough go shopping." Fine associated: acting out under stress of trying to choose motherhood. Doesn't mean it. Shopping an ego-syntonic, anal-erotic activity. For the female.

Filled with dread of his brain exploding, Fine plodded on through the jam-packed day. The Jefferson House patients were adapting well to the pilot study. One of the world's strangest triple dates—The Jefferson; Eli the Hassid (with poodle Lafite) and Stinko; Cooter the Manic and Mary the Crucifix—had seen the X-rated *Pumping Ethyl* Saturday night. All but Cooter had survived. He'd gone psychotic. Refusing meds and Finestones, he was in the Quiet Room. Fine would see him later. Reuben's murder had terrified the Stow psychiatrists. Morning report focused on increasing Mr. Royce's security staff, with emphasis on sealing off the only entrance to the island, the Curley Bridge, and making sure that all staff and patients signed up to have their photos taken for ID tags. Dr. Pelvin, cool and hard, black hair slicked down, announced: "I'm taking my vacation early. I leave now and will be away until five June."

Psychopathic, Pelvin had a great talent for infuriating his wealthy psychopathic patients—any one of whom, psychodynamically, could be the killer. At first the Stow staff were delighted that Pelvin was leaving—none of his dangerous patients would be coming to Stow for therapy. Then they realized that Pelvin's psychopaths would be enraged at his abrupt departure, and, easily outwitting the bumbling Royce, would take it out on the institution, Stow. Envisioning whole armies of killer-patients roaming the pacific Stow acres, staff tried convincing Pelvin to stay. In vain. Mr. Royce—a green-eyed weasel with bushy black hair and a horrible red birthmark on his cheek—said the police were getting nowhere, but tried to be reassuring: "Stow is easily secured. As long as the killer is not one of our own inpatients. Or—" he paused, flicked his eyes insolently around the room like his idol, Chandler's Marlowe—"one of us."

The titter of paranoia rose. Fine himself picked out several potential killers among the staff. And what about Royce himself?

Fine met with Ms. Ando. Repeated experiments confirmed it: high-calcium hoppers learned and remembered better. The news failed to ease his physical pain, his sense of forboding. Seeing his other patients, too, was a burden. Mardell, his pro basketball addict, was argumentative. A nurse had told him of Freud's trial of cocaine. In the gym with Fine, he read from a copy of a letter from Freud to Martha Bernays: " 'Who is the stronger: a gentle little girl who doesn't eat enough; or a big, wild man who has cocaine in his body?!' If your man did it, Fine, why can't I?"

"What are your *thoughts* on why can't you?"

Mardell shot the ball off Fine's gut, hard, and walked out.

Things were collapsing. On the toilet, Fine's straining rebounded hydraulically, blasting against the roof of his skull. His anus bled. Even the suicidal Joy's punctual call—"Where are you?"; *"Click"*—had seemed ominous to Fine, now.

Late that afternoon, on his way to see Cooter, he found himself standing, still, on the hill above Jefferson House, looking over the vista, shivering. The pain had not abated. He was mesmerized by a supertanker drifting in a horizontal band across his line of sight, into Boston Harbor. His eyes felt drawn to it, as if magnetized. He could not turn away. His gaze would sweep, right to left, stern to stem, and then—the movement of the ship so much slower than that of his eyes—reverse direction in a quick horizontal zoom back to stern. Over and over again. Strange. Feeling seasick, he forced his eyes away. He saw his breath in the air, and, strangely in touch with nature, looked around at what the discordant weird cold had meant to other living things: the forsythia and tulips were wilting, the daffodils and violets were barely hanging in, despite their alleged natural antifreeze. Dogwood and cherry were snuggled up tight in buds, sumac asleep. The sea grape waited, while beach pine—Japanese and native—showed no reaction to the past-term spring, spreading over the cliff-edge. The huge copper beech in his front yard, survivor of four centuries of seasons, held its chill sap, its million tiny buds closed up, waiting for winter's fist to open. The wind was from the northwest—rattling the beech's leafless branches like wild palms—and jets zoomed in low over Long Island to Logan. Each glide-path down was a river of lava inside Fine's skull, afterburn screeching like a fingernail on a blackboard. Fine sensed immense discord, felt immense alarm. Where the hell's my wife! Never came home for lunch. See her at dinner. He entered Jefferson House.

From the far corner of the padded, white-walled Quiet Room, Cooter glared at Fine. Good psychiatrist, Fine interviewed him, noticing the signs—pressure of speech, ideas of reference, loose and "clang" (linked-by-sound) associations, hyperacute attention, paranoid thoughts—and made the diagnosis: manic psychosis. Cooter was refusing meds, suspecting them poisoned. (This, an argument against the psychopharm boys—who ignore the data, that patients *don't* take their meds—"When they refuse meds, how do you treat *that?*") Fulminant paranoia. "You're angry Cooter—tell me about it."

"Don't give me that 'angry' crap, asshole."

Fine followed a rule—never let a violent patient get between you and the door—and sat. If he attacks, I run out.

"Ready to run if I come at you, eh doc?"

Amazing, Fine thought, how they can always read your mind. "You're quite high, Cooter. Tell me about it."

"Tell you about your wife—how she was with some other guy all yesterday—surprised? Suspicious? Ha!"

Fine *was* surprised and suspicious, but knew that the statement was a mere projection of Cooter's wish to be with Stephanie. The correct response? Rule of projection: the analyst must get out of the line of fire of the projection. Technique: sit *alongside* the patient, so as to "be with" the patient facing the delusional system together. Fine got up and sat next to Cooter, facing the closed door. Fine tried the "empathic": "How *courageous* of you, Cooter, to talk about these feelings for my wife." Great interpretation, Fine!

"Fuck you!"

Try medication, Fine. "How about a Finestone?" Fine put one in his own mouth: Plop. Suck. He offered one to Cooter, who flicked it back at him, hitting him in the nose. "Ow!" said Fine, realizing, with dread, that to use the rule of projection had been a mistake, for Cooter was now blocking his way out the door. The correct response would have been the rule of paranoia: confronted with a paranoid, the analyst, knowing that the root of paranoia is homosexuality *(Jealousy, Paranoia, Homosexuality,* 1922), must avoid at all costs getting physically close to a same-sex patient, for this will provoke the most violent physical manifestation of paranoid psychosis, the most murderous rage known to mankind—"homosexual panic"!

"So your wife's ballin' some other guy, doc—tell you what—I'll make a deal: you discharge me, I keep it quiet. Okay?"

Fine blocked. All that came to mind was the indexed reference to Freud's classic: *Coll. Pap.*, vol. 2, *Coll. Pap.*, vol.—

"Come on, doc—I *need* you—Jesus I need some fuckin' *help!*"

He reached out his hand, pleading, and Fine's heart went out to him, this poor gorgeous young man crippled by a terrible biochemical disease of the mind. Fine's impulse was to grasp his hand, hug him, comfort him. Absurd. *My* impulses have no place in my work; touching is not allowed. Lot of good all those touchy-feely therapies have done! Professional caring means rebuilding ego boundaries in the rubble of the shattered mind. There are no shadows in the psychoanalytic sun. The biggest mistake I could make would be to give in to my so-called human impulse. My task is to get out of this room in one piece. "So," he said, "let's talk about your meds."

"You won't even shake my hand?!" Fine made a tiny move toward the door. "Hold it! Don't move." Cooter shouted: "Hey everybody—Fine's wife is ballin' another guy! Haha!" He paused. "You don't believe me, do you? You think I'm just crazy, huh?"

Trapped with this crazy man, Fine asked himself: could he be the killer? He's had off-ground privileges, he has a car, money, Southern gun-cathexis, poor impulse control, rage. Try one more empathic, then run for it. "You must really be hurting, Cooter—"

"Jerk!" he screamed, and rushed at Fine.

Fine jumped up and ran for the door and thought he'd made it when—wham!—he went down hard cracking his head on the white wooden floor and seeing stars and managing just one scream: "Help!" And then he felt a blow on his cheek and glimpsed killer eyes slashing away at his own and he tried to cover his head from the buffeting. After what seemed an age, a goon squad of staff rescued Fine, and trapped and medicated Cooter. Fine arose associating: what a great case! I identified the affect, demolished the defenses. The headline? FREUD AND FINE PIN PSYCHO IN TWO!

"Yes, er, no," said Mr. Jefferson, "he thinks your wife is deceiving you? A temptation to us all, no, er, yes!"

Jefferson (black) said: "Love, love, love in the eternity of sin till the time comes for the dead dead dead to die!"

Feeling a sliver of suspicion Fine asked: "You saw her too?"

"Sure did! Sweet l'il woman! She told me her name was *Pat*, and I said: Hi, Pat!" The Jefferson laughed, and the laughter rang on harshly in Fine's head as he climbed the stairs to his office.

Head screaming, Fine tried to listen to Four o'clock, Sylvia of Mistaken Identity. She was obsessed with having found him, her long-lost sweetheart Stuart Fine. Keeping his analytic cool, Fine gave no hint of his real identity, inviting her to explore her fantasies. She did, saying he looked sick, feeling a need to care for him. Fine could hardly attend. The lamplight bored through his eyes into his visual cortex, setting up reverberations—noxious colors, odors. Time moved slowly, despite her fascinating associations: her "daddy" kept animals in cages—a lion, a puma, a boa. Rabbits to feed to the boa. Stun them, throw them in. Dimly, Fine formulated: she's well compensated, given this rural zoo. But where was mother? Where'd she lose her eye? A little masochistic. True masochism is untreatable: patient wants to stay sick. Stay tuned. Time to stop.

Ratman the Obsessive spent half his session associating to the murder of Reuben—anal rage at the money he was spending on Fine made him glad that someone was killing shrinks (!)—and then resumed the analysis of Fine's fart. Fine was quite mum. "Well, you little *hämorrhoi'de*," said Ratman, affectionately, leaving, "this was the best session ever!" Fine asked himself: how do they always *know?*

Free at last! Fine went home. He called his wife's name, and got no answer. He sat in the study, poured himself a bourbon, put an icepack on his head, and gulped four aspirin and two codeines. A madman was at work inside his skull, hammering to get out. He stroked his goatee. Tomorrow, Fine, you see a doctor.

She appeared, and Fine said: "Stephanie! Thank God!"

"What's wrong?" she said, sitting on the couch beside him.

"Cooter assaulted me!" he said, and then, putting his head in her lap, felt tearful. "He said you had a man here yesterday."

"I did—an old friend I met at the show—the senator—"

"Never mind that," Fine said, reassured by her smoothing his hair with her hand, "this damn headache won't quit! Almost a week, on and off—I'm scared it's either an aneurysm or a brain tumor!"

"A *brain tumor?!* Did you see a doctor?"

"Tomorrow. Oh, love—I really missed you!" She looked puzzled. "I did a lot of analyzing after you left. I've had real insights. Let me tell you." She nodded. "I finally understand what you're saying, about how settling down is death. To rush into parenthood isn't a good idea. Sixty-two percent of modern married couples would not have children if they could do it all over again. Lives are not static, but dynamic. Life's too short to see it always stretching on ahead, for soon it will be stretching off behind. As adults our childhood seems an instant. Binswanger comes in here." He took a deep breath. "I too want to say 'Yes' to everything, risk and grow with you. You're the most important person in the world to me, Stephanie. I'm offering myself to you: the new Fine!"

"You really mean that?" He nodded. "Why now?"

"Good question! After termination with Fumbles, I felt abandoned and vulnerable, a normal reaction. Oh—this throbbing! Turn off the light, will you?" She did, and stood at the window. "At home," he went on, "I regressed—I had an incredibly infantile mother-transference reaction to my mother, you see?"

"Fine, your mother *is* your mother!"

"That's what made it so strong! All my negative feelings for her spilled out onto you! I had a fantastic insight—listen!" Fine gulped, and, in hushed tones, said: "We men don't want to slay our fathers and sleep with our mothers, hell no! We want the opposite! Freud got that part wrong! The reason he—and most males—focus on analysis of father?: it's *easier* to talk about pop than mom! Less resistance! Yet unless we face our mothers, we'll never face ourselves!" Feeling ashamed, Fine confessed: "I think Fumbles—a classical Freudian—helped me work through father but only scratched the surface of mother. This weekend at home showed me how much rage I still have for her. Imagine: to displace it onto *you!*" Fine took a deep breath. "I'm sorry, Stephanie, I really am. My rage at my mom has gotten in the way of my love for you, my wife. But the good news: I realize it, *accept* it! I'll change! *With* you! Our marital struggle is classic for male/female asymmetry around intimacy! I'm hot on the trail of seeing it not as Freudian 'self' but as 'male self-in-*relation.*' No more Iron Man

Fine! Know what?—my dad *is* somewhat empathic! If he can hold my mom, empathically, then I, in relation to him, *must* have empathy somewhere inside me, for you! If their fathers can relate to their mothers, men *can* relate to women, and I to you. And the modern father is even *more* involved, right? I haven't fit in all the pieces yet, but I think it's going to fly! With this new insight, we'll work it out!"

"You really mean this, Fine? You *feel* it, deep inside?"

"Deeper than I've felt anything ever, *yes!*" Fine felt her eyes bore into him. She seemed skeptical. Without thinking he said: "Stephanie, am I *ugly?*"

"What?" she asked, as if slapped.

He realized the immensity of his question. "I . . . I feel ugly. Am I ugly?" The silence seemed dense, as if of unearthly weight.

"Fine—you must *never* ask a woman that, do you understand?"

He was crushed. "But you're not 'a woman,' you're my wife!" He thought: how desperate I must seem, how weak. She'll hate me for my weakness. To his surprise, she smiled. He had risked, and won! He felt flushed, happy—things would all turn out okay, no question, now! He beamed. "So, then, what do you think of the 'new' Fine?"

"I want to believe you, but I'm afraid—besides, something's come up—I've got to talk to you about it—"

Fine felt her softening, opening up to him, and said: "A second analysis will focus on my relationship to my mother—"

"A *what?!*" she said, eyes flaring.

"A second analysis—with a female analyst—" His eye caught the clock: "God! 7:41! I'll be *late!* Gotta run—" He got up.

"Late?! What are you talking about?"

"For the Vergessen seminar at the Institute," Fine said, straightening his tie and grabbing his suit jacket. " 'The Anus.' "

"No! Don't go! I need you with me tonight, Fine—"

"No choice. We're working through Reuben's death—"

"Call in sick—"

"Incredible association—know what they'd make of *that?*"

"But you hated Reuben—"

"I hated him! That's what I've got to work through—"

"And what about all you just said to me?"

"I mean it, every word—"

"Stay with me, Fine—I really need you now—"

"We'll talk tonight when I get back—"

"Tonight's too late—"

"How can two hours be too late? You think I need a scarf?"

"Fine, listen: *I need you with me right now.*"

"No need for melodrama, Stephanie. Now is impossible."

"For you, there's never a *now,* now! What a sucker I am: when you said 'most important person in the world,' I believed it!"

"You are, but there's a big difference between analytic—"

"You're a bad actor, Fine, you had me convinced, but you know what's missing? Feeling. Inside you? Nobody home! Cold as ice, Fine, cold as ice! What a sucker I've been! No more! No way!"

"We'll talk later—"

"Like hell, Fine, know why? 'Cause *later* isn't real—"

"Reality's a—wow!" Fine slammed the door before the decanter hit, heard the glass shatter, and associated: mother, throwing glass at father. Once threw knife; stuck in wall; over my head; quivering. Cut glass. My childhood littered with. He rushed across his gravel drive-wife—what a great slip!—to his car.

And just as, listening, he failed to hear, so looking, he failed to see: a ten-speed bicycle leaned against his gate, front tire crossed back over frame like the legs of a man leaning comfortably—even familiarly, proudly—against the wall of the house he'd just bought.

As he rumbled across the old Curley Bridge, Fine found himself quoting Freud's famous letter to Marie Bonaparte: " 'The moment a man questions the meaning and value of life he is sick, since objectively neither has any existence; by asking the question, one is merely admitting to a store of unsatisfied libido.' " And yet, even buffed up by this, at the door of the Institute Fine felt a strange gnawing concern. Like a Hooke's law of the psyche, the further I am from her the stronger I'm drawn back to her. What do I feel? Suspicion. Why? Blocking. He said the day's password —"Oliver Freud"—and was buzzed in. He leaned on the water cooler, wondering if his headache were a migraine, and recalled his first big headache: at Disneyland, with mom and Moe, pop three thousand miles away, at home. He took out one of the assigned papers—*Character and Anal Erotism* (1908)—but his hand shook so, it fell to the floor.

As he bent to pick it up the intracranial pressure increased and ripped at his brain meninges, making him feel sick. And then, as if in a bad dream, his eyes chanced to be drawn to something that cut him down to bone: on the front page of the previous day's *Globe* was a photo: John O'Day, as Petruccio, kissing Stephanie! Feeling faint, he held the water cooler for support. It can't be! It is! Like still photos in a film, Fine saw a dozen pieces of the puzzle clack into place: the helicopter flight back to cover The All-Night Bard/she asleep when he came back, asleep when he got up, gone all day/her saying: "You're a bad *actor,* Fine!"/that bicycle in my yard—*his!*

Dullheaded as a bull, Fine roared back to Stow, fit to kill.

Yet by the time he got back to Stow-on-Wold he had pretty much analyzed it all out. On the one hand, he had the wish to know; on the other, the wish not to. If he didn't know, he could live with the illusion that she was faithful; if he did know, either he carried the burden of the fantasized sexual carnival, or needed to know more, and in the web of suspicion and deceit might lose her. He decided to act like a perfectly analyzed human being: not act at all, but *think.* He parked up the hill, took his binoculars from the glove compartment (stashed there in the guise of "birding"), and snuck down past Jefferson House. He found a hidden spot from which he had a clear view of his house, his bedroom window. Trembling with hope, fear, and cold, in exquisite pain, he sat clasping his knees in his arms in the crisp May night, seeking the sight that might destroy him.

As his eyes adjusted to the dark, he noticed, around him, beer bottles, cigarette stubs, and a neat pile of used Trojans—his inpatients *had* been peeping at him and his wife. The light went on in the bedroom window. Fine's fear streamed out behind him like a parachute that might just open in time, and might just not. He saw, through the gauze curtain winnowing out through the window, the springtime of his life die. There Stephanie was, throwing things into a suitcase; there John, helping her. Perhaps they are merely chatting? Fine lifted the binoculars to his eyes, and saw him come up in back of her, as she bent, and nuzzle her neck. She lifted her head in a slow graceful arc, eyes sweeping the ceiling. His lips brushed what Fine knew was the sensual skin on her shoulder. Shivering, she took his hands and led them to her breasts, her thighs. Fine's heart cracked, as he watched John unbutton her blouse from the back, she laughing; his hands disappeared, she gasped—his fingers were on her breasts, her tender tips! Fine shivered with rage. This is wrong! She threw her blouse into the suitcase, pulled on a halter top, scolding him for playing. They disappeared. The light went out.

Numb, numbly realizing what was happening, Fine stumbled like a drunken ape down the slope toward the front corner of the house, the pumping in his temples redoubled. The pipes were about to burst. He turned the corner of the house just as the front door opened. His head cleared the giant forsythia. Bright light flooded him. Just in time! Here they are, coming out carrying suitcases! Thinking he would stop them, he tried to reach out his hand.

Fine heard a sharp *crack!*—(a gunshot?!)—and then something terrible happened—painless, yet terrible and utterly foreign to life, lifting him out of his thirty-four years into something else. He watched himself in slow motion reaching out his hand toward them. His hand stuck in mid-air. His eyes swung back and forth from the trapezoid of light in the doorway to their backs. And then from their backs to the light. Back and forth, back and forth —not sure if he was doing it voluntarily to get away from the weird feeling inside or if it was all being done *to* him. It seemed to last an eternity, his hand stuck in the air as if in ice, his voice clogged his throat—all the paralysis of a nightmare, running and running and running away, staying right where you are. He heard John say: "Life's too short for Fine—"

And Stephanie answer: "—and Fine's too short for life!"

He asked himself: What is this strange feeling in me and why can't I make my eyes stay still or my hand keep moving? And with a terrific sense of doom he felt something cave in, something of the realm of his spirit give.

The three of them almost touched, but didn't quite. Like wrongly pent-up atomic particles, they flew apart. Through a hot red film he saw the two, unaware of him, get into her purple Jag, and go.

And then the bad feared thing came true: something deep inside split at the seams and something red gushed out into a place it never should have been, draining from a place it vitally needed to be and Fine felt himself in slow silent motion start to fall.

In the short time it took Fine to drop sixty-eight inches to his doorstep, much happened:

He said: this is no false alarm, Fine, this is death. Am I afraid or in pain? No. This proves it real. The mouse lies still in the jaws of the cat, narcotized by endorphins. Euphoric, he noted many aspects he'd read about in reports of those who'd come back from the dead: the sweet good cheer, the tunnel, the gauzy silence, the white light coming, the need not to struggle against, and, finally, the way that he was floating up, higher, lightly higher, until he felt his left ear bump gently against the lowest branch of the immense patriarchal copper beech and there, looking down on himself falling, he paused, feeling much relieved that it was all so fluid and charming and, well, *nice.* He thought he was repeating out loud:

"Here it is Mental Hygiene Month and 'living is an eternal nuisance' (Freud) . . . Israeli cows are able to give milk *three* times a day . . . VISA-spasm!"

From his high perch Fine watched his body lie quite lifeless down on the solid ground, his wife and her lover drive off, and—what's this?!—his Jefferson patients, bug-eyed and wailing, rush down from their peeping place to find him lying on the gravel.

Over the howling of the poodle, Fine, happy, heard someone say: "About calcium you were *right!*" Carried high on the shoulders of the painters of the night, he caught the sweet acrid scent of turpentine, and heard himself murmur: "Death? Death is love lost."

And so the present passed with all the nostalgia of a home movie of someone laughing, seven years dead.

III

FREED

Nettled not a little by L. Boom
(as it incorrectly stated) . . .
—James Joyce, *Ulysses,* 1922

18

JOHN AND STEPHANIE flew to Paris.

From her, later, I was able to piece together the details.

Arriving Tuesday morning, they dropped their bags in her family's flat on Avenue Rapp in the Seventh—a penthouse with a view of the Eiffel Tower—and went back out to explore the City of Light. The day was warm, and, to them, sensual. They strolled arm in arm through the verdant Champs de Mars to the Seine, bantering freely as lovers have always done and will always do, floating through the morning at a level of love. Lightness suffused them, lifting them higher, heightening all senses. Life, whirling before their eyes, seemed faceted with meaning. They drifted over the Pont Alma, up the Avenue George V. John pointed at the people at a café, all facing front like passengers on a boat: "Don't tell 'em it ain't moving."

Yet daylight soon brought out the enormity of what they'd done. They started to feel a need to bury remembrance and guilt, and so they sat and drank. John gulped his wine like beer. Flushed, he said: "Fizgerald was wrong: *only* American lives have second acts."

"Or, maybe, American lives have *only* second acts?"

Exiles, they watched the Parisians parade past in a horizontal

free fall of sensuality: men all thin and dark-eyed, in tight pants
and tinted glasses; women in sharp collars, shirts open down past
bra, the lingerie freeing up bodies for undulation.

John said: "Did I ever tell you my secret?"

"What's that?"

"I love ladies' undies."

"Really?"

"Can't get enough of 'em! Eat two silk panties every mornin'
for breakfast. Yup—I'm lunatic about lace, entirely."

"Nut! You lovable nut! Paris is the City of Nuts!"

"And the City of Lingerie!"

"Let's spend obscenely! Let's go buy sexy stuff!"

Reeling from wine and jet lag, they sailed up the wide Marceau
to the Arc de Triomphe—remarking on the smell of urine, daz-
zled by the nexus of infinitely radiating sunbursts of cobblestones
—and, fighting the deafening swirl of traffic, floated down the
Champs into the Tuileries—a garden filled with evanescent children on carousels and ponies, and senescent bums. They watched
the puppet clowns of Théâtre Guignol, descendant of *Commedia,*
which inspired Shakespeare.

"I wish it were 1920," John said. "We could go to Brick's, hear
Mabel. And wouldn't it be great to do our cabaret act, here?"

"Yes. Yes, it sure would." They walked on for a while. "You
know—I bet we *could!* An old friend of the family runs a club—
she'd do anything for me. Yes!—she's at Brasserie Lipp almost
every night. We'll outfit ourselves for our grand entrance, yes!
C'mon!"

They shopped. Money being no object, they bought whatever
they wanted, including an instant camera with which they recorded, "for posterior," Mssr. O'Day perched in a stone bas-relief
high above a rotary, looking with visionary zeal up a patriot's
horse's ass. The lingerie shop on the Rue Rivoli was a lesson in
tumescence. After several changes, each shown to John—she noticed him fidgeting on his chair as the half-naked women paraded
in and out of the dressing room wrapped only in satin and lace—
she made an entrance: dark-green satin tuxedo-striped pants with
nothing on top but a strapless bra that was nothing but black lace
flowers with two strands of a black satin bow trailing down her
tummy as she stood, posing, and, as she twirled, unfurling out
around her. They laughed. She mocked him with a stripper's

pout. Even the Parisians stared and smiled, for everyone loves lovers.

Everyone, of course, but the one betrayed.

"That's it?" he asked, "I mean, that's all?"

"And this." She snatched a transparent silk shawl, cast it out and curled it around, the colors solid yet delicate, a tropical bird settling on her smooth shoulders, dangling bright feathers down. "What do you think?"

"C'mere." She did; he whispered: "I want the used panties."

"Sold!" she said, and, as they left, handed them to him. He passed them once across his face, and stuffed them into his pocket.

Their frivolity turned to exhaustion. To be tired in a great city is to be truly tired, and they straggled across the tiny ironwork bridge called la Pasarelle into the quiet courtyard of the Île St. Louis. They collapsed into the iron chairs of her favorite bistro, protected by the high seventeenth-century walls, and soothed by the gurgling fountain and the single plane tree stunted by centuries of constantly intermittent light. In this haven of vibrancy and peace, they sipped sharp coffee, wishing their fatigue would ease.

"Here," she said, taking a box from her purse. "Try one."

He looked: chalky white kumquat-sized stones. "What's this?"

"Calcium. Our cortisol is all screwed up from the flight. Calcium will tighten us back up. Watch." Plop. Suck.

"Like sucking stones in *Molloy?*" Plop. Suck.

He asked where she got them. She hesitated, and then said: "Fine."

The word hung between them, limp, dead. They sat in silence for a time. He asked: "You feeling bad?"

"Yes. It's a big thing, this."

"Sure, but we should've done it seven years ago."

"Would've done," she said, "if only he hadn't arrived." Her face fell, her normal side joining her palsied in sadness, and her breathing got harsh. "There's another link between us, now."

"What's that?"

"My father's dead, now, too."

She started to cry. He moved his iron chair next to her, put his arms around her. "It's been almost two years, and I still think of him every day!" She cried harder, and he held her. She felt, over and over again, a pestle grinding on the mortar of her heart:

"Daddy's gone, Daddy's gone, Daddy's gone." After a while, wiping her tears, she felt braver, and smiled. "He was so important to me! There won't be anymore showstoppers in my life, hell no!"

Late that night, at Brasserie Lipp, they made a grand entrance: Steph in her new lingerie outfit, John in his: blue velvet cape with crimson collar, blue velvet hat with crimson feather, carrying a silver-knobbed cane. Steph spotted her friend sitting at a banquette at the end of the bar, and, crying, "Helene! Gerald!" flew across the crowded room to them. She turned back to John, who swept through the room, unfurling his cape to reveal, to all, his T-shirt: PROUST ÉTAIT UNE YENTA! As they drank, John performed. In succession he became Hamlet, Falstaff, and—(!)—Juliet. By evening's end they were on for "American Night" at Nouvelle Eve, Thursday. They'd have a day to rehearse.

And so at three in the morning they stood on the balcony of the flat, watching the Socialist rally fireworks fizzle around the Eiffel Tower. They kissed, tenderly, and, exhausted, headed to bed. Steph used the bidet, and then went into the bedroom and saw him already asleep. Smiling, feeling terrific that she'd actually *done* it—unlocked the cage of Fine and found someone so different, so daring and free, someone she loved deeply in old and new ways both at once—she joined him in bed. She asked herself her father's question: "If you knew you were to die tomorrow, would you have lived today as you have today?" And as she had not done for years, she could answer: "Yes."

Just before dawn they both stirred. Steph, half-awakening, called out: "Fine?"

And was surprised to hear John answer: "Nora?"

In the morning, to the cooing of a horny dove, the chatter of the concierge, and, across the courtyard, the exuberant gushing of l'Institut Aquanude Kinesthétique, they made love. Steph was thrilled—his lovemaking was so different from Fine's—so *dramatic*—he played to her body as to an audience—and so dirty! Lightly stroking her bottom, he said: "I adore this—where the curve of your hip meets the curve of the back of your thigh meets the curve of your cunt—the hottest wettest cunt, I might add, in all the Western world!" She tingled with pleasure, and, taking his penis in her hand, used it as a microphone: "Okay, folks, now we'll have a little stand-up: Two Jews are up in a balloon, and—"

They laughed. How long and thin his compared to you-know-who's. She played with it until he couldn't stand it anymore, and he, feigning affront, rolled away. They frolicked in the bed together, bodies smoothing against each other, laughing. Finding herself perched over him crablike, her back to his front, she settled down on him from above and bent forward and guided him in but then when she sat upright he yelled—"Ow! It don't bend that way, lady!"—and she chuckled and fell down across him and then, with her face in the crook of his neck, she thought again, "How big a man he is!" She felt safe and close, and, making love, she felt free.

Really tired, they both crumpled. He went out like a light—*click*—while she, still high up on the ledge of her arousal, full and empty all at once, eased out like the long day passed—*phshhh . . .*

Later that morning they made love again. And again. And each time, with the repetition, she felt it more intensely, longer, until, just before they firmly resolved to get up for lunch, they reversed the dawn's sequence: she screaming and biting in orgasm after orgasm wanting more orgasm; he, spilled, left to deal with his erect empty sore yearning. He got up to shower. She, as high sexually as ever she had been, flicked through why: because this is illicit, unlaced from past and family, overude—I mean overdue—suffused with ten years of wish, and, of course, because of Fine. How flat the Fine-sex had become! He always claimed it was "age appropriate" to cool off. Guess again, schmucko! The right-hand parenthesis around the dates of my life has moved too near already! Too close for comfort! The hell with you—I'm gonna live!

Finally, in the middle of the afternoon they had lunch and then went to the club in Monmartre. "Know what the French call rehearsal?" she asked him. He did not. *"La répétition."*

"Grand!" he said, eyes widening at the coincidence. "Just grand! This whole damn thing's like a dream come true!"

And Fine? In her mind—freed up by love, lust, drink, rehearsal, novelty—Fine was fast becoming a scrim: depending on the lighting, transparent or opaque. An object of scorn. They picked a postcard from a series called "Paris—Crazy Years—the Twenties"—*Accident de la gare Montparnasse:* a steam locomotive had overrun the barrier, smashing through the back facade of the station, and plunged from the third floor down into the street.

It lay, nose-down in the gutter, linked by the coal car to the third story. Two gendarmes stared. Perfect metaphor. Did they mail it? Their attention turned, they forgot. It slipped from a hand, skidded on a breeze—one sharp arc down, another—lay briefly on oily water, and sank.

"Will he know where we are?" John asked.

"Yes."

"Will he follow?"

"No."

"Why not?"

"He has appointments with his patients."

"So what? His wife's run off with his former best friend."

"So the only thing that keeps an analyst from his patients, buddy, is death."

For her, for most of the time, Fine could have been dead or alive, *cela m'est égal.* For she and her lover were into forgetting.

John quoted to her his great rememberer, Sören Kierkegaard: " 'If a man cannot forget, he will never amount to much.' "

19

FINE SAW CLOUDS, fuzzy white clouds. Fine saw Christ, crucified on a cross. Fine asked: Am I in Heaven? Fine answered: If I am in Heaven, I am in the *wrong* Heaven! The opposing team was right! Beneath the Crucifix was a Bible. Beneath that, a sign: READ THE BIBLE.

"I will!" Fine cried, relieved at the magical sound of his voice. "If I am alive, I promise you, Big Guy, I will!"

Fine, floating on air, felt pure bliss.

I feared for him more than ever.

A squad of doctors in green surgical garb entered. Fine knew he wasn't in Heaven. The white was the walls of a hospital room. They handled his body roughly, as if he were a side of beef. He asked where he was. A pink-cheeked woman said: "St. Elizabeth's Hospital."

"That explains the Crucifixion!" said Fine. They stared at him as if he'd lost his mind. All but the woman doctor left.

"You've had a grand mal epileptic seizure," she said.

He felt a hot stir in his genital zone. "What day is it?"

"Tuesday May ninth, 5:35 A.M. You've been unconscious for six hours. We've done all the tests, and the only abnormality is a sky-high serum calcium—must be lab error." Weakly, Fine chuckled. "You'll be hospitalized until we find a cause."

"No," he said, sitting up, "I'm leaving—ow!—*wow!*" Pain—like a hot steel bar jammed through both temples—made him feel faint. He flopped back down. "Is this headache from the seizure?"

"Nope—it's from the test we did—a lumbar puncture."

"Hospitals!" Fine said. "Danger!" Sitting up gradually, rubbing his head, he felt a tangle of wires. "What the hell?!"

"Eleven stitches. You hit your head." Fine tried to get off the stretcher. "Wait—suppose it's a brain tumor?"

"Who says it's a brain tumor?"

"It's the odds-on favorite." He grinned—to apply odds to a human life seemed frivolous to him.

"You're not worried?"

"Actually, I feel kind of happy."

"That's not 'happy,' that's 'postictal euphoria'—it's an aftereffect of the epileptic fit."

"Wouldn't *you* be happy, if you'd just come back from the dead?" She tried convincing him to stay, but he was firm. Finally, she said: "It'll have to be AMA—against medical advi—"

"Where do I sign?"

"Okay," she said, resignedly, turning to the door, "fine."

"Hunh?"

"What?" she asked.

"Oh—sorry—it's my name." Shaking her head, she left. He was surprised that he'd fallen for the old mix-up, but relieved to recall his name. "The loud ones don't stink" came to mind, but he didn't know what it meant. She came back. He started to sign, then stopped, shocked: "Hey," he said, "I'm left-handed! I'm a lefty!"

"So?"

"So I was always a righty before!" He tried to get dressed, but he was logy, and muffed it. She, a nurse-practitioner named Corey, helped him. She was squat and ugly, yet Fine felt a base animal attraction to her. When his hospital nightie unfurled, both noticed his thick rosy penis, redoubled into a half-chub. She blushed. He made a lewd proposal. She refused, but wrote down her phone number. Feeling great, he said: "Well, I'm going now."

"Good-bye."

"Wait—*where* am I going now?"

"Home. You can get a cab right outside."

"That's what I mean—where is 'home'?"

"Long Island—Stow-on-Wold—you really should stay—"

"Fine!" he said, and answered: "Hunh?" He laughed, and left.

The warm dawn flew in through the open cab window. Fine saw something he thought strange, and asked the cabbie: "What's wrong?"

"Whaddaya mean?" said the hack, a no-neck from Medford.

"Why are all those people running? Like somebody's chasing them or something!"

"Oh them? Yeah, they're crazy. Joggers!"

"Oh. And the ones with the headphones and battery packs snapped to their shorts—are they being remote-controlled?"

The hack, coughing, slouched lower, cursed, sped on.

Fine had forgotten almost everything, and so everything seemed new. He realized this was a "retrograde amnesia": events closest to the fit were most wiped out, those further back, less. In all likelihood, it would be temporary, his memory would return. What luck! To come so *bodily* into such a vital, virginal world!

That morning, back at Stow, he walked the path around the island. Warm rain was falling, wetly greening the tired winter grass, and he felt it a spring rain, soft and promising. Each marking of time—season, month, day, hour—seemed balanced on the crest of its cycle, and locked in sync to some unlocked cycle deep inside Fine himself. He noticed all he'd never noticed: the earthy warmth was kissing to life the immense copper beech, and like millions of little flags, the leaves were unfurling almost before his eyes, and the low sun shone through a curtain of lightening bronze. Flowers were exploding into bloom—he could almost hear the "snap" "snap" "snap" of daffodil, tulip, forsythia. The roses, set above the crocus, snowbell, and violet, were thick with the new season's green-red shoots. Fine floated along the path gulping in deep breaths of sea breeze, feeling at one with the shape of water and skyline and sky. The sounds of birds—raucous gull, soothing dove, insolent mallard, staccato woodpecker, whistling green-winged teal—rang clear and sharp, like the finest glass bells hung on tiny twigs of wind. He felt he'd never been part of a day so fresh and free, so teeming with life. His six senses seemed confluent—a whole new sense. The morning air felt rich as water;

the sea water clear as air. He found himself smiling, chanting in rhythm to his steps: "Lilac will bloom soon, and soon azalea; lilac will bloom soon, and soon azalea." What a sound-shape, that!

He felt himself a perfectly right-hemisphered human being.

Back home, he felt a great hunger. Searching the kitchen, he recalled that he'd been on a high-protein diet, but could not recall why. He drove to the nearest supermarket, and bought all the things he craved. He began eating on the way back—Sunshine Mallopuffs ("With Real Coconut Topping") and Fudgsicles—and at home he began eating in earnest, devouring several bottles of Gerber's applesauce ("Strained, Vitamin C Added") while he waited for the microwave to return his Aunt Jemima Original Waffles ("No Preservatives Fortified with Five Vitamins and Iron"). He drank Pabst Blue Ribbon beer. The brand names seemed so *neat.* He ate reclining on the living room couch. Feeling curious about pop culture, he turned on the TV.

They found him there three hours later, mesmerized by a new game show: "Celebrity Hitmen." Mrs. Neiderman, alarmed that he'd not shown up for his Six o'clock (she, frantic, had been waiting at Neiderman's office door at eight), joined forces with Ms. Ando (he'd not shown for her lab-briefing either) and tried to find out what was wrong. Fine felt nothing was wrong: "In fact I feel all *right!*"

"Poor Duffy," said Neiderman, "she's so crazy about you!" Neiderman began detailing his schedule, but then, sensing his new placidity, stopped, and said: "Dr. Fine, your blackout has left you in no shape to see your patients today. I shall cancel them." He smiled, and said he'd do whatever she thought best. "And there's a murderer loose, remember?" He vaguely did, and nodded. "Security is tight, the day's password is 'peacekeeper.' Take care." She left.

Ms. Ando had brought a cage of high-calcium grasshoppers. She held out two Finestones. He mimicked her: Plop. Suck. She began detailing new research data, on serotonin. Fine remembered his lab work only dimly, but pretended to be on the same wavelength, marveling at her passion to discover things about these shapely insects. Triumphantly, she finished: ". . . and so, the effect of serotonin *plus* calcium?: weight loss, hypomanic euphoria, high IQ." Fine had no idea what she was talking about, and said nothing. She took this to be criticism, and said, admiringly: "Don't you see, your hunch was right: tryptophan is a precursor of serotonin. All those high-tryptophan, high-calcium foods we've been eating—soy nuts, tempeh, tofu, broccoli—they work! Preliminary data show that the high-calcium, high-trypto-phan hoppers are smarter, happier, *thinner!* More energetic—it's why manics and creative artists get headaches from red wine and cheese! Serotonin decreases carbo-craving; high-protein diets in-crease it—they're frauds!" Hushed, she said; "If it holds up, it's the Nobel! If it's sold right—*The Fine Diet*—it's a fortune! See?"

"Yes!" Fine said, not seeing at all. "Right!"

"One drawback: in monkeys, the most aggressive male has the highest serotonin. I better check it out, okay?" Fine said okay. She stared at him, concerned. "Dr. Fine, you're not acting like yourself. An epileptic fit is no joke. Relax. Leave this to me, okay?"

"Okay!" said Fine, as she left. "Nice work!"

He sat communing with his grasshoppers until staff called him over to Jefferson House. His inpatients, like children with an in-jured parent, were hesitant and tentative with him. When he in-vited them to feel his stitches, they drew back. The staff, alarmed at the new free-and-easy manner of the tightest man they'd ever met, sent him home. The head nurse, a big-boned Hessian from rural Pennsylvania, escorted him out. She wore a filmy flowery spring dress. His arm rubbed up against her breast; his penis got hard as a rock. She unlocked the door and he propositioned her. She blinked, put a hand to her throat, frowned. Quick as a flash, he cupped her rump, tracing the solid curve through the light cotton, feeling the sharp edge of her panties. She pressed his hand hard against her encased flesh, whispered "Not here not now—*later!*" and pushed him out the door.

Late that afternoon, Fine was lying on the couch dipping Fritos ("Extra Thin and Crunchy Nacho Cheese Flavor") in Coolwhip ("Extra Creamy New Large Size"), engrossed in the gay quadri-plegic sex therapist on a slick talkshow. The doorbell rang, and rang again, with an ominous insistence. On airy legs, Fine rose to answer it. Before him stood a slim, nut-brown man with sleek black hair, in an olive khaki suit.

"Where is she?" the man asked. He pronounced it: "Vere."

"Who are you?" Fine felt him to resemble some plucky little bird, say, a gamecock.

"Your wife?"

"You're not my vife—err—wife." Fine was relieved to find that he now again remembered his wife, Stephanie. "Where is she?"

"Your wife?"

"Yes. Who are you and what have you done with her?"

"Nipak Dandi."

"What?"

"Nipak Dandi!" he said, impatiently.

"Why has she gone off to Nipak Dandi? On business?"

"It is not a place, it is my name. I am from Sri Lanka—used to be Ceylon—"

"Is it Nepal you're talking about?"

"My name!" he said, hopping up and down. "My *name!*"

"What is it?" asked Fine, feeling befogged.

"Nipak Dandi is my name!"

"Ohh!" said Fine, slapping his slack cheek with his palm, "Yes, of course, not a country, no." He stuck out his hand: "Fine."

"Maybe not!" he said, glaring. "Where is she?"

"I don't know. Do you? No, of course you don't—"

"Cad!" screamed Nipak. Losing control he seemed to explode and, screaming, leaped at Fine, grabbed him by the throat, and began pressing Fine's jugulars, searching skillfully for the carotids.

"Help!" Fine cried. "The killer!" He tried to fight back, to no avail, and for the second time in twenty-four hours he felt the life force drain from him, things growing dim. But suddenly the pressure of darkness was relieved, and Nipak lay on the rug beside him, and standing over both of them was Mr. Royce, Stow Security, and The Jefferson. "Whew!" Fine said. "Thanks!"

"We never sleep," said Mr. Royce.

And then the confusion was cleared up. Following Steph's invitation to visit, Nipak, arriving late the previous night, had been told that Fine had, in fact, "locked her up in the basement."

"What?!" said Fine. "Whoever told you that?"

"A very articulate young man with a Hassidic mein."

"Aha!" He recalled. "Eli! Psychotic—compulsive liar—"

"Oh, yes, I see now, yes. I'm sorry." Mr. Royce and The Jefferson left. Nipak made what Fine thought an eloquent apology, ending with a resigned: "Ah well, it is the passion do you know?"

"Of course. She inspires it!"

"Yes, the birds of the feather are in the same bush. And so where is she?"

"Don't know where in the world she is! She's bound to be back soon. Why not wait? Would you like a drink?"

"But you—you're not jealous of my affection for your wife?"

"Nope. Should I be?"

"No—" he said, quickly, "—you must not start to be, no, and yes, I would love a drink. You probably do not have whole milk?"

Fine's eyes lit up. "You like milk?"

"I love it very much, yes—the State Drink, New York—"

"I love milk too!" said Fine. "Terrific source of calcium!" Saying the word seemed to free up his remembrance of the "calcium story." It was quite intact. He felt it as old deep knowledge.

"But of course, the bones and all that. And so what?"

"Yes, osteoporosis is epidemic in the female," said Fine, "not enough calcium in the diet. And so you know about calcium?"

"I know about milk—what is this, charades?"

"Let me tell you," Fine said, and he went and got a fresh half-gallon, and with a certain reverence, poured two full glasses. In silence, they watched the foam crest on the top. To both, somehow, there was something enormously significant about these milks.

"Look!" cried Nipak, eyes wide, skittering away: "Roaches!"

"No, no," said Fine, calming him, "grasshoppers. Harbingers of deep summer. Beautiful animals, really." He picked up a smart hopper, cradling it in his hand. "See? Exquisitely made."

"Please, sir, I am a professor of Cosmology and History in New York City, an honorable man—I must see her again—I *must!*"

"Those are admirable titles, but I don't know where she is. She's often gone, but always comes back home. Now this hopper—"

"A beautiful, sensual, high-IQ, vital, funny creature!"

"My grasshopper?"

"Your wife!"

"Right!" Fine noticed, then, that his more distant memories seemed intact. Or, rather, that already distinct clouds of recollection were condensing from the sky of amnesia. "Let me tell you about *Fine Theory.*" And as they drank milk and ate cake, the two scholars—one desperate with yearning for the other's wife and the other glad merely to be alive—began an exchange of ideas. For dinner, Fine cooked up some Spam, tempeh-burgers, and Hebrew National knockwursts on his gas-powered grill, and afterward, they took a walk. Macanudo cigars in hand, they strolled out into the warm mulchy night. The breeze rustled the new leaves, shaking husks off cherry and apple. Their airy promenade was soothed by the crash and suck of high tide.

Fine said: "It rained today."

Nipak answered: *"What* rained?"

"And did you know," asked Fine, leading him into the lab, "that J. Paul Getty drank a pint of mother's milk a day? Calcium effects menses, ovulation, pregnancy—even spring fever!" Yet as Fine led Nipak toward a cage of hoppers, the little Sri Lankan said he felt queasy. "Wonderful!" said Fine, taking out two Finestones. "Calcium's a low-salt antacid. Here." Plop. Suck. Plop. Suck.

Fine chatted on about calcium and learning in grasshoppers, and finally, holding a Finestone in the palm of his hand, sighed: "Just think. Sir Humphrey Davy, in 1808, found, in lime, this light yellow metal of the alkaline earths, as ductile and malleable and hard as gold itself—found in nature *only* linked with other elements, this bivalent cation—calcium!" A little sadly, he went on: "Here lies the world's hope. We live in the Disjunctive Age. From cell membrane to psyche itself, we are unraveling. A kid sees a man kill a man for a car on TV; the kid gets a gun sees a car kills a man, 'just like on TV.' No hesitation. No firm links in a chain of morality or thought. We are devolving into animals! We need firming, links, steadying of impulses, patience. Our help lies right in the palm of our hands. Supplies of limestone are virtually inexhaustible." Fine felt a rush of revulsion. "Imagine, my gentle friend: someone is killing shrinks!"

"You must market Finestones at once! I have the best connections in the holistic world—perchance we can form a corporation?"

"Great idea!" said Fine. "I've got the perfect name!"

"Tell me!"

"Fine and Dandi."

"Fine and Dandi, Inc.! I love it very much, yes!"

And as they laughed together, Fine felt a strange attraction to this lithe brown-skinned dark-eyed man, who seemed to exude the deeply comforting scent: cocoa butter. "I'm ravenous," he said,

"why not slip into Boston for an after-dinner nosh at the Ritz?"
On the way out, Nipak stopped at a cage set apart: a single green-
ish-brown hopper stood quietly, munching an apple covered with
a chalky dust. In the middle of the cage was a tiny red fire hydrant. Nipak asked why. "Oh that," said Fine, shyly, "that's just
my smarty assistant, Ms. Ando, her idea of a joke—she has a
sense of humor, not like me—at least my wife says I don't anyway."

"I think you are very funny."

"Why thank you, Nipak."

"But still I do not grasp the humor in the little hydrant."

"Oh. Well, Ms. Ando thinks if you want to get a hopper to lift
its leg, you show it a fire hydrant, like a dog *pishing*, see?"

"Yes, marvelous! And does it work?"

" 'Course not. That's a higher form of learning, one that invertebrates are incapable of. Not even a genius hopper like
him—"

"Good God man!" cried Nipak, bending closer. "Look!"

Fine saw the hopper standing, one leg raised, near the hydrant.
"Impossible!" He bent closer. "They don't have the neuronal net-
works—ugh!" Fine felt a cool gooey film coat his right eye. Taking his hand away, he saw that it was smeared with brown hopper
spit. They laughed, the hopper chirped. Fine reached into the
cupboard. "Have a Mars bar, Nipak, it'll carry us till we eat."
The last look in at the hopper showed him with all legs down in
graceful parity. But for his busy mandibles, he stood absolutely
still.

In the car, Fine, excited about incorporation, took Nipak's
arm: "I've got it!—our slogan: 'Suck Finestones, Live Harder.' "
Fine Lex.

After lunch the next day, the lithe Easterner gave Fine his first
lessons in meditation. *"Vipassana* was Buddha's own practice.
The process is, simply, *becoming aware of what actually is."* They
sat on the rug, Nipak in full lotus, Fine scissored lunkily. "The
instructions: Focus your attention on your breathing. When you
find your mind wandering, then very gently—and without judging
yourself—lead your attention back to the breath."

"And is this transcendental meditation, TM?"

"No!" cried Nipak. "Such fraud, that! To sit, chant like an
idiot, tune out? Perversion! The Buddha tuned *in!* He was totally

in the world, aware of life, practical." He sighed. "Ah, the West. Such abundance of bodily wealth, such impoverishment of spirit. Balance to the East. Now: sit; breathe."

Fine had trouble: his attention sprayed out in colors like light through a prism, but each time, as he noticed this, he drew his attention gently back to his breath. Once, he felt a strange familiar peace. His foot fell asleep, his knee sizzled, he moved.

Sensing his restlessness, Nipak said: "The door that locks you in is the door that frees you. I recall the words of Sri Nisargadatta Maharaj, a resident of modern-day Bombay, maker of cigarettes, teacher, discovered to the West by Maurice Frydman, a Cracow Jew: 'The entire purpose of a clean and well-ordered life is to free the self from the thralldom of chaos and the burden of sorrow.' "

"Nice!" said Fine. "And how does this jive with analysis?"

"Ah!" said Nipak. "I have studied this! Psychoanalysis focuses on self, with two perplexing dicta: 1) self, analyzed, is understood; 2) understanding of self must not be revealed to the other! Vipassana is different—listen—the secret of—"

They were interrupted by a delegation from Jefferson House.

Mr. Jefferson informed Fine that his wife had run off with his erstwhile best friend. They awaited Fine's explosion. It came instead from the little Sri Lankan, who, enraged, shot to his feet, cursed, spat, and asked where they'd gone. Royce said: "Paris."

They stared at Fine, who said: "Not a bad idea. She loves Paris. Family's flat overlooks the Eiffel Tower. Good for her."

"We ain't talkin' no Eiffel Towers, man," said Cooter, now firmed up once again, "we're talkin' snatchola!"

"Good Lord, man," said Nipak, "will you not take action!"

"If it'd been me, good buddy," said Cooter, "I'd kill him!"

"Really?" said Fine, amazed.

"Yes, er," said Mr. J., "and as a token of our appreciation we, yes, no, we bought you this." He handed a wrapped gift to Fine.

"Oh, you shouldn't have—whoops!" Fine dropped the heavy parcel. "Hope it's not breakable." He unwrapped it. "A gun?"

"Not just a gun, doc," said Cooter, "a .44! Ever since the President's wife admitted to carrying her 'tiny l'il gun,' it's all the rage. With the world a big shoot-'em-up, hell, fella, you gotta be crazy not to carry heat! So I went to Boston and bought it myse'f!"

"A handgun's sold every thirteen seconds," said Eli. "Fifty-five million handguns owned, one out of four Americans—*now!*"—he checked his watch—"that was another sale! Every fifty minutes, one person's killed with a handgun; every twenty-four minutes, a murder; every seven minutes, a rape; every ten seconds, a house burgled; one out of every sixty-one babies born in New York City last year will die at the handgun of a killer! Thanks."

"Thank you Eli babee!" said Cooter. "I'm a member of the National Rifle Association. 'Murcans have a right to bear arms!"

"Oh?" asked Eve, anorexic. "A right to wear sleeveless?"

"Yes, er, no," said Mr. Jefferson, "someone is even killing our devoted psychiatrists, no?"

"Yah!" said Stinko, crouching. "Maybe chust von of *us!*"

They each looked around at each other, the paranoia rising.

"Right!" said Cooter, cheerfully. "So Doc, you hop tonight's jumbo to gay Paree, and go for it! 'Cause if'n they got guns, less'n we got guns, they gonna gun us down! Y'all gotta go *do* it!"

"Do what?" asked Fine.

"Kill 'im! Give 'er a coupla whacks wi' the gunbutt too!"

"In France," said Mrs. Bush, a rich WASP patient of Pelvin's, *"la crime de passion* is still a quite valid legal defense?"

"Yes, er, no," said Mr. Jefferson, "a great cuckholding blow to us all." A tear came to his eye, and Mrs. Bush wiped it away with a monogrammed hankie. "You see, we all, well—we all *loved* her!"

They fell silent, verging on tears. Mary began weeping. She crossed herself and wept, wept and crossed herself. Fine asked why she was crying. "I'm crying for the mothers of the killers."

"Now!" said Eli. "One of 'em just got raped!"

Jefferson (black) cried out: "Jesus is inside me, sayin': 'Let he who be without sin throw the first stone.' "

"Well, doc?" asked Cooter.

All eyes upon him, Fine felt pressure to comply. Finally he said: "I'll have to see what takes shape."

"You hear that, guys? He's gonna be a man! Hip hip—"

"Hooray!" they shouted, and, taking their cue from their doctor, they all broke their low-carbo diets, starting to pig-out.

Nipak and Fine shared a cab to the airport. They passed a gunshop marked by a neglected sign:

USE   GUNS NEW GUNS

"Look!" said Fine.

"Yes?"

"It almost seems like a sign!"

He left Nipak at the New York shuttle. As Fine hugged him, his brown body seemed to express the scent of cocoa butter. Without realizing that his brain was trembling freely like voltaic jello, Fine bought three Klondike ("The Original") chocolate ice cream bars, and by the time he'd finished the last he was boarding the Wednesday night flight to Paris.

20

"—it happens all over the world,
It's done in London you're sure to find someone
It happens all over the world,
Yes Texas is just teeming with sexus so
Follow the sun all the world around, and
Keep on the run till your love is found,
It happens all over the world,
The world keeps falling in love!"

Goldie and O'Day waltzed through their finale in top hats and tails, and the Thursday—American Night—crowd at Nouvelle Eve loved it. Flushed with success, they exited.

Yet every exit is an entrance somewhere else; later that night, before they left the club, they received a telegram:

```
LOVED YOU STOP LOVE TO PROMOTE YOU STOP
MEET ME IN EYE OF GRAND LABYRINTHE JARDIN
DES PLANTES FRIDAY DUSK STOP ALONE STOP
BON COURAGE BONNE CHANCE STOP
                    SUPERSTOPSTITIOUS ANGEL
```

"Quel strange!" John said. "Shall we?"

"Yes."

And so late the next afternoon they walked arm in arm from "the Boul Mich" through the small winding streets of le quartier Mouffetard to the Seine. The fading day was lush and warm. At the entrance to the Jardin des Plantes a stone lion lay, caught forever in yawn. They walked past the statue of Lamarck and down the stately *allée centrale* fringed on either side by a pleached arbor of lime trees, the double rows of branches interweaving in trellises of bright green, shading members of the béret generation playing cards, as well as children, grandchildren, the odd fez wearer (la Mosquée was nearby) or very black African, and assorted domestic animals, from monkey through snake. They strolled along, leaning into each other, making up stories about who their "angel" might be. They searched out le Grand Labyrinthe, constructed by Superintendent Buffon in the early eighteenth century on a high knoll of centuries of garbage, behind the zoo emptied during the siege of 1870 when the people ate the animals. They entered the wide end and climbed, *femme et cavalier* entwined, whorl after whorl up the sloping, ever-tightening spiral, until, out of breath, they found themselves at the eye: a circle of thick bushes in the middle of which was a kiosk. (Wherein, at noon, a set of lenses would reflect the rays of the sun and sound a bell.) They sat on a low stone bench, breathing hard, facing the crotch of the path, full of expectation. Their breath slowed. They sat still.

"Steffy?" The voice came from behind them. "John James?"

Startled, they turned.

There stood Fine, crouched like a marksman, gun in hand.

"No!" she screamed, reaching out to him, noticing that he was wearing, of all things, a béret?! "Stop!"

"Don't!" shouted John.

Fine aimed, and fired: "BANG!"

Out of the gun stuck a rod, and down from the rod rolled a banner, and the banner read: "BANG!" As Steph and John watched, Fine rolled it back up, stuffed it back in the barrel, repeated: "BANG!"

"You jerk!" screamed Steph, "that's a helluva thing to do!"

"Oh boy were you two scared!" said Fine, laughing so hard he had to hold his béret on with both hands.

John shrugged, and said: "Well, I can see myself doing the same thing, under the circumstances. What the hell—we deserve it."

"Why?" asked Fine, feeling perplexed.

"Oh cut it out, Fine," said Steph, "you know damn well why."

But Fine didn't understand, and overcome with the concatenate shape of the encounter, he blurted out: "Isn't it great!—here, now, the old threesome back together again!" Feeling awed, he went on: "And last night, you two were super!"

"Okay, Fine," Steph said, "come off it. You're wild with jealousy, right?"

"Nope, Steffy, I'm happy."

"You're crazy!"

"Could be, but I feel happy—"

"What's wrong with you? Is this some new technique you learned in your analysis?"

Fine looked perplexed, lost, and asked: "*What* analysis?"

"You don't even *remember?* All those years of Fumb—"

"Can't you take a joke? Ha! Haha!"

"Come on, Fine," said John, edging toward him, "what's up your sleeve?" Fine looked up his sleeve.

"Stop that!" said Steph. "What's wrong with you?!"

"Me? Nuthin', Steffy." He laughed. His puffy cheeks shook. He calmed. "Why're you so suspicious of my being happy?"

"Because the normal reaction to this is rage, hurt—"

"Since when have you ever accused me of having the 'normal reaction' to anything? Hunh, Steffy?"

"Why're you calling me 'Steffy'?"

Fine, puzzled, said: "It seems the most natural thing in the world for me to call you, that's why."

None of them could know that his seizure had erased not only much recent memory, but also the capacity for "thought." Input/output. Period. Clarity. In some sense, body without mind, man without inner light. Entitling the bearer to a seeming bliss.

Fine, tiring of badinage, felt hungry. "What about dinner? I've made reservations at a very special place—c'mon!"

"Okay, Fine, but you first." She and John followed him down the widening gyre. She said: "God, Fine, you look fatter!"

"Yeah," he said, turning, "I'm back on carbohydrates. That high-protein–diet weight loss was mostly water!—I was dehydrated—gained back twenty pounds in four days!—feel a lot better, more solid, back in shape." They'd stopped before a tall old tree—one of the tallest in all of Paris—the plaque read: *Faux acacia,* "locust tree." "Wow!" said Fine, "look! Know what 'locust' is in French?: *sauterelle d'Orient!* Lovely?!" He stared at his old friend, feeling the warm air of friendship rise. "Great to see you, John James!"

"Call me John."

"John. So, here we are again—the 'Ondt and the Gracehoper' and Steffy! Oh—reminds me—I met Nipak Dandi—what a nice guy! He and I . . ." As they walked back out through the fragrant garden, as they listened to Fine chatter, Stephanie turned to John and said:

"Be careful."

"Why?"

"I think that Fine's gone mad."

The restaurant Chez les Anges was on a grand boulevard near the tomb of Napoléon. The menu cover showed a winged Cupid painting a portrait of a nude woman, and upon his canvas he'd transformed her into a bottle of wine. The inner covers were filled with doodles: "Good food, June 6, 1964—D-Day + 20 yrs, Stanley Eisenhower." Steph and Fine had eaten there when he'd chased her down in Paris. As they drank their raspberry kirs, Fine—for some reason still in béret—scanned the room. Suspicious, Steph forced Fine to taste all food, which he, laughing, did. They chatted about nothing, the lovers smothered by the betrayal that hung almost visibly in the air.

"You know, Fine, John and I are not just casual friends getting up an act—I mean you know that, right?"

"Right." He slithered another oyster down. "I know."

"But you used to get so paranoid about us!"

"Did I ever! Remember, graduation day, when you and he—"

"—and now it's a *reality*—don't say it!—"

"Say what?" Fine did not know what she meant.

"I mean now John and I are together, I mean sexually, and—"

"Yes, yes, as long as you—"

"But it's not just sex, Fine," said John, "we love—"

"—*love* each other, yes! I'd hate it if you were just treating each other like pieces of meat! I don't know—maybe I should be upset, but I'm not. I'm just glad to be together with you both, here and now. Life's too short to lose the ones you love." He took their hands in his: "I don't mind if you don't." He meant it. "I mean jealousy's such a seventies concept, know what I mean?"

Steph, lost and a little irritated that he was taking it so lightly, said: "But in the past you always said—"

"Can't people change?" He thought to mention his seizure, but, not wanting to worry them, unwilling to face it yet, did not.

"You claimed *not:* 'We never do anything out of character.' "

"Well, I've changed. I don't understand it either, Steffy, but all I know is that I feel okay about this, really." He reached into his pocket and, holding a Finestone in each palm, moved them reciprocally up and down, like the scales of justice: "I feel that I'm finally in harmony, in neurophysiological sync."

The main course arrived. Fine was transported to such rapture by his special fish dish, they too got caught up in the food and wine. As they were draining their third bottle of red, Fine jumped up, cried "Lacan!" and grabbed Steph—"To translate—c'mon—"

"What's going on?"

"Jacques Lacan—the 'French Freud'—eats here all the time!"

A little old man sat in the corner, emphysematously sucking at a Gitanes, wreathed in gray-blue smoke. Fine accosted him, the most famous living analyst in the Western world. Lacan, with the impatience of the cultural idol, barked for the host to throw him out. Fine would not be turned: he reminded Lacan of their exchange of letters, and then quoted a seminal Lacanian *écrit:*

"I am not sure that man has an interior. The only thing that seems to testify to it is that which we produce as excrement. The characteristic of a human being is that—in contrast to other animals—he doesn't know what to do with his shit. We are always coming across cat shit but a cat is a civilized animal. But if you take elephants it is striking how little space their leavings take up in nature, whereas when you think of it, elephant turds could be enormous! The discretion of the elephant is a curious thing. Civilization means shit, *cloaca maxima."*

Lacan insisted Fine be thrown out. Fine said: "Wait—I'll predict what you are getting for your entrée—and why!" Fine paused. *"Alose à l'oseille*—shad of Loire steamed in sorrel leaves, no?" The great Structuralist, startled, nodded. "Why? Why do Mexican peasants soak maize in limestone water to make tortillas? Why do Amazons grind up the bones of dead relatives and drink the powder in banana soup? Why do Africans eat fish wrapped in banana leaf whose acidity dissolves the bones and what does this liberate?"

Lacan muttered something which Steph translated freely as: "How the hell do I know, you little *putz?*"

"Calcium! Just as the acid sorrel dissolves the thin bones of this fish and frees up *calcium!"* Fine smiled, held out his palm. *"Le* Finestone! *Je suis* Fine!" Lacan looked puzzled, and grunted:

"Vous? Assez, Le Gros!" Steph translated: not thin, fat.

Chuckling, Fine told him about Finestones. Plop. Suck.

"Incroyable!" said the French Freud, going on in broken English: "I am eating thees feesh deesh for seventy years!"

The French Freud joined them. Fine had read many of Lacan's *hermétique* (at TBI they were called *meshugge) écrits,* and wanted to be the first in America to use what he saw as the brilliant Lacanian technique—for which Lacan had been thrown out of the Internat. Psychoanal. Ass.—the five-minute hour: suddenly and at random, after five minutes of the session Lacan would cough and say: "It's time for us to stop." This was said to have profound impact on the next session.

As the meal passed, Lacan amused them with his world-class associations—combining famed Saussurian structural linguistics ("analysis" = "anal" "lysis"), Lévi-Straussian structural-linguistical anthropology, the *patois* of Oc and the slop of *la boob tube,* TV. The *propriétaire* brought out *le marc de Bourgogne,* a potent house brandy. Soon they were all looped. As they bid Lacan adieu, he promised to give Fine instruction in the five-minute hour, the next day. And then, looking closely at Steph, he repeated his famous *aphorisme:*

"A woman is a symptom."

The troika jolted out into the soft night, brains whipped by French intellectualism, food, and wine.

They were so drunk they could hardly stay on the sidewalk. Throwing out words in three languages for how loaded they were —*"plotzed!"* (Fine), "crucified" (John), and *"fichu"*—"screwed" (Steph)—they moved as if on rollers down the narrow street.

A man walking toward them, seeing them lurching about,

crossed to the other side. But as they closed, the man looked at them and shouted out: "Alphonse? Alphonse!" And rushed toward Fine.

"Oh no," said Fine, "it's happening again!"

And it was. The man mistook Fine for "Alphonse." Fine asked Steph to explain. She looked at Fine closely, and said:

"That's it! *That's* why you're acting so different—you're not you, you're someone else! You're not Fine at all! Alphonse!"

The Frenchman, now sure, cried: "Alphonse!"

Fine protested that he was Fine. Steph challenged him to prove it. Mustering up all sobriety, Fine said: "I know I am Fine because Fine is the only man I know who is often mistaken for other men, okay? And now Fine deigns to continue on his way home."

Fine was staying at the Ritz. At the door of the apartment he parted from them, hugging John, and then, without letting go, drawing Steph in, too, as they had done in their salad days. He turned to go, but she grabbed him by the shoulders and looked him in the eye, probing, asking him again: "What's going on?!"

He laughed. "Oh you—do you have to analyze everything!"

"There's something fishy here, Fine—"

"Hey, you don't have to *carp* about it! I'm just a little *shrimp, flounder*ing around, so *shad* up!" Handing them each a Finestone, he kissed each on each cheek. "So I'll come by at noon?"

"Fine—oh shit!—did it again!" said John.

Spirits soaring, Fine wheeled off down the wide quiet avenue toward the river, whistling, as atrociously as ever, an old sweet song of love.

They watched him disappear into the dark and then listened as his afterimage, his last atonal notes, melded into the silence. They went up to the flat, undressed for bed. She lay in his arms, and they talked about Fine. Steph still suspected that Fine was faking it, scheming, about to pounce. John disagreed: "It's too good an act for someone like Fine. Believe me, he means it all."

"Why?"

"Who knows? Maybe we have flipped him out?!"

"Or maybe he's on drugs?"

"It's weird, that's for sure," John said. "Almost kinky."

"Yeah." She ran her fingers over his smooth chest. "I almost feel like we *should* make love, you know?"

"Let's not force it. Too much booze, love, too long a day."

Neither said what both feared: the problem wasn't booze or fatigue, the problem was Fine. Later, Steph was to say: "If only he'd fired a *real* gun at us! If only he'd cried, cursed, whatever! There was nothing to blame him for!—except his cheeriness! That little putz was spoiling the whole thing! Him there with us, cheerful? It was mad! I felt worried about him! And the worst?: he was adorable!—something about him, then, was, well, almost sexy!"

There's nothing like betrayal to stir up fond feelings for the betrayed.

And as she lay in bed tracing back over the flow of the day, she fastened on one detail: Fine had eaten dinner with his fork held in his *left* hand. Why? Was he pretending to be European? Weird! The trace faded, becoming a faint etching on a glass wall, of sleep, of dream.

At the same moment, Fine stood in the middle of the immense cobbled Place Vendôme, under the column that had borne, on its pinnacle, a succession of greats: Napoléon I as Caesar; Henry IV; a gigantic fleur-de-lys; Napoléon I as himself; and, presently, a replica of the original Napoléon I as Caesar. Fine spun slowly on his vertical axis, a circle in consonance with the seventeenth-century square. At number twelve, Chopin had died. He rotated again, spinning free, a little faster, enjoying the sufi-whorls of time and space and motion. He stopped. He felt dizzy, and the square still circled on. As he wobbled toward the gold revolving door of the Ritz, he asked himself:

"How do humans change? By free will or by fate? Are we fated to believe in our free will? No choice but to believe in choice? Is a man who he seems to be? Is a man ever who he is not?" Assessing, he said, finally: "Humans change by magic."

What did Fine feel? Grand and horny. Grand that the threesome had spent at least one happy night together again. Horny for no clear reason but so intensely that he asked the bellhop about the possibility of a whore. It didn't pan out. Like a glider finding a thermal, Fine floated, circling up on a breeze of sleep, lips creased into a smile.

21

BUT THEY COULDN'T stay in Paris. American Night was a once-weekly event, the French Actors' Union wouldn't let them perform regularly, and, to top it all off, Steph's mother was arriving at the flat Sunday with boyfriend Tray. And so they decided to return to the States. Fine suggested that they all live together at Stow-on-Wold. The others were incredulous. Fine parried their incredulity.

Finally, Steph said: "It's outlandish!"

"Yes!" said Fine. "Take a chance!"

"By the way," said John, "on the Fourteenth—Sunday—I've got to be in Dublin. Forgot to tell you—I was planning to go for the day."

"Why?" Steph asked.

"Oh, nuthin'—just arranged to see some old friends."

Steph scrunched up her eyes. "Come on, what's up?"

"Can't say."

"Why not?"

"Just can't. You'll see."

"A mystery?" said Fine. "Grand, just grand!"

And so on Saturday night the thirteenth they were standing wet and chilled in the spattering rain, outside O'Dwyer's Pub off Merrion Square. John pointed out, in the array of Georgian town-houses, that of the artist Jack B. Yeats, whose *Portrait of a Lady* and *The Clown Among the People* they'd admired earlier that day in a gallery. Fine had changed béret for tweed cap: "Handwoven by D. Flood, Donegal." It never left his head. Across from O'Dwyer's was a huge brick building.

"See that?" said John, "The National Maternity Hospital, used to be called Horne's House, Holles Street. Two chapters of *Ulysses* are set there! Christ!—I'd forgot the fookin' *wet*— c'mon—"

They entered the pub—(called "The Office" because the UCD med students hung out there)—and were swallowed by the warmth and the dialect, filled with—as John said: "t'ick t'uddin' consonants 'n' great loorchin' vowels." At the jammed bar, John ordered Guinness. They watched the ritual filling of glass: fill halfway; skim the spilling foam with ruler; let settle; again fill halfway, etc.

"Hey O'Day, you big bugger!" said a thin curly haired man.

"Noel!" said John. "Always here! Where's the good doc—"

"Is that big Amerrykin fag back again?" said a portly black-haired man with a soft round face, wearing doctor's whites.

"A.J.!" said John. The three old friends greeted each other, and were introduced to Steph and Fine. They chatted, awhile, until it was time for Noel to sing. John and he had performed in pubs together. With little coaxing, John sat down to do a song.

The uilleann pipes began to whine, the concertina wheeled out a harmonic, and John came in with eight bars of guitar. Fine recognized the theme: Tchaikovsky's *Pathetique*. And then, in a high fresh tenor, edged like a slant of sunlight, he sang:

> "When midnight comes, good people homeward tread,
> Seek now your blanket and your featherbed;
> > Home is the rover,
> > His journey's over,
> Yield up the nighttime to old John O'Dreams,
> Yield up the nighttime to old John O'Dreams . . ."

Fine sensed a great power in his friend, as did the others: John's voice was so clear and light, the words so freeing, the crowded room turned still as a field at night. Here was a shape edged with magic—a man, *his* own song—and the magic wasn't in the words or in the music, but all around and in between, like an unseen breeze ruffling wheat. He sang the last verse, eyes glistening:

> "Now as you sleep, the dreams are winging clear,
> The hawks of morning cannot harm you here;
>> Sleep is a river,
>> Runs on forever,
> And for your boatman choose old John O'Dreams,
> And for your boatman . . . choose old John O'Dreams."

"Wonderful!" Steph said, as he sat back down with them, to applause. "Right from your heart! What's it mean? Tell us."

"Ah you know the Irish—mad romantics altogether!" Despite her prodding, he kept the secret of his sincerity to himself.

They chatted and drank until the phone behind the bar rang, and A.J.—his specialty was "Obs and Gobs"—covering the hospital for the night, had to leave for a forceps delivery. The Americans left with him. He stood on the sidewalk, looking up at the huge hospital in his charge, and said: "Work is the curse of the drinkin' man! Wouldja like to come pull out a few babies before bed?"

"How do you know there'll be other deliveries going on?" Fine asked.

"C'mere," he said, drawing them in. "See that buildin'? In there they average a baby an hour, the whole year round! Jayzez!"

They accompanied him in, past the huge Virgin slammed against the wall of the lobby, up the rickety open-sided elevator, to the delivery room on the top floor. John and Steph declined to go further. Fine donned a white coat and went in. Attended by midwives, each on a curtained-off stretcher, rump on pillow and knees wide apart looking down over a great hill of belly, lay eight women in various stages of labor. Fine watched the process, amazed—he'd never seen a birth ("Obstetrics" not required at Harvard Med.)—and when a mother delivering child number nine flashed a raw-gummed smile and said: "Every baby costs you a tooth," he thought calcium, and smiled too. Yet by the third episiotomy, the fourth placenta, Fine felt nauseous. A.J. took him to the door and asked, "What kinda doc are you then?"

"A shrink," said Fine.

"Ah yeah," A.J. said, smiling, "figgers."

As Fine and Steph and John stood in the waiting area, a first-time mother—hardly more than a girl—was wheeled out past them, her firstborn in her arms. They talked with her, they touched the newborn's tiny soft hands, feet, teeny nails so sharp. The mother smiled, and left.

"God what a beautiful smile!" said Steph. "And is it the happiest moment in a life?"

"By far!" said Fine. "But where are the fathers?"

"Home," said John, "dreaming."

"Dreaming?" asked Steph.

John lapsed into a thick brogue, and, joking, said: "Fer all fathers are dreamers, shurly?"

As they walked through Stephen's Green to the hotel, John cried out: "Ah life! Life as it *is,* not as it seems to be! That's what I found here, all those years here, yes!"

"So why'd you ever leave?" Steph asked.

He didn't answer. Unless they could have read his answer in the *clack, clack* of his boots on the wet worn stones, or the melancholy whistle of a flute wafting out from an alley into the hush after the rain, or the verse of his song, out of beat with the flute, and so all the more mysterious to Steph and Fine.

And on Sunday morning they followed him across the Liffey and up O'Connell Street and past the Rotunda into the maze of streets lined with decaying row houses, near the famed Eccles Street where Leopold and Molly Bloom had "lived." Dublin on Sunday was a city of Masses, and of wrecked abandoned baby carriages parked in gutters, and, of course, of Dubliners. John stopped outside one house of many identical ones, and, pulling himself together, climbed the few steps of the stoop to the door. He paused, and then, rang the bell.

He waited, tugging at his blond cowlick, shifting his feet, smiling uneasily back at his friends. He rang again.

A woman opened the door and stood there with her hands on her hips. A big woman, with her hair mussed. Her eyes were an exquisite aquamarine, like a tropical sea. Fortyish, she'd once been pretty. Perhaps even a beauty, once. "An' is it you?" she asked, her voice tremolant, so that she put a hand to her throat.

"It is."

"The man himself. An' I'm t'inkin' it's not like you to come all the way here in porson."

"It's fourteen May and I—"

"Tomorrow is the fifteenth, and you said—"

Behind her skirt there was a rushing, and then a cry: "Da?"

And a little boy shot past her and crashed into John, his face in John's pants and his arms hugging him behind the knees, tightly. John reached down and picked him up and lifted him up against the sky like a prize, turning away from the woman, and said: "John James!"

"Da!"

And the father brought the son down to his breast and then cradled him in the crook of his neck and bent his head over him and closed his eyes into the little boy's light hair, and they saw his big body shake with sobs.

22

ALL SUNDAY AFTERNOON, they fought the turbulent westerlies back to Boston.

John James Michael O'Day II was almost six. Deprived of his father for the past nine months, he clung to him, like a duckling to a mother duck. As they'd stood in line to board, John James had stared up at his father and asked: "Da, are you bigger'n God?"

Fine and John laughed, and John said: "Nobody's bigger'n God, luv, nobody in this world."

Stephanie, in silence, moved further up the line.

To Fine, the love between father and son was so big and thick it seemed almost visible: a wire coiled between two spirits, so that as they moved further apart, it drew them closer together again. Stretched tight, it seemed almost to sing, the attachment fiercer for the boy's freedom from his mother. "It's all so sweet!" Fine said to John, his eyes rimmed with tears. "What a great kid!"

"Think I oughta keep him, then, eh, Uncle Fine?"

"Keep me, Da, keep me!" the boy said, with real fear.

"Right, then, I shall!" The three males laughed, and John, beaming, said, "Grand, just grand!"

"You know, John," said Fine, "there's a sense of completion about this, about the next generation sitting right here with us."

John asked, suspiciously: "You really mean that, Fine?"

"Yes! With all my heart!"

"Oh boy!" muttered Steph under her breath.

"Sure it's a surprise, and yes you're a pecker for not telling us, but it's bringing us all back together again! Isn't it?" They didn't answer. "Besides, stepfamilies are almost the norm in America, now. John James will feel more at home!" Looking down at the little boy, Fine smiled, and in his mind's eye traced the penetration of his old friend's genes: the flaxen-white straight hair; the face just beginning to elongate through the infant's roundness; the delicate female lips, a sign, in the boy, of the woman in his father's soul; the body, too, while still chunky, could—judging from the big feet (in clunky cheap shoes)—lengthen to his dad's height. The other shapes were those of the mother: aquamarine eyes; broadness of chin; pug nose. And the thick Irish brogue.

John James had never been to America. He wanted to see real cowboys and Indians, *Superman* and guns, and eat hot dogs and swim in the warm ocean and spend every day with da and Granny Katey.

Fine, feeling so childlike himself, felt the child's excitement as his own. His heart went out to the little boy. Sensing this, John James latched onto Fine in a big way.

It wasn't until John James conked out, an hour from Boston, that Steph had a chance to talk to John alone. Carefully shifting the sleeping child to Fine's shoulder, John followed her forward to the bulkhead. Fine watched the pantomime, seeing the anger flare in his wife's eyes, hearing snatches of accusation and hurt, watching John reach out to her and she turn away and disappear into the bathroom. John, shaken, came back, sat down. He said: "What a mess! You think I should've told her before?"

The child stirred. "Shh! Little guy needs his sleep!"

In a whisper, John told Fine the details: he'd met the mother when both were acting at the Abbey, the year after graduation. She'd gotten pregnant. He'd married her. After a few years it had become intolerable: alcohol, fistfights—the works—and he'd moved out, traveling, coming back as often as possible to see his son. She'd gotten an anullment, remarried, had three more children, and for the first time had agreed to him taking the boy to America for the summer.

Steph stood in the aisle, eyes red. Fine said: "It's not the little boy's fault, Steph. Besides, he's beautiful, isn't he?"

"Beautiful?" She paused, smiled. "Hell, he's gorgeous."

Fine recognized the white flag, a truce. "Okay, guys, let's decide where we're going to live."

"We?" said Steph. "Forget it."

"Why not?" said Fine. "Just like old times."

Steph rolled her eyes. John said: "My mum expects us—John James and me—to stay in the attic at home. I guess that's out, now."

"It sure is," said Steph. "How 'bout a hotel?"

"I can't see my boy living in a hotel."

Silence. They looked to Fine. He beamed. "Let's all stay out at Stow! There's plenty of room: you two in the master bedroom, John James next door—the room's just meant for a kid—I'll take the nanny's room, next one down. Perfect. What do you say?" They said they thought it was pretty weird. "Yeah, but what choice is there? At least let's try it, at least for tonight. Where else can you go when we land? It'll give us all time to see what's what."

"I suppose we could stay there tonight," said Steph, "and use it —temporarily—while we looked for an apartment. But listen: it's got to be secret, I mean the question of who's with whom, okay?"

"That's why it's got to be at Stow. The place is known for deception. And know what? I think it's gonna be fun!"

"Fun?" said Steph, eyes wide with amazement. "Fun?"

"Sure," said Fine. "Come on, guys, take a risk!"

The boy awoke. Fine excused himself and headed straight for a large Aer Lingus stewardess. He'd been attracted by her long red hair, creamy freckled face, and stature—as he went up to her she loomed a good eight inches taller. Kay, from Galway. He took in her solid thighs and rump, her large solid breasts that, as he flirted with her, seemed to expand, the right nipple stretching the layers of clothing, popping up near his nose. Up close, he saw a thin line of red fuzz on her upper lip, which suggested a very busy pudendum and got him hard. They flirted in a gentle, innocent way until he dared suggest they adjourn to the bathroom. She blushed and turned away, but in a flash he slid his hand up under her skirt toward the front feeling the satiny-covered thick pubic hair rustle against his palm like a hidden scrub brush. She grabbed his hand, but before she let go there was a tug-of-war back and forth across her genitalia. She turned, smiled, winked, and went up the aisle toward the lav. Fine doffed his cap and popped it over his erection and, seeing Steph and John staring, smiled, gave a thumbs-up sign, and followed country Kay in, punning to himself: "Aer Yoni."

Fine had become body: concupiscent, phallic, free.

Hot and humid, thick and sensual as a steambath, was the sea-level Boston air. In their absence, the weather had turned, and was now perched on the hot edge of oppressive. John James, unused to heat, gulped his breaths and said he had to pee. On their glide-path down over Boston Harbor they'd noticed a mass rally on Museum Wharf. Fine, at the wheel of Stephanie's Jag, detoured to it, and they found themselves on the edge of a crowd gathered for one of many nationwide Mother's Day rallies of Women's Action for Nuclear Disarmament. Surrounded by clowns and balloons, they saw Dr. Helen Caldicott hold her six-month-old baby up to the crowd and say: "My drive is fear for my kids. Our children know for a fact they are not going to grow up. The secretary of defense shows an abnormal lack of emotional involvement." And her husband: "There's got to be a change in men. There needs to be a redefinition of courage in men. For a woman, a courageous man is one who can admit he made a mistake."

Fine listened, touched, recalling how homey President Reagan seemed on TV, spouting "freedom through strength" in the amiable primary colors of Norman Rockwell. Yet behind the mask loomed George Orwell: "war is peace." Fine shuddered. He felt he now could—*must*—use his new artfulness to address the nuclear issue. "Incredible! Everything's fitting together—everything, everything!"

"What are you talking about?" asked Steph.

"I'm going to write another letter. Culmination of all I've learned—I'm going to *do* something, something of use!" She asked to whom was Fine writing. "The President—for release to all media." They laughed. "You laugh, but hey—you just wait."

"Wouldja tell 'im sumthin' fer me too?" asked John James.

"Sure," said Fine, bending down to him. "What?"

Eyes wide, he said: "Tell 'm not to do it afore I'm big?"

"That's just what I'm going to tell him, yes." He rose. "I start tonight, after dinner. Au WANG, Citröen! C'mon!"

On the way out to Stow, John told the boy that they'd be staying with Uncle Fine.

John James asked: "Not with Granny Katey?"

"Nope. This'll be more fun."

"Will we see Granny Katey tomorrow, Da?"

"Maybe. If not tomorrow, the day after."

Armed guards stopped them at the mainland end of the Curley Bridge. The killer was still at large. Mr. Royce was tightening Stow security. They had to get out of the car, and, while a German shepherd sniffed for explosives, Fine and Steph identified the two others. They were told to get their photo IDs. Shaken, they drove on. John, as gently as possible, explained the situation to his son, ending with: "So if a stranger comes up to you, you run, y'hear?"

"Aw Da," said the boy, showing his street smarts, "y't'ink I don't know that? B'Jayzez!—it's just like in the *fil'ms!*"

Later that night, kissing "Aunty Steph and Unky Fine" goodnight, John James was taken upstairs to bed by his da. Steph and Fine sat out on the porch overlooking the harbor. For the first time since she'd left, they were together alone. They sat in silence, as the lush darkness lifted the heat up just high enough to be comfortable. Across the bay, the city was Sunday-night dark, the skyline nudging rather than cutting the sky. The air was heavy with the scent of new blossoms—the full blast of lilac, the subtler fruit trees, others—set against the tart dark-green undercurrent of pine. In the first blush of warmth, everything had rushed to bloom. Even, Fine mused, the Form of Bloom. No mosquitoes yet. The waves lapped at the shore. The only other sound was that of Fine chomping and slurping a Swanson Turkey ("Mostly White Meat") Entree, "With Gravy and Dressing and Whipped Potatoes" ("HUNGRY-MAN, for the Hearty Appetite"). He licked his fingers, clicked the deck chair to the last notch back, and burped four times. Looking up at the sky, he said: "Look—all the planets nearest Earth, visible at once: Venus, a yellow spark in the west; Saturn, dim red in the east; overhead, Mars, Jupiter; next month, Mercury! Rare. Know what it's called?"

"Fine, I don't know what's going on with you, but I do know one thing: we have to have a little order around here, a little discipline—no gossip, no telling secrets to anyone, you hear me?"

"Right, but—" A song floated down from the boy's bedroom window. They'd heard it before, sensed it was special, yet had never guessed the obvious—it was a lullaby:

> "Both man and master in the night are one,
> All things are equal when the day is done;
>> The prince and the plowman,
>> The slave and the free man,
> All find their comfort in old John O'Dreams,
> All find their comfort in old John O'Dreams . . ."

They listened in silence until Fine said: "You're hurt, aren't you, Steph? I mean you didn't expect this, did you?"

"Hurt? Why of course not, Fine, I'm overjoyed! What could be better for me than to just slip right into a ready-made family?!"

"Well, I hope you can avoid getting bitter, Steph," he said, concerned. "I mean that's the worst, in life: to get bitter."

"Sure, sure."

"Anyway, it's called 'szxygy.' " She asked what. "The kick-line up in the sky: conjunction of two or more heavenly bodies. In a few days, full moon—the tides will be rising in all of our limbic lobes—I'll have to up the dose of calcium. Amazing, isn't it?"

"What's that?"

"The body. Suddenly I'm seeing what you were saying all along —the importance of body. I feel like shooting all the analysts who see psychological causation as greater than that of the body. Just because analysts neglect their own bodies is no reason not to free up the body in my own life—all our lives—is it?"

"Fine, you really have changed. I don't understand it."

"Me neither. But 'understanding' is such a nineteenth-century concept. Ah, I dunno—guess I'm not so much into dyads anymore. The dyad is dying, eh? Ha! Let's just have some fun, okay?"

"Easy for you to say," said Steph, getting up. "I'm going to bed." As she passed Fine—he slouching down looking up at the heavens—she reached out her hand and through his tweed cap ruffled his hair. "What the hell?!" She ripped off the cap and discovered the sutures on the top of Fine's head. "Fine, what happened?!"

"Oh, nothing."

"Come over here to the light!" Under the porch light she saw it: like a black insect flattened against his shaved white scalp, a row of stitches spread across an ugly-looking wound. Voice tight and scared, she demanded: "Come on—tell me the truth."

Under pressure, he did.

Her face went white with shock. "Why didn't you tell me?!"

"Didn't want to worry you. Besides, it's nothing—"

"Nothing? Everything! It's a total change of personali—"

"There's no connection between—"

"I mean what is it? Is it like a—" She paused, as if afraid to mention the word, "—like a *stroke?*"

"No, not at all—I told you: a grand mal epileptic seizure."

"Well, what caused it?"

"Don't know. Or, rather, no cause was found."

"It could be serious—we've got to find out the reason—"

"Oh come on, it's not like a brain tumor or something—"

"Brain tumor?! Who said brain tumor?"

"It's nothing, I'm all right—"

"Nothing? It's like a lobotomy! It's brain damage, Fi—"

"I'm *not* brain-damaged—"

"Maybe even brain *death!*" Fine laughed. "You're not in your right mind!" She let her breath out in a tight harsh stream. "To-morrow we go to a doctor—that's *we*—you alone are not capable anymore. The best doctor in town, you hear? No wonder!"

"Why are you angry at me?"

"Because you didn't tell me—Christ what a mess! My husband's had a stroke, my lover's had a child, I've quit my job and I'm too upset to even *think* comedy, and you say it's gonna be just *fine?*"

"Hunh?"

"What?"

"Oh—sorry—I keep hearing the word as my name."

"Oh my God! Dear God help us! I've had it for today—I'm going to bed." She walked away. "Oh boy! Oh boy, oh boy, oh boy . . ."

Fine sat alone for a while. He heard them start to bicker. Unwilling to eavesdrop, he got up and went through the thick night to the side door of Jefferson House, heading for his attic office.

A man on a mission, he was unaware, climbing the stairs, of his right foot dragging behind, not quite clearing the lift up each step to the next.

In his office he went for the box of Finestones, and soon feeling high and firm, he slipped a systems disk into his WANG, and like a pet glad to see its master, it went *buzz, mmm, rr—rrr,* and then, with a cheery *bleep!,* told him it was ready.

THE NUCLEAR MIND

With relief he found that now only events directly before his seizure were still lost. Like an old jalopy coming out of a car wash, his memory sparkled brighter for its recent blur. He recalled word for word talks with Steph about recent Presidents (she read the biographies).

He had a sudden insight: the last three elected Presidents— Nixon, Carter, Reagan—had nearly identical (psychologically) mothers, fathers, birth orders, childhoods, character!: the "nuclear mind." None of the three were firstborn. Their fathers had been weak, absent, drunk, early to die. In the shadow of an older brother or sister, in father's absence they'd each been abandoned to the care of a powerful, ideological (often religious) mother. Trapped, scared to be like mom and yet scared to free themselves from her, they fled the love/hate conflict, isolating themselves from relationship. They were like John O'Day—with self untethered and floating free, they'd mimed distant heroes (priests, sportscasters, past Presidents), slipping into the actor's disconnection from the world. Nixon, the stress of his resignation unmasking his paranoid character, summed up with his hateful: "My mother was a saint!" And Reagan himself often quoted A. Lincoln: "All that I am or hope to be I owe to my mother." What better proof of their ambivalence toward mother than Pat, Rosalynn, Nancy—their exhausted, soldierly First Ladies.

Fine could see the three lives—like time-lapse flowerings—unravel into President: isolated from real feeling, each had a magical relation to the world, seeing the world as part of self, bending reality to narcissism, devoid of relation. The image, so vivid compared to the real, freed each from the complexity of real relation-

ship. Denying so much of themselves, they deny a real world
("America is back, standing tall . . . with courage, confidence,
and hope"). "Male" in the sense of "bigger than" (not phallic;
penis the least of it), they split the world into opposites, lacking
skills to see it from the other side. Having the same goal as the
Soviets—preserving humanity—they'd be damned if they'd work
with them toward it. The only hope in the nuclear age was dia-
logue; the only fear, bombast. Yet the bombastic posture—a cry
from the dead soul within—was that of the commander in chief.
Is it inevitable, given this world? Fine's mind slipped back twenty-
five years: the family sits in the TV room, the venetian blinds
turning them into zebras, hearing the nice host of the TV show
say: "Here at General Electric, progress is our most important
product." And now he's "hosting" America. The media had nicknamed Reagan the "Great Communicator." Yet they'd never
pinned him down as to *what* he was actually communicating. Fine
knew: denial. Denial of logic, denial of feeling and doubt, denial
of reality. In a video era of mass happy endings, people don't want
Carter's "malaise" of reality, they want a strong affable grandpa
saying: "It's okay, it's okay, it's all gonna be okay!" In history—
world and intrapsychic—denial inevitably fails. Sure makes you
question democracy, when the people's choice seems as blind to
the real as a despot. Except given the alternatives. Is all power,
deep down, the power of transference?

Possessed by a feverish intensity, he recorded fluidly, on into
the night: 1) Introduction; 2) The Nuclear Age; 3) The Nuclear
Family—"Pop"; 4) The Nuclear Mom—The "Hi Mom!" Syndrome; 5) The Nuclear Mind; 6) What to Do Now. Fine ended
with an anecdote:

> . . . and then my wife said to me: "You men would find a
> way to relate, if you realized your lives depended on it."
>   And so, Mr. President, I leave you with this alternative
> to the *either/or* thinking of the nuclear mind: listen to the
> women; they will teach you the meaning of *and*.

He printed it out, sealed, addressed, and stamped the envelope,
finishing just before dawn. He made a note to call Nipak, and Ron
from NASA. Stiff, starting to rise, he realized how much of what
he'd written had come straight from Steph. He felt overwhelmed

with love for her. He sat and punched the GO TO PAGE key. To the cheery green phosphorescent query WHICH PAGE? he punched PAGE 1. There, laying the pulsing cursor underneath the title, he punched INSERT and to the query INSERT WHAT? began to type the dedication.

It was so clear, true, and loving, that as he read it over his eyes filled with tears.

23

MODERN AMERICAN LIVES are difficult to leave for any length of time, and Fine's life was more difficult to leave than most.

To ready himself for the Monday onslaught, Fine fulfilled his promise to Nipak, and sat in his office meditating. Each time, he'd been more able to focus attention on the world around him, and this time he felt quite truly *in* life. His senses intermingled, as if the wires of his brain had regrouped in bold new parity; he could almost hear the sunlight splashing on his arm, see the songs of the birds at dawn. Hungrily, he got up to go to breakfast.

In his waiting room sat an exquisite blond woman. As Fine entered, she stood, seeming glad and surprised to see him. Fine knew he knew her, and struggled to recall how. His mind reverberated: she's dressed in the colors of change, she's dressed in th—

"Dr. Fine!"

"Dora?" he said, without thinking.

" 'Dora'? I'm Duffy!"

As she stood before the window, the sunlight slanted through her filmy dress, edging the shape of her body: facing him in a widespread stance, the jointed flow of both legs up to where all seams meet, and, as she bent to pick up her bag, her breasts hanging freely down. Yet Fine, rather than as before being attracted to parts, was now aroused by the whole—body and aura. Aroused gently, subtly—as, he felt, a woman might be.

She seemed as sensually *there* as if she'd reached out, unzipped him, and cradled him in the velvet of her palm. He got hard. Seeing her seeing his erection bulging his too-tight khakis, he blurted out: "God you look great!" She stared at him. He smiled; she smiled back. Biting her lip, she smoothed her dress down over her hips, threw back her shoulders. He stared, and said: "Tit for tat."

Blushing, hips swaying, thighs going *swish swish* with each step, she led him into the office and lay down on the couch. He sat behind her. Looking up at the ceiling she began to associate (Fine felt this now as odd, the method so *distancing!*): "I've been worried sick, Dr. Fine. Gone for a week with no explanation! My fantasy?: you were sick, hurt, even dead, or—worse—you were fed up with me."

"Sure, sure—but what did you really think?"

Startled, she said, "Don't you want to hear my fantasies—"

"Did you miss me?"

She paused. "Yes. Very much. You're so important to me."

"Am I?"

"Yes. The sudden loss made me realize how much I rely on you. Did you see the papers?—without you, the Federal Reserve went nuts!—the dollar got depressed, the Deutschemärk inflated! For the first time I can say it: I love you. 'Course I know it's safe, here—nothing will happen, despite the attraction between us—I couldn't help noticing you were, uh, excited to see me again . . . I'm desperate to be close to you—emotionally and physically— and I thought that if only we could actually touch—if you'd take my hand, or hug me, or hold me—or even, yes, make love to me —as gentle as I know you are—it would once and for all make me whole. Right now I wish that you'd do that to me, for me, with— *ahh!* What are you doing?!"

Fine sat on the couch facing her, his hip against her thigh.

"Doing?" He felt good, touching: sensual and close.

"Sitting here doing?!"

"Doing what you want me to do." She lay with her hands folded upon each other on her lap, a scared look in her eyes. "Your hands there seem so peaceful. I can almost feel vibrations from you, through them, to me." Smiling, looking into her brown eyes, he lifted his hand and, slowly so as not to frighten her, moved it toward the mound where they rested, two small birds nesting. She stared at him, eyes widening, as in slow motion he placed his hand on hers. He felt sparks fly at the touch. He pressed, gently. "Do you feel it?"

"Y . . . yes . . ."

"Feather soft."

"Oh." She closed her eyes. He pressed down. Her hips moved, so slightly as to be missed except through the crackling in his fingertips. He was startled by her frankly sexual motion, marching in over the gentle gestalt. He could almost see the Fine homunculus spread over his sensory cortex—giant lips and fingers fed by millions of tactile sensors. "I feel such vitality in you. You're a beautiful, sensuous young woman who wants to be held, loved freely. Life's too short for chill, deception. Why hate this body?" Tenderly, his palm on something unimaginably soft, he massaged. His free hand began a delicate *effleurage* up her thigh. "Your body is you—"

She opened her eyes and stared at him like a child awakening to a molester. She cried: "What the hell do you think you're doing, Mister?! I'm not a body, I'm a person—let go!" She flung his hand back—bam!—it hit him in the nose! She jumped up, ran to the door: "I'm reporting you, Fine! You're through! Pervert!"

The pain in his nose brought tears to his eyes. "Wait—I didn't mean—I was just doing some body—"

"Fruitcake!" And she was gone.

Fine sat, puzzled, her accusation ringing in his ears. I hadn't violated her. It wasn't just sexual; it was a new—female—route to her blocked eroticism. He saw headlines—FRUITCAKE DOC BAGGED ON MORALS CHARGE—and felt a twinge of worry. It soon passed. After all, hadn't we learned something?: a wish, fulfilled, vanishes.

Feeling light and airy, he lurched heavily downstairs. He was intercepted by the five Jefferson House early risers and Lafite. They had all gained a lot of weight. They now wore photo ID tags.

"Hey rump buddy," said Cooter, "how they hangin'?"

"Low to the ground, pal," said Fine, "for speed."

Cooter, startled at this, fell silent, mouth agape. Eli the Hassid
said: "Dr. Fine, how'd you get so fat so fast?"

"Discipline." How bloated we all are, even the doggie.

"Ha!" said Cooter, recovering. "So you din't kill 'm after all,
didja doc? We seen 'm, up there in your bedroom winder—"

"Yes, no," said Mr. Jefferson, "we'd never *peep,* would we?"

"If'n you got Jesus in you," said Jefferson, "no need!"

"So Doc," said Cooter, "shoulda been heah for Mother's Day!"

"My mother came," said Eli, weakly, seeming ashen, as if
caught in the delusion that he had recently lived through Dachau.
"Her breasts *are* still growing! They're huge!"

"Bigger'n the Federal Reserve!" said Cooter.

"Dynamite!" said Eli. "Touch them, they'd explode!"

"Sabotage!" screamed Stinko, crouching. "Keel!"

"*Booby* traps?" said Fine, laughing.

Shocked, they fell silent. Their chronic psychotic body gestures
(some, "tardive dyskinesia" from years of meds) exaggerated into
a twitching, shuffling dance. The elder statesman, decked out in
sailor's whites, said: "Yes, er, no, strange words—do we *know*
you?"

"C'mon," said Cooter, "Fine's weirded out. Let's to chow."

"Ciao!" said Fine. Staring at him as if he were mad, they scut-
tled off, jaggedly, stopping from time to time to glance back.

Chuckling, full of affection for them, Fine walked through his
row of cherry trees—all chuffed out in pink puffs—up his path—
now lined with creeping phlox, hardy violet, and the rising shoots
of roses—ducked under the purple racemes of wisteria hanging
over his porch, ignored the *Globe* on his stoop, and went in. Alone
in his kitchen, he unbuckled his too-tight belt, foraging
voraciously for food.

Soon John James joined him. Rubbing sleep from his eyes, he
asked: "Can I have a hot dog?"

"You got it. Here—dip these in that while I cook it up." They
sat at the table chattering, finishing off a bag of Doritos dipped in
La Victoria Salsa Ranchera. Steph and John came in. The menu
changed abruptly. For the lovers, the situation was tense. Yet
Fine, as full of wit and spunk as a kid, soon had them all laughing.

Mrs. Neiderman and Ms. Ando came in, dragging with them

the chaos of the usual. They were puzzled and furious. He'd neglected his work, he'd neglected them. In the week he'd been gone, all hell had broken loose. Grasshoppers and patients had regressed. Ms. Ando said that several of the hoppers had stopped eating, stopped learning. She'd been getting calls from all over the world—even Tibet!—about Finestones.

"What's this company they ask for?" Fine asked what company. "Fine and Dandy, Inc.—what is it?" Fine started to explain, but she got up to go back to the lab. She glanced sharply at John and Steph, and then sweetly at the boy. "What a cutie." She left.

Mrs. Neiderman's news was worse: his patients, abandoned, were decompensating. The Jefferson Housers had gone off their diets and were getting fat. "Your patients all come into my office, moon around—as if I can help them! Everybody's on edge, worried that this mass murderer will strike—the paranoia's unbelievable! Off the wall! Between your poor patients and the tight security by that mad idiot Royce—it's become a real Twinkie factory around here! Oh—that reminds me—the Institute called—asking why you missed last week's seminar, 'The Anus'—do you believe it?—and quote *suggesting* you go tonight." Fine asked what was tonight. " 'Oedipus'—and the police."

"The police?"

"The police artist—he's going to try to use you analysts to sketch a 'psychoanalytic portrait of the killer.' It's mad!" Her face softened, she tucked in her blond hair. "Look, I'm glad you're back. Please, Dr. Fine—we need you—help us—get to work!"

"Hold it," said Steph. "He's had an epileptic fit! He's not going back to work until he's seen a top-flight neurologist."

"Not to worry," said Fine, "there's nothing really wrong—"

"It's so wrong you can't even see it!" said Steph, her voice quivering with tension. "This is a matter of life and death!"

Using professional courtesy, she got an appointment right away with a noted Mass. General neurologist. And on the way to the car John James had his first encounter with Jefferson Housers. He stared, sensing their bizarreness. Frightened, he hid behind his da.

"Yes, er, no," said Mr. Jefferson, "a son."

"Get Jesus inside you," said Jefferson, "or else!"

"Hot damn I 'clare," said Cooter, "jes like me—a boy!"

"No—a goy!" said Eli. "Look at that Aryan hair!"

"Woof!"

In the car, the boy asked: "Can we see Granny Katey today?"

"We don't have time today, John James," said his father, "we've got to take Uncle Fine to the doctor. Maybe tomorrow, okay?"

"No!" said John James, pouting. "Not okay at all!"

While father and son sought to ease the wet heat of the day with an ice cream cone and a ride on the swan boats in the Public Garden, Fine was being given the world's most complete neurological exam. The neurologist, Dr. Gersh Berg, a balding, inquisitive genius, found in Fine the answer to his prayers: the switch in handedness meant a switch in hemispheric dominance from left-brain to right; the right-hemisphere qualities—spatial awareness, intuitive shape-perceptions of people and things, creative vision—were ascendant. Fine revealed his other symptom—his increased sex drive—and Gersh peppered him with barrages of closely cropped questions. When Fine told him how, yes, since the seizure he'd been attracted to sensual wholes (body aura of Dora) rather than to parts (breasts, nipples), Gersh beamed: "Testosterone! Male hormone—you've shorted it out! Your left *planum temporale* is on the fritz! Brain-wise you've become more female—amped up the woman inside. Yet you're still hotly male—witness your erections. Fascinating case!" Fine asked about this *planum temporale.* "Oh—it's the center for language and speech."

"Men and women speak different languages?" asked Fine.

"Ever been married? Left-handed women are in orbit!" Steffy's left-handed, Fine thought, listening, entranced, to *The Berg Theory.* "And so," Gersh finished, "testosterone jazzes up the thymus, which through the immune system distinguishes self from other."

"What?!" Fine cried, jumping up. "Is it empathy?!"

"Empathy?"

"The missing link!" said Fine, seizing him by the shoulders, looking him in the eye. "Between biology and psychology!"

"Quick!" said Gersh, excitedly. "Let's have it!"

"Males have a sharper edge between self and other—a guy can't *feel* what the other guy feels. The 'nuclear mind' is testosterone-jammed—but I've found that calcium, in Finesto—"

"What the hell's going on here?" Steph stood in the doorway, staring. Fine realized how strange they must seem—two intense

Jews nose to nose, flushed with triumph—and let go of Gersh. Reluctantly, as bored by the usual as he'd been stirred by the unique, Gersh told her about Fine's epileptic fit. She asked: "What caused it?"

"Don't know. The tests they did were normal."

"What could it be?"

"Could be nothing—epileptic fits are like marriages—we're each entitled to at least one." Steph asked what would be most likely. "Statistically? Hm. Some god-awful mess like brain tumor, yes—"

"Brain tumor? Oh my God!"

"But it might be nothing, right Gersh?" Gersh nodded.

"He's a totally different person! Is it from the seizure?"

"Could be." Gersh fiddled with his reflex hammer. "Happiness is rare in modern society—his *could* be postictal euphoria." Steph asked if Fine were responsible for his actions. "Hm. Was Dostoevsky responsible? Mohammed? Both, temporal lobe. Shrouds of evidence, even, for Jesus. Responsible? Dunno."

"His new personality—this euphoria—how long will it last?"

"Hm. Could end the next second, could last out his life. Which, if it *is* tumor, might not be all that long anyway, right?"

"Right!" said Fine, rising. "I'm gonna make every minute count! I'm so happy! So so happy!" He fell down, hitting the back of his head, hard, seeing stars. Steph stooped to him. He chuckled.

"Oh—that reminds me," said Gersh, looking down at them, "there *was* one hard sign—his right foot is partially paralyzed."

"Paralyzed?" said Steph, heart sinking. "Like a stroke?!"

"No. Here—" he wrote a prescription. "Go down to Prosthetics—get a leg brace. I'll schedule a CAT scan for next week."

Steph paled with fear. "And it can happen anytime again?"

"So what if it does," said Fine, airily. "I love it!"

"Hm. I wouldn't be driving, or underwater, at the time."

They found themselves in a basement ring of hell where robust physiotherapists tried to temper the decay of the body with gleaming chrome steel. Fine was led away, and Steph sat watching the parade of the bracers and the braced, the battle of nature against nurture. Riffling through the events of her life, she formulated the law of Stephanie Caro: Everything happens with maximum irony.

"Steffy?" She turned. "Lo—The Iron Man."

Fine stood across the room. His right pantleg was rolled up, and there, from knee to toe, was a shiny slatted-and-hinged brace. In his hand was a cane. He looked from her eyes down to his brace, and then back. He saw her face rise in shock, and then fall. Trying to cheer her up, he said: "Watch!" Taking a step—*clunk!* —he felt a shock wave ride up his spinal cord and bounce off the top of his skull. "Ow! This damn thing's awful!" He looked up at her, and saw in her face a faint tracing of stress lines, like the lines of grief that push through the skin of new widows, aging them, and as she rose he saw her mouth wrench down and her eyes fill with tears. Not sad for himself, he felt sad for her. As she came up to him, reaching out her hands, he too felt tearful. He bent his head, she put it on her breast, they cried together. After what seemed an age he said: "It feels good to be held by you, again, Steffy."

"Oh Fine—things seem so fragile—everything's going wrong!"

"I have changed, Steffy, and it is strange, yes. But somehow it's no great disaster. I feel like I'm sitting in a backyard at a picnic— a family picnic on a beautiful sunny day and everyone's getting along—and if I died, well, it'd just be like someone erased *me*, but the picnic would go on. Whatever happens, happens, okay?"

"But you can't see how bad this all is. I'm scared, Fine, scared for you, and me, and for John and that gorgeous kid! I didn't bargain for this. I don't know what to do!"

"But we're all so happy!"

"Dream on! And don't say I didn't warn you. All right, come on, gimpy, let's go." He stood there, staring. "What now?"

"You look like a clown."

She took out her mirror and saw the black lines of mascara carried down her cheeks on her tears. Wiping them away, she saw him in the mirror—his mustache and beard split by his inane broad smile—and despite herself she laughed. She turned to face him, saying: "Remember Pearl Harbor?" He was puzzled. She kicked his cane out from under him: "Sneak attack!" He stumbled, chuckled.

"So when are you going to get back to stand-up?"

"That's all I need now," she said, "comedy."

"But you do—you made a great start—Goldie—go for it."

"C'mon, my little Moonie, let's just face the next wreck."

Rejoining John and the boy, Fine made light of his brace. Out in the rising heat and bright sunlight he ogled women. "Amazing! After the winter, women sprout armpits, and tushies, and boobs!"

"And the men," Steph said, "suddenly have necks."

The boy was cranky. They told him they were now free to do whatever he wished. He said: "I wanna go see Granny Katey!"

"Except that," said John, "we'll see her tomorrow."

"Promise?" John said yes. "I wanna go on the Giant Coaster!"

They drove south to the peninsula of Nantasket, to Paragon Park. They sought the Giant Coaster. Fine bought the tickets. The vendor was a gray-haired dwarf with thick glasses, almost blind. Fine stared; the dwarf's eyes wobbled back. Fine felt weirdly simpatico.

O'Days in the front car, Steph and Fine behind, they were cranked up higher and higher. Apex. As if slung from a net in a hollow of the wind, they rested, magically safe. Dizzily they scanned the panorama—Boston, Stow water tower, Quincy shipyard, hook of Hull, vaporous Atlantic. Steph said: "John James, if you click your eyes open and shut, like a camera, you'll remember this picture forever."

"Really?!" said the boy. "I'm doin' it, Auntie Steph—*now!*"

"Hold on," said his father, "you hold tight! Whoa-ahh—!"

The strings that held them loosed, and down they plunged, screaming and floating and rolling and feeling like puking on and on and on until, gasping and wide-eyed and screaming, they leveled out, coasted in, stopped. The boy wanted to ride it again. John and Steph, queasy, refused. Fine said: "Let's go!" Afterward, the four strolled the midway, swinging hand in hand. A hot day, getting hotter, humidity chased by a flicker of breeze off the sea. To the boy, his father was the bad guy and Fine was the good. On the rides and in the games, Fine and John James were paired.

"He used to be scared stiff of heights!" said Steph to John as they watched Fine standing up rocking the gondola at the top of the Ferris wheel, waving down at them. "It's incredible!"

"I can't stand it. He's better with John James than I am."

After the bumper cars, the wet heat, noise, and slamming were too much for Steph and John. They tried to get Fine to leave.

"After the Tilt-a-Whirl," Fine said.

There he engaged the attendant: a tall, tough-looking black

woman who, joint in mouth, danced the rolling metal-slatted deck of the ride, opening and closing the whirling cars with a graceful aplomb. Fine shared her joint and after a couple of rides he too stood with her, dancing on the sea of buckling iron, high as a kite. Her name was Serena. Fine invited her to visit him out at Stow.

On the ride back the boy napped. When they got to the house, they woke him up. He took Steph's hand and said: "I did it!"

"What's that?"

"Took a pichure with my eyes at the top, 'n' I kin still see it all! You tol' me and it works!" He hugged her. When John tried to carry him inside, he said, "I ain't no baby, Da, leggo—" and ran in alone. John followed him up to his room. Returning, he told Steph: "You made a friend."

"So did he," said Steph. "What a terrific kid!"

"You and Fine are *it,* for him. What'm I doing wrong?"

"Don't try so hard," said Fine. "Don't try to entertain him. You don't have to go for the Academy Award—just be yourself."

"Grand," said John, sarcastically, "just grand. I'll just ignore him, will I? Better yet, I'll just hand him over to you?"

"Oh come on," said Fine, "get the 'Celtic Pride' out of it."

"What makes you such an expert on fathering, anyway?"

"Me?" Fine nodded sagely. "Women's intuition, I guess."

The phone rang. Fine picked it up.

"I'm going to *kill* myself!" said a woman's voice.

"Where are you?" Fine asked, glad Joy was alive. "Wait—" *"Click."*

He smiled. "Almost forgot—I've got to go see my patients."

"What?" said Steph. "Like you are now?"

"You'd rather I see them like I'm *not* now?"

"At least wait until you're better."

"How could I ever be better, hm?"

Steph covered her eyes as if in pain. "Just goes to show, Fine, you were wrong: reality's not a crutch. Reality's a cane."

He chuckled, and left. Stopping just outside the screen door to adjust the brace so it didn't chafe, he overheard her:

"Poor guy! He could be dying! He's like a time bomb, waiting to go off!" Fine smiled beneficently. Who isn't?

With cane and brace he made his way—*tap, clunk*—through the muggy afternoon—seeming to hear in his pores the heat rising —to the gym.

24

PRIAPISM WAS NEW to Fine, and not unwelcome.

He was surprised to feel attracted to Mardell. Fine stood in the doorway. Mardell, in a silvery Cavalier warmup jacket, was taking out his anger at being hospitalized, with a series of slam dunks. Fine thought: what grace! In the far corner, gun on hip, was the vigilant Mr. Royce. Fine nodded, wondering why he was there.

Mardell was frazzled. Drug-free for the first time in two seasons, he was talking fast, mostly about the murderer. He spotted Fine H-O-R-S-, and made his first shot. To their surprise, Fine hit it too. And so it went. Mardell was having a hard time putting Fine under. Fine, still relaxed from Serena's weed, made a few hoops. "He gotta be nuts—who else'd want to kill you little pricks? You don't do nuthin' to make nobody off you—don't do nuthin' at all." Fine felt angry. The game was tied. He let fly with a hook shot. As the ball went up Mardell kept "jukin'," but as it came down his pro eyes told him the worst: *swish!* "Mother fucker!"

"I believe our bet is a 'nickle'?" said Fine, using drug slang for five grand. "Your shot." Mardell came over, spinning and dribbling the ball as if it were part of his huge hand, cursing. He dribbled, spun, and seemed to lay the ball gently up into an arced channel through the air toward the hoop. Long before Fine did, he knew. "Fuck!" *Clang*. Fine laughed, and held out his hand, palm up.

Mardell, his opiate receptors raw, exploded, standing over Fine, threatening to strangle him. A goon squad appeared. As he was led off, he said: "You're a sittin' duck, Fine, so watch out!"

Mr. Royce walked Fine to Jefferson House. Fine asked why he'd been in the gym. "We never sleep," said the grim paranoiac. "That man could kill." Fine, feeling light-headed and wanting to try and cheer up this morose man, asked why he thought so, clapping him on the back. Startled, he felt under his fingertips a hump! A hunchback? "Oh I don't know," said Royce, pulling out quickly from under Fine's touch, scowling, "just a hunch." As Royce walked off, Fine shivered. Such a deformity breeds rage, arrogance, drug and alcohol abuse, madness! Concealment signifies its festering. Most murders are committed on drugs. Expert in guns. Could it be?

By the time Fine made it up to his office, it was almost five. There in the waiting room was a small, mousy-haired woman with an aquiline nose and something wrong with one of her eyes.

"Well!" she said, rising. "It's about time!"

Fine couldn't recall her, which must have meant she was someone he'd begun seeing nearer the time of his seizure, for those memories were still partly wiped out. "Yes," he said, "go on in. I'll be right with you." She went into his office, he into the bathroom. He cradled his turgid penis as the Stow-on-Wold bells— replica of those of Stow's Cotswold namesake—rang the changes —four chords, five chimes. Fine came out into his waiting room.

The woman walked out of his office, shaking her head in disbelief, one eye flared in anger. Fine asked: "Why, what's wrong?"

"I was sitting in your chair and some guy with a big nose and a bushy wild hairdo came in, lay down, and started talking stuff— sick stuff—about his mom. He needs you more than me. I'll wait."

Fine went in, sat behind the couch. The furry supine man took no notice, and continued associating, obsessing about a novel, often saying: "Yes, but I—" Cute, Fine thought. His eyes fell on a paper—*VII: Anal Erotism and the Castration Complex* (1918)— and he recalled: Maurice, a writer; nicknamed Ratman the Obses-

sive. Had Neiderman said something about his coming in, keeping
the analysis going, while I'd been away? Ratman acknowledged
Fine's presence, but minimally. Bored, feeling the deadness of the
analysis of this constipated fellow, Fine clicked on what he would
do. Thinking of Paris, he checked the clock, and then mouthed
the countdown: six, five, four, three, two—

"It's time for us to stop."

"What?" said Maurice. "Did you say something?"

"It's time for us to stop."

"Yes, but it's only five past the hour—"

"It's time for us to stop!"

"Yes, but I'm paying for the whole fifty—"

"Cut the shit, Maurice. *Stop!* Out. Now!"

Wild-eyed, hair quilling out like a raging peacock, Maurice flew
to the doorway: "My lawyer—I'm gonna sue your ass but
good—"

"Stop!"

He went. Fine smiled. The first time in American history that
Lacan's five-minute hour had been used in treatment. Lawyer? So
what? Hadn't they learned something?: a symptom, stopped, goes.

Smiling, Fine opened the door to Four o'clock.

"That was quick," said the woman, sitting down opposite him.

"New technique," said Fine. *"Trés* continental."

"I've been so worried, Stuart!" Her sallow face showed her
concern. "I happened to be there when you had your fit—you
okay?"

"I feel a lot more like I do now than I ever did before."

"Oh good—*what?*" He repeated Eisenhower's joke. She wrinkled her nose, laughed. "Same ole Stu! And listen—I *laughed!*"

"Yeah, so?"

"Don't laugh much now. My sense of humor seems to've died."

"They used to say that about me, too."

"Right—it drew us together—our not getting the other kids'
jokes, didn't it?" Fine remembered now that she'd mistaken him
for her long-lost Tuscaloosa boyfriend, Stuart. She stared at him.
"You know, your leaving last Wednesday reminded me of your
leaving me after high school to come North, and—" she hesitated,
"—and my giving myself to you, that once."

Fine felt her accusation, and fidgeted. She went on, but he
found himself only half-listening, preoccupied by her face. The

prosthetic eye was so ill matched—like a child's "glassy" picked up and used—it threw the whole face into discord. As if in the contest of "good looks" she went around conceding defeat. She was talking about how, after high school, abandoned by "Stu," she'd fallen apart: sleeping around, pregnancy, marriage, baby boy. "When he was two months old, my baby died. Crib death. I just about gave up! Drove my husband out, clear back to Mississippi! Almost killed myself!"

"Where were your mother and father?"

"Daddy was nearby, busy with Green's Wild Animal Farm. Momma?" She took a deep breath. "Never knew her—gone when I was two."

"Died?"

"Left. How could you forget that?"

"You poor woman!"

"Only thing I remember, is, like, a blanket being pulled off my bed, leaving me shiverin'." She fell still. "Did I tell you how I was training for the Boston Mounted Police? Special program, for the handicapped. What I don't know about horses there isn't to be known. It was a great job! And then, after three months, tax cut, no money, they fired me! Do you believe it?"

"Sylvia?"

"Yes?"

"How did you lose your eye?"

She gasped, and fell silent, bowing her head. Fine watched her body tense as she struggled with whether or not to tell him. She looked up; one eye was reddened. "Know what's the worst?" He asked what. "I can only cry out of one damn eye!"

"Tell me about it."

"That's enough for today," she said, rising. "Walk me out?"

He did. They stood at the gate of Fine's house and saw, on the broad emerald lawn flowing down to the sea, John and John James playing soccer. Backlit by the low sun, their blond hair shone, their faces wet with sweat. The father moved with the grace of a natural athlete; the boy, arms and legs flailing, battled for every kick as if it were a matter of life and death. Screeches and laughter rang up the slope. A voice came from Fine's house, and he and Sylvia turned: Steph was on the porch, calling John and John James to dinner.

The boy hesitated, wanting to continue, but the father scooped him up onto his shoulders. Settling himself there, the boy, like the mythical Irish hero Cuchulain rising from the sea, rode the man up toward home.

"What a sight!" said Fine.

As if talking to herself, she said: "After my baby died, I took my neighbor's—just for a day—it helped me get by." The boy and his father came nearer. "Can I see you again tomorrow at four?"

Fine said yes.

At dinner, John told them he'd gotten a call from the Shakespeare Company. In financial trouble, they'd compromised their ideals by taking ten grand from an LA group to showcase *Mother Coward,* a musical comedy with lyrics by Brecht and Coward and music by Weill and Manilow, all set in old Casablanca. The lead couldn't tap-dance very well in water, and so the director, in hysterics, had called John, offering him the role.

"I really want to do it," John said, his eyes bright, the old energy returning. "Got to let him know in half an hour, and be at rehearsal tonight. We go up Saturday. It's only for two weeks."

"It sounds like garbage," said Steph, *"drek.* Is it?"

"Worse: *Drecht."*

"I can't see you doing drek," said Steph.

"But I need to prove I can! I need exposure. Do you know 'The Five Ages of an Actor'?" Animated, he played a series of producers: "Who's John O'Day?; Get me John O'Day!; Just like John O'Day!; Whatever happened to John O'Day?; Who's John O'Day?" They laughed. "You laugh, but my career's stuck! To make it in America I've got to move on from classics and star in garbage. From garbage to garbage, till I get my big break: Broadway-TV-film—*Big-Time Garbage!* Big green bucks! Then—then! —back to Shakespeare, Chekhov, okay? Theater folk are drek— just like me. This could be it!"

"But what about our act?" Steph's voice showed her hurt.

"Look," he said, taking her hands, *"you're* the stand-up, not me. I can't do it, you can. You've got to get up there alone."

Fine was struck again by John's crassness, and falseness. His friend had joined those who were leaching reality from the real world, overlaying it with image. Surprised at John's not considering the effect on the boy, he said: "What about this little guy, eh?"

"Right," said John. "I'll only do it if it's okay with him."

"You mean actin', Da, like you did in Dublin?"

"That's right—remember you came to the Abbey to see me?"

"An' mum, too! It's okay, but fer one thing." He laid his head on Fine's shoulder. "Will Unky Fine stay here wi'me?"

"Sure I will, kiddo," said Fine, "sure."

"Wait," said Steph, "don't you have a seminar tonight?"

"No problem," said Fine, "I'll take him with me."

"What?" said Steph. "To the Institute? You will not!"

"Tonight's 'The Penis/Oedipus'—he's the perfect age!"

"Hold it, Fine," said John, "I don't want a bunch of shrinks putting weird ideas into my son's head."

"Relax—analysts never *do* anything." He ruffled the boy's hair. "We'll show 'em, eh kid? Presenting, live, in the flesh: Oedipus. Reality testing. Psychoanalytic history in the making."

Fine being at risk for another seizure, Steph refused to let him drive. The four went into Boston together. Dropping John at the Shakespeare and Fine and John James at the Institute, Steph went to check out what the *Globe* called the "boom" of comedy clubs.

Fine and the boy stood between the two blossoming magnolias. The buds were the size of blacksmith's hands, and a *soupçon* of lavender came through faintly, like a zephyr of pine scent through a humid night from across a wooded lake. Fine tried to recall the night's password. He'd gotten it from the TBI secretary earlier in the day. She'd told him of the latest scandal: the director of the Freud Archives had been dismissed for quoting an unexpurgated letter from Freud to Fliess that suggested that Freud's abandonment of the "seduction theory of neurosis" (the women *really* were seduced), in favor of the "intrapsychic theory of neurosis" (the women were *in fantasy* seduced), stemmed not from Freud's objective scientific enquiry but rather from his wish to cover up the reality of his own father's "perverse acts." The fired archivist said: "Psychoanalysts would now have to recall every patient since 1901. It would be like General Motors recalling the Pinto." How silly, Fine thought, it's not *either/or,* it's *and.* To have been *really* in Auschwitz; to have *fantasized* being in Auschwitz—*both* are of vital import to a human, to humanity. Any theory that fails to encompass both, artfully, fails. Why do humans insist on hacking the world apart, crating it up? Then, recalling the letter suggesting Freud's schtupping his sister-in-law, Fine said: "Minna Bernays."

The door opened.

Fine sat John James in the hallway with a *National Geographic* and a Drake's Ring-Ding Junior. Having missed "The Anus" last week, devoted to working through Reuben's death, Fine knew that, except for his ally Georgina and the neutral Vergessen, he was entering enemy territory. He took a deep breath and went in.

Three policemen were in the room. One sat in the corner sketching the psychoanalytic portrait of the killer. Late, Fine sensed the castigation, and sat next to Georgina. As usual they were going around the table in order. He'd missed his turn. As the last three analysts-in-training free-associated out loud, it seemed to Fine an impossible task for the artist to sketch anything coherent at all. Just before eight, Vergessen called a halt. The police artist—a slim gay Irishman—ogled the handsome young men in their pinstripes, and then, with a flair for the dramatic, whirled the sketchpad around. There were gasps, and then silence.

It was quite a good likeness of Fine.

25

They all stared at Fine until Vergessen cleared his throat and said: "Yes, and as Freud put it: 'Psychoanalysis is the study of self-deception.' If the police will leave, it is time for Oedipus."

Suggesting that, since clues were few, they'd appreciate Fine's coming by the station the next day for a chat, the cops left.

"Why do we kill?"

Vergessen introduced the theme for "The Penis/Oedipus" and sat down. Dr. Leon Bergeneiss, the Jungian with the pocked face and bushy black hair who'd been Reuben's ally, had volunteered to take over, and was pitted against Fine as codiscussor. Dr. Pete Gross, bald, big, so good with the dying, began the précis of the text:

> "Das Ich und das Es, 1923: I. Consciousness and Unconsciousness. In this preliminary chapter there is nothing new to be said and it will not be possible to avoid repeating what has often been said before. . . ."

As Gross plodded on, Fine floated off. Being so much into body, he felt impatient with this speculation on mind. The truth, Oedipal or no, lay in the flesh. One can't be down or bored or in combat with an erection. He turned to Georgina. She was facing away, seemingly absorbed. She wore a sleeveless blouse, and as Fine watched, she raised her arm and stroked her punky, geld-streaked—God what a slip!—*gold*-streaked hair. Castration complex indeed. His eyes were drawn to the shape of shaved armpit curving into breast. He felt himself surfing down that wave of skin, in under the bra, pushing against the soft blancmange with his "divining rod." He no longer yearned to *do* something to a part of her, but rather to *be* with her, skin to skin, cock in cunt, sensually. He scribbled a note, passed it to her: "Hey, Titty Babee, wanna feel Me?" As she read it her neck flushed red. Nonchalantly she wrote: "Where and when?" Fine grinned: "Here and now." She: "If you can hide Your Big Cock under the table, sure!" He moved his chair—*scraack*—closer to her, and unzipped. She reached over, touched it—*zing!*—a jolt of electricity shot through him! She fondled him gently.

> "Pathological research has centered our interest too exclu-sively on the repressed. . . ."

Up and down she milked him, sometimes tickling the little orifice with the nail of her pinky. Fine slipped his hand up under her skirt, nails digging into her thigh. They went on, kids playing doctor, hiding it from the grown-ups, until—

"Dr. Pintzer?" said V., calling her out of turn.

Amazingly, without taking her hand from his penis, she quoted the seminal passage describing the ego in relation to the id:

> "It is like a man on horseback, who has to hold in check the superior strength of the horse; with this difference, that the rider tries to do so with his own strength while the ego uses—*(squeeze)*—borrowed forces. . . . Often a rider, if he is not to be parted from his horse, is obliged to guide it where he wants it to go; so the ego is in the habit of trans-forming the id's will into action as if—*(hard tug—whimper —Fine)*—as if it were its own."

What a trooper, Fine thought, and zipped up.

Leon spoke, making solid, insightful points laced with hard case material, about the Oedipus, the pivotal conflict in Freud.

"To put it colloquially: little boys wish to slay their fathers and sleep with their mothers." He went on, his only deviation from Freud being, lastly, a mention of Jung: "The Oedipus is an *archetype,* i.e., has existed across culture and throughout history forever. Thanks."

"Dr. Fine?" asked Sean Vergessen.

Fine rose. "Know something? I'm not so sure that the Oedipus is accurate anymore. Freud, alive today, might agree." There were murmurs of disapproval. Fine chattered on, ending with: "Maybe we men wish to slay our mothers and sleep with our fathers? How scared we are of intimacy with mother: how keenly, as babies, we felt mother's distance, as she first looked at her little boy and said to herself: 'Oh my God!—I'm the mother of a future *man!*'"

"That, Dr. Fine," said Leon, "is the most ridiculous thing I ever heard! Every bit of analytic data points to—"

"Why not let him finish?" asked V.

"Why so upset? It's a loving act—a body act—we go *toward* father out of love, not out of fear of castration. Ever seen a little boy play with his dad? The evidence is before your eyes!"

"What evidence?" asked Leon. "Where?"

"Glad you asked," said Fine, clunking out, hearing in the hallway their riled voices. He returned with John James.

"What's this?" asked Leon.

"This, Leon, is a little boy, almost six. By your timetable, in the throes of wishing to kill his dad and sleep with his mom."

"Too far, Dr. Fine," said Leon. "This is unethical!"

The boy took one look at Vergessen and said: "Jeez, Unky Fine, he looks just like Santy Claus!"

A hush. The boy had said what each had thought—even said behind V.'s back—but to *say* it to him? What would the great V. do?

"What's your name, little feller?" asked V., smiling, his voice twanging. Shock spread round the room. Hick talk, from him?

"John James Michael O'Day the Second."

"Can we ask you a few questions?"

"Aye."

And the most remarkable thing happened: under psychoanalytic cross-questioning, John James said that no, he did not wish to kill his father. Nor did he want to sleep with his mother. In fact he was happy to be with his da again, relieved to be away from his mum. "Yes, sir," he said to one of Leon's questions, "I *wanna* sleep with da! 'e said I could, too, if 'e wasn't sleepin' with Aunt Steph. So tonight I'm sleepin' down the hall, with Unky Fine." That did it. The boy was led out. Things got ugly. Hanging dirty laundry in the Institute?

"Wait a second," said Gross, "who are the players here? Don't I recall that this Steph is Dr. Fine's—"

"The child," said Georgina, staunchly, "confirmed Dr. Fine's viewpoint: he's moving toward his father out of love, not fear—"

"He's saying that because he's repressed," said Leon, scars flaking white on his cheeks. "His castration anxiety is sky-high!"

"Castration anxiety?" Fine smiled. "Another myth."

"What?" Leon looked, smiling, at Sean Vergessen. "Oh, yes?"

"Freud said," Fine went on, "that fear of castration is greater in the male, making for a more punitive superego, a stronger morality in men than women, right?" They agreed. "Yet this is not so. Look around: which gender's about to blow up Mother Earth? And which gender's holding up their babies, saying: 'No, it's immoral, stop! We won't be this generation's "good" Germans, hell no!'"

"Dramatic, Dr. Fine," said Leon, "but let's leave sociology to the sociologists. Query: has this boy been analyzed?"

"Why should he?" said Fine, "he's a normal five-and-a-half."

"Can't be," said Solarz, expert in narcissism, "he's not in a *normal* Oedipus." He grinned as if this were a genius-class comment.

Leon said: "Come on, Fine: has he ever been in treatment?"

"Don't know. But it's not exactly the rage in Ireland."

"Which may explain the violence there," said Gross.

"Words are so fickle," said Fine. "I'm more into the body."

"The 'body'?" asked Gross, puzzled. "What do you mean?"

"Body is *it,*" said Fine. "Your body is *you!*"

"Not mine," said Leon, edgily. "I'm no body, I'm a self!"

"Tell that to your acne," said Fine.

Leon's eyes popped, his hand went to his face, and just as it seemed he'd explode, he said—"Bermuda!"—and fell still. No one knew what to say. The silence hung heavy over the group.

"It's time for us to stop." All left. No one said good-bye.

Fine left with Georgina, and, taking John James by the hand, strolled along Commonwealth Avenue to find the boy an ice cream cone. Georgina said she'd heard rumors of his seizure, and asked about it. He rolled up his pantleg, showing her his brace. When she heard the details, she lit up: "Let me do some body work on you!"

"What?" asked Fine, envisioning another few rounds in her bout to work through her vaginismus. " 'Body work'?"

"You bet," said Georgina. "I'm learning Feldenkrais Body Awareness—get at the mind by digging in through the body. Away from the glandular, into the musculo-skel—penetrate that body armor! Your head's seized up, right?" Fine nodded. "Let me free it, okay?"

She drove them to Stow. As they tucked John James in he said: "Them people down there made me t'ink 'a St. Brendan's."

"St. Brendan's?"

"The asylum behind where I live. Same look in their eyes!"

Stripped to his striped boxer shorts, stomach-down on the living room rug, Fine subjected himself to Georgina's hands. For some reason, even though the turmoil was in his head—on the left side at that—Georgina went for his right shoulder blade. She moved it up and down, back and forth, and then, using fingers as blunt instruments, dug in under, rocking the fascial planes. At first, unaccustomed to the sensation, Fine yelped with pain and struggled away, but with her saying he had to "go into the pain and through it, freeing the pain to move around," he relaxed, and felt a calm come, spreading from his right shoulder blade across the spine and, yes, up into his skull. Her words lulled him: "Ida Rolff is rough and tough, Feldenkrais is funky; Ida Rolff is rough and tough . . ."

Just when Fine began to feel suffused with a syrupy inner wholeness—similar to what he'd felt occasionally in meditation with Nipak—Steph and John came in.

Steph was shocked: "Oh no—what now?"

Fine rolled over, sat up, and said: "Hi! I'm being Feldenkraissed. Remember Dr. Georgina Pintzer?"

"Christ, man!" said John. "What's happened to your ears!"

"What do you mean?" Fine asked.

"They're bright red, and big as Dumbo's!"

Steph handed him her pocket mirror. "Incredible!" said Fine. "But I thought we were going for my clotted left hemisphere?"

"We are," said Georgina. "It's coming out your ears!"

They adjourned to the basement of the gym, the padded bench used for electroconvulsive shock. She finished him off.

Feeling full of oxygen-rich blood and affection, Fine walked Georgina out to her car. The morning paper had brought news that a scientific study had proved that trees do in fact send out warning signals when threatened by insects, and as Fine and Georgina stood beneath the massive copper beech, feeling the salty wind winnow the husks from the leaves, Fine felt so sanguine, so brimming with warm cuddly Spinozan love for all things living, that, with his arms around her waist and her head nesting in his goatee, he pressed their two ears against the gray trunk. "Ah my elephant!" said Fine. "When I was a kid, I saw on TV how they tamed a wild elephant: they put one tame elephant on either side and walked around the stockade, sides touching, until the wild one got the idea. I keep thinking therapy should be like that, shouldn't it?"

"Like parenting, yes. Oh, Fine, I feel so close to you tonight! With your marriage breaking up, the door's open, right?"

"I'm not into dichotomies. No more taxonomy, okay?" He too felt close to her, and was startled that the closeness itself—more than, say, the weight of her breasts on his wrists—gave him such pleasure. Tactile pleasure! Are women wrapped in different skin? Do they *feel* so differently from men? He hugged Georgina tenderly, nibbling her nape. Nuzzling, they parted.

On his answering machine was a message from the Aer Lingus stewardess, "Naked in Phoenix and wet as the dew in Skibbereen." At eleven, as he sat in the living room with milk and cookies and Chef-Boy-Ar-Dee Shark's Fin Soup while watching a beautiful blond newscaster narrate a filmclip of six cocoa-skinned people being shot, there was a bang on the window—the killer?—and he hit the floor. Hearing his name, he edged over and saw, in the black, the gleam of white teeth. Who should it be but Serena, of the Tilt-a-Whirl Serenas. Fine let her in.

She did not want to chat. As they turned to climb the stairs they saw the little boy scurry back to bed. In Fine's bedroom Serena lit up a joint and took off all her clothes and lay down on the bed. Her breasts flattened to the side like flat tires, but Fine was pumped up. He unzipped his pants and out sprang his penis.

"Hey, hey," said Serena, "not bad for a li'l honkey." Fine smiled. "Whachu call it?"

Never having called it anything, he blurted out: "Caesar!"

"Yeah? Lookit it throb! Yeah!"

"Now, now," Fine said, grandiloquently, "we come not to praise Caesar, but to bury him."

"No foolin'. Le's do it!"

And with a squeal of delight Fine leaped to the breech. He thought: I'm doing it! For the first time I'm actually doing it with another woman besides Steph! At that thought, Caesar dropped as if shot. Serena chuckled. Fine tried to focus all his attention on the limp bird lying in her bush but the more he focused the more limp it got until his whole being was straining hard, hard at work on the one vacationing part. The harder he tried the softer it got. Serena was just about busting a gut laughing. Fine suggested they "rap" about it, but, rolling another joint she said: "You kiddin'? No problem, happen all the time. Here—you puff on dis, I be puffin' on dat."

They did. They did it. The noise they made doing it, Steph was later to describe, was like someone sawing wood—*"wshzt, wshzt!"* It awoke both John and her from a sound sleep. At first they had no idea what was going on, until they heard a woman's voice—"Ree ree ree—" and they knew. Was it the plump Georgina from the Institute? The sound turned into a Motown song: "Ree ree ree ree-*spect!*, jes a li'l bit!" Not Dr. Pintzer of the Institute at all.

"It can't be!" said John. "The one from the Tilt-a-Whirl?"

"Sick!" said Steph. "Totally unbalanced! Sick!"

Fine, ecstatic, said to himself: "I did it! I tied his record! I've slept with at least as many women as Sigmund Freud!"

Later, as they slept, Serena arose, picked the house clean of valuables, and walked out happily into the warm, mossy night.

26

"GRANNY KATEY!" shouted the boy. Jumping from the scraggly grass border down onto the coarse, mussel-shell–strewn sand, he ran across Carson Beach and plunged into the lap of his grandma. She'd come to Ireland several times. They loved each other intensely.

It was noon the next day. John, Steph, and Fine followed him, slowed by Fine's difficulty negotiating the sand with his brace. John said: "A Tuesday, and the beach is packed? Nobody works anymore at'all!" John reintroduced Steph to his mother and her friend Mrs. Curley. The two tiny grande dames, despite the rising noontime heat, were bundled up in hats and veils, perched like queen birds in the midst of their colony of Irish. Katey received Fine and Steph coolly. She still viewed them as the two who'd led her son astray at Harvard, away from her and his roots. Steph had arranged an interview at a comedy club—to be followed by an afternoon's shopping—and soon took her leave. Fine and John walked her partway back to the Jag. She stared at Fine—Panama hat, florid Hawaiian shirt, jungle-green shorts—and as if talking to a child said: "You must be careful, Fine. Stay with John; don't do anything without asking him."

"Why should I have to ask him?"

"Because you've lost your balance!" she said, care mixed with exasperation. "You're not in your right mind. John—I'm holding you responsible, understand?" John said he did. "I'll pick you up at about three." She left. They rejoined Katey and the boy.

"Well, Mrs. O'Day," said Fine, cheerily, "how are you?"

"I'm fine."

He stared at her. For a man mistaken for other men to have so many others looking him straight in the eye and saying—"I'm Fine"—was still troublesome. He felt his new reaction to be a message from his revved-up right hemisphere: in each and every other person there was a person *like* him. He saw himself as having more of, or more clearly having, this harmonic: Fine. Life? Fine tuning.

"I wanna go in now, Da," said John James, "pleeze?"

Katey stripped him to his trunks. John and Fine stripped too. Fine was wearing a day-glo green bikini. His gut bulged down over it, and it bulged down too, as if holding significant weight. The old women looked away; the young women, toward. The boy, all plump legs and rubbery knees and churning arms, ran into the water, splashing, spray arcing rainbows into the steamy daylight. John followed with a flamboyant bellywopper, and the two began flipping and rolling in the sea, slick white seals at play. What fun! Fine thought. Yet as he watched he felt apprehensive: John again was performing for, not playing with. The little boy seemed shy, even cowed. Fine turned his attention to the parade of flesh. He zeroed in on the pubescent girls, and felt mixed yearnings: to make love to them; to *be* them. Vagina envy? He drew genitalia in the sand with his cane.

John, nervous about giving the boy his freedom to chase the newborn tiny crabs with a boy named Mickey, sat with Fine and the ladies. The wind was such that the jets screamed down low over them, cutting swaths through the conversation. Katey said their room was all ready for them—after all, hadn't she expected them the day before? "Ah, to have my boys safe under my own roof will be grand!"

Unwilling to tell her yet, John glanced at Fine and picked up the tabloid, the *Herald*. The governor had won the trifecta at Wonderland Dog Track. John asked, "How's the tax protest going?" Coyly, Katey told him to turn to the centerfold. There they saw a photo of Katey and Mrs. Curley roped to the wheel of a firetruck in the D-Street station. "Hello—what's this?" he said. "Your man on the committee's been indicted for kickbacks but refuses to resign?"

"And why should he?" asked Katey, indignantly.

"How's the poor politician to make a livin' anyway, at the salary they pay, unless he's taking a bit extra?" said Mrs. Curley. "They all do it; if it didn't go to him it'd go to someone else."

"If it weren't for it," said Katey, "who'd take these jobs then, eh?" She seemed angry. "The real pain is the mayor—"

"Oh! I'd love to kick 'im in 'is wherevers!"

"Kevin's corrupt?" asked Fine, innocently.

"'e's sly!" said Mrs. C. "They'll never get 'im! 'e's layin' off our boys—laid off my Jimmy, an' after all he did for 'im too!"

"But," said John, "you voted to cut spending, in Proposition Two—"

"No we did not! We voted to lower taxes, right, Katey?"

"But then you have to cut services," said John.

"Who says?" said Mrs. Curley. "Who said that?"

"There's no money to pay them!" said John, hotly.

"There is!" she said. "There's always money, oh yes!"

"Where?"

"Payoffs," she said. "Why's 'e lettin' *firemen* go? How's Jim to live? He should let less essential ones go—like his chauffeur—"

"Cousin Fingus?" said Katey. "You'd 'ave 'im out of work?"

"Oh!" said Mrs. Curley. "Sorry. What about Parkman House?"

"What? Why those jobs 'ave been The O'Nack's for years!" Katey thought hard, and said: "Kevin's personal secretary?"

"Tooty McToole? Our own 'go-through'? Katey! Shame!"

"Oo!—I didn't t'ink—must be this terrible heat!"

"See?" said John. "Everyone's on the payroll! You can't fire anyone in Boston! Cut taxes and keep jobs? Never happen!"

"My relation—James Michael Curley—did it, didn't he? We're sittin' on a beach he built, are we not?" Her eyes narrowed. "If Hahvid hadn't stuck those aristocratic notions into your 'ead, Johnny, you'd not be lookin' down your nose at your own this day!"

John blew up. "Curley? The most corrupt mayor in Boston history? Curley makes Kevin look like Snow-fookin'-Wh—"

"John!" said Katey, "you hush!"

"Troublemaker!" cried Mrs. Curley, taking off her hat and waving it toward a group of beach chairs. "Billy Curley, c'mere!"

A big-bellied pig-eyed man carrying a Schlitz and wearing a "Thank God I'm Irish" hat arose and came splayfootedly toward them. Fine, sensing trouble, gathered their clothes, and tried to drag John away. Billy arrived, and Mrs. Curley told him of John's insults. Billy suggested Fine and John might wish to "move along."

"Well then Billy," said John, "I see you're at work today?"

"I'm warnin' ya, Johnny—"

"Dr. Fine, you see before you a miracle: this man is present in two different places at the same time: while he seems to be here at the beach, there are those who will swear on the Holy Bible that he is, at this very moment, guarding the door of the State House—"

"Argh!" roared Billy. "Faggot actor!" He attacked.

"No heavy lifting, thirty grand a year, and who's paying his salary?" said John, dancing away. "Us! You, me, these two ladies —Ow!" He fell back, caught by a haymaker. Billy rushed him again, but John, crouching, ducked under the swinging arm and, battering his head into the fat gut, used the hulk's momentum to lift him and toss him up, over his head, and throw him down— whomp!—on his back. He lay there gasping, the wind knocked out of him. Fine tugged frantically at John's arm, until he saw Billy turn on his side and retch. John swept Fine's Panama in a courtly bow. They went toward L Street.

Exhilarated, John said: "Who'd've thought it?—stage fighting actually works? God that felt great! I taste blood—where—?"

"Your lip," said Fine. "A little cut on your lip."

"Grand, just grand! Let's go to the Bellevue—The Uncle always said I never got into enough fights—wait—where's John James?" They saw him playing near the L. They called, he came running with his new pal. They said they were going to the Bellevue.

"I wanna come too, Da."

"You can't—it's a bar. Go back to Granny—"

"It's Th'Uncle's bar—lemme come with ye—"

"Go to Granny Katey, now—"

"No!"

"Yes! Go on, right now, y'hear?"

The boy looked at Mickey, puffed out his chest. "No!"

"Hey, kid," said Fine, "watch." He pressed his finger on the boy's shoulder, bringing a cry of pain. "You're already sunburned, you go back there and get covered up."

John James kept saying no. Finally John, fed up, really let loose, screaming: "Shut up—*right now*—and go do as you're told!"

The boys—and Fine—fell silent. Without a word, the little guy turned and walked off. From a safe distance he yelled: "Dingus! My da's a *dingus!*" He walked down the tideline with his buddy.

"Christ what came over me? I was a monster! He hates me!"

"It's okay. Kids always forgive."

"I didn't. Shit!" He walked away fast, so that Fine, limping, could hardly keep up. At the mouth of L Street they looked back. The boy was staring at them. Seeing them stop, he turned away. The silence was a shroud—heavy, dark, gloomy. Fine felt John's pain:

"You're thinking of your own father, aren't you?"

John looked at him, surprised. He sighed. "Yeah. This place—this heat—brings it all back. On a day like this he walked away, and I never saw him again. Never *alive* again. Father O'Herlihey decided I was too young to visit him in Boston City. Next time I saw him, two months later, was the wake. He looked like he was made of wax. People were telling stories, laughing; a few, crying . . ."

"You never cried?"

"How could I? He wasn't my da, he was made of wax."

"You never got to say good-bye to him."

"Nope." He looked down at Fine, his eyes pleading. "Fine, I'm scared. I don't know what the hell I'm doing with him. I don't know when to come down hard and when to lay off, I don't even know when to be with him and when to leave him alone. It's bad, man, bad!" Fine began to reassure him. "No, no—it's something fucked up about *me*. I'm an actor; I can act but I can't *be*. Real and acting get all mixed up inside and I can't tell the difference anymore."

"Just because you're a gifted actor doesn't mean—"

"Not even that! I always thought acting was dissembling, pretending to be somebody else. Not at all! Real acting's the opposite of dissembling—it's being, onstage, not seeming to be. Me? I just put on a mask—trade my offstage mask for my on."

"Oh come on, don't be so hard—"

"That's why I'm doing this garbage. I can't act, but maybe, with my looks, if I'm lucky, I can get into film or TV. There's no real acting in film, 'cause it's not live. No wonder it's taken over— a dead medium for all the dead souls. 'Twitch' acting—get in a close-up and twitch. I'm a failure, Fine—I can take failing as an actor—but to fail with my own *son?*"

"You are not a failure with—"

"Listen—I don't know how to be a father! I was okay when he was younger, but—" He shook his head, amazed. "Time's so different when you have a child!—six years ago seems like last week, and last week seems like six years ago! There's always such commotion, with a kid—you never seem to take the second step in anything—nothing seems to happen—and then you look up and suddenly it's his fourth birthday party! Last summer in Dublin, things began falling apart: for the first time, I didn't know how to be his da. It's like a cancer, now—cold, clawing at me. I feel so confused. Why?"

"How old were you when your own father died?"

"I was six and—" John stopped, surprised. "Is that it?"

Fine smiled. "You never got it, so how can you give?"

"A repetition? *Unreal!*" He hesitated. "But can I learn?"

"Can't help but learn. As long as you just show up. I'm starting to think that showing up is half of life—at least half—"

"And *not* showing up is the other half. That's why theater sucks—theater folk are rarely *there*. But can I change?"

"I'll help you; so will Steph, and so will the boy. We'll pool what we know. And what we don't know, too. Deal?"

John stared down at him, and Fine felt, for the first time again, connection, the rebirth of the old friendship. Fine opened his arms to him. John bent down and put his head on Fine's shoulder. As they had done in college—joking, then—the little guy hugged the big. They stood there. Passersby stared. John straightened back up, biting his lip to keep back tears. "Why aren't you jealous, Fine?"

"Don't know. It seems right for you to be with her now."

"Is it?"

"Seems to be."

"I always thought that if a man had a dream, he'd be all right. But now, believe it or not, I'm thinking the opposite."

"Why not both?"

"Yeah. How 'bout a drink?"

"First, these." Fine reached into his pocket and came out with two Finestones and a cat's eye marble. He handed a Finestone to John, took one himself. Plop. Suck. Plop. Suck. He stared at the marble, tried to figure how it'd gotten there—the boy?—and, failing to do so, followed his pal firmly into the Bellevue.

The Uncle, having nearly mangled Fine the last time they'd met, the night of John's birthday party, was surprised to find Fine so much changed: "You're actin' like a human bein', lad, God bless you!" He wanted to talk about the "murtherer." Detective O'Herlihey and The Uncle had been meeting regularly to try and solve the case, and the homicide detective had just been there, before being called away suddenly a short time ago. There on the bar—stained with brown circles of dried Guinness—was a map of Greater Boston: an attempt on their part to find a pattern in the events. "See?" said The Uncle, proudly, "we found it—a *locus!* Do you see it?"

"The map? How could we miss it?" said John.

"Not the map, man, the *pattern!* C'mere, c'mere." Fine blocked his nose to the warm gummy breath. The Uncle explained: each damp circle of beer was centered on the location of a murder. The first, in Brookline on Sunday April second; the second, five miles east on Lewis Wharf, Sunday April thirtieth; the third, Reuben, between the two, May first. "You see the pattern?" asked The Uncle, craftily. They said that they did not. "Oh Jesus, listen: between the first two, four weeks passed exactly, and the killer's moving east! An' tell me: what is it that 'appens every twenty-eight days?"

"The moon," said John.

"Yer menstrual periods, aye! So it's got to be a . . . ?"

"A woman?" Fine said.

"Herself! And is she not movin' east, toward . . . ?"

"The ocean," said John, "all this blue on the map."

"Not so fast, Mr. My Nephew. There's an island in the way."

"Stow-on-Wold?" said Fine. He felt a chill.

"A place crawlin' with headshrinkers, is it not?"

"Wait," said Fine, "what about Reuben, this circle here? One day later, and in between the two. There's the end to your pattern."

"Not if the pattern is *mental,*" said The Uncle, craftily. "At first me and The O'Herlihey were t'inkin' the next hit's a month off, out at Stow. And then this 'appens, and we t'ink some more— we may've banjaxed our brains completely, t'inkin so hard—how does it fit?" They asked how. "That's what I'm aboot to tell ya, men!" The Uncle leaned over, clopping each in back of the neck. "The killer's headin' toward Stow. An' who's the only shrinker from Stow who's a candidate at the Frood Institute on a sartain Monday night the forst a' May?" He turned his gap-toothed face toward Fine. Pressured, Fine asked: "Me?"

"Is it you?"

"Yes."

"Just as we figgered! Yer locus points to only one porson—you! An' isn't it the thruth that you had words with victim Reuben just 'afore the killin'? Aboot a sartain matter you shrinkers call the 'transistence' I do believe?"

"My God!" said Fine. "But why wasn't *I* the one to get it?"

"That's the braintwister!" said The Uncle. "Why, man, why? It's almost like she's stickin' up fer ya, settlin' yer scores!"

"C'mon, Uncle," said John. "The thing doesn't fit."

"But it does—Dr. Fine's the only porson linked to 'im."

"Why me?"

"Why indeed?"

"Strange," said Fine, "but I *have* felt the threat coming closer. Each victim has been closer, in credo, to the Institute."

"One t'ing's clear: the killer is someone who knows ya."

"A patient of mine?"

"Who said that?" The Uncle was indignant. "Don't jump to the false conclusion, man! Stick to yer locus, y'hear?"

"Sorry," said Fine, pulling at his goatee.

"Forgiven. Yer not as versed in this as The O'Herlihey an' meself. Now—there's one top-secret clue—what they call the key to the case, cuz it's kept from the press—suggestin' the woman's been in therapy before—c'mere—" They leaned in. "The killer writes, in blood on the victim, a message: 'Therapist = The/rapist.' Amazin', in't? Sets the old steel balls clackin', does it not?"

Fine shook himself, as if to awaken, and said: "But I can't

believe that anyone I know would actually murder someone, no way."

"Dammit *listen:* not someone you know: someone who knows *you!*"

Meanwhile, I was later to learn, Katey, seeing the sunburn on the boy's shoulders, had gotten him to go inside. The sun was hot. The next day was supposed to be even hotter. A heat wave was coming. They crossed Day Boulevard and headed toward the house. Mrs. Curley peeled off toward City Point, promising to call later. They passed a church with a high brick wall. Upon the wall was written: NIGGER GO HOME!

"What's 'nigger' mean, Granny?" asked John James.

She told him. He told her about the big black man, Jefferson. She was mildly interested. He told her about Serena. She was very interested, and asked more about her. The boy had been warned by his father not to say anything about Stow to anyone. Gleefully, he said: "Last night I seen Unky Fine go sleep with Serena."

"Oh? And where did your da sleep?"

"He slept with Aunty Steph."

That was that. She led him upstairs to his room for his nap and waited for her son to return.

Fine and John walked right into the blast. Katey let loose with a torrent of anger and hurt, ending with: "—and my grandson will not spend another minute with you perverts, no!"

"He will," said John. "He'll do what I say he'll do—"

"Over my dead body! I'll have the police on you! Mrs. Curley always said they'd get you on a morals charge—and you were tryin' to talk to *me* about corruption? For shame!"

The boy, awakened from his nap, wandered in, and Katey held him to her and said: "Don't you want to stay here with me, Johnny?"

"Oh can I? Yes!"

"Hands off!" said John, reaching for him. But she held on, and they started screaming at each other, and soon the boy, tugged this way and that, was crying. "I'm his father—"

"What kind a father are you? I'm callin' the vice squad—"

"Don't take me away, Da, pleeze!"

"See that? Your boy knows what's right!" She blocked the door with her body, spreading her arms, leaning back against it.

"Get out of my way!" John said. "Now!"

"You'll 'ave t' kill me forst! If your own da were a—*oops!*" She fell backward as the door swung open.

A short, solid, elegantly dressed woman stood there.

"Nora?" said John.

"And in luck," said Nora, "where the hell have you been?"

"Best not to come in now, Nora," said Katey.

"You've got your car?" asked John.

"Bodies like this don't ride bicycles," said Nora. She looked around, saw the carnage, and said: "The motor's runnin'."

"Let's go!" said John, and, pushing Fine ahead, carrying the boy in his arms, started for the door.

John James squirmed out of his grasp: "No! I don't wanna—"

"Hush!" John screamed at the top of his voice. "You hush! Not another damn peep outa ya, John James, or else! Now c'mon!"

The little boy, scared, fell still, and then turned and marched out on his own. John followed. As they got into the burgundy Rolls they heard Katey shouting:

"You never learnt it, but it's the truth: 'The Kingdom of God is within you!' And furthermore—"

Her words were lost as the four doors went *thunk!* The boy, sitting between Fine and John in the cool black leather back seat, folded his arms in a proud and colossal sulk.

27

NORA LIVED IN a mansion on the highest hill in Newton, a suburb west of Boston. They got out of the air-conditioned Rolls, were smacked by the wet heat, and entered the cool stone villa. Her two children—Christina, ten; Conal, seven—soon led John James back outside, to play with a yellow-green Nerf-ball. While Nora organized lemonade, John and Fine followed them out. The sudden panorama took their breath away: every vista, free space! Far below to the east, gauzed by the heat and the haze of pollution, the toy buildings of Boston. The kids, after chasing each other around the towering white flagpole, hit the jungle gym and swings, sculpted out of a pine grove that fenced Nora's land. The friends strolled after them. John told Fine about Nora—this was the first time he'd seen her since the All-Night Bard. Fine, stimulated by the verdurous shape of garden—white-blossoming apple, mimosa, cherry, dogwood starting to bloom, mimosa again, red-leaved Japanese maple, all set against the gray-pink marble mansion floating on a lawn napped smooth as a putting green—listened, his attention loose, free.

The kids ran to the edge of the plateau, down from which stretched a long steep slope toward a pond. They hesitated. John James said: "It's like Howth Hill! Watch me!" He lay down and, with a shout, rolled over and over, shrieking and bouncing, down, all the way down to the pond. Nora's kids had never done this, and were hesitant to try. John James, out of breath from the climb back up, dared them. Still they hesitated, until Fine said: "Oh come on, it'll be fun!" And plonking himself down on the edge, he giggled and pushed off. Over and over he went, sunlight flashing off his brace, until, at the bottom, he stood up facing them on the edge of the pond, and then, gyrating, fell backward, in! They laughed, until he started thrashing and yelling: "Help! I can't swim!"

"Come on, John James," said John, "we'll rescue him!" And cradling the boy in the hoop of his arms, he rolled down with him, followed by Conal and Christina. Just when they were about to jump in and save him, Fine stood, smiling, the water only up to his waist. Clowning, they trudged back up the hill for a repeat.

Nora appeared on the veranda, calling John. He glanced at Fine, shrugged, and went to her. Fine watched them for a while, their animated body language saying all. He went to swing on the swings.

From the top of his arc, Fine could see over the low blue picket fence into the neighboring yard. On the lawn, between a grand stucco Victorian and a charming red-shuttered carriage house, was a grouping of white metal chairs, table, and yellow shade umbrella. A woman in an ovoid pink bikini bottom stood at an easel painting, back to him. Her red hair sparkled in the sun. Christina, excluded from a feverish soccer game between the boys, joined Fine on the swings. When she pumped up to sync with him, he asked who lived next door.

"Some weird doctor!" she said.

Fine swung higher, and saw the redhead turn, bend—her body spilling out of the bikini top, a pliant flesh-shape framed by the rigid pines, voluptuous in the muggy afternoon. "Boy I love it hot!" said Fine. "We've gone from thirty-four to ninety-two in only forty-eight hours!" Pumping higher, Fine saw, in the shade of the umbrella, in white long-sleeved shirt buttoned at the neck and broad-rimmed white hat and wraparound sunglasses, a man smoking a cigar, posing for his portrait. An albino? Could it be? "Say, Christy, his name isn't Vergessen, is it?"

"How'd you know? The Vergessens are wicked weird!"

Without thinking Fine pumped—once, twice—and with a jungle cry—"Eee-yahhh!"—catapulted out into free space. With the magic slo-mo of a dream he felt himself suspended in air, soaring. Barely clearing the fence he crashed, wind knocked out of him: "Oomph!" Dizzy, he lay on the most obsessively kept lawn he'd ever seen, trying to right his jolted brain. He noticed before him white tap shoes, pink socks, and, looking up, a plump knee, plumper thighs, a few curly red hairs escaping from a bulging pink bikini bottom, and small conical breasts, the string of the bikini top stretched like a guy wire across their apexes so he was looking up through her cleavage to her chubby chin. Her red hair was cut short: boyish, even punk, androgynous. The whole seemed vague, fuzzy, a sensual meld of "girlboy." She dropped the paint brush on his bare stomach.

"Oops!" she said, and then, staring: "Ooo!"

Fine followed her gaze: below the chartreuse paint smear his own bikini had pulled down, exposing his penis, which before his eyes, was inflating, struggling to raise itself up off his left thigh like a drunk off a sidewalk. Fine snapped up his swimsuit. Embarrassed to rise while erect, he crossed his legs, leaned nonchalantly on his elbow and looked away from the source of his arousal toward Vergessen, thinking: what a hot ticket! To have this sexbomb for a wife?!

"Dr. Fine, have you met my daughter, Miss Sophie Vergessen?"

"Hi, Dr. Fine," said Sophie, "call me 'Sunny.' "

"Hi, Sunny," said Fine, astounded. The daughter of his hero, free game? *This* is the reason for V.'s hidden address and unlisted phone: not his fear of TBI candidates coming by to slip prayer-messages into the chinks in his walls, no—this honeypot! "Sorry to barge in—was—by chance or fate I don't know which—um—next door."

"Yes," said V., "aren't schlemiels powerful in this world?"

"I'm delighted to meet your family, Dr. Vergessen."

"Well," said V., "bright red apple, wrong orchard perhaps?"

Fine wanted to talk to Sean about his finding out that the killer was someone who knew him, but Sunny, with her chatter and body language, made it impossible. "I guess that my fellow candidates are pretty mad at me," Fine said. "The police sketch and all."

"Yes, but isn't all fair in love, war, and analysis?"

"Listen—I think the killer is someone who knows me, and—"

"Really?" asked Vergessen, sitting upright in his chair. "Why do you—" Sunny barged in, and Sean gave her all his attention. Fine watched, thinking: he treats her as an analysand. Sean clearly hadn't a clue as to how to control her, as she revolved around them. To Fine she seemed starved for company, like a kid kept ten years in a closet. Sheila, Sean's wife, came out. A tall, neat, black-haired woman, she at once took charge: "Sunny, we'd love you to stay here and talk."

"Going into *my* house." Sunny headed for the carriage house.

"Oh, and while you're in there," said Sheila, "why not put on your really *tiny* bikini, the light citrine one, you know?"

"Mother!" said Sunny, pouting like a teenie—to Fine she seemed anywhere from thirteen to thirty. "Stop! I'm getting dressed!"

Sheila, clearly used to being a buffer between her analyst husband and the world, fended off any serious talk, and once again Fine was stymied in trying to ask this wise man what he should do. Sunny came back out dressed back up: a cute tanktop over a firm bra, the "V" down the front embroidered with hearts and flowers; tan shorts; boating sneakers; bright red lipstick, green eyeshadow. She frowned.

A sharp whistle cut through the thick air, from Nora's. John stood outside the house, fingers to mouth, whistled again. "Fine! C'mon! Phone call! Hurry up!" John turned, calling: "John James?"

Apprehensive, Fine excused himself hastily, saying he looked forward to talking about his concerns in supervision Thursday.

"Nice to have you come," said Vergessen, his direct statement raising Fine's hopes for a more personal relationship, but then dashing them again by equilibrating, "and nice to have you go?"

As he climbed the stile back over the fence, he noticed Sunny following. Sheila called out, cheerfully: "Sunny?" They looked back. "Glad you're going with Dr. Fine. Have a nice time."

She stopped, balanced on the fence. Fine knew it would be a faux pas for her to come. "Sorry, Sunny, you can't go with me."

"The hell I can't!" said Sunny, moving toward him.

"No, you can," said Sheila, adamantly.

"Oh?" said Sunny, indignantly. "Then I won't!"

"Yes, you can't!" Fine said quickly, puzzled that he was falling into this strange, inverse semantic.

"No, I am!" said Sunny, coming down on Nora's side of the fence.

"You're not!" said Fine, firmly. Sheila shouted—"No, you go!" —and Sunny hesitated. Fine laid down the law: "No way, Sunny, go away!" Fine limped off; Sunny bounced along. "I'll be your cane," she said, taking it, and, pulling his right arm around her slender waist to lie—as if, Fine felt, it had always meant to lie— on her rump, bumping her healthy left hip against his lame right, she walked him up the lush, newly thawed lawn to Nora's.

Fine failed to see it: Sunny was a flagrant example of the ana- lyst's child syndrome, less parented than analyzed (Sheila too an analyst). Rather than firm clear limits, Sunny had gotten clouds: "What are your fantasies, hmm?" Without ballast, she'd become a floater, a balloon carried to and fro on the prevailings. If once she censored an impulse, next she censored the censor and freed it. Sent as a child to a child analyst, her doubt had been mirrored, doubly reflected. Desperate, she clung to a rule of opposites: if she felt like it, she did not; if she felt not, she did.

Fine cupped her rear end, feeling it undulate on his palm. Her body felt like a meld of genders. Much aroused, he lost his fear of transgressing, and curled his pinkie under her shorts. A ridiculous pun floated in: "Is this real, or a pigment of my invagination?"

"What's up?" Fine asked John.

"O'Herlihey called The Uncle, who called here. They found another body."

"What?! Who?"

"Serena."

"Oh my God!" Fine's head spun. "Where?"

"Stow. Let's go."

The sun sulked under the covers of haze as the Rolls, despite its exquisite shock absorbers, clanked across the Curley Bridge. An ambulance with its siren off passed them going the other way. The water below, seeming so near, was sluggish, beaten down. Few sailboats were out. A single behemoth leaked a rainbow of oil in its wake, heading for the storage tanks at Neponset. At the Stow end of the bridge was a crowd—police, Stow staff, and several of Fine's Jefferson House patients. They got out and looked.

There, on a flat granite slab at the water's edge, The Uncle and O'Herlihey stood with two uniformed policemen. An outline of a spread-eagled body, centered on a dark red blotch, was drawn on the rock. O'Herlihey called to them. They pushed through the crowd. To Fine the two older Irishmen seemed out of place, as odd outdoors on a hot sunny day as bats. "The word is, Dr. Fine," said O'Herlihey, "is that you knew her?" Fine said he did, and then told him the little he did know. "Right," said the detective. "Except for the fact that she was not a psychiatrist, every detail of the murder is the same. This forces us to the obvious conclusion, does it not?"

"What?" Fine asked, feeling scared.

"The killer knows you, and is watching you, intimately."

"But why me?"

"Why indeed?" asked The Uncle. "Think aboot it, will you?"

"Of course," said Fine, "I will. I guess, I mean it's crazy but the obvious . . ." He gulped. "The killer is a patient of mine?"

"Let me impress on you, Dr. Fine," said O'Herlihey, "that in all my years on the force I've not seen anything quite so brutal as these murders. I mean Mental Hygiene Month is one t'ing, but this is anuther! Take care. I wish we'd money for police protection of you, but the tax cuts have us strapped. You're on your own."

"Listen, Johnny," said The Uncle, teeth yellow in the light, "it don't seem it's Fine himself at risk, but rather those around 'im— Reuben, this floozy. That means you, and the little lad. Why not come 'ome 'n' stay with your mother and me till this blows over?"

"Thanks, Uncle," said John, tensely. "I'll think about it."

They climbed back up the rocks to the roadway. The Jefferson House patients were panicked, flagrantly psychotic. Lafite had found the body, leading the others to it. Mr. Jefferson held out his hand, palm up. In it lay a small lump of spongy pink stuff. "Yes, er, no, a brainy lobe. Wonder what it's thinking now, no?"

"Gone to live wid Jesus!" said Jefferson. "Or wid Myrna Loy!"

"*Souvenir,*" said Henrietta Bush, "in French: 'to remember.' "

"Throw it back," said Fine. Morosely, he did.

"Well," said Cooter, starting to walk away, onto the iron bridge, "I'm a goin' into town, doc. Gonna buy me another gun!"

"Germans!" cried Eli. "Fourth Reich! Third World War! *Now!*"

As the Rolls pulled into the gravel driveway, Fine saw Steph standing on the porch, her hair frizzed, her face flat and hard with tension. How surprised she was to see them emerge from the luxurious automobile! John James rushed to her, hugged her. Glancing skeptically at Sunny, she told them that when she'd gone to pick them up in Southie, she'd run smack into Mrs. O'Day. "Your mother is not pleased," she said. "What happened?"

"Later," said John. "You heard the news?"

"You got a hair frizz!" said Fine, wanting one too.

"Yeah," said Steph, "it's absolutely awful!"

"It's not!" said Fine. "I love it. Where'd you get it?"

"Oh, my hair? Yeah, I got it for my act."

"Any luck?" John asked.

"As a matter of fact, yes," she said, smiling, pleased with herself. "I've got a spot Saturday night at The Comedy Box."

"Grand!" said John. "Just grand!"

"Hi, I'm Sunny Vergessen and I'm with Fine." Steph's eyes popped, her mouth fell open. The boy, having had enough of his da, wanted to go play outside. John told him: only in the walled-in backyard, and only if someone went with him. The boy wanted Fine or Steph; Sunny volunteered. "No, Sunny, you stay—" Fine began; "Yes, I won't!" she said, and led John James out the back door.

"Fine," said Steph, "tell me she's not Vergessen's daughter?"

"She's not Vergessen's daughter."

"Thank God!"

"But she is." Steph looked heavenward. "Cute kid, no?"

"She's not of age, Fine!"

"Oh come on—John's barely of age, either! *Ha! Haha!*"

None of them wanted to open that up. Instead, they talked about the latest murder. Those close to Fine being at risk, he said it might be best for Steph, John, and the boy to leave. With clear and denied irrationality they reasoned out why they should stay. The clincher?—Royce's Security had finally sealed off the island quite hermetically, making it safer than anywhere else. No one ever said the truth: their bond, recast, was too strong to break, yet. They would stay together, for the time being. Did Fine have any idea who it might be? "No. Even if I did I couldn't talk— 'confidentiality,' you know? I'll work it out with Vergessen in Thursday supervision, day after tomorrow." He got up to see Three, Four and Five o'clock.

None of whom showed.

Fine sat, fiddling, wondering why not. Six o'clock, that morning, had failed to show, as well. The analytic dogma: failure to show means wish to show, a defense called reaction formation. Well, yes, Fine thought, they are angry at me: Dora for my touching her, Mardell for my beating him in H-O-R-S-E, Sylvia—no, I hadn't picked up her anger yesterday; in fact, as we'd watched them play soccer on the lawn, she'd softened, asked for an extra session?—Ratman yes, furious for my Lacanian five-minute hour. Fine went through his patients, looking at each's potential to kill. He soon stopped. Knowing each in actuality, he could not envision any as a killer. To take an actual gun, load it with actual bullets, track down an actual, harmless, trusting human being and there, face to face, actually pull the actual trigger to actually kill? To stick a real finger in the gore and scrawl "Therapist = The/rapist"? No. Such things are not imaginable. Yet like the Holocaust they are. Perhaps it's not a patient but someone who—like Hinckley, Jodie Foster—never met me but has a psychotic transference to me, tracking me. Can't be anyone I've sat with: a *real* me would melt such a transference. He thought of the wild *Herald* headline from the trial of the kid who shot the President: HINCK'S SHRINK STINKS. Have I too become celebrity enough to be stalked by a crazy killer? For the first time since his seizure Fine felt scared. He locked the office door. If Ratman did show, late, he could knock.

The phone rang. Nipak Dandi. Fine was delighted, remembering that he'd forgotten to call him about *The Nuclear Mind.*

"You must be telling me, my friend," said Nipak, "what happened with your wife?" Fine told him, and Nipak got angry. "I must come up there at once!" Fine said that would not be a good idea. "Why not? It is the free country, as they say, is it not?"

"Yes, but there's been another murder, and people around me seem to be at risk. But listen—I need your help in solving the—"

"Ah yes, the *Times* had a piece—I'll wait a bit—but listen: we are ready to roll!" Fine asked what he meant. "Fine and Dandi, Inc. I am getting the calls from all over the world—American Cyanamid, Marion Labs—they are making the calcium pills for the ladies' bones—the ADA, AMA—"

"The ADA?" asked Fine.

"American Dairy Association. New studies show homogenized milk has oxidases that turn Western arteries hard. Milk is too-high cholesterol, as well. They seek alternative calcium, may wish to 'ground-floor' it with Finestones. What is cholesterol content?"

"Cholesterol? It's a rock, there's no cholesterol—"

"Very excellent, yes! There will be no attacking hearts—"

"We're all being oxidized anyway," said Fine mordantly, feeling that by now, from the rays and carcinogens, his sperm must be all bent out of shape, "from the environment, through the food chain. Or is it reduced? Whatever—it all comes out as all these cancers—"

"Yes, yes, but even the government rang up—the Pentagon or some such agency, I know not why—but as to production of—"

"Ron from NASA?"

"Yes, NASA—however, my fellow, did you know?" Fine was shocked—Ron, uninvited, nosing around? From Nixon on, every paranoid suspicion about the dirty tricks of government had proved an underestimate. Nipak chattered on, wanting to see *The Nuclear Mind.* Fine said he'd send it. And then he told Nipak of the new clues, asking for advice. Silence. Finally Nipak said: "I remember some words that may prove useful—from the Maharaj."

"Yes?"

" 'When a man is killed, the tragedy is with the killer.' "

"How does that help me find who it is?" Fine asked.

"Search for the one with the greatest tragedy. Yes, that's it: find the most god-awful tragedy of the life, man, and there is your killer, yes. Oh, I wish I could shuttle up, be with you and your wife in this desperate time! But not yet. We will keep in the most intimate touch, will we not, my friend?" They hung up.

After dinner, Steph and John went out to rehearsal. Fine and Sunny played with John James and then put him to bed. Fine did not want Sunny to sleep over. The more he tried to get her to leave, the more insistent on staying she became. He sighed, followed her upstairs. A feather in her cap to bed one of her father's boys. As he watched her girlyboy rear end wiggle up the steps before him, he thought: I've never met anyone so upwardly nubile.

In the bedroom, Sunny said: "I am Sunny and I am enough."

"What?"

"I am Sunny and I am enough." She crossed her arms as if

hugging herself, and then began to roll her top up over her head. Fine tried to keep her clothes on, but she scurried away, pushed him roughly onto the bed, unhooked her bra and let it fall. Her neck and upper chest were pink tan, her breasts stark white, boyishly perky, the nipples set high, almost horizontal, triangulated by the ultrawhite negative of her bikini, bumps circling poached nubs, very red, as if sore from sucking or pulling. She unzipped her shorts, unrolled her panties, and stood legs spread wide and arms akimbo, breasts pointing out, curving up, and said: "I am Sunny and I am enough!"

"Sure are," said Fine, aroused again by her whole body, drawn only to her vagina—that puffy hair, those reddened, labile *labia!* —wait—her breasts look far from mature; is she even of the age of consent? "But are you *old* enough?"

"What are your fantasies about how old I am?"

Oh God, a teenie analyst. "Cut the analytic stuff—"

"I am Sunny and I am enough. Now you say it about you."

"I am Fine—" he caught himself "—uh, and I am enough."

"Good. That's the self-esteem tape. Let's go for it!"

She dove for him, and before he had a chance to roll away she pinned him. He could feel her nipples digging into his chest, her hip bones cracking against his, and her pubic hair scrubbing at his penis. "Sunny, I don't think we should make love."

"I do!"

"No! I hardly—"

"Yes!"

"—know you! I won't treat you like a piece of meat—"

"Come on, big boy, fuck me like a T-bone!"

Fine felt funny, sexually compromised, as if her eroticism were too rough, an attack on something delicate in him. Her touch felt coarse, uncaring. What the hell's going on with me? Caught in a storm of strange new feelings, puzzled, he tried talking, but this strong young woman, clearly a video kid, became even more inflamed by his words. She became wild, freely animal, covering him with her body like a big frantic bird a nest. Okay, Fine thought as his arousal built, fuck delicacy. Oral, anal, genital, first one position, then—as if by choosing one she saw the other as better—another, sucking and cursing and fucking like in a porno film. On and on into the night they went until their bodies, oiled with glistening excrescences, were as humid as the wet air. The last time, Fine was under her, half-crazy with a butcher's son's lust, screaming "Fuck me to *death!*" She spread her arms wide and grabbed Fine's hands in hers and somehow, almost prehensilely, enwrapped his feet with her own. Fine was like a mirror image of her: palm to palm, locked ankle to ankle, bodies—the same size—layered on each other, held in a deathlock stillness but for one moving part: the base of his cock on her clit. *Two* clits! Back and forth, back and forth she gyrated, teaching him how to move just that part until the real butchery began, a sadomasochistic slashing and smashing bonded tightly to each other but for the gristly rub in the center between their legs, which felt to Fine like the center of his *being*. He went wild! Fine felt this orgiastic body-instant as the closest ever he'd gotten to heaven, or maybe to Myrna Loy.

They crashed. Once, later, when she got up to pee, Fine, overheated, went to the window and stood looking out at the sea. There was no breeze, and the outside was as hot as the in. Fine thought of Freud and felt smug, envisioning headlines: YOUNG DOC OUTPOONS FREUD/THATCH IN SNATCH CALLS SIG NO MATCH.

When Sunny came back in, she was carrying a large Phillips screwdriver. He asked why and as she handed it to him, she dropped it on his foot. He winced in pain, and they lay back down in bed. He felt close to her, but when he tried to hug her, she moved away.

Down the hall, hearing for the second night in a row the erotic carnival, Steph felt furious. She took it out on John by some vigorous sex of her own, winding up on top, bucking hard back and forth—"riding the bull" she called it—pummeling John to get back at him, and Fine. Spent, she rolled off, feeling a soreness between her legs, and slept.

Screams—terrified, blood-curdling screams—cut through the heavy air—the boy's room!

Fine jumped up and rushed in, Sunny behind. John and Steph came in from the other side. John James was sitting up in his bed, wild-eyed, pointing at the open window, screaming: "A face! I saw a face lookin' in at me through the window! A face, a face!"

"It was just a dream, John James," said John, sitting on the bed, trying to take him in his arms, "a nightmare—"

"No it weren't nightmeer! It was real! Hurry—go see—"

"Can't be real, it's the second floor—"

"It was! She was there, lookin' at me!" He looked around at the others—Sunny and Fine stark naked, Steph in a nightgown and John in his pajamas, and said: "Unky Fine, tell 'im it's true!"

"Go put on some clothes!" said Steph to Sunny.

"I will not put on—"

"Shut up and do it!" said Steph, taking her by the shoulders, turning her around, and pushing her into the room, "Now!"

"C'mon—we'll get 'er," said the boy, heading for the door.

They went downstairs and out into the hot humid night. The scent of lilac hung heavy, mixing with the sour smell off the sluggish, polluted harbor. The moon fought through the thick air, almost full. Fine felt a sharp sweet pain on his arm—first mosquito bite—and, slapping it, seeing blood on his palm, felt a summery pleasure. They went along the side of the house, turned the corner, and looked up at the window of the boy's room. They saw nothing.

"See?" said John. "Nothing there."

"Ain't them vines messed up?" said the boy, pointing to the ivy crawling up the side of the house.

"Nope," said John.

"Are too! She climbed up on 'em, like in the fil'ms. She was standin' right there on that ledge."

"They're a mess all over the wall," said John, "see there?"

"You think I was dreamin', Da, but I wasn't neither! Why doncha believe me?" The kid marched determinedly off by himself, disappeared around the edge of the house. They followed.

"Oww!" Fine said, stepping hard on a round pebble in the grass, feeling a sharp pain in the sole of his left foot. "Wow!" He sat on the grass, peering at his instep to see if it was cut.

"What?" said Steph, running to him, her quickness and scared tone showing how tense they'd all become. "What's wrong?"

"Stepped on something—a stone or something. Caught me right in the middle of the arch—woo-wee!"

She helped him up. They were alone. "Fine, what the hell are you doing?"

"What do you mean?"

"Messing around with her."

"Her? What's wrong with her?"

"She's ditzy, a total airhead! She can't be even sixteen—it's illegal! You're out of your mind, Fine, do you know that?"

"How can I know it? I'm out of my mind!"

"Stop it, will you? Cool off till you're better again—"

"It's my life, Steffy, I'm free to do as I please—"

"It's not moral, what you're doing!"

"And what *you're* doing is?" His jealousy surprised him.

"Well, well." She stared at him for what seemed a long time, eye to eye in the murky moonlight. He couldn't read her, but knew he'd hit home. Her voice was somber: "Yes, I see. C'mon." They walked along the wall, turned the corner, up on the porch, in.

John James wanted his father to sleep with him. Steph kissed the boy and went alone into her bedroom. Fine hugged and kissed him, and then asked what the woman in the window looked like.

"Didn't see her too good, but she looked weird! Aye, she looked like in the fil'ms—like a *monster!*"

Fine glanced at John, and then left.

Soon the house was as still as houses are after wild commotions. Fine heard the boy's prayer:

"And please, God, please help Da 'n' Unky Fine see things bettern' they do, please? 'Cause You 'n' me know what I saw amen."

Whether because of the pain in his left sole or the hour of the night or the excitement about the nightmare or the tense contact with his wife, Fine had never noticed, as he climbed the stairs to the second floor, that his palsied right foot had cleared every step.

And none of them had noticed that an intruder could have come down—easily could have come down—to the window of the boy's room from above.

28

THE NEXT MORNING Fine sat in his office waiting for Six o'clock. He was beginning to worry. The killer had to be someone who knew him, had access to Stow, had seen him with Serena. Most likely it was a patient, former patient, or staff; if an inpatient, one with privileges to go off the island. Fine made a note to check hospital records for patient passes on the nights of the murders, but then realized that O'Herlihey must already have done so. Yet even if cleared, the inpatients were suspect: slip-ups were common, alibis could be forged. His mind spun with the endless possibilities. Statistics crowded in: most murders are committed on drugs or alcohol; the most common motives are money, revenge, love, drugs, psychosis. A mass murderer was likely to be psychotic. But Fine's psychotics were the least likely to take action in the world; and none of his outpatients were that sick. Freud was of little help: if every symptom has many motives, to analyze either symptom or motive doesn't narrow the field. Yet the murders might well be symbolic repetitions of childhood experiences—as Nipak had said: "The life with the worst tragedy will bring the worst tragedy to life." *Fine Theory* predicted the killer's defect to be in empathy—to catch the killer, find the least empathic person. Are these murders, spun on transference, murders of mothers? But then, why males? Fine recalled snippets of gossip: each of the first two victims was expert in some kind of gender conflict: Myer, expert on gender, a secret cross-dresser; the first, Wholer, expert on bisexuality, rumored bisexual. For an instant everything fit: each expert in gender dysphoria *was* secretly gender dysphoric; the killer, because of problems with gender identity, had sought each as therapist—no, she'd not have been their patient, for then she'd be on their books; unless she used false names, disguises—anyway, in each of them she found, through surveillance, the hidden perverse sex life; betrayed, hurt, angry, she lured them to their offices on Sunday afternoon and then, high on drugs or booze—the kill.

I too am expert in male/female. Has one of my patients sought me out for that? Peeping on me? Fine's skin crawled. But wait— Reuben and Serena break the pattern—why them? The hypothesis fell apart. Fine's fear edged toward paranoia. Speculation, all of this. Theory would be of little help, but for one thing: to find the killer he had to search out—with empathy, in reality—tragedy.

Can I be empathic? How can I feel empathy for one who feels none? It'd be like hugging a corpse. He shivered: that's how I'll know—by failing. And suppose, provoked, the corpse comes to life? He looked at the clock: 6:50. Six o'clock had not come. Suspicion on the rise, Fine opened his desk drawer and stared at the .44 Cooter had given him. He picked it up, his hand trembling. How slight a movement on the trigger ends a life, changes a world! The gun is the great modern weapon: kill from a distance, cleanly. As he got up to leave, Fine recalled Dora's rage at his touching her. He stopped cold. Could it be? The metaphor of her analysis was frigidity. The icy rough parenting, the molestation by Uncle Savage, the failed marriages, sexual doubts, rage at men, abortions—all there. The Federal Reserve would be a perfect cover. Empathy? Calling him "pervert," she'd cut him off cold. What clearer motive than her rage at all the therapists she'd gone to prior to Fine? For the last four months she'd been regressing, filled with wild childlike affect. Drugs? Most killers are high on drugs. We each have our drug of choice—mine, now, carbos— God I'm fat! A nation of addicts. No wonder we massacre each other. Was Dora on drugs? Maybe coke. Like everybody else. Queasy, he realized it could be.

Warily, he went down to breakfast. The sole of his left foot was badly bruised, and he limped even worse than before. The others were eating. When she saw him come in, Steph said: "Here comes the little Hebe—lock up your women!"

"Not funny," said Sunny, miniskirt flaring out as she spun up off the stool. "C'mon, kiddo, let's play." They left. Steph took a paper towel and wiped the stool. Fine asked what she was doing.

"Cunt prints," she said. "She's leaving them everywhere."

Fine felt her hostility, but said nothing. Mrs. Neiderman appeared for the morning briefing. Bringing her into the living room, Fine felt that both she and Ando were prime suspects: always around, resenting psychiatrists, seeming so happy, and yet, in idle chatter, each had admitted to him her misery. Neiderman was heartbroken at being childless; Ando, miserable in love. Thinking he was doing it subtly, Fine asked Neiderman about her personal life. Out it poured, one tragedy after another. On he probed until, as he asked about drug use, she resisted. He dug in, harder. And then, to his chagrin, she caught on. "What?" She stopped, stared at Fine. "Wait—you don't think that I—oh my God!" She got to her feet. "You think it's *me?!* Unbelievable!"

"Now, now—you know I think you're a prince among women—"

"You think you can just play with other people's feelings, don't you?" She shook her head in disbelief. "Dr. Fine, have you lost your mind?" Fine didn't know what to say. "I used to think you had all this warmth and depth in you—of course I needed a nuclear submarine to get at it, yes—but now, I'm not so sure!"

Shaken, Fine went to the lab for his meeting with Ms. Ando.

"Hai!" she cried, excitedly. *"Hermissenda!"*

"Hermissenda?" asked Fine, puzzled.

"Hermissenda crassicornis! Shell-less marine snail, a gastropod mollusk. My friend spies in Dr. Alkon's lab, Wood's Hole. Listen!" She told Fine that Alkon had trained snails, and recorded electrical activity from inside the cell that learns. "And guess what rises inside the cell membrane?"

"Calcium?"

"Hai!" From under sultry tucked lids, her dark eyes glowed sensually. "Calcium! Proof! During learning, calcium rises, increases enzyme phosphorylation, altering the shape of the cell membrane, which increases calcium channels even more—result?: better learning, memory! Dr. Fine, I'm so excited—we're *right!"*

Fine sat, strangely unmoved. "The biological basis of learning!
The Nobel! Mind control! Look—" She held up a jar, containing a
human brain. "Mr. Able's back from Texas! Guess what electron
micrographs show?"

"Calcium?"

"Hai! Mr. Able used to be a fat, dumb schizophrenic, remember? Three years of Finestones, and he was a thin, smart schizophrenic. And now! Inside his brain cells? Look!" She took out
three photomicrographs, laid them side by side. "Grasshopper,
Alkon's snail, Mr. Able. Go ahead—tell me which is which."
Fine looked.

"I can't."

"Neither can anybody else! *Schistocerca, Hermissenda, Homo
sapiens*—all the same! Calcium is it! But Alkon might beat us!
We've got to go all out! *We have got to get to work!*"

Obsessed with the murders, Fine couldn't get excited. He tried
opening up Ms. Ando, but she too soon resented his questions.
Her anger flared, and she began berating Fine for his recent er-
ratic behavior, his sexual acting out, and, most of all, for his
neglecting his grasshopper work. Exasperated, she cried out:
"Kichigai!"

Chastised, Fine left. Yes, we've found the unit change, constant
in ontogeny and phylogeny, which underlies learning; yes, it's
calcium. Compared to a killer at large, so what? And is it ethical,
this "mind control"?

At Mr. Royce's morning security briefing, Fine entertained fantasies that Royce himself, or Pelvin—allegedly still on vacation in
the Allagash—or another Stow psychiatrist was the murderer. He
sat in the last row, rear protected by the wall, on guard.

By afternoon, Fine's paranoia was blooming.

The Jefferson House patients were the most likely suspects by
far. Their tragedy in life started before life itself, in the murky
gene pool of their heritage, and the brutality of their childhoods
would make a slaughterer wince. In murders of psychiatrists, almost all are psychotics, of a paranoid subset. Such thoughts went
through Fine's mind as Mr. Jefferson asked him to come with
them on an outing that afternoon. For the first time, Mr. Jefferson
was offering to take the whole hall out on his "small" boat, the
thirty-five-footer, *The Jeff.* This boat was "a mere mote in the eye,

yes, er, no, compared to our Tall Ship, our brig *The Thomas*.
Good fun, yes, er, no, for even Zeus was at the mercy of the
snake-tailed Chthonian winds!" For months Mr. Jefferson had
fantasized about sailing *The Thomas* up from Duxbury on Memorial Day, for the Tall Ships. This would be a dry run. Despite his
fear of being caught in an enclosed vessel out on the open sea at
the mercy of a chronic psychotic Brahmin, how could Fine say
no?

And so after lunch Fine, Steph, John, Sunny, and the boy left
the metallic sheet of shade of the mammoth copper beech and
followed the Jefferson House patients down the wide, deep-green
lawn toward the Stow jetty—a long stone arm reaching out into
the bay. The day was hotter and more humid than the last—even
steamy—and the flowerings even more wild: the last lilac, the
dogwood beginning to fleck its black limbs white, redbud and
English hawthorn and the golden chains of laburnum and even
the mountain silverbell; willow, red oak, poplar, the soft lime-
green buds nested on the ends of fir, boxwood, and pine; the lawn
itself, freshly mown, gave off a quintessential spring scent: chloro-
phyll-and-dog-turd. Plump bumblebees sucked nectar from flowers. As he strolled along Fine tried to calm himself with a "walking meditation"; his mind, untethered, floated into a vision of
May as Life: like childhood it begins in an orderly, step-by-step
progression—bud, leaf, crocus, daff, tulip; then the first heat stirs
the hormones, bringing the chaotic bloom of adolescence; next, on
a steadily growing plateau, flowers and blossoms mature, prevail;
finally comes the mass wilting, Memorial Day. Looking back,
those first brave buds seem the closest, the only immortals. If only
you could catch them in your hands, those crisp fearless infant
blooms, and hold them there, forever? Fine sighed; prophylacti-
cally, he gave out Finestones. They cast off, The Jefferson at the
helm.

They soon found themselves becalmed on a plate-glass sea. The
city rose from it like a metropolis from a Steinberg drawing. In
the gentle rock and calm, they felt lulled. The sun beat down, and
most of them sought shade. Sunny, flagrant flesh in her skimpy
bikini, wreaked havoc among the psychotics, despite Fine's efforts
to keep her with him away from them. Male and female alike
were wrenched with arousal. John James, when he'd seen Jeffer-

son (black) close up, had started to cry: "I never saw nobody more big'n my da!"

"There's always someone more big, kid," said Fine. "There's always someone *more* anything, believe you me."

Now the boy stood over Fine: "You look like a piggy bank." Fine asked how. He pointed to the fresh scar on Fine's crown where the sutures had been. "You got a slot in your head for the money."

The Jefferson seemed to Fine to be going awfully far out into the bay. Leaving the ship in command of Mrs. Henrietta Bush, The Jefferson came to Fine: "Yes, er, no, a confession to make." The white-clad sailor gulped: "I did it. Murdered them all. Unfit to live in society, er, yes, no. Please bury me at sea right now."

"Jesus told me to do it," said Jefferson, "I did it too!"

"Oh come on," said Fine, "you couldn't have—"

"Unwise, Dr. Fine, to spurn a true confession, er, no, yes." Mr. J. began mumbling angrily, and reached under a compartment. Fine thought—yes—it's him!—he's going for a gun! Fine drew his .44. and said: "Hands up!" They stared at him, in shock.

"Yes, er, no," said Mr. Jefferson. "I was only seeking a linchpin, yes, for my jib has begun to flap, no?"

"Jesus Christ!" said Jefferson. "Doc Fine's the killer—"

"Hey you muthas, it ain't him, it's *me!*" Cooter, wild-eyed, hopping up and down on the bow, started screaming that he'd killed them " 'cause they's he'pin' the little fuckers take over my world!"

"No, stop!" yelled Fine.

Too late. With a horrific cry, Cooter plunged over the side and started swimming ferociously away. What he lacked in skill he made up for in rage, and as they watched him grow smaller, panic broke out, everyone screaming and threatening to give in to the impish, perverse urge—like being high up on an unrailed balcony —to jump in after him. The Jefferson, true captain, kept charge: with a startlingly cool authority he restored order, radioed the police, and began tacking deftly toward shore. Fine felt puzzled, ashamed. Was it a mistake, drawing the gun? Yet it had provoked Cooter, and he—intermittently sane and psychotic, of violent Southern stock, gunsmith, hater of shrinks who had in fact clobbered Fine in the Quiet Room—could well be the kind of guy who'd kill someone and walk away sucking a lollipop. Empathy with a manic? No way.

By the time they'd docked, the police launch had corralled Cooter. The mental health workers and Mr. Royce ushered the panicked patients back to the locked hall. "I keel heem!" said Stinko. "I keel theese shrinkers weeth my bare hantz!" Like the others, under the strain he'd again lost the edge between self and other, and, imagining that he was locked up with a killer, had become him.

John James was frightened. On land, he looked up at Steph and said: "I hate you!" She was startled. With a tense laugh he said: "That means I love you! Walk with me, will you, Aunt Steph?"

John and Fine followed them up the lawn. Sunny was shadowing the Jefferson Housers; Fine told her to come with him, but she said: "I've had enough of you! I'm leaving!" And she did.

Steph and John went into Boston to rehearse. John took the boy with him. Fine, holed up in his locked office, was surprised to hear Five o'clock knock on his door.

Ratman the Obsessive, under the strain of the five-minute hour, had regressed to psychotic levels. Nevertheless, he first tried to behave normally, lying down on the couch, associating. Fine, however, was intent on finding out if Ratman could be the killer, and he began to go at him directly. Ratman tried to ignore him, associating on, but Fine would not be turned. Finally, the anal rage came out, and the small, fuzzy-haired Jewish writer exploded: he shot to his feet, ran to the door, blocked it with his body, and began railing at Fine for "pulling that shit on me!" On and on he went, spittle dotting the corners of his mouth, screaming "betrayal" and "taking legal action." Appalled, Fine tried everything he knew to pacify Ratman, including, finally, suggesting vipassana meditation and, when that failed, Feldenkrais. This flipped Ratman further over, and he began to make threats. So venomous was the abuse—which, in *Vampire Mom,* had amused a million Americans—Fine felt that the Rat was the killer. Worse: Ratman's compulsively neat summer suit *did* have a bulge in the breast area—could this be a gun? Fine got very scared. Ratman was apoplectic. Nothing Fine said had any effect. And then Fine did a terrible thing: "Listen Ratman, you've got to . . ."

"*Ratman?*" He paused, wiped a thread of drool away. There was a deadly silence. Fine knew that Ratman knew. "Did you say—"

"No, no," said Fine. His blush betrayed him.

"You asshole!" screamed Ratman, starting in again. And then Fine too lost control, answering him in kind. Back and forth they went, screaming, calling each other all kinds of names, until as Fine watched, Ratman reached for the lump in his jacket and Fine knew he was going to die. Out came his hand, clutching something. "A notice of suit!" said Ratman, waving the document in the air, his nose, whitened with rage, rising from his torqued red face like an ax. "I'm suing you for all you're worth, you little shit! Here are the first eighteen interrogatories." He threw it down at Fine's feet. "Go shit in your hat!" Like a borderline adolescent, he slammed the hell out of the door.

Stunned, Fine tried to recall if he'd paid his malpractice premium. To calm himself, he opened the Moroccan box and reached for a Finestone. He was surprised to find another cat's eye marble! Why did he keep finding these? He tried to remember where and when, but it was fuzzy. He sat, massaging his sore instep: I found one in my office carpet, one in my pocket, yes, and—*thump!*—Fine's heart beat hard—a clue? Hard fact?

He stumbled downstairs to his house. He went around to the side, to the lawn under the boy's window.

On hands and knees, he searched the grass. Yes! Digging it out of the ground where he'd stepped on it, scraping the mud from it with his fingernail, he held it up to the sky: a cat's eye marble! The boy had not been dreaming—the killer, a woman, had been at his window! A woman who had access to his office and was leaving these cat's eyes for him! Why? Why marbles? He put it in his pocket, looked around in fright—as if the killer were watching—slunk back into the house, called O'Herlihey and told him all.

Late that night the threesome sat in the kitchen, talking. Tension was high. The two performers had had bad days: Steph was in no mood to do comedy; John, his show opening Saturday, was down on it: "I should be happy—it's such execrable garbage, it's bound to go to Broadway, to film and TV. Because it's Weill, they all think they're great geniuses—but they're no different from the herpes-and-cocaine crowd of Hollywood. It's what's killing theater now: playing from the outside in, playing for the laugh. Everyone's writing from the surface image—there's no heart now, in anything! Style, no substance—sick!" At the rehearsal, there'd been another tiff with John James. The boy, sitting in the hot theater, had been impossible—talking, taunting, running up and down the aisles—and finally John had had to take him out and spank him. "It just about killed me!" John said. "This sweet little kid, and I'm making him cry! Like my own dad, drunk, did me—he called booze 'false courage.' You're not helping me break this cycle, Fine, come on!" He shook his head, sadly. "All the way home he sulked, wouldn't talk to me, and then he ran out into the yard. What's he doing out there?"

"He's got some planks and cardboard—he's building a fort up against the brick wall—his 'Dublin hut.' Normal for his age."

"I'm really screwing up with him, aren't I?"

"Well," said Fine, "to tell the truth: yes."

"Nothing I do seems to have any effect."

"Yeah," said Steph, "that kid has a whim of iron."

John didn't laugh. "So come on, what should I do?"

"Maybe it's a mistake to be away so much, doing this show."

"I told them I'd do it, I've got to go on." Steph and Fine said nothing. "Don't look at me like that! I'm not thinking of myself, I'm thinking of him. It's a hard time. I'm doing this for my career, to make money, to provide for him. His mother won't, you can be sure of that. You saw how she lived—it's unhealthy! And now, with her new husband, new kids? We need money! One TV series and that's it—for *life!* Let them eat residuals! I'm doing it for the boy! You hear me? For him! Not for me, for him!" He went on, morosely: "Even when I'm with him, he's unhappy, right? But I asked him, first, before I took the show. And asked you too?"

Steph and Fine looked away, saying nothing.

"The hell with you, then!" said John. "You're not helping either! You know, I'm beginning to wonder about all this. I ask myself: what the hell am I doing, living in a loony bin with two crazy Jews? There's nothing wrong with John James. He's gonna be just grand!"

The first clear sign of the depth of their trouble came a short while later: John James, sleepwalking, came in. Without noticing the three adults, he went straight to the refrigerator, opened the door, pulled out his little penis, and urinated all over the vegetables.

29

AFTER THE FIRST nightmare since his seizure—being stabbed, and hearing someone say: "Cocky! You had to be cocky!"—Fine awoke at dawn on a stifling Thursday the eighteenth, feeling suspicious and vulnerable. He didn't know whether he was closing in on the killer, or the killer was closing in on him. Cat's eye marbles; access to my office; the face in the window a "monster," maybe a woman. Unlike in a thriller, neither solution nor plan appeared. As he made his way through the humid morning air to his office for Six o'clock, Fine felt delicately balanced, and very fragile. Like the day last July on Martha's Vineyard when his friends Ben and Cris had gone on errands, leaving their baby Zach in the stroller with Fine. Entrusted with the precious cargo, Fine had felt terrified. What agony to cross the street! How slow the time passed! Rather than being reassured by Zach's happy cooing, Fine had become ever more wary, attending less to the infant than to the infanticidal world. Now Fine faced the day vigilantly, edging toward paranoia. This, from his childhood, was familiar, even a strange comfort. Each life he'd looked at seemed to have tragedy enough. Empathy was hard to find in anyone. Are all of us, deep down, killers? Yet actually to kill—unless saving your own life or that of your child—you'd have to be psychotic.

Or "wired" on drugs. Fine felt ashamed of the way he'd acted with Cooter and Ratman. Yet hadn't the son, in *Vampire Mom,* chopped the mother up into linguine and fed her to his pet bat? The rigidity of Ratman's defenses is a tip-off to the power of his rage.

Fine oscillated back and forth between paranoia and trust, logic and feeling. Dream seemed more vivid than reality, and then, suddenly, reality more vivid than dream—the line between blurred. Scared, he medicated himself with food. His body was swollen, turgid, bloated. He felt, inside his skull, the shorted-out, damped-down brain cells starting to reignite, realign in new patterns. Euphoria would flip to dysphoria, and then flip back. But for his constant, ever-deepening paranoia, Fine felt as if he were living in a foreign body. His thinking about his thinking helped little. He felt lost.

As Nipak Dandi was to say: "The fish is the last to know that it is out of water."

Six o'clock came back. Precisely on time, without makeup, blond hair in bun, in a dull brown business suit, she went to the couch without looking at Fine. She covered her genital zone with her purse. Feeling her hostility, Fine sat behind her in the analytic position, hand on gunbutt. She associated to his transgression: "How many times had you told me: touching is not allowed? And then *you* do it—why? I tried working it through on my own: maybe Fine's just human, maybe it's my fault for being seductive? Then I thought of daddy. Remember I told you about Uncle Savage, his brother, touching me?"

"Yes," said Fine, apprehensively, reading from her body language—hands at her sides, fists clenched—her rage.

"Well I . . . I lied. It was him. My own father . . ." Her hands were white with strain. "He tricked me! Mummy was so cold, daddy was so vibrant, he seemed to be promising me that if I were only his buddy, I could be like him, and . . ." Her voice sharpened: "Liar! He's the most self-centered bastard you ever met! He betrayed me! And then, when I sensed it, felt his revolting touch, I tried to go back to mummy—but I . . ." She paused, sighed. "Like when I was a little girl, one summer in Pride's Crossing, swimming in the ocean: I swam out, far far out, beyond the bounds of sounds, of callings to me from shores; I swam far out, and couldn't get back. Too far from mother to ever get close,

again. Why wasn't she there, protecting me? If you can't trust
your own mother, who the hell can you trust? What a coldhearted
bitch! Who started me when I was only twelve on these goddamn
diet pills I still take now? Mother!" Fine was stunned: amphet-
amine? There's a drug to kill on! For the first time ever, her anger
did not melt to tears, but grew. He shivered: it's her. "Your touching me brought back *his* touches! I opened my eyes—and saw
him! Men! Fucking men!"

Fine watched her cross her arms over her chest, as if her right
and left sides were hugging each other. He was scared, immobi-
lized, and broke out in a cold sweat. The door seemed far away.

" . . . they sent me to so many therapists! Sometimes I get so
crazy—I hear a phrase over and over in my head like a broken
record: therapist equals the rapist—it's—"

"Time for us to stop," said Fine, rushing to the door.

"What?" she said, sitting up. "It's only ten past—" Fine ran
out, hearing her shout: "What the hell are you doing?"

Fine limped to his house and locked the doors and windows.
He saw her come out, hurry to her bottle-green Mazerati, and
screech off down the hill toward the bridge. He dialed the police,
but hung up—confidentiality is a sacred trust. Before you break it,
you've got to be *sure*. Could there be an explanation? But if you
suspect a patient is dangerous and you fail to warn the potential
victim, you're criminally liable. Fine called Vergessen—no answer
—he'd ask him that afternoon, in supervision. He notified Royce:
Duffy, if she came back, must be stopped at the gate, and he must
be called. He wouldn't see her alone, no. "I think I've solved it,"
Fine said to the others at breakfast. "We're safe, now. What a
relief!"

By noon, the day was the hottest on record for that date. Fine,
John, and Steph sat on the porch sipping drinks, sweat pouring off
them. The boy sulked, refusing to talk to John. Yet he was all over
Fine, like a cheap suit. Missing the cool wet summer of Ireland,
the boy complained of headaches and stomachaches, picking at
his food. He was hard at work on his shelter in the backyard, his
Dublin hut built up against the seven-foot-high brick wall enclos-
ing the yard. That morning, unbeknownst to him, Granny Katey
had come to fetch him, Father O'Herlihey in hand. Alerted by the
guard at the gate, John had persuaded Steph to take the boy off

for a swim. Facing his mother's threats and pleas and O'Herlihey's prayers, John had sent both back to Southie more furious
than ever. Fine felt nervous that he hadn't called the police, but
he also felt proud: he'd cracked the case.

The noon sun, seen from the porch, was a yolk at the apex of
the sky, oozing gold molt down—a steambath. As if the sun itself
were getting too hot, and seeking cool, hiding behind the shadow
of the haze. Time itself, as if cracked, seemed to have died. The
full moon, pale in outline opposite the sun, flaunted its spacial
chill. Fine could feel it tug at the water in his brain, carrying on
its tide florid thoughts and feelings, leaving odd fantasies to pool
in new hollows and transient eddies—desperation, rage—now
here, now gone.

Fine got a lift with John into town, to the Institute, for his
Thursday supervision with Sean Vergessen.

As he climbed the stairs to V.'s office, he felt his right leg to be
stronger. What does this mean for the shape of my brain?

Vergessen sat behind the largest desk in the Institute. Frau
Metz was rumored to have a larger desk, but that was chez Metz,
on Beacon Hill. Chubby and hot, Vergessen had removed his
jacket, and his whiteness—skin, hair, short-sleeve shirt open at
the fat neck—against the dark oak paneling made him seem to
Fine an essential white, a wise old swan. Fine stared at his idol,
warm feelings rushing in. This kindly old guy has tried his best,
with total integrity, to help people for forty years. Despite
Semrad's warning—"It's hard to sit with sick people!"—he'd
plodded on: good-hearted, trustworthy, reliable. He's always *accepted* me. Yet Fine felt awkward at having seen him at home, at
taking his daughter away for the night, and wondered what V.
knew of his personal life. The penultimate blank screen for Fine's
projections, V. sat quietly, and then pulled his famous gesture—
leaning his cheek on his closed fist—and Fine knew this was a
sign for him to start associating about his two control cases. The
Institute made no distinction between analysis, supervision, and
seminar work: all was conducted as an analysis.

"I've found the murderer!" Fine said. "And guess who it is?
The woman you've been supervising me on—Six o'clock!"

"Umphgh?"

"My hysteric—listen!" Fine told the story, ending with her in-
criminating "the rapist" line that morning.

After a long associative pause, V. asked: "Paranoia?"

"Paranoia?" asked Fine.

"Don't we always, with you, have trouble with the paranoia?" Vergessen rose, went to the shelf, pulled down a volume of *The Standard Edition,* sat, opened it. "Hypervigilance? Isn't your fantasy that this murderer is somehow connected to you?"

"Yes—I mean yes she *is*—I mean it is her—"

"Oh?" asked Vergessen, clearing his throat. "Yes?"

Fine felt hot. Vergessen was taking the time-honored route, assuming that any problems in the analysis were not with the patient, but with the analyst: that Fine's own neurosis was distorting his perception of Six o'clock. Analyze the analyst to analyze the patient. Stung with disappointment, Fine sat mute.

Vergessen found the passage: " '*The Case of Shreber.* Part II: Attempts at Interpretation.' Here, Freud quotes Goethe's *Faust:*

> *Und seine vorgeshrieb'ne Reise*
> *Vollendet er mit Donnergang.*

Literally: 'And with a tread of thunder he accomplishes his prescribed journey.' " Sean nodded, and before Fine could express his puzzlement, he paged forward, and read again:

> "Part III: On the Mechanism of Paranoia: On the basis of this clinical evidence we can suppose that paranoiacs are endowed with a *fixation at the stage of narcissism,* and we can assert that the amount of regression characteristic of paranoia is indicated by the length of *the step back from sublimated homosexuality to narcissism.*"

"Do you believe, Dr. Fine, that the emphases are Freud's own?"

"Homosexuality?"

"Narcissism?"

"I tell you I've found the killer, you tell me I'm a fag?"

"Why so pejorative?"

"Sorry. Anyway, I want to call the police, to tell them—"

"And break confidentiality? What on earth for?"

"What?" asked Fine, startled. "Why, because she's the killer!"

"She is not."

"What?" exclaimed Fine, again. "Of course she is—"

"No," said Vergessen, firmly, "can't be."

Fine felt a wave of apprehension. "But how else could she know about the mutilation of the body?"

"The word play?" Fine nodded. "Isn't that from Nabokov?"

"Huh?" Fine felt a queasy slosh in his gut, a sense of doom.

"Didn't you tell me she was an avid reader of the émigré anti-Freudian, V. Nabokov?" Fine said yes. "Yes, and isn't that particular verbal game from *Pale Fire?*" Fine thought he was going to throw up. V.'s brow knit up in concern, he shook his round white head: *"Tsk! Tsk!* To even *think* of breaking the confidence of an analytic control?"

"But look at her history—as a child she was molested—"

"Yet is she not now a success? Don't, sometimes, the ones with the worst history turn out the best? And, sometimes, the ones with the best, the worst?" Who did V. mean? Fine? Himself? Sunny? Vergessen was looking deep into Fine's eyes—was this the legendary "attention" that V. was said to show his patients, so that they could feel it even while lying on the couch facing away, coming from behind, percolating down through skull, brain, heart, gut, uterus, ovaries, balls? Fine felt naked, and ashamed, and glanced away.

Vergessen went on: "Is touchy-feely enough? The sixties and seventies crowd thought they'd discovered the touchy-feelies, but had they? Haven't we seen every meshugge therapy there is?— and do they work? Try giving people 'corrective emotional experiences'—how far do you think you'll get?" He sighed. "You think the answer is in touching patients? It's not enough merely to put your arm around."

Fine felt accused. "Who says I've been touching patients?"

"Why lie?" V.'s complexion darkened. He seemed to Fine querulous, like an old woman, a Greek. "Don't you know by now that the world is a funnel to me?" Fine nodded. "There's a movement to throw you out. Take care. Life, unlike fiction, has no narrative."

"We make our own narrative."

"We do our best. Each person always does his or her best, no more, no less. No blame, no guilt. Our best."

"You think," Fine said, "that we're no more free than that?"

"My daughter?" His voice gave the slightest hint of pain.

Fine gulped. "She came of her own free will."

"The longer I live, the more I ask: is there such a thing?" He fell silent. His attention seemed to vaporize.

Fine's brain felt twisted, like a Möbius strip. Gastric acid burned his esophagus. "If not, then how do people change?"

"How do you imagine people change?"

"It's mystical—kind of a magical event that just happens!"

"Your own story?"

"So far."

"Women?" V. asked, in a quizzical tone. Fine failed to follow his association. "As Semrad always said: 'It's amazing about the Rockettes—that anyone can get so many women to do the same thing at the same time.' It's not Six o'clock. The killer's still loose. Remember: it's not enough to put an arm around. Psychoan—"

"But it's not enough *not* to either," said Fine, firmly.

"Hunh?"

"It's not enough *not* to put an arm around, either."

"Isn't psychoanalysis the best we have?"

"So far."

"Yes? As Metz once said to me—I was about your age—'Show me a hero, I'll show you a dream.' It's time for us to stop."

Fine found himself back out on the hot skillet of the day. He tried to shake his brain back down into shape. Feeling defenseless, as exposed as an agoraphobe, he squinted into the glare, as if searching for a landing strip. Something deep in his gut twitched —in the zone of his spleen. He hurried to the cab stand at the Ritz, filled with a colicky sense of dread.

Meanwhile, Steph, alone at Stow, had gone to Fine's office. It was the only air-conditioned room around, and she wanted to practice her comedy act. She saw that he'd put her picture in front of Freud's and Vergessen's, and was touched. Idly, she punched a few keys on his WANG and—*buzz, mmm, rrr-rrr, bleep!*—it came alive. The dark screen filled with green phosphorescent text:

THE NUCLEAR MIND

Dedication
For my dear wife, Stephanie:
When I die, you will read this and know:

I always did love you,
And I heard you.

"You men would find a way to relate,
if you realized your lives depended on it."
—Stephanie Caro Fine

"How sweet!" she said out loud, moved deeply. He had listened, after all? Feeling like she were reading someone's suicide note, she hit the NEXT SCREEN button. It was unlike anything of his she'd seen before: as opposed to the usual academic cool, it was warm; as opposed to the constricted analytic contempt, it was expansive, compassionate. She read on, hungrily. Finishing, she stared at Fine's chair: "Have I ever really known you, Fine? Why, schmucko, why the hell couldn't you have shown me this you, before?"

Late that night while the others were away rehearsing and John James was safe in his bed, Fine was surprised to find himself walking alone around the island. Despite Vergessen's doubts, he felt sure he'd found the killer. Maybe he would call the police after all. He felt relieved that at least Duffy would never get back onto Long Island without him knowing it. His loved ones were safe, for now. Yet he felt a disquiet, a restlessness, a sense of his own mortality, even, yes, a nearness to death. Once, concerning his wife, he felt the claws of the green-eyed monster—jealousy. He found these feelings hard to understand, as if they were attached to someone else.

His actions, too, surprised him.

He went into the lab, and took two cages of smart grasshoppers from their shelves, leaving only one last cage of smart hoppers behind, out of respect for Ms. Ando. As if pulled along by a wire, he walked with the two cages up to the top of the hill behind Jefferson House, where the grass was wild, unmown, and, it seemed to him, fragrant. He held one cage up, and unlatched the door, and he said: "You are free."

One hopper, a sleek male, peered over the edge, hesitating. Then, with a chirp to the others, he took the leap off the edge, into the night, into the grass. Gone. One by one the others followed.

"You're free," Fine said. "You're safe."

Silence.

He took the second cage of smart hoppers back to his office, concealing them in a false panel of his bookcase, like slaves in an underground railway. He'd spent years of his life training them to lift their legs, raising the calcium level in their endolymph and tiny brains—they were priceless, irreplaceable, really. These hoppers, too, now, in a different way, were safe.

And the last thing he did was in some ways the most bizarre. He had a feeling that his wife was failing to recognize him. At two in the morning he got up and went into the bathroom and shaved off his beard. He'd grown it upon falling in love with Freud, when he'd joined the Boston Institute. Gone. He ran his palm over his cheeks. Soft as a baby's foot. The person in the mirror was so young! Good. Once again he looked as he had when she first fell in love with him, such a long time—that is to say, so many ages— ago.

30

"—BUT I TOLD YOU, Sylvia," said Fine, finally letting out his anger, trying to pierce his one-eyed patient's illusion, "I am *not* your Stuart Fi—"

"Oh come on!" she said, coquettishly, "no need to pretend, sweetie. Why, without your beard you look just like you did back in high school. Now hush up 'n' listen—I'm close to a breakthrough, y' hear?" She went on about Green's Wild Animal Farm.

It was half-past four on Friday. All day long the heat had grown, and by late afternoon it was searing, wet, oppressive. The fifth day in a row—each hotter than the last—of record temperatures, a staggering heat wave. During each day, day after day, the heat had grown, as had the stillness. Friday was a lull. The birds were flying high up in the sky for insects, a sign of a storm. Yet with no storm in sight, it was spooky. The forecasters were flummoxed, their computers variant, down. Floods in Los Angeles, snow in Knoxville—something bigger than human was screwed up. And now, a lull, portending. All living things sensed the portent; none knew what the portent was. Yet portent alone brought out the bizarre.

Fine had spent the day fighting against himself. Duffy had not shown up that morning at six, and she'd failed to show up at the Federal Reserve—highly unusual for her. Fine had tried various other ways to locate her, but she'd disappeared. Clearly, her running away was proof of her guilt. He'd left a message on her machine, saying: "It's urgent that we talk. Call me at once. Insist that you be put through, no matter what." Safe at Stow, feeling out of danger, he was torn by conflicting feelings about calling the police. While he was still struggling to understand his session with Vergessen and his own weird actions, it was as if someone else had been doing these things. Most troubling were his flashes of jealousy: at random during the day, sometimes with Steph and the others, sometimes alone, seeing in his mind's eye the image of his wife, naked, legs spread, arms held out to John—at this, his scrotum would tighten and he'd feel a tremendous surge of rage. Yet with the surge, the rage left, wiping out the image. As if in his brain a dirty spark plug, firing once, had been shorted-out by igniting, leaving a stalled hot engine behind, as empty of memory as metal.

With only a few minutes to go until the end of the hour with Sylvia, Fine felt frustrated by her denial of who he really was.

"—'member when my daddy died, when I was thirteen? That 'accident,' with the shotgun? And then, after you left, they dammed up Lake Tuscaloosa, the farm was under water, an' my favorite tree, that umbrella magnolia, drowned. So I picked myself up, came North—New York City, imagine, me? Worked in the Central Park Zoo. And—"

He stared at her face. Unlike other one-eyed people where there was always the disconcerting question of which eye was real, hers were ill matched. With her mousy brown hair and hawk nose, it gave her a disjointed look. Looking into one hazel eye, he felt the other—like another person—watching him. He searched for affect. Sensing in her facial disjuncture a skew of soul, he said: "How horrible for you, to have your child die? Tell me about it, will you?"

"What?" She was shocked. "Lay off! I'm talkin' 'bout a zoo!"

Dummy, Fine thought, what's wrong with you? She went on about working with animals—she liked having them under control, lined up in their cages. On her days off, an expert equestrian, she'd ride in Central Park. Kept her own horse. Made friends with the carriage drivers and their horses, the ones outside the Plaza Hotel.

"If you liked it so much," Fine asked, "why did you leave?"

"Had to."

"Tell me about it."

"It's not right what you did, Stuart, not right at all. I can forgive your leaving me, way back then—I mean sort of forgive you—we were kids, what the hell, right?—but I can't forgive you for what you've done to me since I've been seeing you in therapy."

"What do you mean?"

"You know damn well what I mean!" Her face tensed, as if chilled. "Don't play innocent, it doesn't become you, sweetie."

"I don't know what you're talking about."

"Your sex life—every night a different woman—what the hell's come over you?" Fine was stunned—how did she know? "We were so close, once, and now we're gettin' close again, and you take up with sluts? Fornicatin' like a damn marmoset? For shame!"

"Surely," Fine said gently, "my personal morality is my—"

"No it is *not!*" Her voice, ice-cold, kicked out through rigidly set lips. "It's the concern of God, and of us on earth who know God! You're doin' evil! The Lord won't allow this much longer!" At first Fine thought she was merely a born-again Christian, but as she went on he felt something else: her quick shift from love to hate was so discordant, so brutal, it must be a sign of tremendous hatred underneath. His heart sank, he felt butterflies in his stomach: oh my God—is it *her?* The tiny vestigial hairs on the back of his neck crawled, as if a breeze were blowing across them. His paranoia floated up. Her good eye fixed him, unwavering. His heart beat hard in his chest, he felt a flush creep up his throat, and, dimly, heard her ask:

"What's wrong?"

"Nothing." His voice was furred, as if covered in moss.

"Come on, come on, tell me."

His bowels felt watery. "Tell me how you lost your eye."

"You don't give a damn—it's technique. I've had it with your batting my questions back. Tell me about *you,* or I swear I'll show you something that'll turn your stomach but good. C'mon—talk!"

Fine could barely think. "I told you: you are mistaken—"

"Come on, come clean." Fine felt caught in a vise. His mind froze. She sat between him and the door. He wanted to glance there to judge the distance, but dared not. She seemed to sense his wish to escape: "Scared of me? Good! Come on, talk." Fine panicked. He sat mute, trembling like a netted bird. "Dammit, you pulled this silent treatment on me once, leavin' me without so much's a good-bye—like my mother, and daddy too." She took a deep breath, and like a hawk swooping down for the kill, said: "What you did to me back then—it wasn't seduction, no. It was *rape.*" She perched on the edge of her chair: "There, it's out. Now stop staring and talk—or else!"

Fine felt her savagery, and tried to control himself. No, this actual person, even if sick, cannot be a mass murderer, no.

"Okay, you asked for it—I'll show you somethin' to turn your stomach but good!" She bent her head, and with a quick movement of her hand she plucked out her glass eye. She sat, glaring at him, tossing her eyeball up and down, taunting him. "Pretty ugly, hey?"

And then Fine knew: cat's eye marbles.

Instantly it came clear: her symbol, an object with psychotic meaning, marking her passage through the world, a fetish defining her self. He imagined her laying the cat's eyes at the site of the murders, calmly, to defuse her fury, a signature on her art. She is that rarity: a female psychopath. Without the glue of empathy, she flicks over into a killer-self. Fine knew he was now in grave danger. In her purse would be her gun. He had an ominous thought: if she knows I know, she'll kill me, for my knowing would be a final abandonment. He heard in his mind: "if your life depended on it," and knew he had but one chance: find a human shred in her, to relate to, feelingly, right now. And so he said: "How painful it must be for you, to have to face the world this way?" He felt it was false. Did she?

"Save your pity for someone who needs it. No pain in a dry socket." She stared at him, her one good eye seeming to darken, as the flecks of black coalesced. A welt arose, white, on her cheek. Fine was scared stiff. "What's wrong? What are you thinking?"

Fine looked from the scarred socket to the live eye. He felt his life hanging in the balance. "Sylvia, I'm scared."

"Am I that ugly?"

Fine felt a sliver of connection to her.

"No, that's not it—"

"What's in that cruel mind, eh?" Fine tensed. "I see," she said, in a tone that Fine suspected meant she'd come to some bizarre private conclusion, or even decision.

He felt desperate, and could say, only, "See?"

"Oh Lord!" She lifted her purse. "Why'd You make this—"

A sharp knock on the door. They both jumped. The door opened and Steph rushed in: "I'm sorry, but it's an emergency—"

"Who're you?" asked Sylvia, popping her eye back in.

"My wife, Stephanie—" said Fine, rising.

"What?" said Sylvia, "you're *married?* But . . . but you don't wear a ring! Why, what—" she stood up. Fine reached toward Steph. "But she's with the blond guy—and whose little boy?—you deceiver!"

"Steph, watch it!" yelled Fine.

"I'm gonna get you!" said Sylvia, looking wildly from one to the other. "Not right now—I'll let you suffer—but you—all of you—I swear to Almighty Jesus I'm gonna get you in the end! For the Lord will have His revenge! Yes! Yesss!" Hissing, she ran out.

"It's her," Fine cried, "get down!" He slammed the door and locked it and hit the rug, pulling Steph down beside him. He fished for the phone and called Mr. Royce, who—issuing photo IDs to Stow Dietary—failed to act fast enough to stop the beat-up Ford from speeding off Long Island, through Squantum, to disappear down the maw of the Southeast Expressway, into the body of the world.

"You're white as a sheet!" said Steph.

"Thank God you came when you did!" Fine shivered with terror. "And that she didn't start firing! Was that close or what?" He dialed O'Herlihey. "Why'd you come in? You've never done it before."

"A woman named Duffy called the home number—said you insisted she talk to you. She seemed concerned about you—"

"Damn! How could I've been so dumb?" He sensed his life starting to crash down around him. He got O'Herlihey, told him what had happened. The detective agreed—this was the real thing. Fine hung up, got out the bourbon. Pouring drinks, his hand was shaking. "At least, now, we're sure, right?" Steph said yes. "And since we know what she looks like, she'll never get out

here again, and we're safe, I mean, out here on the island we're
safe now, right?"

"Uh huh." Her dark-blue eyes looked straight into his, and her
voice trembled: "Oh Fine—what a *tsimmes* we've made!"

"No joke." The bourbon burned, warming him. "Now what?"

"Let's get out of here." She hesitated. "How 'bout a swim?"

"Swim?" He felt panicked—how close they'd come to death!

"Yes. It'll be all right." She took his hand. "C'mon."

They went out into the blast furnace of the day and walked down
the rusted railroad tracks toward the far end of the island. The
railway had been built during World War II to carry supplies to a
series of bunkers carved into the limestone hill upon which the
Long Island Light stood. They tried to match their strides to the
ties, and failed. The day, sizzling hot, immaculately still, seemed
to Fine both harsh and gentle. The heat made talk an effort. Fine
felt bloated. His belly, squeezed by his belt, oozed over the rim;
sweat poured off his head, neck, and chest and pooled in his
crotch, fat thighs chafing. Gaining weight had started to bother
him. So many things, now, seemed to be popping up, declaring
themselves, confusing him. He wished she'd take his hand. He
was reluctant to take hers, for she was no longer his. He felt a stab
of jealousy—lasting, lasting—and he looked out to sea. It seemed
solid. Only when he focused in could he see the undulations. Sailboats and tankers moved in slow motion. A jumbo jet slid more
slowly than seemed possible down a bevel of thick hot air. Fine
caught the scent of wild grass, thought of his freed grasshoppers,
and felt happy for them. At his feet, a single red tulip wilted over
a rusted rail. Wild roses thickened in bud, unfooled by the false
summer. Fine said: "It's hard to hold onto anything in the world,
isn't it?"

"Yes," said Steph, "but it's not as hard as letting go."

At the rail's end, a wall of a bunker had fallen in, exposing a
white-tiled shower room. The path forked: left to beach, right to
Long Island Light.

"I bet there's a breeze up there," said Steph. "Let's go." She
took his hand and started up. He felt a thrill—to be touched by
her again! They struggled, pouring with sweat, up the tamped dirt
path to the base of the lighthouse, and, puffing, stared up at the
peeling paint of the black-and-white checkerboard. Fine unlocked

the door, locking it after them. Like kids doing the forbidden, they climbed up the circular stairs, each turn darkening, smelling of birds, up and up until the spiral began to lighten again and then each turn lightening as they breathed ever more heavily until it was blindingly light and there was an explosion—*whoosh!*—as dozens of startled pigeons clattered off into the air. Drenched with sweat, breathless, they looked out as if from on top of the world.

After a while, from across the room she said: "I want you."

Fine felt the circular room spin, and held onto the rail, his head reeling, old and new feelings jangling together. And then she unzipped her jumpsuit partway down the front. She was naked beneath. Fine felt a rush of arousal, but then saw a terrible image: the cut a *diener* makes on a corpse, chin to crotch, for an autopsy. Sickened, he put a hand to his mouth. How beautiful, and how terrible! He looked away. She embraced him, kissing him with open mouth, her tongue sucking at his own. And yet he felt her touch as rough, her coming at him this way as harsh. I want talk, a feathery caress, lightness. Is this how women feel men? Is macho felt as rape? With astonishment, he realized that he was feeling her as a woman might feel a man! *That's* what he'd felt with Sunny, yes! Talk about wires being crossed, inside! He tried to break away: "Wait—no."

"What?" Aroused, she held him, moving her body against his.

"It's not right—I can't."

"It's no big deal—maybe it's the full moon, or the heat, or what a sexy animal you've become—I always liked you fatter—you're more solid—and without your beard—it's like turning back time—"

"I shaved it off because I thought you didn't know me."

"What?"

"Thought if I shaved it, you'd love me again like before."

"We won't talk love, Fine. This is *lust,* animal magnetism, no strings attached—I just really want you, right now—"

"Please n . . . n . . . no." He stuttered, shaking, feeling a chill.

"What?" she asked, worried. "Are you still scared?"

He lied: "Yes. St . . . st . . . still terrified, yes."

"Oh." She relaxed her body. "Poor kid."

"Please, Steph, just lie with me, and hold me a little, and let me hold you, please?"

"Sure."

And so they lay down, and she held him. After a while, he began to stroke her, gently, calmly, delicately, her shoulders, her breasts, her thighs. He felt he was touching her as a woman might, and as a woman might want to be touched. Feeling close to her for the first time in weeks—years?—he said: "Is *this* what women want?"

She laughed. "You really have become a funny little putz."

They lay still, together, looking up at the rafters, sensing the breeze, and, far below, the world. She even napped, and he felt, then, motherly. The pigeons returned, roosting. Sunlight slanted through the dusty air, glanced off Steph's silky black hair, and filled the room with red-gold light. She awoke, and Fine whispered an aphorism: " 'I am like a child trying to grasp a sunbeam: I open my hand to find, with amazement, my palm empty, the light gone.' "

"This was nice," she said, "but don't get any big ideas."

They walked down the darkening spiral, out.

At dinner, everyone was tense. Steph and John were in a rush—he was off to dress rehearsal, she to The Comedy Box. Both were opening the next night. The boy still wouldn't talk to his father. Only because Fine had cooked his favorite meal—hot dogs and french fries and peanut-butter ice cream—would he eat with them. He wolfed down his dinner and got up. John said: "Tomorrow, fresh vegetables, you understand?" The boy went out to the backyard.

John looked at them, disconsolate. "What can I do?"

Ever since the tryst with Steph, Fine had felt a bitterness toward John, and said: "You shouldn't've taken on the show."

"I had no choice."

"There's always choice," said Fine, "always."

"That doesn't help me now, Fine."

"It might. Suppose you quit."

"What?" John looked amazed, as if Fine had suggested he quit life. "That's ridiculous. My show's opening tomorrow."

"Your show with your son is already closing."

"I'm doing it for him."

"For the greater glory of yourself—at least admit it, okay?"

John, looking hurt, stood up. "C'mon, Steph, let's go."

"Kids will always forgive you, if you just give 'em a chance," said Fine. "If you quit, and stay here with him—"

"He won't even talk to me!"

"Stay, and he will."

"I've tried—I've spent whole days with him—doesn't work."

"How can it, when he sees you go off at night to something you love more? Look—it's not your fault, John—you've got problems seeing others as separate from yourself—me, Steph, your boy—all of us are reflections of you—this is an opportunity to free up your—"

"Grand," said John, derisively, "just grand! Ripping up my personality right before my biggest opening night—just what I need."

"Your son needs you and you're leaving," said Fine, angrily. "A little boy needs you and you're acting like a little boy yourself! You may've been the *wunderkind* at Harvard, but now it's more *kind* than *wunder,* if you ask me." John narrowed his eyes, seemed about to attack. "Hey, I'm sorry, but . . . don't be reckless. He needs you."

John's knuckles whitened on the back of the chair. Without a word, he stormed out. Steph got up, took a plate and put it in the sink, saying: "It doesn't suit you, Fine, it really does not."

"What's that?"

"Contempt."

He caught her gaze, and wanted to hold it, but she looked away, and started for the door. "Hey—how's the comedy coming, eh?"

"Remember what I said: don't get any big ideas." She left.

No one noticed that Fine had eaten dinner with his right hand.

Before he went to bed, after making sure the boy was safe, Fine felt a strange premonition. Remembering that he'd forgotten to look in on his hoppers that day, he went to the lab. He turned on the light and failed to hear the happy chirps of the males in the one cage of smart hoppers he'd left in the lab. His heart sank. He went to the lab bench.

All the grasshoppers were dead, ripped apart. A head here, a torso there, and everywhere, limbs, some still twitching. She'd done it *before* she'd come to see him! He screamed, ran out, and found himself under the copper beech, beating his fists against the trunk as if his punishing it could bring back his dear little creatures. And then, remembering his last cage, he ran up to his office, opened the secret door, and—yes—there they were, safe. He sat staring at them, rage and grief swinging back and forth inside.

His last smart hoppers, as if sensing a great wrong, stood quite silent and still.

He hid them again, ran to his house, locked all the doors and windows, checked once again on the boy, and sat, trying to get the arms of his mind around the vileness, the depth of viciousness, of the monster, Sylvia Green.

31

OF ALL THE Jefferson House patients struck down, those continuing to cry, scream, and whimper were the ones most easily found.

"Kidney stones?" Fine asked Ms. Ando.

"From Finestones," said said, sadly. "Excruciating pain." She was distraught over the massacre of the grasshoppers.

"But I told you to keep them hydrated—"

"They wouldn't listen—they were too upset."

Several of Fine's inpatients, failing to drink enough water during the heat wave, had come down with kidney stones. Torn apart by the events of the month, they and the others—barometers of the psychic weather—had regressed to early stages of development and were curled up in fetal positions, hiding in the labyrinth of tunnels carved under Stow during wartime. Fat Sadie, enraged at being disturbed with her cache of food, assaulted the staff, and in the scuffle, her bones weakened by gallons of high-phosphorus diet soda, had broken her ankle and was now in a cast, wigged out on morphine, sure she'd been wounded in "Viet-Salvador." Eli—betrayed by the howls of the poodle—had been found hiding in a secret room in Dr. Pelvin's house, and assuming the identity "Eli Frank, Anne's missing brother," screamed at the mental health workers: "Nazis! Never again!" Fighting them, he forced them to act like the Nazis he feared. All day Saturday Fine, Steph, John, and John James were haunted by the screams echoing up through the maze of tunnels, decreasing stepwise as yet another terrorized psychotic was found, locked up, tranquilized, and hydrated. Cooter, Stinko, Mary, Eve—all were still missing.

Brutally hot and eerily still, with no birds singing and no live things stirring, the day seemed damaged, an ominous defective day that darkened as it went. All day long Fine flashed on repetitive childhood memories of places and times, perhaps dream, perhaps wakefulness, filled with foreboding. He sensed dimly, in the haze, a threat. Yet the worst seemed to be past. There were cracks in the dome of tropical air. The usual orderly progression of change of weather—hot, storm, cool—was on its way. Hadn't the horizon, by noontime, shown those fuzzy free-form curls of dark clouds? You could see the storm on its way, as you can see air in convection currents over radiators. And, just as in winter cats seek warm beds of sunlight, all day long humans sought cool.

"What am I doing here?" John asked Steph as they sat in the den watching Fine commune with his smart hoppers. "Why am I living in a madhouse, listening to a man talk to trained insects?"

"Why?" Steph said. "For the same reason that I, depressed, have to go out tonight and make the louts of Boston laugh. I feel so bad! I wanna pig out on Pepperidge Farm, and fall on my fork!"

John and Fine laughed. They'd made a testy peace. There seemed to be a new, sullen edge to Fine. He'd spent the day apart from the adults, playing with John James.

And so at the end of an early dinner, John and Steph got up to go upstairs and get ready for the trip into town for their debuts.

"Do me a favor, Fine, will you?" John asked. "Go get John James? Bring him inside before I leave, before the storm."

"Right," said Fine, rising, "I'll go get him right now."

"Thanks." He sighed. "You're right. After the run—it's only two weeks—I'll take time off, spend it with him, just him and me, a real vacation. It won't be too late, then, will it?"

"Never too late, with a kid, no."

He smiled. "You'll see—it'll be just what the doctor ordered." John followed Steph upstairs. Fine went toward the kitchen.

Yet just then Fine heard, from the front of the house, the first soft roll of thunder. He turned and took a few steps toward it before he stopped, and, feeling responsible for the little boy, turned back again. This time he got as far as the back door before a flash of light shot through the screen door in the front of the house, down the long hallway, transfixing him. Lightning? He waited for the thunder, and heard none. What then? He'd take just one look and then come back for John James. There, again, as if meant for him, the flash of light. Drawn by an invisible thread, he walked to the front door and out onto the porch.

The west was darkening rapidly, as if angry, the black clouds rising, higher, higher, fighting the heat, shielding the setting sun. Again a flash, and Fine knew what it was: the Long Island Light.

He was drawn down off the porch and found himself scurrying up the hill behind Jefferson House, to see more freely. And then, up on his high perch, all at once he felt very strange.

He stood there, drawn to the repeating cycle: flash/black . . . flash/black . . . As his eyes followed the strobe, he felt dizzy, deep down inside. Queasy, almost seasick, as if something was about to tip, spill. The bars of light and dark seemed like a cage, beckoning him in. To stay out seemed the height of folly, intolerable. In the western sky, the chimneys of cumulus were being crushed down by the high pressure whizzing in from Canada, the last sunlight slipping in under, glinting off the water like a million fireflies, the distant glints as sharp and clear as the closer, all quanta the same. Fine looked away, toward the full moon. Strangely, he was unable to focus on it freely, and so he looked down to the ground. But no relief there, for the moon shone off the twin rails and led his eyes once again to the lighthouse and then to the light—the only movement in the stasis before the storm. The sweep of the beam was asymmetric, the dark longer and more intense than the light. Fine flashed on his oldest dream: trying to grasp an infinity of shifting, fluid, free-form shapes, and, over and over again, failing, the points vanishing, the lines warping, the planes tilting, the solids shaking like gelatin so there was no solidity left. Were my childhood days so painful? Is this why I have nightmares? Drawn to the flashing light, Fine felt a terrible aura: he was about to have another seizure. A second fit would confirm the worst: brain tumor. Scared, he cried out: "Please, Big Guy—not now—I'm not ready, yet!"

To prevent the onslaught of the light, he shut his eyes and turned away. Like a blind man freed in a foreign city, he used his cane to feel his way down the paved path, playing real blindness to ease his terror: *tap, tap, tap . . . tap?*

As if in answer to his plea but in answer from the wrong sector, through his lids came an even more potent flash of light: lightning? *Ba-dum.* Thunder? What a world! Useless even to be blind! He opened his eyes and saw in the sky the jagged sizzle of a terrific bolt, and then, counting—each second meant the eye of the storm was a mile away—one one thousand two one thou—*ba-doooml!*—less than two miles off and coming in fast! Fine's body felt heavy yet empty, energy flowing up into his head, his brain. His hands flew up to his temples, as if to stem the tide. A flash came that lit up the whole island with an eerie harsh light and then, a second behind, borne in on a rush of cold air—*ba-DOOoommmm!*—the first real crack in the skin of the hot crippled day. Fine stood, transfixed, legs whipped by branches of low bushes. And then the lightning came hard and fast, one bolt after another, welding earth and sky, and in on a wave of icy sulfurous air came a sheet of rain and hail.

Fine stood, drenched, hailstones raining down on him, while high over his head bolts of lightning drew him up. The whorls of electricity crackling in the air sent wondrous currents through his body. He could feel the ions in the air interacting with his surplus free calcium—the reverse of the famous hot desert winds—sirocco, sharav, chinook, Santa Anna (during which, he recalled, murder rates increased). He watched the icy crystals hit the pavement and pop back up into the watery air, he saw a tree limb crack, rip from its socket, fall with a crash, shaking the ground, and he was staring at the tree's gaping white wound when, in the wake of a tremendous bolt, a switch came unstuck in his brain and voltage surged through the browned-out parts and he could almost *see* the pathways come alive: step by step at a zillion synapses calcium ions switched *on* and a tide of current rushed right back up the reductionist ladder through the hippocampus into the fornix and the mammilothalamic tract and the many-pronged anterior thalamic nuclei and, with decreasing resistance, blasted into the cingulate gyrus whirled in ever-higher wattage through the cephalons of evolution—*insecta, reptilia,* things that rely mainly on smell or gills or wings to get along—all the silly fishes and bats and birds and crafty monkeys shitting into their hands and pelting travelers from trees and—*whooosh!*—the ho-

lographic wave came roaring through the prestigious de Broca
cortical layers—the Palm Springs of Neurotopology—VI, V, IV,
III, II, I—"Ignition we got a go Houston the thing is flyin' bee-
you-tee-ful!" (Whaddaya call a Jewish astronaut? [a beat]
Schmuck!) and then the phantasmagorical wave crashed down
over him—the poor little *pisher* from Columbia New York USA
The Earth Milky Way Galaxy The Universe—and Fine broke
free, and took off:

"I have been betrayed!"

He cracked his cane over his knee and started to run down
toward the house. Encumbered by the brace, he bent to remove it,
and then, freed from it, he really ran, through the sheets of rain
and blasts of thunder and hailstones and whipping tree limbs, into
his front yard, up onto his porch, in through the screen door, and
face to face with Steph and John, who, dressed up, were coming
downstairs to leave. Fine blocked their exit, screaming: "You bas-
tards—you betrayed me!" He saw the shock come over them.
What a sight he must have been: soaking wet, roaring like a lunatic: "Monsters! Both of you are fucking monsters!"

Thunder blasted again, shaking the beams. The chandelier tin-
kled and the rain hammered like a dozen madmen on the roof.

"Well," said Steph, "it's the old Fine, back again—"

"How could you? In my *bed!* In my house in my bed—"

"You didn't seem to mind, these last two weeks—"

"I was sick—"

"When I said that to you, you told me you never felt bet—"

"Because I was sick! I had no choice, none! And to do it in
front of the little boy? John—you should be ashamed."

"Okay, okay, maybe I should," said John, "but we've got no
time now. Where's John James?"

With a sinking feeling, Fine remembered that he'd forgotten
him. "I . . . I don't know."

"What?" said John. "But you said—oh shit! Search the house!"
He grabbed an umbrella and rushed out the back door. Steph
went upstairs. Fine, paralyzed, watched John go into the Dublin
hut and come back out, white as a sheet, and then begin racing
around the high-walled yard. Fine went shouting through the
downstairs and cellar—no luck. John, back in the kitchen, eyes
frantic, screamed: "Goddamn you Fine, I told you—"

"I've looked everywhere," said Steph, breathlessly, coming downstairs. "He's not here."

They went out onto the front porch, trying to see through the rain. The storm had clouded the moon.

"Goddammit, where's the fucking light?" said John.

They waited, and Fine, heart in his throat, prayed for a bolt of lightning. And then it came, a great jolt, seeming to lift them by their hair, lighting up the whole vista. Their eyes strained to see before the curtain of dark came down again.

"Look!" said Steph. "There—the jetty!"

"Oh God no!" cried John, and started to run.

Fine saw the figure of a man in a wide-brimmed hat, running away from the house, carrying over his shoulder the limp form of the boy. Chloroformed? Dead? He was already at the base of the lawn. And there, moored at the end of the jetty, was a speedboat.

John grabbed his bicycle and raced off through the pelting rain down the lawn. Fine and Steph started after but Fine screamed through the storm for her to call the police and then ran after John.

As he ran down the slope, Fine could see, as if in slow motion, a terrible drama unfold. The man trundled toward the end of the stone jetty, John gaining on him all the time. Just when it seemed he would catch him, the bike slipped its chain and jolted to a sharp stop, sending John tumbling over the handlebars onto the grass. Dazed, he got up, started running, but the man had dumped the boy into the boat and was casting off. John reached the end of the dock five seconds too late. Fine saw him look toward the boat, and in a blast of thunder, reach down to take off his shoes to leap in.

He never straightened back up.

Fine got to him just in time to save him from vanishing into the sea. He lunged, grabbed John by an arm and a leg, and pulled with all his might, tugged and tugged for what seemed an eternity, trying to keep John's head above water, always on the verge of falling in himself until, suddenly beside him, Steph too pulled and they got him up, back up onto the pier, and, panting, laid him on his back. Fine, hands soaked, wiped the sweat from his face.

Breathless, Steph bent to tend to John, but glancing at Fine she stopped, and stared, eyes wide with fright. She pointed to his forehead: "Look—blood!"

"What?" He looked down. His hands were covered in blood. Shocked, he asked: "Mine?!"

"No! Oh my God—"

Feeling a wrench deep inside, deep in the core of his being, Fine looked down and saw, in a last withering flash of light, where his friend's chest had been, a dark mass of flesh and blood, and there, below, glistening like maggots, a mass of guts.

John, lying on his back, was trying to talk.

They bent to him to hear, Fine cradling his head in his arms. John looked down at his raw intestines, moved a hand as if to touch himself, and in disbelief, said: "M . . . Mine!?"

"You'll be all right—" Steph said.

"No, there's an ebb." Blood bubbled from his mouth. "Sorry."

"It's all right," said Fine.

"Dear God sorry forgive my sins . . ." A cough—black stuff —Fine could feel the life force dimming. "You take care of John Ja . . ."

They felt—first in their fingertips touching him and then throughout—they felt an aery tingling as his soul slipped off, away.

Steph screamed, and screamed again. Fine felt his own body turn inside out and a bolus of horrible stuff fly up in his throat and he leaned over the pier and vomited.

The speedboat cut a white slash in the black sea. The wake spread. The wave crashed into the jetty, seeming to rock it, them. The rain beat down and beat them down, and then eased. The storm eased, and left the outer world clear and crisp and sweet scented, as if they—and all things—were good. They heard: *tap, tap, tap*—water dripping—as if the living, swinging white, red-tipped canes, were trying to find their way.

Their silence was immense, as deadly as their freedom.

After the rain
each hears
a bird.

IV
AWARE

My friends, life is for living.
The purpose of life is to live.
There is no other purpose than to live.
And to live is to be related.
     —Vimala Thakar, *Newsletter,* 1983

32

"THE UNIVERSE ALWAYS WINS," said Nipak Dandi, crisply, out of the blue.

Beethoven's Sonata No. 12 in A flat—*Funeral March*—had just come to its quick clear end. Nipak had chosen it. He had played it over and over. To Fine it could have been a kid banging pots and pans, or "Alexander's Ragtime Band." So much dull noise. The three sat on the porch after dinner Monday night the twenty-second. Steph and Fine had not eaten. Nipak sat alone on the white wicker couch. Fine sat alone on a white wicker chair at one end of the porch, Steph sat alone at the other. The day had been immaculate: clear, sharp, bright. A bluejay swooped past. Others might call the last light "exquisite."

"Always always wins." Nipak seemed perky—a spirited little water animal, say, a fighting fish. He wore a white cotton suit. His sleek black hair shone. In his handsome cocoa-butter face, his dark eyes sparkled. He jabbed the air with a cigar. He pronounced "wins" like "vins." Fine thought: so what. Fine's heart was numb. With effort he swung his eyes to Steph. She too seemed dead at heart to this "universe" crap. The frizz in her dark hair seemed wrong. Her lids, thick and low, hid her eyes. Her complexion was dull. Her defective lip gave the illusion of her being close to tears. Neither she nor Fine had cried. In her he saw his own nullity.

Fine sensed he'd reached the lowest point of his life.

I had hope for him at last.

Nipak had shown up on Sunday morning. He claimed to have had a "sixth sense" of something wrong. He'd tried to ring—line engaged. He'd caught the first shuttle from New York.

He had appeared just as John's mother and uncle had begun to attend to the grisly business of gathering up John's things. Katey was silent, enraged. The Uncle served as usher. From the doorway of the bedroom they watched Katey open the closet. She saw her dead son's shoes. With a cry she folded down onto the floor. The Uncle went to her. Fine and Steph went away. Katey left the house without a glance or a good-bye. The Uncle laid a hand on Fine's shoulder. They would wake John Tuesday and Wednesday, bury him Thursday. He wrote down the name of a funeral home, a church. He left.

Saturday night and morning had been spent with the police. Detective O'Herlihey was livid. Clearly there was now a fresh and vital interest in the case. It turned out that Sylvia had worked for the Boston Mounted Police for a short while. She was expert in horses, firearms, power boats, disguises. This explained her man-in-brimmed-hat disguise and her beating the Stow blockade by coming by sea. A vicious, sly, capable murderer. And yet there was some hope: Steph's call to the police had set things in motion, and the airport, harbor, bus and train terminals, and major highways had been sealed off. There was little likelihood that she'd gotten out of Greater Boston. She was hiding somewhere close by.

"How can we find her?" Fine asked.

"Wait for her ransom demand," said the gray-skinned, blue-lipped detective, over a wall of cigarette smoke.

"Ransom?"

"When she finds she's trapped, she'll deal. Meanwhile, Dr. Fine, stay out of our way, and be careful. If you remember anything about her—tell us." Fine looked puzzled. "You shrunk her, right?" Fine heard this as an accusation, and lowered his head in shame. "So if you think of somethin' specific—deep down in her warped mind, you call, you get me?" At sunup Sunday the morose detective trudged down the lawn for a last look at the scene of the crime.

Trying to recall Sylvia, Fine found his mind almost blank. Exhausted, he couldn't sleep. His senses replayed the murder. His suffering was worse for his not feeling it. With numb curiosity, he awaited the pain to come when the novocaine wore off.

Whenever Fine tried to make contact with Steph, nothing happened. They kept apart. They moved about without purpose and in silence, like two species of animals. If they chanced to come face to face they stared. Not eye to eye, but askew. To him she seemed dead. Or, if living, alive in the wrong element. A creature of air fallen to water, gasping in the syrupy surround. Fine wanted desperately to talk. Fine sensed that if he talked, she'd not hear.

"I'm tired," Steph said. "Oh, but I am tired."

They kept apart.

For Fine the whole thing was unreal. It had not happened. Look—the real lawn, the real jetty, the real sea and sails and city and sky. Any minute now John and John James would reappear.

The real weather, too, seemed to mock them. After the hard storm, the day had bloomed lush and full and rich. The sky was meticulously clear, and sharp, and light, as if something wonderful had been born from all the rain, and lightning, and thunder.

Nipak Dandi tried to help. At first his quiet presence—a buffer between the two—had been welcome. He cooked for them. He answered the phone, scattering the media vultures. Yet by Monday night Fine was fed up. Nipak too had an agenda. He'd encouraged them to meditate. Like puppets, they'd acquiesced. Sitting, Fine's silence was chaotic. His mind kept scurrying back over the events, repeating, repeating: What if I had gone straight to the boy when I had planned to? Would *I* be dead? Would the boy be safe? Would John still be alive? What if this? What if that? Nipak and Steph took long walks together around the island. Fine, saddened, sat.

And so when Nipak brought up the "Universe" Fine exploded: "The Universe? Don't give me the 'Universe'! My best friend died!"

"What died?" asked Nipak. Fine, sinking under waves of contempt, snorted. "Why don't we pay as much attention to where we were before we were born as to where we will be after we are dead?"

"A cruel, senseless death. The world's coming apart."

"The problem is not in the world, but in you."

"Tell that to the little boy, wherever he is."

"Life goes on. We are still here—"

"Six million Jews aren't. Peace? Love? Try pulling a Gandhi—lying down in front of Hitler's tanks—see if they stop!"

"And so *we* should do the same? Learn brutality? Become Hitlers ourselves?"

"Freud himself—a delicate, sensitive intelligence—crushed by the Nazis!"

"Freud lives on—"

"The world stinks! The world stinks and is about to end!"

"In the Buddha's time, the world stank and was about to end. The world has *always* stunk and is *always* about to end! So we must—"

"This is worse—worse than Germany in the thirties."

"Hardly. We have now a rebirth of the spirit—"

"If, in Munich in '34, someone told you that in a few years they'd be gassing millions of Jews, would you've believed it? This'll be worse—it won't seem to be happening to *real* people, but to these little people on TV. The first time was a warmup—we got TV and nukes, now. I want to *kill* her. I'm gonna learn to shoot that gun!" He paused. Again the wave hit him: "Oh God—he's dead! Oh my God! Everything in my life's gone wrong—everything, *everything!*"

"Join the crowd," said Nipak.

"Oh fuck off."

"Fine," said Steph, rising, "he's just trying to help."

"Like he was just trying to help by getting into your pants in New York? You can't trust anybody. Hitler was a guru too."

"You think that lives go well?" asked Nipak. "That you can live without suffering?: 'Life like the charmed'? Lives do not go as we plan. Our quest for permanence in an impermanent world is the root of all our suffering."

"Great," said Fine. "Why even make an effort, right?"

"Effort has no place in reality."

"Zen bullshit!"

"Look—here—" Nipak was pointing over the porch rail toward the cliff edge. "Look at that gull—what do you see?"

"I don't want to look at a fucking gull," said Fine.

"And would you want to look at your not wanting to look?"

"Please, Nipak—just leave, and leave me alone?"

"Oh but the mind is shameless!" said Nipak.

"I'm tired," said Steph, opening the screen door slowly. It cried out on its hinges. "Good night." It slammed shut.

"And I'm tired, tired of talk," said Fine. "I want to act."

"Yes! Most definitely!" said Nipak, jumping up. *"Act!"*

"So much for your 'effort is unreal,' eh?"

" 'Right' action takes no effort. We must employ 'Full-Catastrophe Zen'! Use our power to find the woman, save the boy!"

"How?"

"I do not yet know how. The answer is inside you—us—us *in the world.* When it comes, it will hit us like the bullet in the nose!"

"Terrific," said Fine, rising. "You sound just like the analysts: the problem's never 'them out there,' it's always 'us in here.' Well *I* didn't murder him—that cunt Green did! I'm fed up."

Fine went to his car. Nipak followed, asking where he was going. "To the Institute. I'm codiscussor at the seminar."

"In the world! As they say: 'Never forget your zipcode!' "

"Jerk!" Fine cried, as he drove off. It was as much to get away from them and Stow as to go to the seminar that he left. The TBI password, diluted down the Freud family tree, was now "Lady Caroline Maureen Blackwood." The door buzzed. Fine went in. The subject was "Countertransference": how the analyst's perception of the patient is distorted by his own early infantile neurotic conflicts. Freud had written little on this—his Nürnberg Congress paper (1910); a few helpful hints in tonight's *Observations on Transference Love* (1915).

All were there. Georgina, puffy eyed as if she'd been crying, patted the seat beside her. V. posed the evening's question:

"What about how *we* feel?"

Dr. Pete Gross, the ex-pathologist, solid as a rock, began:

> *Bemerkungen Über die Übertragungsliebe,* 1915: Every beginner in psychoanalysis probably feels alarmed at first at the difficulties in store for him when he comes to interpret the patient's associations and to deal with the reproduction of the repressed. When the time comes, however, he soon learns to look upon these difficulties as insignificant, and instead becomes convinced that the only really serious diffi-

culties he has to meet lie in the management of the transference. . . .

To Fine, Freud's words seemed comic and unreal. What use is
this? John's dead. Fine sat numb, staring at nothing. Gross then
dared comment: "I submit that in the passage that follows, Freud
used the famous 'sausage metaphor' both as a counterphobic exegesis of his own castration anxiety, and as the earliest documented
presagement—'throwing a single sausage onto the (dog)track'—of
the Great War."

"For the doctor, ethical motives unite with the technical
ones to restrain him from giving the patient his love. The
aim . . . is that this woman, whose capacity for love is
impaired by infantile fixations, should gain free command
over it; that she should not, however, dissipate it in the
treatment, but keep it ready for the time when, after the
treatment, the demands of real life make themselves felt.
He must not stage the scene of a dog race in which the prize
was to be a garland of sausages but that some humorist
spoiled by throwing a single sausage onto the track. The
result was, of course, that the dogs threw themselves upon
it and forgot all about the race and about the garland that
was luring them to victory in the far distance. . . . It is
not always easy for the doctor to keep within the limits
prescribed by ethics and technique. Those who are still
youngish and not yet bound by strong ties may in particular
find it a hard task. Sexual love is undoubtedly one of the
chief things in life, and the union of mental and bodily
satisfaction in the enjoyment of love is one of its culminat-
ing peaks. Apart from a few queer fanatics, all the world
knows this . . . ; science alone is too delicate to admit it."

So what? I don't care. I'll leave town. I'll buy a farm in Iowa.

"It is not a patient's crudely sensual desires that constitute
the temptation. These are more likely to repel, and it will
call for all the doctor's tolerance if he is to regard them as a
natural phenomenon. It is rather, perhaps, a woman's subtler and aim-inhibited wishes that bring with them the dan-

ger of making a man forget his technique and his medical
task for the sake of a fine experience. . . .

A *fine* one indeed. How new my own name seemed, just after my
fit. Something valuable happened, then, but it's all fuzzy, now.
Gross handed the floor to the codiscussor, the acne-ed Jungian,
Bergeneiss. Strangely, Leon ignored the paper and began presenting a case. The patient, now twenty-two, at age nine in a car
accident had seen her mother decapitated. Cool and precise, Leon
told the story marvelously, making it seem a spellbinding, exciting
analytic challenge. In treatment he had confronted the patient,
pounding away at the layers of "repressed material" until out
came, in minute detail, the memory. He spoke of how hard it had
been for him to keep his own feelings out of the analysis: disgust,
pity, anger. He claimed the case was poised on the edge of breakthrough. Although she'd not shown up for the past two weeks—
claiming she was "quitting"—Leon thought this a "final acting
out" and awaited her return. Had he shown his own feelings, the
analysis would have failed. Fine's heart beat faster—he sensed the
poor nine-year-old's horror. How could she recover from that?
Enough she's still alive, after her Auschwitz. He looked around
the room. All but Georgina were sitting stolidly, many chomping
cigars. Georgina clutched his hand. With each awful detail, she
squeezed harder. Leon gave a brief account of his "countertransference distortions." As he'd sat with the patient, he'd analyzed
out his revulsion: "a *shadow,* in Jung's collective unconscious."
At this, Fine looked into Georgina's eyes, saw her horror, and
began to crack.

Fine got up to speak. His sense of unreality fogged the room.
He stood, in silence, looking numbly into one set of eyes, then
another, sensing their contempt. He turned to Vergessen. His idol
seemed far away, smaller, like a place from childhood. A child
sees her mother beheaded. What could there be to say, to do? I
saw my best friend die. I put my hand into his guts. I held him
and felt his spirit ebb. I am too numb for words. For talk.

As used to silence as they were, Fine's was oppressive.

At last Fine said: "Two nights ago, my best friend was murdered." He paused. "My best friend is dead and I am to blame."

He looked into Georgina's eyes and saw them start to glisten. A
sick feeling rose up in his throat and, fight it as he might, his lips

turned down and his eyes welled up and he felt a raw grating pain
clawing at the bridge of his nose and he tried to choke back his
tears but could not. He stood before them, silent and immobile,
arms at his sides, palms turned out, tears trickling down his
cheeks.

Shuffling of feet, coughing. Dully he sensed their reactions:
How could this be? What next? This is not the way "Countertransference" seminar should go! Talk, not action; insight. Can't
Fine control himself? The tension was almost palpable. V. said
nothing. Georgina wept. Fine, deadened by their silence, dried up.

He stood there, re-numbed, isolated. After what seemed like
ages, he said, bitterly: "He died! It's my fault! Can't any of you
help me?"

"Perhaps Dr. Fine would wish to step out and compose himself?" asked Leon, a note of compassion in his voice.

But Fine just kept standing there like a schizoid until, finally,
Georgina arose, held out her hand to him, and escorted him out.
They stood in the hallway. Through the door Fine heard them
arguing, Leon ending with: "—dirty laundry here? Ménage, black
prostitutes, *murders?* Perhaps poor Fine needs a second analysis.
I hear Dr. Gold has time. At the very least I motion that Dr. Fine
be severely censured by TBI, if not expunged." A gasp; a long
silence.

"Yes, well," said Vergessen in that kindly, enigmatic tone that
assured that what followed would be subject to a whole rainbow
of interpretations, "only losers know the meaning of life."

Georgina led Fine out onto Commonwealth Avenue. The night
was warm yet crisp. Moonlight glinted off a piece of glass in the
gutter. Fine thought he caught the attar of wild roses, but knew it
was far too early, yet, and that it must be her perfume. She suggested a talk. In the bar, she said: "How brave to do what you
did."

"What did I do?" Fine asked, fuzzily. He again felt only the
same null void, the frozen heart.

"Showed them," she said, proudly. "The problem with countertransference is that we hide it!" Fine grunted. "It's so male!; 'if I
show her what I feel she'll *get* me.' It's not that men don't hear,
it's that they don't *respond*. Listening is only half; telling—in a
feeling way—what you heard is the other half, and dammit you
did it—right from the *kishkes!*"

"You don't understand," said Fine, rising laboriously, as if the atmosphere had turned to mud. "Enough talk. He's dead."

When Fine got home Detective O'Herlihey was waiting with Nipak and Steph. Sylvia had sent a videotaped ransom demand. O'Herlihey stuck the tape into the recorder. There she was, in her wide-brimmed hat. Beside her, gagged, eyes big with fright, John James.

"Oh the poor little kid!" cried Steph.

And Sylvia said: "Get me Stuart Fine."

33

THE DISASTERS IN Fine's life began breeding. The Jefferson House patients were flagrantly psychotic from the morphine given them for their kidney stones and from the murder of someone they knew. Several Jefferson families were considering legal redress. Mrs. Neiderman, loyal and concerned, said that there were rumblings of Fine's being suspended from Stow. His outpatients were shaken by John's murder and by Fine's connection to it, and were demanding extra sessions. Ratman was holed up with his lawyers, and his editor was calling Fine about the writer cancelling his contract for *Vampire Mom II*. Dora, decimated by Fine's behavior, had yet to go back to work at the Federal Reserve— prompting Brazil to default on IMF loans and Germany to say okay to Pershing II nuclear missiles—and was on the phone constantly with Neiderman. Mardell his Cavalier addict had escaped. And Joy his suicidal borderline ("Where are you?" *"Click."*) had failed to call Monday, for the first time in a year—an ominous sign. Fine felt his patients depending on him, and it seemed a great burden. And a cable arrived that next morning:

FINE MATTER BEING REFERRED TO FRAU METZ STOP SUG-
GEST CONTROL CASES BE PUT ON HOLD TILL METZ MOVES

STOP KIND REGARDS STOP COMMITTEE ON EVALUATION
AND ETHICS STOP

                                                    BE WELL LEON

Fine cabled back: GET FUCKED FINE.

Yet even that backfired, for as soon as he sent it, he was filled
with regret: throwing away psychiatry too? Putz!

Fine was avoiding Nipak. Steph was avoiding Fine. The only
hint of what she was feeling had come after O'Herlihey played the
ransom-demand tape. Steph had said: "But even if you find Stuart
Fine, he won't agree to be involved—it's too dangerous!"

"Cross that bridge when we come to it, darlin'."

"Wait," Steph said, "you *wouldn't!*"

"Good night." said O'Herlihey, leaving, "and God bless?"

"Did you hear that, Fine? They're going to use him without
telling him! We've got to stop them—or find him and warn him!"

"All I care about," said Fine, "is getting that bitch dead."

The first time Fine fired the rifle it knocked him down. Red-faced,
he took Ron from NASA's outstretched hand, and was helped
back up to his feet. Always, with lanky, athletic Ron—from that
very first time, aged ten in Columbia—Fine felt the total klutz.

"It's okay, good buddy," said Ron, chuckling, still cheery and
crew-cut, his age betrayed only by the deltas of wrinkles in his
tanned Houston-based face, "always happens, first time. Try
again."

To escape the cascade of disasters and to take one step closer to
taking action, Fine that Tuesday afternoon was at the Moon Island Police Firing Range, just across the Curley Bridge from
Stow. Ron had shown up that morning. This time he had no
stumper for Fine to solve, but had come " 'cause I heard 'bout yer
troubles, bub, thought we might jes he'p." Fine told Ron he
wanted to learn guns. Ron turned out to be not only a scientist
but a trained marksman. As he taught Fine guns—the .44 revolver, Ron's .38-with-silencer (the "liquidator"), rifle, and Uzi
machine gun (Ron kept both in the trunk of his car)—Fine recalled that he'd never known what Ron actually *did* for NASA.
Could Ron be from the CIA?

After the knockdown, Fine progressed rapidly. He was thrilled
at the kick of the revolver butt against his palm, the blast of the

rifle in his ear. What power! When he walked to the target and saw the confetti where the heart had been, he felt a grim pride.

"Ooo-whee!" Ron whooped. "You got th' fucker!"

Ron knelt on one knee in the dust and took out a pack of Marlboros. Fine asked for one. The day was so still, the match flame, barely seen, hardly wavered. An air of unreality returned: Fine felt like the Marlboro Man. He said: "I want to kill that bitch!"

"Easy 'nuf to get her," said Ron, "but with a hostage it's a mite tricky. Shoulda called us, back when she was alone. We'd'a took care of 'er for you. Coulda found her within twenty-four. Guaranteed."

"But I didn't know it was her."

"Shoulda called, bub. Why you keep doubtin' your gov'mint? 'Bout time you realized jes how good we are!" Fine asked what he should do now. "Wait'll they bring in Stuart Fine; go from there."

"They'll never find him—"

"Find 'im by tonight."

"It's been twenty years."

"Find 'im by tonight. 'Member that equation a' yours, waves through that damn torus, way back?—you started sumthin' big, 'n' now we use it for everythin': dragnettin', nuculer deterrence—" Fine rankled at the thought. "Shitfire! Thanks partly to you, boy, we're good—the best. Find anybody, anywhere. Within twenty-four. Guaranteed."

Sobered, Fine walked back to the car. On the drive back to Stow, Ron said: "Fine, the President's interested in you."

"Me?" Fine was startled. "Oh—so he read *The Nuclear Mind?*"

"No, he can't."

"What? He can't *read?*"

"The *time*—can't find the time. Listen up: he's real interested in your grasshoppers. We want you to tell us all about 'em."

Fine felt so numbly fatalistic, he could care less why his "gov'mint" wanted to know. He led Ron to the laboratory, and got his last cage of smart hoppers from his office, setting it down beside a last cage of normal controls that Ms. Ando had secreted away. Ron stared at the two cages for a while, and then said: "Hermissenda."

"Hermissenda?" Fine was surprised that he knew of Alkon.

"Crassicornis, bub. You bet. Hermissenda's the first time ever that we got, for sure, the biological basis of learning. And what's the key?" Ron smiled, opened his palm: a Finestone. "Damn but you were *right!* Now listen up: we gotta get MC befo' Russia!"

" 'MC'?"

"Mind control. You think they don't have it already?"

It took just an instant, and then Fine saw it—the whole proof, spread out before his eyes. He said: "It's impossible."

"What?" said Ron. "You joshin' me, Fine?"

"Nope. Logically impossible."

"Why?"

It was as if his seizure had wiped his slate clean, just for this. His words flowed out smoothly: "A 'unit change' takes in learning, involving calcium in nerve-cell membranes. But the unit change, by definition, is not specific—it's an on/off switch, the same in each membrane. 'Mind' is, by definition, specific—specific brain-wiring patterns at birth, specific learning patterns in life."

"Hold on—calcium makes us learn faster and better."

"In general. It's like changing the water in the tank."

"What about depression?" Ron asked, betraying his expertise. "Drugs work in depression, mania, schizophrenia—specifically."

"Generally. Drugs change all units—all transmitters of a certain chemistry—uniformly. You're changing the water in the tank."

"But these are different, specific mental illne—"

"How many transmitters are there? Six? Ten? So you can put ten kinds of water in the tank, and when there is a general chemical imbalance—mania, depression, psychosis—you blitz all synapses, sit the brain in clear water, level out. You do nothing directly to alter specific *human* qualities. Nor *can* you. Logically impossible."

"Hold it. It's logically impossible to change minds?"

"With drugs. The proof is an integration of Gödel and Turing —gains in consistency are losses in completeness—having to do with science as general laws, mind as specific instance. We now know a law of unit learning change; we'll soon know a law of each pathogenic transmitter; there can never be a law of a person's mind."

"There's no way to change human min—"

"Two ways," said Fine. "One: map all, or most of, a particular human brain onto a controllable network—say a computer, and you'd need one as big as the universe—bit by bit; i.e., repeat it, build a 'double' you could control; two—" Fine paused, surprised at the intuition: "—psychotherapy. The art of psychotherapy, yes."

Ron stared at him hard, and dropped his "good-ole-boy" mein. "You're sure, Dr. Fine? A lot is riding on your answer—at this point in time your word holds a lot of water in your government."

"Dead sure. Mind drugs alter things in big, inhuman ways. Like nerve gas or nukes—might as well just gas 'em or nuke 'em, Ron."

"But the Soviets have drugs for mind con—"

"—can't have. It's a bluff, a deterrent—like having your finger on the button." He felt angry. "Why the hell don't you *stop?*"

"You reckon there really *is* a button?" Ron asked, sharply.

"What?" Fine was stunned. "You mean that it's all a—"

"Best gov'mint in the world, bub. Believe it." His eyes were steely, like gunmetal. "One last time: you're sure?" Fine said he was positive. "An' all yo' own work on calcium 'n' hoppers—"

"Calcium is key; Finestones work, grossly. So what? I'm through with research. I don't care about anything, anymore."

At dinner, Fine, Ron, and Nipak got into an "if-Hitler-were-in-your-gunsights" argument. Fine argued heatedly that there was no argument. He and Steph left late for the wake.

Neither had ever before been to a wake. They clanked across the Curley Bridge, not talking. Finally Steph said: "I'm scared."

Fine felt nothing. He asked: "Katey?"

"She'll hate our being there, won't she?"

"Most likely, yes."

"Please, Fine, let's try, tonight, to help each other?"

For some reason he felt angry at her. He said, only, "Okay."

The night was crisp, autumnal. A long tunnel of light burrowed through the sea at them, tracking their moving eyes as if alive, the reflection of the sun's reflection in the moon. The stench of raw sewerage—storm-water overflow channeled through the Calf Island Pumping Station across Moon Island and dumped untreated into the harbor—smacked them across their faces.

To Fine the Byrne Funeral Parlor seemed a mere facade, as two-dimensional as a set for a Hollywood movie. John's body could not be in there. Cars blocked the street. Pimply faced young men in cheap black suits directed Steph's purple Jag off toward Carson Beach. They got out and stared. They had played together here.

The funeral home seemed just as unreal inside. Too neat and clean and, Fine reflected, unlived in. They followed the "O'Day" signs and stood in the portico of a large clean crowded room.

In the back half of the room were a row of folding chairs. People were sitting there chatting, occasionally laughing. At the other end of the room was the casket. There lay John. Steph grabbed Fine's hand, clenched tight. His stomach churned. This is barbaric. If a Jew, he'd be under already and we'd be fighting and eating.

The casket seemed to float on a sea of flowers. A woman went up to it, knelt, prayed, touched John's face, rose, went to the women in black sitting along the wall—Katey, and John's sisters —offered condolences. Without looking at him Steph asked: "Ready?"

His mouth felt full of cotton. He mumbled: "No."

"Ready?" she asked, hoarsely and as if she hadn't heard.

"No. That's not him. That's a corpse."

Neither could force themselves to move toward the body. They stood in the center of the room, staring down at the cheap navy-blue carpet. They felt eyes upon them, and dared not look.

Suddenly the room seemed too quiet. Fine sensed that something was wrong. He looked up. Hushed, people were staring at Katey, who was walking slowly toward Fine and Steph. Fine bowed his head again. He felt Steph's hand tighten, her body tremble.

Fine thought: all these people know what I did.

Katey stopped just before Fine. He feared she'd slap him. He braced himself. He looked up.

In her red sore eyes he saw sorrow. He felt a pain in his heart, both sharp and dull. His chin started to tremble. Katey's eyes filled with tears. She started to cry. And so did Steph. And so did Fine. He put his head down on his chest and covered his face in shame and wept. His body shook. He wanted to scream hard and he cried softly as if afraid to awaken someone. The room seemed deathly still and the stillness boomed like surf inside him.

Fine felt a rough hand in his. The old lady was leading him to

the casket. She would show Fine her son. She knelt. Fine and
Steph followed. Fine was too stunned to pray. How? Why? How
could Katey take her hatred and spin it to compassion? Kneeling
beside her he sensed—palpable across the gap between them—a
flow of energy like the flow he'd felt as her son had died in his
arms. Was this her "faith"? He felt her rise, and then Steph rise
too. He saw Steph bend over the casket, kiss John, move away.
Fine rose, stared at the body. John looked like John and yet not.
He did not look asleep, or of wax, no. He looked just as he actually was: a corpse. Fine had seen autopsies. Fine knew that John's
heart, guts, brain were whole in bottles and sliced thin on slides—
this was mere shell. He tried to create back from this outline to
John. He saw him alive onstage, and heard him and repeated now
to him: " '. . . but once put out thy light/Thou cunning'st pattern of excelling nature/I know not where is that Promethean
heat/that can thy light relume.' "

Going down the row of family—the sisters, The Uncle—Fine
managed no words, only tears. Face to face again with Katey,
Fine said: "I—we—we are so much to blame."

"No, no," said Katey, firmly, "it's God's will."

"But how could He let—" Steph caught herself, stopped.

"It's not for us to know His ways," Katey said.

"Mrs. O'Day," said Fine, "thank you for what you just did."

"He'd have wanted it so."

"Why?" Fine asked. "Why did he die?"

Her dark eyes lifted to his, and seemed to lighten, even to grow
lambent, so that Fine felt a trickle of warmth seep in under his
skin, and she said: "He died so we might live."

"Your son—"

"He died to bring us alive."

Her words bit into his heart. For the first time he sensed what
others got out of Jesus. Yet he felt cynical, lost, ashamed.

The rest of the wake was blurred by grief and booze. No one
from the Shakespeare Company showed. Their own show must
have had to go on. "So much for stage love, John, for your stage
family," Fine said, bitterly, "all about as real and as human as
stage blood."

Fine and Steph wound up with The Uncle and others at the
Bellevue. They listened as others, laughing and crying, told stories
about John. Detective O'Herlihey came in and announced that

they'd found Stuart Fine. Amazed, they asked about him, but he'd tell them nothing. Steph again objected to using him as bait. O'Herlihey said: "Johnny O'Day was a dear son of Southie, yes, a dear boyo to us all. Sure and we'll settle it all very soon."

"At least let me meet him," said Fine, "and talk to him."

"Stay the fook outa this! Ya done all ya can. Ferget it now, 'n' leave it to us professionals." Fine persisted, until finally O'Herlihey said: "Christ but I t'ink you're still missin' a few shingles offa yer roof! I'm telling ya: stay out of it!" He left.

Fine looked at Steph, and said: "I wonder what he's like?"

It turned out he was like everyone, and no one. He was a veterinarian, a minor functionary at the Roman L. Hruska U.S. Meat Animal Research Center in Clay Center, Nebraska. His main claim to fame was in assuring that the slaughterers of pigs kept up the facade of humane treatment. The hot issue was making sure that the handlers did not break pigs' snouts for the final trip to the slaughterhouse, to prevent fighting. His motto: "No Cruelty to Swine!" Stuart Fine, DVM (U. of Neb.) had a wife, five kids, and was a member of Temple Beth El (Reformed), American Legion, Moose, and Rotary. An avid bowler with a 173 average, he coached bowling at Clay County Regional. Having had sexual trouble with his wife he'd had a long-standing affair with his secretary at the USDA plant and having had sexual trouble with her, too, was looking around for new meat. He was a man who'd risen from humble origins as a Jew in Tuscaloosa to a life of great ordinariness. He'd procured the American Dream—albeit in southeastern Nebraska—and was floundering around in that usual half-light of mid-life that, if he could have put it into words, would have been something like: "Is this *it?!*"

In appearance he was virtually the mirror image of Fine.

Stuart Fine was primed for excitement. He was startled when the FBI arrived. He was curious as to why they told him almost nothing about why they wanted him to come with them, but having been in government all his adult life, he was used to following orders. He'd been scared to go inspect that slaughterhouse in Bagdad, Arizona, also, hadn't he? What a time he'd had with that lady Pima!

Besides, he'd always wanted to visit Boston. The big time at

last! He was relieved that his plaid suit had just come back from
the cleaners. He packed quickly and went eagerly along.

Luckily for the Boston police, he was to remember his high
school sweetheart Sylvia fondly, recalling little cruelty in their
love and totally repressing the "rape." Sure he'd be glad to see her
again—not knowing why, no questions asked—if it would be of
service to his country.

34

FOR THE FIRST TIME Fine felt the sense of a religion: we shatter, it holds. I myself had felt comforted. Yet it was her religion, for me brief comfort. Katey's faith was genuine and not mine. Like a landscape seen in a flash of lightning, her faith first was clear, then blurred, then gone—gone but for the afterimage of my own distortion. Is blind faith visionary? Who cares? Whatever works.

By the time he and Steph got back to Stow he was numbed out and worried sick about his life, Steph's life, the boy's. He kept trying to recall something about Sylvia that might tell him where she'd be hiding, but nothing came through. The postictal euphoria was now a lost patch of life. He sensed that if he could bring it to light again, now, he might find her, kill her, and heal.

Steph and Fine entered the house in silence. Nipak and Ron were asleep. Fine wondered how he could get rid of them. He felt a deep need to isolate himself, to get safe alone.

Yawning, Steph kicked off her black pumps in the foyer at the base of the stairs. Fine thought her face looked old. He imagined the two of them old, shuffling down the street arm in arm, and felt a rush of tenderness. But it might not be! He shivered. Distractedly, she was unbuttoning her white blouse. Fine watched as it peeled back, revealing her lacy bra, white skin, dark nubbins.

She noticed the silence, looked up. Surprised, she covered herself, buttoning fast, blushing like a schoolgirl. "Oh!" she said, beet red, "I forgot." Her hands dropped to her sides and she stood facing him. Like, he thought, standing naked the first time at their Crik, two lifetimes ago. Such sparkle, then, in those deep blue eyes. He raised his hands to take her in his arms. Her eyes now showed exhaustion and fear, and he held back. He said: "You look so hurt!"

"You too."

"Can I comfort you? Sleep in the same bed?"

"I wish."

"We need each other."

"Yes—but—oh Fine, I don't know who you are!" He saw his shock reflected in her own. She said, "Who I am—who we are. Lives aren't stories—we can't know what comes next. I'm all unraveled now—so are you. Ever since—" She covered her mouth with her fist, swallowed. "Unless we ravel back up in a new way, we're lost, through."

Fine stared up at the cobalt-and-rose stained-glass skylight over the stairwell, tuning out. He yawned without covering his mouth, and said: "Yeah, you know I'm amazed at that Katey—such faith! —such—what?—*wisdom* in a lower-class, uneducated, ordinary woman."

"What's so surprising about that?"

"She goes along her whole life yearning for the new Chevvie and the big new color TV—putting in her six-hours-a-day in front of the old set—her reality shaped by the commercials, the soaps, the self-help idiots—and *bang:* out she comes with something profound."

"How do you know what she feels?"

"She feels for Sylvania, Buscaglia, and the Chevvie—she's bought it, all of it—worse—it *is* her, it's crawled into her brain like cancer—Orwell's *1984* Newspeak!—'Big Brother Is You Watching.' To her, vulgarity is sublime."

Steph's eyes flared. "Katey's right in the thick of life—not like us. She's lived in the same house for a generation—she has friends, she goes to wakes, christenings, hospitals, town meetings —how many friends have *you* had die? She knows life; we know nuthin'! You're so out of touch with real life you can't even see it!

All the wisdom in your head would fit under one of that woman's fingernails!"

"Right, right—just 'cause I'm an analyst, right?"

"No—I'm sure there are enlightened analysts out there too."

"Well there's a switch! What makes them enlightened?"

"Who knows? Maybe something to do with their mothers."

"Right—and I suppose you're different, in 'wisdom'?"

"I got locked up in school, too—and I met you—"

"And ran off with my best friend!" Fine stared at her, watched her eyes harden, wanting to hurt her as much as he could.

She looked down. "Fine, I've got something to tell you: I think I'm going to New York for good, to try stand-up. I just—"

He exploded: "Sure, that's it—run! Run away again—like you ran from me to John, like you ran from your father's death to comedy, and like, way way back, you ran from your ridiculous mother!"

"And what'd I find out?—the worst was you!"

"Oh you found out all right—what'd you find out about affairs? You found—"

"Love!"

"Bullshit! You found the same bullshit you always found, and are finding, and always will find—because you found yourself!"

"Well—back to Freud, eh? Back to the old analytic—"

"The problems in this marriage weren't just *me!* Your problem isn't having a dream, it's getting it. You were even more unhappy with John—admit it!"

"My unhappiness came from *giving up* my dream—first for you, then for him. My mistake was leaving you for another man— I should've left you for *me*—stayed in New York and done stand-up, alone."

"Alone? You? You latched onto Nipak like there was no tomorrow! Alone? You're a dilettante: ten minutes of this, ten of that. Alone? *Ha!* You can't be alone for an hour, let alone a whole night!"

"Because I happen to be *related* to other—"

"Because you can't stand yourself!"

"No more, Fine! I'm through looking to anyone else. It's all me, me alone, from here on out!"

"Just like your narcissistic mother!"

"Go to hell!" she screamed, her voice shrill, wavering, seeming to rattle the beams. "Go straight to goddamn hell!"

She turned away. Fine felt something boiling, up around his ears. "If only you hadn't gotten in touch with John, if only you'd stayed away, he'd still be alive today. It's your fault!"

She turned back, her eyes shining with fury. "You *wanted* me to find him again and you know it!"

"What?!"

"Admit it."

The thought was so outrageous he was stunned. Something was hanging, balanced, but he kicked out the support: "Never!"

"It's as much your fault as mine."

He screamed: *"Never!"*

"I *had* to!"

"You did *not!*" He stood there staring hard into her eyes, attuned to the slightest movement, like a predator of the deep. He felt her tremble, and he trembled: we could kill each other now.

She broke the spell with a Yiddish-accent setup: "I got good news, I got bad news: the good news is, is that finally this is who we are, without all the crap; the bad news is, is that this is who we are, without all the crap." She sighed, and raised her eyes to the heavens. "You know, Fine, God must have been playing a joke."

"What joke?"

"Putting men and women together."

She lifted herself wearily up the stairs. Only when she was out of sight above him did she let loose. Her cries rained down on him. He felt them—edged and glinting, like shards of glass.

"Dear God," he said, calling up through the funnel of stairwell to the skylight, to the sky, "why did this have to happen to us?"

35

FINE AWOKE AT attention from a nightmare at five the next morning, Wednesday the twenty-fourth. That first moment of wakefulness is a moment of truth, and when he realized where he was and who he was and what had happened to him—and his wife—it was as if a vise clicked a notch tighter around his ventricle. He felt overwhelmed, obsessed with worry about John James. A need for distraction drove him to his office to see Six o'clock. After the way he'd treated her he didn't know if she was still showing up. He climbed the stairs wearily, catching his breath at each landing, puffing like an old man after a coronary. He sat, leaving the door open. The room—a messy nest of books and memorabilia—seemed the room of the deceased.

At twenty past, Six o'clock appeared in the waiting room. Seeing Fine slumped in his chair, she came in. He saw her dimly, without detail, noting only that she seemed older, sobered, less sexy. She walked to the couch slowly, as if following a funeral cortege. Before she lay down she looked at him: "You look terrible! Like you're a person from a nursing home or something!"

Fine sensed he hadn't shaved and was wearing the same rumpled shirt he'd worn to the wake—actually, since the day after John's murder. Why am I here with this woman? This "therapy" seems unreal, false. How can I, in the shape I'm in, help her? He thought of the analytic reply—"Tell me your thoughts about how terrible I look"—but revulsion swam up his throat. He said nothing. She lay down. "I know how you feel—Mrs. Neiderman tells me everything—" Great, Fine thought, so much for my being a blank screen. "—horrible what you've been through—I feel so bad for you!" She paused. He, a corpse, could not reply. "But last night when she told me how you always say you've lived a 'charmed life'—I almost fainted!" So Neiderman's wrecked the analysis, so what? "—I thought that about *my* life, too—not that I'd ever tell anyone, but all my life, on the surface, things seemed to go so well—valedictorian, Harvest Queen, super dates for the Yale game—even now, the Fed *looks* like a fun job—and nobody knows—except you and her—that every night I go home alone and cry myself to sleep. I do my best, and then I wake up and find out I've made all the worst choices. My life's a wreck and it's all my fault! I'm so lonely! My life's so dead. It's too damn hard! Why live? Why live at all?"

Good question, Fine thought, even excellent.

"—so why am *I* so sensitive? Why do *I* take things so personally, get so crushed? Other people don't feel so bad—why *me?*"

Fine felt a shudder go through him, realizing: *I* feel the same way! She's talking about *me!* And for the first time since John's death he felt, in his core being, a wrench of real pain.

"—but for me to see that you're in bad shape, too, that *your* life, underneath it all, is a mess—it was like, I don't know, like a revelation!" She paused. Without thought he blurted out:

"You think other people don't suffer like you do?"

She let out a little cry, like a child surprised by an honest answer from a parent, surprising him. What has she picked up in his tone? She half-sat, as if to turn and face him, but then settled back: "I . . . I never thought . . . you mean it's just the same for them?"

"You'd be surprised how many of 'them' go home and cry into their pillows at night."

"Really?" She fell silent. After a while she began associating, talking about her losses: father dead; mother in the bestial, tormented world of Alzheimer's presenile dementia—she visited her every other weekend in New Jersey, holding her hand, her mother not even *knowing* her!—Uncle Savage disgraced; the loss, one after the other, as if fated, of two husbands, countless men. "I started to trust you, but then, when you changed—started missing sessions, acting weird—when I realized I'd lost you too—I felt it was *me*, that I'd driven you away by my sexiness and all my crap —I felt so bad! I felt like killing myself!"

Fine was surprised to find himself so totally caught up in her story. He saw that her losing him was the pivot on which her other losses had been set spinning. Attending to her, his own losses started to spin—John, the boy, Steph, parents, self. He could feel what she was feeling, and he felt it as his own.

As he looked at her—a desperate human being searching for a meaning in her life—he felt sad. How badly I've treated her—my cold-hearted analysis *of* her, my crude postseizure thaw, my failure to show up at all, my jumping up and running out when I thought she was the killer—and still she comes back? What *resilience!* He recalled John saying that when John James was born, it was as if the baby had an extra little sac around his heart, filled with love, and all a father had to do to get it was to be there with him. Fine flushed, warmth creeping up his neck, making his ears and scalp tingle. The human spirit—you can't kill it! Even the Ukrainians, after a while, rebelled against taking actual guns and pressing them into the backs of actual Jewish necks and actually pulling triggers and actually being spattered with pieces of skull and brain as actual bodies fell into actual mass graves. Even the Ukrainians rebelled! (Prompting the Germans to perfect a cleaner killer, Zyklon B.) I feel so *with* her now, as if it's me lying there, my story she's telling, as if there's still something left in my own little childhood sac.

His heart felt warm, like a heat pump, his ribs radiators, and the warmth in his chest seemed to spread his ribcage and flow out, bridging the gap between him and her, so solidly present, he thought, you could reach out your hand and touch it, take a Polaroid of it, even. This warmth seemed so vibrant and real, he sensed she must feel it too. No, that's ridiculous. A Polaroid would show the back of her head, period. It's mine, not hers; she feels nothing.

"Wait," she said, suddenly, "what's going on here?" She sat up on the couch and stared down at her feet. "I . . . I feel something here, in the air. Something's wrong. I . . . I'm paying too much attention to myself. I mean *you're* really hurting, Dr. Fine, I can feel it." She raised her blue-gray eyes to his. "Aren't you?"

She *had* sensed it? What a shock! Her eyes showed her opening her heart to him. Ashamed, he looked away, tried to think: now what? The analytic response?—ask her to "explore" her "self"? No, he finally saw that for what it was: a defense against connecting, a mask for separateness, hiding a deep contempt for and deeper fear of being *like* the patient, of being *touched.* I've laid the groundwork of trust; no choice now but to be real. We're in it together, now. Go.

And yet still Fine could not answer from his heart.

"Oh, Dr. Fine," she said, voice cracking, "you look so sad!"

He looked up into her sadness for him and tears welled up in his eyes. "I am. I'm hurting a real lot."

After he said it, he realized what a risk it was—it could ruin everything. He was in her hands. And then her eyes clouded with tears, and then the tears ran down her cheeks, carrying black mascara, and he felt her sorrow. As if for the first time he saw her as she actually was—every detail from her sober pinstripe blue suit to the first lines of age round her eyes and the first thinning of her blond hair—all the etchings of fading beauty—every detail became clearer, not only of her body but also of her self, and not even of her self alone but of her self-with-others, and through history—for all at once he saw with great clarity where she had come from, and where she would go. He sensed a deep acceptance of her.

To his amazement, she stood up and came around and sat on the raised head of the couch, one foot up on the rung of his chair, and she held out her hand to him, open palm up. He took it, closing his eyes. At her touch a wave flowed through him, and he shuddered. The silence seemed enormous. Gently, she laid his head on her lap, and covered his cheek with her other hand. The room lost solidity, seeming to pitch, roll. His breathing communed with hers. Rocked as if on a sea, he felt safe for a while from the pull of the dead.

"God, look at the time!" she said, "I'll be late!" Opening his eyes, he realized how awkward he felt, and quickly got up. She too seemed embarrassed, and moved stiffly to the door, taking the doorknob in her hand. Fine felt fond of her: she's someone I'd like to really get to know. How contemptuous, to call her "Six

o'clock"! "Remember the day you made that doorknob comment?
That was the turning point, 'cause then I knew there was a real
live person in there, hiding." Fine tried to smile, but the dull
numb was again rising. "I'm the same way: I put out my little
feeler—my pseudopod—put it out in the world and—*bam!*—get
stepped on. Do I like my job? No. Will I go to work? Yes. To save
Brazil." She chuckled. "Do I like who I am? No. Can I help it?
Again no. Who can? I guess you're right—we all hurt. So why do
I think I'm so special?"

"To keep yourself apart," Fine said. "Like all of us."

"Feeling I'm better than others?"

"And worse than others—anything but feeling the same."

"From now on, let's do the whole session like this, on the doorknob, okay?" She laughed, he smiled. "Tomorrow." She left.

By the time the door closed behind her Fine was trembling.
What the hell was that all about? He'd never cried with a patient
before. Crying is one thing—Vergessen himself was rumored to
have done so—but putting your head in her lap? Are you nuts?
That's not therapy, that's touchy-feely bullshit! What next? Off
with the undies? Great, Fine, terrific—you've really done it now.
Sure, you and she were feeling good, but *feeling* good by itself, far
from being the cure, is in fact the disease. Just look at California!
Check out our Santa Barbara president! (Favorite saying:
"There's nothing better for the inside of a man than the outside of
a horse.") *Feeling* better often gets in the way of *getting* better—a
malignant inversion of Freud's death instinct. Fine sensed a slippage, down toward dread. To calm himself, he took a Finestone.

Plop. Suck.

Okay, okay: something vital had taken place, but was it therapy? You made deep contact with her, what was the sense of it?
Overwhelmed, Fine struggled, knowing that if he could only get
his mind around the session, it would point him toward something he wanted desperately: a vision of himself as therapist. Try
as he might, like a fish blind to water, he saw only part: she gave
to me; I passively got. But how does this fit with everything I've
learned—and others have learned by trial and error throughout
history—about being a therapist? He felt a wave of contempt—for
her, for their little *folie;* he needed to order this chaos, spacially.
He sat at his WANG:

1) Each life is a story.

2) It's always the same story.

3) Therapy's like dancing—she leading, I following. Therapy is becoming aware not of self, but of self-in-relation. Therapy is like dancing on deck.

4) What distinguishes the therapist? The therapist is responsible: for the ship; the deck; the course; (?) the music.

5) For the patient to grow, the relationship must grow; for the relationship to grow, the therapist must grow. It's mutual.

6) How does the therapist grow? Same as anybody else: I get hurt out in the world, and so I am open to her pain.

7) Question: I got, but did I give? How do I?

8) Question: what is the transference?

9) Conclusion: that was touchy-feely nice, but it was not therapy. Think of the effect on *her!* I am in big trouble.

10) Comment: Nu, Big Shot, what now?

Yet Fine was surprised—the session had energized, rather than, as usual, depleted him. He felt he had risked, and taken a giant step toward seeing what therapy actually is. He sensed a surge of power, and shouted:

"Get out! Get out! Bang into others out in the world! Only *live!*"

At breakfast, Mrs. Neiderman and Ms. Ando were sitting with Steph, Nipak, and Ron. Nipak and Ron were already at each other's throats. Neither could fathom how Fine could tolerate the other.

Mrs. Neiderman, looking somber, said: "Duffy stopped by on her way out, and told me. You do quite beautiful things."

"All I do is try to make us aware," Fine said, distractedly.

"Oh," she said puzzled, "you mean why we do things?"

"*That* we do things."

"That's *all?*" She seemed disappointed.

"Believe me, that's enough." Fine made more coffee.

"Yes," said Nipak, "more than. For we are blind, asleep."

"Well, then how do we wake up?" asked Mrs. Neiderman.

"If we are aware," said Nipak, "life itself will awaken us."

Neiderman shook her blond curls. "I don't get it."

"Excellent!" said Nipak. "Ignorance is the best beginning. Be aware of who you actually are, and you will grow—"

"Beware of who I am? Too hard." She took out her notepad. "Now, Dr. Fine, 'Family Feud' called—they want you and your family on the show, because of the murders; the movie studios keep calling—I never knew there were so many! It's unbelievable, if you ask me."

Nipak said to Fine: "Something is happening to you, yes?" Fine, irritated at his perkiness, poured another coffee, but Nipak snatched it from him, saying: "Caffeine destroys the peace of mind!"

"And the trigger finger too," said Ron, picking up the carrying cases in which was enough firepower to eliminate all of Stow. "C'mon—time fo' Guns II. Only way to heal is with cold cold steel."

"No, no," said Nipak, sharply, "rather, with awareness."

"Yeah? An' I s'pose awareness builds bridges too, hun?"

"Awareness *is* bridges," said Nipak, firmly.

"C'mon, Ron," said Fine, rising.

"Fine," said Steph, voice edged from the night before, "don't you see a conflict between learning meditation and learning to kill?"

"In this vulgar world," Fine said, "I need both."

After his stint on the firing range ("Guns'r 'user-friendly' now," Ron said, and it was true—already Fine was less gun-shy), Fine fled the TV cameras, sheltering behind the locked doors of Jefferson House with his inpatients. He was relieved to find that they too were trying to balance: the recent carnage; and life.

"Yes, er, no," said Mr. Jefferson, "like a nuclear attack?"

"Jesus told me," said Jefferson, "to tell the world He's about to destroy it, yeah, with nukies, and that I had to build me an ark! Christ knows it—I can tell things befo' they come true!"

As he listened to his inpatients, Fine felt sad: what hell they'd been through! The pilot study was a wreck, Pelvin was in hiding, they were frazzled and psychotic. They were reassured to see Fine, and once again he was aware of how much they cared for him, and—from his own near-psychotic euphoria—how close to the surface is the psychotic in us all. I am more *like* them than not. When I dream, I live their lives. He said: "I'm sorry if I've let you down."

"We went a-Maying," said Fat Sadie. "We did not get dis-Mayed."

"Yes, er, no," said Mr. Jefferson. "Given the recent traumatic events, I propose a special plan, a holiday day."

The group had never heard him so emphatic, and fell silent.

"Yes, er, I propose an outing. I suggest we enter my family's 'rigger, *The Thomas,* in the Memorial Day outing, the international flotilla in Boston Harbor on Memorial Day, five days from now, called The Tall Ships." He faltered. "Yes, er, no, am I adrift? Aground?"

"Not at all," said Fine. "Sounds good to me."

"Er, we're cleared to bring *The Thomas* up from Duxbury?"

"You are," said Fine. "Go for it!"

"The Tall Ships!" said Mr. Jefferson, grasping his dream.

"The Tall Shits!" said Jefferson, in awe.

"The Tall Shits!" they shouted, happily, "the Tall Shits!"

Fine continued trying to seek refuge in his patients, feeling a strange relief and comfort in being attentive to their lives. He looked forward to seeing Five o'clock.

Yet Maurice began as usual with the deathly obsessive drone of associations to Fine's troubles. Bored and fatigued, Fine napped. At 5:40 Maurice accused him of napping, awakening him—associating to the time Fine "cut that fart." So exhausted was Fine from the strain of the past few days, the whole thing struck him as funny, and despite himself he laughed. Maurice, shocked, tried to go on free-associating, but Fine suddenly saw it all as so comical he cried out: "Oh God I can't stand it! It's so damn *silly!*"—and burst out laughing, hard. Maurice sat up and turned around, in his eyes a question: has my analyst gone off the deep end? Yet seeing Fine trying to hold back, Maurice could not, and let out a sharp cackle. Fine guffawed, and the contagion spread, back and forth between them until both were laughing uncontrollably. They laughed about the fart, the five-minute hour—analysis itself! How ludicrous, life, their lives! What a joke!

Maurice rose to go. "Unbelievable!" he said. "You stopped acting like a doctor, and I stopped acting like a patient!"

Fine looked at him, and—as if a veil had been lifted—sensed he

was actually *seeing* Maurice: the thick body, short legs, hairy
wrists, mustache, that nose!—a nose to make a mother—

"Hey—*yours* is just as big," Maurice said. "You might want to
try those new kosher nose drops—the king size?—dynamite!"
They laughed. "I guess after what you've been through, Fine, if
you didn't laugh, you'd cry. I really feel for you—in a lot of ways,
we're a lot alike." He left.

Fine felt touched, comforted. Nice guy, the kind you'd like to
meet for a drink, and really get to know. Dancing on deck, yes.

And then all at once Fine realized how much he cared for these
people, these poor trusting souls who came to him in pain, looking for a way to change. Feelings rushed through him—shame,
love, grief. There's a sacred act going on here; it's a privilege, this
meeting of humans and being with them as part of their lives, and
each session is almost what you'd call a spiritual event. I *have* to
be responsible. I have to captain the ship, watch for storms, tack
the safe course, play the danceable tunes. He sensed the immense
responsibility of being entrusted with actual human lives, and was
filled with doubt. "I want—really really want—to help them! But
how? Who am I, what is my technique? What is the theory?
Where are the lines on the court—on *my* court—the fat new
chalky ones that I *must not transgress,* for therapy to work?" Lost
in his questions, he found himself staring at the photos—Freud,
Vergessen, Steph—and then he knew that, for him, each of these
dear teachers was part of his answer. "Please, Big Guy, show me
the way?"

When he came back to the house that evening, he found Nipak
sitting alone under a lamp, writing. Fine asked what he was doing.

"The lucubration: nocturnal meditation to promote action! The
words with the powers to shake the figs from the trees! I am sick
and tired of being sick and tired about this kidnapping! We *must*
—do you hear me, man?—we must find her!"

"Find her and kill her," said Fine, surprised at how stone-cold
sober he felt, "save the boy and kill her dead."

36

GATE OF HEAVEN CEMETERY spread itself over a hill in South Boston. The variegated headstones tilted out from the dark-green curvature at odd angles, reminding Fine of transplanted teeth, teeth growing chaotically in a deformed, monstrous embryo. The day was sunny, bright, breezy, and cool. Everyone was dressed darkly. At first Fine thought the sunshine wrong for a funeral. Yet the death was so wrong that wrongness was welcome. Three or four crows, feathers shining oily purple, hectored the gloomy humans from a wrought-iron fence. The mourners' dark clothes collected the warmth, taking the bite from the morning air. Good, Fine thought: no attention need be paid to weather; all could be focused where the raw pain lay.

There. In the hole in the ground, there.

The crowd was large: John's family, Nora, friends, scions of the notorious Curley, many O'Herliheys, police and firemen and city dignitaries, even the mayor. Immaculate, His Honor stood in the front row, cradling a hymnal gracefully, as if it were an appendage. He'd yet to find out whether the U.S. Attorney's investigation into corruption would come close enough to bar him from reelection, and so was still politicking. Steph's hip touched Fine's. As if shocked, she moved away—still locked in recrimination, their contact seemed wrong. What wasn't wrong? A big laughing man was gone. The troika was dead.

Yet she stayed close enough for Fine to hear: "How can a person be alive, then not? Isn't he alive, still, somewhere?"

Father O'Herlihey talked about "the Resurrection and the Life." Fine stared at Katey—a tiny black-veiled sagging person, black hankie to nose. He tried to understand how her bigotry went together with her compassion, her hate with her love. He failed.

It was during the mayor's professional, arrogant, and wrong eulogy that Fine's attention wandered out over the bay. The breezy clear day had bred sails on the water and jet plumes in the sky. Boston itself seemed pristine, as if it really had fulfilled John Winthrop's dream: "A city of God on a hill." His eyes swept the harbor islands, settling on Spectacle—from this height shaped like a pair of spectacles—lying between Southie and Stow. And then, as in a dream a face appears—a face seen once in a crowd and never given a second look—he saw in his mind's eye a recent letter to the Globe: a photo of a cop standing, watching smoking ruins, a brick smokestack poking up like a candle in a cake. And he saw before him the caption:

> All that remains on Spectacle Island of the horse-rendering
> plant is a smokestack. This particular island was used as a
> garbage dump and horse-rendering plant for more than a
> hundred years. It is almost barren of vegetation, and is
> about as ugly as an island can get. . . .

Ugly? In all his time with Sylvia, he'd felt connected to her only once, when she'd asked him: "Am I *ugly?*" He himself had asked Steph the same question before his seizure. Now he could feel what she, so disfigured, had felt about herself; even, now, feel it as his own—and then—*horses!* Sylvia loved horses! "Horses!"

"What?" Steph asked.

"Oh, sorry—nothing." She looked at him quizzically. He glanced away, unwilling to get her involved. His mind raced on: "There are no negatives in the unconscious"—Vergessen. Sylvia both loved and hated horses; to ride, or to render them to glue—it was all cathexis. She was *attached to* horses. He put himself in her shoes. Yes, if she'd discovered the ugly, horse-rendering island, she *would* have been drawn to it. A hundred years of garbage meant no one else would go near it. And there it lay, right next to Stow!

As right as this felt, Fine began to dismiss it. Look: the casket was being lowered into the ground; the women began to keen; sobs shook bodies; men blew their noses, coughed, and tried to clear phlegm from their throats. This is the actual, Fine thought. My little intuitive head trip is mere fancy, a defense against my grief.

So watery were Fine's self-boundaries at the time, he felt sure of nothing, least of all himself. Struggling to resurrect his life, he was opening up, feeling pain, too much pain to sense, in his sorrow, the shearing forces of change. A wind shears a sail, a keel shears a sea; twisted by torque, we move. Fine at that time had few clues to the nature of his nature. Few clues, and less faith.

The pebbles danced on the coffin lid. Everybody cried.

The Uncle, shaking his hand good-bye, could barely speak. Fine knew that if he did decide to act, he needed one more bit of information, and this was his chance. He asked The Uncle how Detective O'Herlihey was doing. "Good. They're readyin' yer man Stuart Fine for action, and, mind you, it'll be soon." Fine feigned nonchalance, and asked where this Stuart was from? "Nebraska, do you believe it?" Fine breathed a sigh of relief. He pressed the meaty hand, looked into the bloodshot eyes—how old he seemed! Fine smelled the same old gummy breath and felt sad. They parted.

All the rest of the day, back at Stow, Fine tried to put the matter out of his mind—he was unused to acting on intuition—unused to acting at all. And yet every time he went outside he was drawn to the outline of Spectacle Island, and each time, his hunch had more a sense of right to it—as a found bone or stone or cloud is "right" in nature. A plan coalesced, as real as the sight of the island: the police would have arranged a meeting between Sylvia and Stuart, probably today, tonight. She'd be expecting him. If Fine were dressed like this Stuart, he could approach her. Stuart was from Nebraska. Fine would dress Midwestern, say in wash-'n'-wear plaid. He would *act* Midwestern, altering his gait and mein toward, say, "lunky." Polyestered and inept, he would be able to get in close enough for the kill. And John James? Fine recalled that Sylvia, in the chaos after her own child had died, had

kidnapped a little boy, but returned him unharmed. We *do* repeat
our pain; she won't harm him, no. Why not go for it? Fear? No.
Danger? So what? I feel half-dead now. My thirty-fifth birthday
won't be too painful, if I'm already dead at the time.

And so for the first time in seven years Fine chose to act.

He was amazed to find an ease to his deception. He sought out
his sailor, Mr. Jefferson. Yes, in his sallies he'd once sailed into a
hidden cove at the bridge of Spectacle, yes. The stench of rotting
garbage had prevented exploration, but he'd glimpsed a dock and
ruins, yes. Fine got the key to the powerboat from Mrs. Bush,
swearing her to secrecy. He apologized to Ron for denying him
access to Ms. Ando, and suggested that Ron pick her brain that
evening—sushi would loosen her. Fine asked if he could borrow
the guns for target practice after his Five o'clock. Ron said sure.
As they parted, Ron laid a tan hand on Fine's shoulder and said:
"Fine?"

"Ron?"

"Bub, you're a great American."

Fine told Nipak and Steph that he was going off to target practice at six, for "dusk training," and not to hold dinner.

Maurice failed to show—Duffy hadn't shown that morning either—clearly having had trouble with the last session. Fine took
the guns, got into his car, and drove off as if to Moon Island.

He stopped, changed into the plaid suit and strapped the holster to his chest. Thinking senior prom, he put on glasses and
stuck a red carnation in his lapel. He slung the rifle and ammo
over his shoulder and, carrying the machine gun, snuck down to
the path along the shore, turning east toward the jetty. The powerboat *Corky* lay at dock, chrome alight in the hard slanting sun.
He mounted the machine gun in the open center-panel of the
windshield, running the clips back into the cabin. He crisscrossed
two belts of ammo over his chest like the photos of Pancho Villa.
He patted the cool hard bullets. Me, a small Jewish man from
upstate New York, armed like a Mexican bandit? West Point at
last! He admired himself in the dashboard mirror. Firing the engine, he turned back to cast off.

There stood Nipak and Steph. Their words were lost in the roar
of the engine. Steph jumped in and Nipak grabbed the mooring
rope. It soon became clear that they'd not let him go off in the
boat alone. Finally he gave in. He throttled up and they were off.

Once on the water, he told them part of what he was about to
do. They tried to dissuade him, but it was no use. He steered them
out into the mouth of the harbor, and then down its gullet. The
skyline was backlit, the sea choppy. Fine acted calm, seeming to
be just another plaid-clad man out for a dusk spin in his fiberglass
boat. The water traffic abated as they approached Spectacle Island. Fine knew from Mr. Jefferson where the secret cove was. As
they got closer, downwind, they caught the stench, and knew why
no one ventured here. By the time Fine eased toward what looked
like the sheer cliff—the bridge of the two lenses—it was twilight,
light enough to see, dark enough to be obscured. The stench, and
the forboding rocky aspect would have kept others from exploring
this place. And yet as he eased on in, Fine saw a break in the
sheerness, a declivity opening up like the true passage in a hall of
mirrors. What seemed cliff was cleft. Fine floated in on the current, and around, and up under the rocky escarpment. There!—a
dock!—no time to lose! He told Nipak and Steph to get down out
of sight. He put on his plaid jacket and pulled tight the ring
around his Western-style lanyard necktie. He patted the gun in its
holster.

The stench was less, here. Yet the rendering of a hundred thousand horses and the dumping of a hundred feet of garbage had
taken its toll on what once, clearly, had been beautiful. The plan,
Fine had told them, was to cover him with the machine gun. They
protested—they hadn't the slightest idea how to work it. Fine told
them there was no "idea" required: you aimed, pulled the trigger.
The rifle with the infrared sight—same thing. He made for the
ladder.

"Fine, don't!" said Steph, holding him back. "I'm scared."

"Let go!" he barked, not wanting to think. "And stay down!"

"There is no boat here," said Nipak. "Perhaps you're wrong?"

"Shush!" Fine said. He climbed up the ladder and stepped gingerly onto the narrow ledge along one side of the cove. The earth
seemed to shiver, giving off heat, as if something buried was fer-
menting, waiting for a spark, to combust. He walked along the
dock, up, and down, nerves on edge with an old—almost atavistic?—spooky sense that he was being watched. He saw, around
the bend at the end of the railroad tracks, the brick chimney of
the glue factory. Leading into the chimney was a small brick
building. Fine thought showers, and shuddered. Given the his-

tory, seeing the rails, the smokestack, sensing the aura of slaughter—how could he not think of the Camps? Enraged, he vowed revenge. With a final glance back at the boat, he began walking—lunkily—toward the factory. With all the clarity of déjà vu, he could almost see her coming from—

"Fine! Fine! Here!" He heard calls, then sounds of a motor, and gunfire. He raced back and rounded the corner—a second speedboat was tearing away from the far side of the cove, leaving a savage curl of wake. Shots were coming from the figure at the wheel, and with a heartsick feeling he saw a second figure lying inert in the bottom of the boat. Bullets chipped at the granite mooring and Fine, keeping low, tumbled into the *Corky,* started the engine, banged off the dock, and shot out after the other boat into the darkening bay.

At first the two boats seemed evenly matched—hers fifty yards ahead. They dared not fire, for fear of hitting the boy. Her boat seemed to go smoothly through the chop while theirs, with a rough up-and-down motion, bashed the waves, rolling side to side as if about to capsize. Foam splashed over them, drenching them and the machine gun. She was heading toward the city, now a hive of lights. Meticulous and paranoid, Fine should have known that she would prove even more so. She'd tricked him, knowing somehow he'd be drawn toward the smokestack, all the while watching from a camouflaged mooring, set to run. Had this been the wrong time, or place, to meet Stuart? What if she thought the police had tricked her? What did it mean for the boy? Fine felt sick at heart. He took out his fury on the boat:

"Come on, goddammit *Corky—move!"*

The spray in his face made him feel powerful. Grimly, he thought: my intuition was right. If only there were a radio on board!

They could barely keep her in sight. The speck of her boat shot straight through the throat of the harbor toward the Charlestown end of the Mystic River Bridge, where "Old Ironsides" was berthed. It seemed to take forever for them to get there. Sure enough, her speedboat floated listlessly next to the huge old square-rigged battleship—she'd gone to land. Fine slammed the dock, jumped onto the ladder, patted his holstered .38, and reached back for the mooring line. Knowing every minute was vital, he yelled "C'mon!"

"Oww!" Nipak tripped, fell, ripping his white pants. Blood oozed out. Steph bent to him. "Oh, shit! It is the trick knee!"

"Take care of him, Steph!"

"Fine, you can't just run after her!"

"Call the cops!" he cried. "Now!" Waving his gun in the air, he lurched off down the dock.

37

FINE RAN DOWN a dark tunnel between two warehouses. Slabs of shadow obliterated all light. He plunged on through, under a ramp of the Mystic River Bridge, and found himself again on a lit city street. Out of shape, he stopped, gasping for breath. Sylvia would have had a backup plan, a second hideout, on land. Even faced with the labyrinth of Charlestown, Fine sensed he would find her. Fueled by despair, his hope was sky-high. He feared nothing, no one.

He ran a few more blocks to the Bunker Hill Monument, a smaller replica of the Washington one. The square around it had been restored to Georgian neatness. She might well be here. The monolith poked up from Breed's Hill. Ever since the Bicentennial when a group of Charlestown whites had pulverized a group of black schoolchildren visiting from Washington DC, the park had been a focus of racial battle. Fine ran up the path toward the stone spike. He would *win!*

He was mugged. Tripped, he fell hard, feeling skin rip at elbow and knee, feeling brain jolt against skull. Shit! Her? From Ron's commando course he knew to roll. He shot back up onto his feet.

"Yoke 'im!" cried a voice from behind.

Fine's throat was caught in the crook of an arm. He started to choke. The light dimmed. He felt something cottony and fragrant shoved into his mouth. A hand closed over his nose, suffocating him. The outer world got mottled. He heard sounds of voices as if from far off, felt hands rip at his clothes—or his body, he couldn't tell which, for it was as if he were etherized. Thrown down again, he felt a cracking pain, heard laughter, then footfalls, fading.

He went under, lost hold of consciousness, and then fought back up to the surface. A new Bunker Hill slogan swam in: "Don't shoot till you see the eyes of the whites!" Woozy, he spat out the gag—the red carnation. Rolling over, he saw a duo running back toward the lit-up city. He lay still, assessing. They'd taken everything but his blue-and-white striped boxer shorts, string tie, and black socks—even his shirt, his pants, his shoes. He tried moving. Despite the hot jolt of pain in elbow and knee, he was relieved that his body was okay. He began taking inventory of what he'd lost, but then it didn't really seem to matter, and he stopped. Plastic, so much plastic. Better off without it now. Down to bare essentials. I feel lighter, ready.

Dazed, in shock, Fine was completely unaware of just how dazed and shocked he actually was.

He sensed that Sylvia would stash John James at her apartment and come back out hunting for him, perhaps in another disguise. From the theory of stochastic processes, he knew that a "random walk" was the optimal way to cover ground. He got up shakily, surprised at how solid his legs actually were. Bloody from the fall, that's all. The moon, past full, wet the pavement, buildings, and bridge with a fluid, tinny light. Things seemed coated in metal. Fine felt he'd never been out in a night so lustrous, and whispered: "Galvanized!"

He began to wander. He spent a long time at "Old Ironsides," staring up at the network of ropes and furled sails, hearing, in the creaking of the rigging as the retired warship rocked at its berth, murmurs of its ghosts. A clock struck two. He found himself at the end of a rundown pier in the abandoned U.S. Naval Shipyard, near a massive pylon of the Mystic River Bridge. Across the channel the city sparkled. Overhead, the bridge loomed large. As he stared out over the harbor, the sea seemed silvery, phosphorescent. No ships were moving. A jet sank, screaming, to Logan, then quieted. The night, as if balancing, fell still.

Footsteps sounded behind him—he turned. A figure—in jeans,

wearing a cap—not fifty yards away—walking toward him! He realized he was defenseless, exposed, open, totally vulnerable, and a chill shot through him, up his spine, prickling the hairs on the back of his neck. How dumb I am! Is it her? "Who's there?" he asked, feebly. "What do you want?" She came on, stalking him, moving deliberately through an ellipse of lamplight, and he saw a glint, as if off metal. She had the fluidity of an apparition, and her movement toward him had the fated smoothness of a dream. He thought: This is how I'm going to die. What could he do? Run past her? Dive into the harbor? The water was thirty feet down. He knew from Ron that he must stay calm—reach for the mythic solo male ideal of "grace under pressure"—but a desperate need crashed over him, a need for the strength of others, and he cried out:

"Help! Somebody—help!"

The figure moved into the dark again, toward him. He knew he was about to die. What will be the last thing I see? My killer? This dark? He turned away. He looked out over the water. A white-blue mercury light wriggled toward him from across the channel in Southie, riding the undulations and sliding on the patches of oil. Fine was mesmerized—he'd never seen anything so beautiful in his life. He refused to bend his neck, close his eyes. I will go open-eyed to my trench.

He could not have said how long he stared at the water. When he turned back to the land, she was gone.

Saved, Fine thought, I am saved. Suddenly he realized what a risk he'd taken, chasing her, coming out here alone, naked and unarmed, in the middle of the night. He was amazed at himself. Why? Why did I do this, come this far, put myself in this danger, why? And then, as if he'd been holding his breath for a long time —his whole life?—he seemed to let an immense breath out. In the stillness before the next breath in, he realized how cautious he'd always been, how scared, always holding on, holding in, holding back, paralyzed by fear, breathless with fear, suspecting others of their worst at his expense, hardly enjoying anything for being so on guard. In that long still instant he saw himself as a traveler in a foreign country, so suspicious of the natives, so busy patting his wallet to make sure it was still there, that he never really saw the sights. Why? What am I so afraid of? Why am I always running away from experience, from life? Why do I dig in my claws so tight? Why am I always so busy worrying about saying good-bye that I never really say hello? Is this what Steph meant, about learning to say 'Yes'? Is this what John meant, dying?

Fine felt himself ease. His senses, as if flayed, became hyper-acute, opening him up. The little piece of the world he found himself in—this pock-marked dock, this sallow light and quicksilver moonlight, this harbor smell and this salt-roughened wood against his palm, this lapping of waves against the pylons—drew his attention to it with a raw, dreamlike intensity that allowed no waver. He let go of everything except attending to the world. Attending, he began to feel himself letting go.

He got up and walked. Taking a new pathway inside himself, he let it reverberate out into the world, and lead him. First he let go of his tags—job, wife, family, keys, passport, Social Security, Carte Blanche, estimated tax payment, periodontist, etc., etc. Next he let go of his will to analyze letting go. Then, his feelings about letting go. Finally he let go of his need to let go. Each discard strengthened his hand—for the death of the part the whole came more to life. Like Fumbles telling him about, in college, being in the ring with a one-armed boxer: "You think that arm wasn't *strong?*" For each part unraveled, another knit up anew—he pictured delicate, supple commissures across hemispheres. Like a traveler setting down heavy bags, he felt the arms of his being, lightened, rising.

He no longer feared the night. As he wandered, he realized that through his action he'd taken his fear and exploded it to bits. He was facing his despair at John's death. He sensed that, while he would be many things from now on in his life, he would never again be afraid to act.

The night sped past. Toward sunup he found himself climbing an enclosed steel ladder up a pylon of the bridge. Up and up he went. The cool sea breeze began to sweep hungrily up the channel, so that, pausing for breath, he felt caught in a net of three elements—earth, water, air. Soon he would be high enough to see fire—the fire of dawn. He climbed on, up and up, until finally he reached the catwalk under the roadbed of the main span. He took the last rungs lightly, and popped up a grill-hole onto the road. From his Rip Van Winkle toll collector days, Fine had a fear of heights. Yet here, at the trembling apex of the long span, two hundred feet up over the water, he was amazed that he was not afraid. He turned east, toward first light: *Fine Lux.*

Still clad only in boxers and black socks, the lanyard round his neck whipping in the high wind like a fangled bird, Fine started on off toward home. His step was springy—jaunty, jolly—for he felt lighter, curious, exhilarated, even awed. The glow of red paled to a golden and then a yellowing halo, and then the round edge of the sun rolled up over the flat edge of the earth. "The rising of the sun? No," he answered, recalling John, Steph, and their racing the receding dark toward the Cape on graduation day, "the turning of the earth itself." Cut by a chill crossbreeze, he shivered, and sensed an old immense sorrow. And finally he knew: my sorrow is the same as every other poor bastard's on the face of the earth.

For the first time in his life Fine felt humble.

The sky and sea and glass-and-metal buildings sprouting from the land were washed by the watery gold of the sun. The night, like atomized, elemental calcium, was deliquescing to day. Fine inhaled the fresh sea air, knowing the odds were he was breathing some of the same oxygen molecules as passed through the nose of Moses. Thank God I got mugged! He tingled, head to toe, tanked up. Awed.

Not that Fine thought he'd found answers; rather he sensed himself being pried open just enough to let in slivers of light by which, back in his usual world, he might begin to see more clearly. Risking all, losing all but his pants, he was beginning to let go of his baggage, let go of I am this or I am that, I am a doc or I am a Jew or I am a spouse—let go of Steph too, for he loved *her,* apart from himself, at least enough to let go—or I am a short or I am a white or I am a man or even I am a human being. A strange peace came over him, leached out in words as:

"At least I am."

It felt solid, right. Yes, I'm ready to make sense of, to *accept* my life: my roots, childhood, love, analysis, dead marriage, her affair, my fit, John's death, the kidnapping—where I came from, where I am, where I will go. He was bursting with excitement. Is my disease, simply, holding on? My cure, simply, letting go?

And so, over and over as he moved toward the toll booths with a light fluid tread, he repeated:

"At least I am . . . at least I am . . . at least I am . . ."

Seeing this near-naked, smiling man walking toward him chanting, the toll collector locked the booth and called the cops.

38

"BY GOD, MAN!" said Nipak, staring at Fine. "You are streaming with light!"

Clad only in his boxer shorts, Fine was walking from the flashing police cruiser across the gravel driveway toward the front porch of his house at Stow. He asked: "What do you mean?"

"Do you not see it, Stephanie?"

"Could be—but what in the world happened to you, Fine?"

"I got mugged, but I'm all right—just cut and bruised."

"Did you find her?"

"Nope."

"Did you find out anything? Where she is—how he is?"

"Nothing." He felt, deep down in his heart, a sense of his failure. "Sorry." Nipak was on Fine's crutches. "What happened?"

"The knee—it has blown up like a purple balloon! We were misinformed, old man: it is not that reality's a crutch, no; rather it is that a crutch is reality! I am about to attend to it."

"A special meditation?" Fine asked.

"No, a cortisone shot—the miracle drug! But come—there is a distinct change we see here—tell us what you've been through?"

"Can't, now—I'm already late for Duffy."

"Hold it," said Steph. "You can't see her like that."

" 'Course not—I'm going inside to get cleaned up, and—"

A shout cracked the still dawn air. A second police car roared up the driveway, spitting gravel. Out tumbled O'Herlihey, face puffed and red, apoplectic. "You!" he shouted at Fine, storming up the porch steps. "You had to be *sma't!* You had to play TV cop, dincha? Well now you've done it! She's gone, now, vanished into the city and we've lost the crucial element—bein' in touch, t'negotiate! Jayzuz Christ!" His spotted hands and cyanotic lips trembled as he lit a new cigarette from the last. "The lad's in grave danger—we're fooked! 'Is blood'll be on your hands, not ours! On behalf of the police and the remainin' O'Day family, I curse you to fry in Hell!"

Fine was shocked, awakened all at once to how stupid he'd been. "I . . . I'm sorry," he said, trembling. "I really am."

"Grand," said O'Herlihey. "Tell it to the poor little lad!"

"Maybe it'd help," said Fine, "if I could meet Stuart Fine?"

"What?" said the detective, his mottled moon face wobbling with incredulity. "No chance! We sent 'im back to Nebraska!" He turned, then stopped: " 'Ere's an idear: *you* go to Ne-fookin'-braska too! Holy Mary I almost forgot why I come out here—I come out here to *threaten* ya: if I catch ya doin' anythin' else, I'll arrest ya!" Fine asked for what? "For bein' 'er accomplice, dammit, that's what!"

Fine watched him drive off. He put himself in O'Herlihey's shoes, and saw the enormous hubris in what he'd tried to do. Shame swept over him. "He's right. Oh my God, what have I done?!"

"But what has come over you, man?" asked Nipak. "Tell us!"

"I've got to go," said Fine, moving toward the door.

Nipak threw a crutch across his path: "Please—a few words?"

"Oh I don't know," Fine said, sighing, feeling deflated. "I guess, before, I was sleepwalking through my life, and now—I don't know—now I can *see* this little, chubby, Jewish man—middle-aged Jewish man—sleepwalking through *his* life. So what? I'm screwed."

"That's it!" said Nipak, excitedly. "And when the sleepwa—" But the cry of the screen door cut into his words. Fine had left.

Fine took his time getting dressed, for he felt too opened up to deal with Duffy's reaction to the previous session, when she'd comforted him in her lap. She was dressed sloppily and looked haggard, as if she hadn't slept, and she avoided his eyes. Fine sensed she was deeply troubled by what had happened. She began associating: "Sure it felt good to comfort you, Dr. Fine, but ever since I did it I've felt so ashamed! Like I'd betrayed you. Through this whole analysis—even the time you sat on the couch and touched me—I've felt you with me, taking care of me, and then, just because of my pissy little need to take care of others, I wreck it! I drag you down to my level, get you to cry, and then act like the nice, in-control, WASPy little mummy! God I can't *stand* myself! I make myself sick!" She paused. "I've decided to quit. This is it. I'm saying good-bye."

Fine was amazed. That's not the way it had happened at all! *He* was the one who'd brought about the transgression, and yet she's blaming herself? She's distorting what happened in the relationship in a way that's coming totally from her: dragging in the pain from her past, turning a loving, giving act against herself. What an incredible thing, transference! From their many hours of struggle together he felt he really *knew* this woman, that he was finally stepping around to *her* side of the mirror, and being with her empathically. He felt how she felt, and he felt it as his own. Yet still himself, he could see the transference, and knew it was up to him to take action, preserve the relationship, be the ballast that would right the listing ship. Without thought, carried on a current of intuition so inevitable it was as if he were merely a filled-up vessel pouring out, he said: "You're blaming yourself for comforting me? What makes it hard to accept the idea that you can nurture someone else?"

She fell silent. He felt his words sink in. "Yes," she said, "I always blame myself, for giving."

"Who does that come from in you?"

"Father. He always fought hard with mother, and then came softly to me. He'd get me to comfort him, and I'd feel—yes!—like I did with you. I'd pat his head, his cheek. He'd even cry! I'd feel so ashamed of myself, after—like I did something dirty, wrong."

Fine realized how stupid he'd been to insist—far too early in the analysis—that the transference had been mother. He asked: "And so your shame is a way of taking yourself out of relationship?"

"Is that it? You mean, comforting others is a way of my isolating myself?" She fell silent. He sensed he'd hit home. How deli-

cate, our hearts! Again he felt flushed, like crying. She said: "Yes
—I see it—no wonder!"

"What?"

"No wonder I turn to ice with men!" Trembling, she went on.
As a girl "playing doctor" she'd wanted to get caught, and never
had. Both father and Savage had fondled her, threatening her into
silence. Her life with men had been much the same: repeatedly
seeking that which would bring her shame. "Know what, Dr.
Fine?—I always put you up on a pedestal—like I did father—and
thought that you knew the answers for my life, and that if only I
could get close enough to you, you'd tell me. Well, guess what?:
you're not up there, you're down in the dirt same as me. Your
life's probably no happier than mine—I can even imagine *you,*
alone, crying into your pillow at night! What a thing to see! Like
the first time I looked in a mirror and saw an older woman looking back!"

Touched, Fine attended. Together, each coming part of the
way, they were using the break in their relationship to knit it up
more strongly, new. He felt the time go along in a kind of stately
way; not filled with high drama, not scraping in sadness and rage,
not even knotted by shame and guilt—just going along.

As she was leaving, their eyes met. He held her with a hard,
sensitive gaze. Their connection felt *sober.* She set her lower lip
firmly, and nodded her head slowly up and down, as if saying: this
is who I am; life's rough, but we're still here. Fine mirrored her—
lip, and nod. After she'd gone, he realized that he'd gone through
the session without trying to *analyze* her: he'd attended not to *the
analysis,* but to her. She'd felt his attention. His responses had
been intuitive. Is this what it's all about? The chalk lines of reliable time, place, analyst as ballast? Attending, empathically; responding, intuitively; working the transference? If you've built
basic trust, the transgression is part of the journey. Yet he felt
uneasy. Something was wrong. He'd misled her before. Is this
"good" feeling my own distortion? The more I know, the more I
know I don't know. I wish I could talk to Vergessen.

By the end of breakfast, the magnitude of their sorrow had
sunk in. Steph, Fine, and Nipak sat quietly, exhausted, immobile,
like unstuffed dolls. Steph got up to get her car keys, to drive
Nipak to Mass. General for his knee, saying: "I keep picturing the

poor kid, and I . . ." She stopped, fell silent, but then burst out: "I can't stand it! Damn that woman! Damn her to hell!"

Fine felt pressure on his sternum: a heart attack?

"So many sufferings!" cried Nipak. He burped, twice, and grimaced. "It gives me the burning of the heart! Right now, in Sri Lanka, civil war! The Tamils and the Sinhalese butcher each other! Why? Isolation! The crime and the punishment are the same: isolation!" Fine asked what he meant. "This!" Nipak waved a mimeographed sheet in the air. "In yesterday's post was *Newsletter* from Vimilaji. As always, she is right on! Listen!" And he read:

> "Living is expressed in the movement of relationship. In isolation there can be physical existence and physical survival. But under whatever pretense one may isolate oneself —religious, political, whatever—there cannot be the movement of relationship, and therefore, there cannot be living."

"That's it!" Fine exclaimed, "that's exactly what I've been discovering, on my own. She's wonderful! Who is she?"

"And right, too!" said Nipak. "And right!"

"So how does it help?" Steph asked, getting up. "It can't. No way. C'mon, Nipak, let's go." She left the room.

"Yeah," Fine said, "right—it doesn't help in real life."

"Let go of the consequences!" said Nipak, and then, pulling Fine nearer, whispered: "You can shun me and my ways if you like, but listen: you and she are in different realities, with little hope for the bridging, okay?—here she comes—quick!—if she has a dream—a nightmare—you must *not* go to her, do you understand me?"

"The way things are between us, I wouldn't go to her any—"

"You would attempt it, and awaken her. But listen, man: let her go through the dream, first to last, on her own, for—"

Steph came back in. She and Nipak left for the hospital.

Exhausted, Fine wanted more than anything to go upstairs to sleep, but he was accosted by Ms. Ando with an insect emergency, and so, feeling sore and woozy, he followed her to the lab. She led him to the two last cages of hoppers. He peered in.

A large, hairy, maroon wolf-spider *(Lycosa tarantula)* was in each cage. The fatter one rested on the floor of the cage of normal controls, two half-eaten hoppers at its feet. The other hoppers were spread like debris from an explosion on all six surfaces of the wire mesh cube. Each was an easy prey. The spider was fat and happy and was having and would continue to have a field day until the last hopper was eaten. On the floor of the other cage the spider seemed thinner. The smart hoppers were in a ring—rather, in a sphere—around it. Male and female alike hung on the cage's six sides, facing in toward the menace. Fine and Ando looked closer. A remarkable drama was being played out: a male would chirp; the spider would move toward it; the hoppers behind it would pounce, and nip at a rear leg. All for one and one for all! *Liberté, égalité, insectivore!* The arachnid was down to three-and-a-half legs, and the tarsi of two of those were gone. Fine felt proud of his smart hoppers. Never again! But oh, the poor normals! Angrily, he asked Ando: "Who did this?"

"Royce says Ron. But why?"

"Why?" Fine put on a glove, grabbed the spider, handed it to Ms. Ando. "This is our government's idea of good-bye."

"But do you see?" she asked, happily. "They work together!"

"Isolation," Fine said.

"Isolation?"

"A killer." He went to take a nap.

He slept the solid, dreamless sleep of the tired child, and was awakened by Mrs. Neiderman in late afternoon, to go see Five o'clock. Getting up out of bed sent waves of pain rolling through him, splashing over raw nerves within. In the mirror he saw a puffy face with shocked somber eyes, one eye ringed by a violet shiner—he looked, he thought, uncannily like one of Freud's lapdogs.

Maurice surprised him. He came in looking frazzled, and barely glanced at Fine. Flopping onto the couch, he seemed intent on putting distance between them, denying the closeness they'd found by laughing together.

"I can take a lot of shit, Fine, but I can't take your laughing at me like you did!"

Fine was dumbfounded—that wasn't how I'd seen it at all! Maurice raged on, weaving a net of accusation around his view of the last session. For the first time Fine felt what it was *like* for him

—this poor short hungry Jewish man, craving for love. And then, as quickly as he'd blown up, Maurice fell silent, sulking.

Fine said, from his heart: "How really shitty for you to feel that way, Maurice!"

"What?" he said, startled.

"To see our having fun together as a criticism of you? How terrible for you to react that way!" Maurice fell silent. Fine sensed his silence as his struggle to let go and accept Fine's *knowing* him, by knowing his pain. And when the pain-silence gave way to relief-silence, Fine asked: "Who did you feel was laughing at you?"

"My mother." And in a tone Fine had never heard from him before, Maurice began talking about her, about how he heard anything coming from her toward him as a "critique." As they talked, Fine sensed a deep, loving—it was the only word—contact. The time flew by. At the end of the session, watching the little guy step confidently out the door, Fine felt proud. Never had he connected with patients so intimately! But wait—what does *my* pride have to do with his therapy, his life? I'm missing so much! All the nuances of—

The phone rang. It was Georgina. She told him the rumor that the Institute was in fact working to "expunge" him. He *must* prepare for the last Vergessen seminar next Tuesday—"Saying Good-bye." His future would depend on his showing against Leon. She offered to help.

Hanging up he felt angry: just when I begin to understand, to sense the depths of being a therapist and the real wisdom of Freud, begin to integrate my world experience with essential technique, and really *need* help—*need* the Institute to learn from— they kick me out? Feeling more and more embittered, he went out for a walk.

Morose, he brought a new lucidity to the day. Crisp, summery yet not yet summer—he could tell by the roses—the day's qualities were sharp as cut-outs of colored paper. It was the time of purples and blues: sky and sea, bearded iris (the best replica, in a flower, of a woman), grapey wisteria, blood-purple tree peonies, and purplish-pink bleeding hearts. The first rhododendra were in bloom—even they seemed atint with blue. Fluffy tamarix and ruby chestnut were out. The buds of mock orange fattened. He thought he scented first honeysuckle. Thinking of colors past and to come, he tried fitting the roll of the spectrum to the tilt of the season. Gloomy, he soon stopped this thinking, this fitting. Oh but the mind is shameless!

He stared at a white dogwood set against a solid dark wave of pine. The black limbs were almost invisible, and the wafered white flowers speckled the blue-green like flecks of surf. He searched for old reliable, the ruling copper beach. He could see only its topmost leaves, whirring in the wind as if gossiping with a thousand birds. Shameless. The Stow water tower with its painted white cloud was now nothing but that: tower with cloud. He heard a cry, and turned toward the beach. A gull hung on the wind. He saw it with such clarity he felt he could have described it just as it actually was, down to its most minute detail and including even its prismatic, ineluctable *essences,* and he also felt he could not have described it at all. He said, only: "The gull is."

Standing outside Jefferson House he could see his porch, and upon it—like a mirage—sat his mother and father and Steph's Aunt Belle. Steph came up beside him, and explained: "Nipak called them—to combat isolation—he thought we needed family now."

"Family, yes," said Fine, apprehension rising, "but Jews?"

"Oh come on—Belle's a real trooper. I'm glad she's here."

"Where is Nipak, anyway?"

"The knee man admitted him. It's worse than we thought." She took his arm. "Come on—let's at least put on a good act."

He walked along stiffly toward them, carrying his baggage, thirty-four years of dread: they would be perplexed by their son, of no comfort and less help. Yet as he walked closer, as he watched them catch sight of him and rise from their wicker chairs, as he read in their body movement their expectancy, their hope, he was shocked: they were being revealed to him. He stopped, stunned. They are no longer the mother and father of my childhood. Like places of childhood, they seem smaller. Look!— my pop is actually a plump, balding, dark little Jewish man with melancholy eyes who, loathing butchery and loving New York City, is stuck like a Chekhov hero in a disgusting job in a provincial backwater, fighting tooth and nail for a move to Boca Raton, Florida, doing his best. Look again!—my mom is actually a large, sagging, red-haired oldish Jewish woman, hating the butcher shop and loving New York City, fighting tooth and nail against a new life in Boca, doing her best. Her seductiveness is the mirror of her suffering—the same pain that's been wedged like a calcified lump of stuffed *derma* in under my own heart for years. Hate her? Fight them? Debate? Instruct? How foolish! He could see it from their side, now, as if he too were a parent. He'd moved from loving them or hating them to accepting them, and that was that.

This happened in an instant, as he saw in their eyes their yearning to love him, their one unfathomable son, and to be loved by him. Soberly he sensed the curve of their lives: where they'd come from, where they'd go. Boca or not—it was all the same; we are all swimmers, swimming. It was as if he were already looking back at a photo he'd just taken of them—they rising, eyes searching—from twenty years on, they both dead. Parents are older humans on their way to die. Like us all.

They embraced. They began to talk.

"You're all black and blue!" said Anna. "You poor boy! My friend Mrs. Storch says that with *two* muggers you make sure to . . ."

Despite Belle's steadying influence, with the usual Fine tact they went right for the meat and were soon elbow-deep in the gory details. Fine did his best to attend. Yes, as usual they've taken over, tried to give advice, moved on from feelings to things —Anna's endless stories about Mrs. Storch and the Storchettes, Leo's moody kosherings of meats and hapless thwackings of Titleists—but Fine knew something had changed. He sensed them sensing his care and attention. They were able to listen to Belle talk about Marxists in Central America, to share her outrage at the USA's covert war. They *are* being a comfort, imagine? You give, you get. Family is like religion: we shatter, it holds. Toward them, he felt paternal.

Anna had brought shabbas dinner, and when everybody went to wash their hands, Steph and Fine chanced to meet in the hallway.

Face to face, Fine felt awkward, and said: "Hi."

She squinted, trying to puzzle him out. "I don't know what's gotten into you, schmucko, but you're doing okay with them."

"I know—it's weird. I keep seeing them as dying, and it helps —shows us what we're here for . . ." He fell silent, unsure of himself, unsure she wanted to hear. He sensed that for her to ask

him to say more, now, would be to connect again—something
they'd both avoided since their fight. He saw that she knew it too.

"Yeah?" Her voice trembled, just a bit. "What do you mean?"

Relieved to be in contact with her, he sighed. "I realized something: they lead us into life, and we lead them out."

After dinner, they again sat out on the porch. A first cricket
chirped, tentatively. The sea made a *shhh—USH* sound on the
shore. The gaps between waves seemed long. Leo turned to Steph:

"You know, when I think of that night before the briss, I still
laugh! And I got a new one: Two Jews are down in a submar—"

"Leo, please," said Anna, softly, "with the tragedies?"

"What better time? You think they didn't tell jokes in the ghet-
tos, the Camps? Like I always say: There's more to life than eyes
the meat!" No one laughed. Steph didn't ask Leo to finish his
joke. Still trying, he asked: "So how's the comedy goin' anyway?"

"It's not."

"Oh. Okay." Leo turned back to the paper, whistling "Some
Enchanted Evening." Anna began on brother Moe's big, strong,
baby, but suddenly Leo slapped his forehead with his palm, saying: "Oh you! Whaddaya mean no comedy? You got your picture
in the paper! Look!"

Sure enough there she was—with two other comics—"Goldie
Fine." Leo read aloud: " 'Appearing at The Comedy Box Satur-
day night *blah blah blah* and a hot new woman comic named
Goldie Fine.' So—a big New York cable show tomorrow night!
You was puttin' us on!"

"No," said Steph. "It's a mistake. I told them no."

"Why, dear?" asked Belle.

"Are you kidding? With all that's going on?"

"So?" said Belle. "So with tragedy, can life stop?"

"You actually think I should do a comedy show *now?!*" Belle
and Leo said yes; Fine and Anna abstained. "Are you crazy?!"
Belle and Leo said no; Fine and Anna again abstained. Face
scrunching down in disbelief, she said: "My best friend drops
dead in my arms, you want me to do comedy? The cutest little
boy in the world is kidnapped—out there somewhere suffering—
and you want comedy? The world's come apart, the marriage's
come apart—*I'm* coming apart!—and you want from me comedy?
And my cat gets run over by a ten-ton truck and it's lying there,

looking like a pepperoni pizza, crying, and you want comedy? Well, the hell with you—I'm not in a comedy mood!"

Silence.

And then Belle laughed.

"This is no joke, Belle, this is what I feel!"

"Oh boy!" Belle said, laughing harder. "That's funny!"

"I'm serious! My life's at rock bottom and you want jokes?"

"Yes!" Fine blurted out, without thinking.

Her eyes, so dark a blue in the twilight as to seem black, locked into his. She raised a hand to her face, hiding her palsied lip. Fine had seen her do it countless times, yet this seemed the first. Her whole life lies there. Her voice was challenging: "Why?"

His heart pounded: "Because John would."

"John would tell jokes?"

"John would want *you* to." Her eyes wavered, then steeled. "The hell with John! I can't live in this world! Not being funny when I'm sad. I wish I'd never been born!"

"Yeh," said Leo, "but who's so lucky? Maybe one in a million?" Belle and Leo laughed; Fine smiled; Anna abstained.

"I'm falling apart!" she said, ferociously, rising. "My heart's broken, I feel like killing myself, and you want comedy? The hell with you, leave me alone! I'm damn well not in a comedy mood!"

Her fierceness quieted them, and they sat in silence. Fine felt balanced on the edge between crying and laughing. To keep himself from laughing he bit his lip and looked down at the ground. A few seconds later he heard Belle say, gently:

"Besides, dear, I happen to know: you never had a cat."

Fine looked up at Steph. He saw her palsied lip twitch, and knew she was barely holding herself back. Steph looked at Belle, then at Leo, and finally at Fine, and then she just couldn't help herself and burst out laughing—laughing and protesting all at once.

Belle, Leo, Fine, Anna—all joined in.

"Great," said Steph, "laugh. My life's a total failure!"

"You know something, dear?" said Belle. "Everybody's life, if we could see it from inside, would look like a failure too."

Later that night, Nipak called from the hospital. He sounded far away, drugged, slurring his words. He'd suffered a complication from the minor surgery and they were scheduling major surgery

the next day to treat the complication. Fine told him not to sign
for the operation, but Nipak said "my room is neat like the pin,"
and hung up. One by one the others went up to bed. Fine found
himself sitting across the kitchen table from Steph.

"This light's too bright," she said, turning it off. They sat in the
wavering yellow light of Anna's two shabbas candles. "So even if
I wanted to do it, what would I use for an act?"

"You've got an act."

"Yeah, what?"

"What you just did."

"What do you—?" she understood. " 'The hell with comedy—'?"

"It was *funny.*"

"It *was* funny, wasn't it?"

"*Very.*"

"With the cat and all?"

"The cat was dynamite."

"That?" She seemed skeptical. "I mean, that's all?"

"That's a lot."

"Could be, could be," she said, considering it. "And then, at
the end, when they're laughing, I stomp off?"

"Why not? A few shtick jokes, you're in." She smiled—in the
shadows a tired, middle-aged smile. She seemed beaten down,
struggling hard to right herself. He felt himself beginning to
watch her in a whole new way—holding on and letting go, both.
"I just want to say, Steph, that it's okay with me if you go off to
New York."

"What?" She leaned in closer; the candles filled out her angular
dark face, paling it. "You actually mean that?"

"You need space—it's the one thing I can give you."

"And what about you?"

"Me? My place is here. I'm getting a lot back from my patients,
now. They're giving comfort to me. Imagine that?"

She stared at him—the incisive stare of Mrs. Sullivan, the only
grade-school teacher who'd sensed the Fine promise behind the
Fine paranoia. "What the hell's gotten into you, Fine?"

"How do you mean?"

"You're different. You can't see it?"

"Sort of. Be my mirror—what do you see?"

"I feel you paying attention. I see you looking right at me, hear you listening—even responding. You never did that before."

"Maybe that's it," he said, gingerly.

"That's what?"

"That's . . ." He stopped. It'd be a risk. So? What's there to lose? Having her, letting her go—all the same. "That's love."

Gingerly, she picked it up: "What's love?"

"Love is paying attention."

"That's all?" she asked.

"That's a lot."

"Yes," she said, softly, "yes it is." Her face loomed blurry in the glowing half-light, like a large sea-creature surfacing, and, strangely chilled, he couldn't read her expression. But then he felt something moving out from her toward him, like the edge of a blanket being wrapped around a blue-lipped shivering child. The shadows flickered on the walls. He sensed her, stripped of this and that. He said to himself: I am sensing her just as she is.

"Life's hard!" she said. "Life is just too hard!"

He felt her pain, and it seemed to lift up to the ceiling and then sift down again, brush the flames, burn with element-colors and settle, as ash. All the dead, Fine thought, filling the earth, packing the earth each winter, feeding the seeds, exploding each spring, newborn. The pain and remembrance and comfort of the dead. He sighed—his mother's sigh after lighting the candles—and said: "You said I *wanted* you to run off with John—what did you mean?"

"I don't know—I just sensed it. Our love was dying, you weren't going to do anything—except keep on analyzing—it was up to me. I thought I did it to hurt you, but maybe it was to help you, you and me both—somehow get back to what we three had? Who knows." She too sighed. "There's nothing left, now, is there, of romance?"

"Unless 'nothing left' is what romance really is."

"We all die," she said. She went upstairs to bed.

Fine sat in silence. The long night awake and his nap had flipped his diurnal clock, and he felt energized. He let his mind wander over his adventure, his failure, his blasting out into the world and then coming back. He realized that he was going back and forth, back and forth, therapy to life, life to therapy, shuttling back and forth, trying to string wires across, bridge the gaps in his life—even to bridge the chasm between the living and the dead. The candles went out. He sat in the dark, vision failing, aglow.

In the early hours of the morning he heard her cries—at first muffled, then insistently louder—she was fighting through a dream. He got up to go to her, but stopped, startled, remembering what Nipak had told him about not awakening her. He sat back down.

Yet then, realizing that the others would wake her, he went upstairs. There in the dim hallway were Anna and Belle, so pale and haggard without makeup, they seemed like ghosts of themselves.

"It's okay," he said. "I'll take care of her. Go to sleep."

He went into her room and sat by her bedside, watching her lie rigid—the clenched musculature of REM sleep. Sometimes she mumbled unintelligibly, and once she cried out: "Help!" Watching over her, he felt an old glow inside. He felt caring. Maternal.

After two, she became agitated. He held her shoulders as she thrashed up out of the deep end of sleep until wild-eyed, disoriented, flailing, she awoke. "Oh! What a dream! What a bad dream!"

"What was it?" A strange sensation came over him, as if he already knew what she was about to say. His excitement mounted.

"A baby—I couldn't care for it—you took over—I screamed for help!—a woman came and—" She stopped, stared, eyes widening.

Fine said: "Her?"

"Yes! Sylvia! But more!—listen—I saw how to get her!"

"How? Come on—before you forget—"

"She reads the papers—she'll've seen my picture, the story about the comedy show, right? She'd come—I know it! Wouldn't she?"

"Oh my God!" He was shaking. "She might—she just might—to flout us—to see you—to keep up some sick, psychotic connection to me—she'd leave John James behind, disguise herself, and sneak in—"

"And then we get her!"

"How?"

"That part's up to you. I'm just the bait."

"We can't use the police—it'd scare her away. How many entrances are there to the club?"

"Two—one down an alley, one in the front."

"Okay—I'll take the front, and—" He stopped. "Hold it. It's dangerous—she's desperate for revenge—if she can't get *me*, she'll—"

"I don't care," she said, sharply.

He sensed the depth of her despair. She didn't care, no, not even about living, anymore. Well then, he thought, *I* have to care, *I* have to take care of her. He said: "No, it's too risky—"

"Are you with me?" she asked, challenging him. "Or not?"

He stared at her, sensed something opening. "Yes. Yes, I am." She relaxed, yawned, shivered. He felt awkward with her, at once both distant and close.

"You really think it's a good act, Fine?"

"Dynamite." He yawned, feeling a wave of exhaustion.

"And then, at the end, I just stomp off?"

"Whatever." He rose to go. "As long as you keep the cat."

39

At eleven o'clock that same Saturday morning, as he raised his razor to his lathered face, Fine's tic reappeared.

And reappeared with a vengeance, for no longer was it a wink of one side of his face, but now—like the lid of an open trunk—his whole face slammed shut—blackout! What the hell? His eyes started to open and then again—blackout!—like being plunged underwater, breath held in a tight grimace, then letting go, coming up. Oh no, not again! Why? Fine felt a morbid fascination: is this a residue of my seizure, a sign of a simmering tumor? Or is it psychogenic, a product of feeling, of stress? He remembered how, in his analysis, he'd understood the tic to have been a symptom of his repressed rage at his isolation. ("You want to sulk, so sulk"—Fumbles.) Falling in love with Steph, he'd joined the human race, his tic had disappeared. Is that proof of a psychological cause? No, for even back then it could have been a sign of a slow-growing tumor, blooming this May. If it's psychological, what am I repressing now? John's death has brought intense feeling—guilt, shame, anger, sadness. So why the tic? Fine raised his eyes—which slammed shut: "Hey, Big Guy—how could You do this to me now, just when I'm starting to see things clearly?" The usual silence, the deistic gap. "Okay, Big Shot—is it that I opened my eyes too wide and, like a survivor, saw too much?"

But then he realized that what had seemed clear, that night of "Old Ironsides" and the bridge, now was not clear at all. Clear? Far from it! Already hazy, clouded over. Has anything changed? I feel a glimmer of understanding of my wife, parents, patients, but the basic fog, doubt, freed-up terror, and entrapment, and blindness to myself and to life? Still the same. Worse—now I've got a *tic!*

Marked, he faced his wife and parents with embarrassment, angrily rejecting their questions and concerns, lashing out sullenly. He was plunged into a twitchy gloom, and moped around all day as he'd done as a pre-Steph adolescent, hiding in his room ("You want to hide in your room, so hide in your room"—Fumbles.) The phone: Georgina.

"Metz!" she exclaimed.

"Metz?"

"Frau Metz! Rumor is she'll be at the Vergessen seminar, Tuesday night, as the final judge. Don't give up—get to work!"

"Metz?"

"Metz! What's the matter, have you gone deaf?"

"Worse—got a tic." He described it. "It's the pits."

"Oh." She paused. "Look, maybe you *should* give up. I'll still love you if you do. What do you need those jerks for anyway?"

"But I do! Now, right now when I'm seeing how hard it is to be a good therapist, when I'm desperate to put together intuition and solid technique, now's when I really can *learn* from them."

"From *them?* From Leon? From that ape, Crusher Gold?"

"At least they *try.* How many of us, now, in this crazy world, actually try to understand, on a human level, human beings?"

"Not many."

"Exactly. At least they're not trying to drug people with pills, or diets, or do-it-yourself books, or hugging poor schmucks on TV—they've resisted the evangelism and hype of the age. They're still trying to do the hardest thing: help people to change. There's a lot of experience down there—Tuesday could be a great chance."

"Chance?"

"Metz." He felt a quiver of excitement—I *can* fight the killers of the spirit, I *can* shake my fist at death. "Let's go for it! Come

out here tomorrow, we'll use the WANG to run the world literature on 'termination'—okay?"

"It's a deal! We'll show 'em. Luv ya, Fine—bye."

Yet not long after Fine hung up, he was pushed under again by
despair. I won't be able to save myself. They'll never believe my
experience, never value how I've brought it into therapy. Dora's
lap, laughing with Ratman—forget it. I'm so confused, I'll be
incoherent. Ironic: just when I'm beginning to love being a therapist, when I'm on the verge of finding out how to be a therapist
and know that they can help show me the way—they show me the
door? Blackout! Terrific—that's all I need now, to have *them* see
my tic. Proof that I failed analysis number one; I'll get the
Crusher for number two. Why do analysts see symptoms as cancers? Aren't symptoms a sign of health, of being both vulnerable
and courageous? A symptom tells the world: here is one of the
walking wounded; here comes a suffering human being. Why
can't we wear our symptoms proudly, like badges of honor? Or,
rather, humbly, as acceptance of the way things are? Why else
suffer anyway?

And so all day long he hid in his room, but for a brief conference with Steph to plan out the night's comedy act. In the light of
day the plan lost solidity, but Steph was firm, and they agreed to
try. Nipak had been unable to stop the Mass. General surgeons
from cutting him, and was in "serious" condition. They acted
alone.

Arriving at The Comedy Box a few hours before the show, Fine
slipped a twenty to the bouncer at the alley door, who promised
to keep all unknowns out. He himself—disguised in white linen
suit, fedora, glasses, and beard—stood sentry at the front door,
watching the crowds stream past to the nearby theaters, searching
each face. No sign of Sylvia. At ten, the show began. Just before
her spot, Steph came out to tell him, and introduced him to a
leering, oily man—Rosensdork—a New York agent who'd seen
her at Catch. They went in, Fine standing guard at the back of the
room just inside the door.

"Goldie" came on. After a good start, as she was moving into
the body of her act, she was assaulted by a heckler: a short wiry
man with bushy red hair springing out from under a Celtics cap,
sitting alone, taunting her in a drunken "Eastie" accent. She ignored him, but he wouldn't let up. Fine watched her squirm in the

spotlight, felt her panic rising. Goldie was dying! She couldn't follow her routine. The audience felt the tension and got edgy. Leo—sitting with Belle and Anna—tried to quiet him, and was cursed out. Rosensdork sat pat, a tiny smile on his face, as if saying: "Let's see what you're really made of, eh?" Everyone knew that it was up to her, and her alone, to deal with the heckler. She faced him: "Well well—I see my dad's out there in the audience toni—"

"I ain't your dad and you ain't funny!"

"That joke was funny till you—"

"That joke was crappy—old and crappy!"

"You're a crappy man—"

"You're a crappy comedian!"

She paused. "So—o—" her voice shook. "So where you from?"

"East Boston."

"What's the matter, did they—"

"—'close all the bowlin' alleys early'? Give up, turkey!"

Taking a deep breath, she looked away, toward another part of the room, and said, politely: "You know, folks, a stand-up comic has to learn techniques to handle hecklers. First, you merely use the very . . . *gentle* . . . insult." She paused, then whipped around to face him and screamed at the top of her lungs: "Hey fella *fuck you!* Okay?!"

"Give up, Goldie, you ain't gonna make it! No way!"

Something in the voice set Fine's teeth on edge—could it be *her?* Before he could move, Steph went on: "And then, folks, if the gentle insult fails, you simply do this—" She yelled *"Banzai!,"* charged out into the audience, and started beating on him with her fists! "All part of the act, folks, all part of the—"

"No it ain't!" The drunk laughed. "Call the manager! Help!"

The fight turned playful. With one last "clip" on his jaw, Steph went back up onstage, and was applauded. Talk about "breaking the fourth wall!" Fine thought, sensing her power. Blushing, she laughed despite herself, and then, as she tried to resume her act, burst out laughing again. She couldn't keep a straight face! The audience, sensing the actor no longer acting, laughed too. They were *with* her—they could see themselves doing something like that too. Magic, Fine thought, like magic she's letting go of artifice and just being herself, here and now with us in this room!

Flushed, she seemed to glow, making him—and others—feel a glow too.

She went on, relaxed, working the crowd, cracking put-downs and one-liners, playing one heckler off of another, even using her "bombs" to keep the fire burning: "Did somebody laugh? You, sir —would you mind taking that laugh and spreading it around the room?" She segued into "My life's a wreck and you want comedy?" and used it as a scaffold, fleshing it out, going with their responses. And then, to Fine's surprise, she started talking about *him:*

"—yeah, *you* can laugh, but do you know what it's *like* to be married to a shrink? You wake up in the morning, and you go: 'Hello.' And he goes like this." Steph rested her chin on her hand, her elbow on her other palm, and sighed. "In bed! And he gives you this look." She stared perplexedly out at them—a look of mock seriousness. "And then, this." She mimicked his tic! They roared! "Next, there's this, like, tape delay, okay?" Steph paused, drumming her fingers. "And finally—" She imitated Fine's psychoanalytic voice: " 'Yes, and what do you *mean* by 'hello'?" They loved it! "That's just 'hello'! You should hear 'good-bye'! And sex?"

"Nuthin'!" said someone in the back.

"Ah!—another analyst's wife in the room tonight? Why, just looking at you reminds me: what's the most useless thing on a woman?"

"What?"

"An Irishman."

They loved it. And then she began using John.

He watched her snatch up her sadness and rage, her shame and guilt, and spin it out in comedy. And it worked. Fine could sense the feeling zinging through the room, linking people, even, yes, healing. She's up there healing. In seven minutes she's done more than Fumbles did in seven years. Shared laughter lit up shared spirit, shared spirit snackled through the room like current, so *live,* Fine thought, you'd think you could reach out and touch it. They laughed, they elbowed each other in the ribs and pointed at her and laughed. She was showing them *them.* He could almost hear them thinking: That's *me* up there on stage! *My* life's just as ridiculous as hers! Didja hear her?—her life's a wreck and I'm laughing? She's me! She's us all! He felt proud of her. Such art.

When the time came to close, she sat at the piano, and Fine
knew what she was going to do. A lump rose in his throat. As he
heard the opening bars, he felt a surge of immense sorrow. She
sang:

> "Carry me back to old Manhattan,
>   That's where my heart belongs,
>   Give me a showspot to hang my hat in,
>   Sing me those Broadway songs . . ."

As she sang the rest of the verses, even from the back of the
room Fine could see her eyes glisten. He was the only one there
who knew what it meant but everyone there felt what it meant.
The room fell still, shared feeling rippling its surface gently, like a
moonlit pond shirred by swimmers. Deep silence bathed them all.
  She finished, and they gave her a standing ovation. On and on
they went. Yes, he thought, joining the crowd, clapping wildly,
she *is* a comic, yes! And being a comic is great! He knew then that
something he'd learned, that weird night, was still with him: he
no longer had a plan for her, or a plan for him and her. He loved
her and he was ready to go on with her and have a child and he
was also ready to let her go. She *should* become a comic, yes.
Wifing me and not wifing, mothering a child and not, having and
letting go—all the same, all the same. Sadly, he realized that she
would leave him, go to New York, be a big success. Her life would
go well, his not. He felt jealous, his face went off—a three-tic
repeater.
  Fine went outside. They'd arranged to meet out front after. It
was as if he were out in a city night for the first time ever. How
fresh it all is: the glitzy neon of the "Combat Zone"; the theater
crowd streaming from the latest pre-Broadway drek; the cars
honking, whores hooking, crowds milling—singing snatches of
song—city lights splashing the dome of sky with an eerie, vanishing florescence.
  Steph came out from the alley. She seemed all lit up inside. She
searched for him in the stream of people, and then saw him and
started fighting her way through to him. And then, just before she
reached him, he saw, down past her on Kneeland Street, the boy.
  He was being led by the hand by a man who could only be
Sylvia. She was approaching a cab. Fine started to run, thoughts

flashing past—she came *with him?*—how crazy can you get?—had
she tried the comedy show and gotten scared off?—was she, like a
cat with a mouse, toying with us?—was it all incredible chance?—
sick!

She was arguing with a touristy couple about who'd seen the
cab first. Fine knew what he'd have to do and that he'd have only
one chance to grab the boy and run. He had to time it just right.
Sylvia was trying to shove John James into the cab; he was balk-
ing. Do it, Fine, right now. He hesitated. What if I miss? I'm so
damn clumsy! He felt like a kid on the high diving board, fearing
the hard cold water, walking to the edge, walking back, letting
others go first, trying to force himself to let go and leap in, failing,
holding back. How to have the faith to take the leap, how to cross
that span of air from high up down, into the unknown below?
Unlike a film, this might not work. Come on, Fine, you got no
choice!

He moved. Much faster and much slower both than he'd ever
thought possible, he barreled through the crowd across the sidewalk and saw her give one more shove to the kid, who—thank
God!—resisted just enough so that Fine before he knew it had
smashed into Sylvia from behind with his shoulder ripped the boy
from her grasp carried him like a football hugged tight into his
body and kept on running as hard and fast as he could down the
street all the while listening for the shots and fearing the sear of
the bullet in his back. Running and running the boy light as in a
dream and feet light on the pavement dodging people and then
breathless he knew he was safe because there was no way in hell
she'd be able to chase him and no way she'd fire into the crowd
and so—puffing—he stopped in a doorway—puffing—huge
breasts (photos) protecting him on three sides (for it was a porno
parlor in the Combat Zone)—*tic*—looked back.

The tourists were sprawled on the ground. The cab was bucking traffic toward the gaudy red and gold pavilions of Chinatown.

The boy stared at him. His fear swung to joy. He yelled "Unky
Fine!" and was screaming and crying all at once. Steph came up
breathless, saw the boy and he her, and the three put their heads
together and screamed and cried and held each other tight.

After a while John James stopped crying. He asked:

"Where's my da?"

40

FINE TOLD HIM.

He stared in disbelief, and then horror, and then Fine saw him crumple up inside, and the spark go out. He became quiet, solemn. Steph asked him if he'd been physically hurt and he said no. Fine took his hand and they walked to the car. The little hand in his felt thin, lifeless, papery, as if a cut-out of cardboard.

Steph went to a pay phone, called Katey and told her. They drove the familiar route to the old three-decker on Carson Beach. Katey was waiting. She hugged the boy, tried to comfort him. Then, sensing his shock, she let him be, tending to the practical matters at hand—asking if he'd like something to eat, or a bath. Nothing. They found themselves sitting in the parlor, stiffly formal as if waiting for someone to call. Watching the boy sitting quietly on the sofa, Fine had a sense of unreality, of sitting in a purgatory filled with specters of people, without purpose. The boy said he'd like a glass of milk and that he'd get it for himself. They watched the little guy get off the sofa and march stiffly—as if his legs and arms had been unstrung—to the kitchen. They stared at each other and saw the desperation, the realization of the total aloneness—deadness—of death, and tears came to their eyes. John James came back with his glass of milk. He wasn't sad, he wasn't angry, he was just now partly dead. He took a sip of milk and in a hollow voice asked how his father had died. Fine told him.

"But where *is* he?" the boy asked.

"His body's close by here," said Katey, "up on the hill overlookin' this house, and our beach. And his soul's with God."

"He's buried already?"

"Yes. Thursday. And would you be wanting to go see?"

"No." He fell silent. "Granny?"

"Yes, luv?"

"Kin I stay with Fine 'n' Steph?"

She paused, and then said: " 'Course you can, luv, yes."

And so they took him back out to Stow. The police came, and O'Herlihey interrogated him. Dully, he told them all he knew—not much, as he'd been blindfolded or drugged most of the time. They finally left, leaving the three of them alone. He wanted to sleep in the same bed with Fine. In the early hours of the morning, when they finally got into bed, he snuggled up close. Fine asked was he going to say his prayers?

"No."

That night he awakened screaming, not knowing where he was. Then, recognizing Fine, he remembered, screamed again—"Da?" —and started crying. Fine held him, rocked him for hours, though not really back to sleep. The nightmare opened the gates of grief. The little boy was finding out for the first time that life can be more horrible than any dream. All day Sunday they tried to comfort him.

He noticed Fine's tic. "What's the matter with your face?"

"Oh, it's nothing. I think it's just telling everybody how bad I feel, that's all."

Sunday night at bedtime, John James did get down on his knees to pray. Fine joined him, remembering how, as a child, he'd reserved prayers only for when he'd wanted something from God.

"Please God, take care of my da. Cause he's good. 'N' take care of me. 'N' Unky Fine 'n' Aunt Steph 'n' Grandma Katey 'n' my ma. 'N' The Uncle." He knelt awhile longer, and then added quickly: " 'N' kill her too amen."

Fine read to him, the boy's favorite book, *The Wind in the Willows,* his favorite chapter: "The Piper at the Gates of Dawn."

Fine too was comforted by it. While John James slept, Fine read on.

Hours later the boy awoke, fighting through a night-terror, scratching and clawing at Fine as if possessed. Fine struggled to hold him, marveling at his strength. Seeing who it was, he clung to Fine, his body trembling. But he wanted Steph too. And so Fine carried him into Steph's room, awakening her.

"He wants to sleep in here with you."

"With *both* of you! Please?"

Steph opened her arms to the boy, and he came to her. Fine stood by the edge of the bed, feeling awkward, as if trespassing. John James insisted he get in on the other side of him. With a shrug, Fine did.

"Keep a little light on for me, will you?" the boy asked, and, snuggling up to Steph, soon fell asleep between them, hand on Fine's tummy, chin in Steph's neck. Fine glanced across at her, his wife. The weak low light showed her first wrinkles. Sad. She reached out her hand; he touched it, lightly.

"Reckless," Fine whispered, letting go, lying back. "He really *was* reckless, wasn't he?"

"Sure was."

"And false."

"True," she said. "As reckless and as false as me."

"As all of us."

The two old wind-up alarm clocks ticked loudly. The night, pressing against the sound, seemed far too still.

"We both loved him," said Fine.

"Yes, we did."

"I feel like such a failure, Steph."

"I know."

"And I feel so much alone."

"Yeah," she said, "me too. Join the crowd."

The three slept, wrapped close in the comfort of sorrow.

41

"THE TALL SHITS!" cried out Jefferson.

"The Tall Shits!" cried the other Jefferson Housers, as the Jefferson family brig *The Thomas,* semaphored "Sail!" by the harbormaster out off Deer Island, tacked to catch the easterly "sailor's wind" and take her turn in a circle of history, the parade of sailing ships in Boston Harbor on Monday 29 May, the celebration of Memorial Day.

John James cuddled in Fine's lap. The boy had run the gamut of feeling and come back to fear, clinging to Fine closely. His eyes had coalesced around silent questions: Dead? *Why?* What did he *do?* But now, safe in Fine's lap on the ship in the harbor, he seemed less afraid. He sat looking out at the spectacle of tall sailing ships. He smiled. Once, he laughed. Please, God, thought Fine, stroking the boy's velvety, whitish-blond hair, please let him start to heal.

They were sitting in the stern, under what Fine had learned was the gaff and boom of the fore-and-aft sail rigged from the brigantine's square-rigged main (or aft) mast. Mr. Jefferson, decked out in starched white and gold braided captain's hat and old shiny metals, was standing proudly and solidly behind the wheel, giving orders to the helmsman, who else but a white-uniformed Jefferson (black). The joy in Mr. Jefferson's face—in his whole *being!*—made Fine reconsider: is chasing the dream less important than getting it, after all? No, for Mr. Jefferson's dream is "the sailing" not "the sail"—journey not arrival, dreaming not dream. The gerund rules. Ports are finite, sailings infinite.

And what an expert Mr. Jefferson has turned out to be! Here he is, captaining a complex and subtle creature, his 136-foot brig, *The Thomas*. With the help of a few Jefferson family retainers, he'd taught the Jefferson Housers to crew. They'd motored down to Duxbury, practiced for two days, and sailed on up to Stow. That morning, when he'd sighted the huge elegant ship docked at the jetty, Fine had been astounded. He'd stared up at it—all ropes and knots and masts and furled sails and gleaming brass and hatches and who knows what—marveling at its intricacy, feeling that he could no more have fathomed how to set it in rightful motion than fly from its crow's nest off into thin air.

Mr. Jefferson knew his ship: "Yes, er, no, like the sole of my foot! 'Brig' short for 'brigantine' from the Italian *brigare,* to quarrel. Square-rigged on the fore and main masts, yes, er, but the added fore-and-aft rigging, schooner like, yes, makes 'er swifter and more maneuverable than bigger ships. Was, er, pirate and robber ship, yes, like a galleon or galliot. Family shame, yes, er, but family fortune too, no? The tides and winds familial!"

Fine was amazed. Keep Mr. Jefferson—all of them—on this ship, they'd have no need for treatment. Bring back the Ship of Fools! Let them sail in grand historical pirouettes off the coasts, circling, circling. The others had responded to Mr. Jefferson's clear firm orders: Eli, Cooter, Stinko, Mary, Mrs. Busch—with her Stow Auxiliary chum, Mrs. Mustin—Eve, Fat Sadie—even Neiderman, Ando, and Royce—all were at work. You'd be crazy to think they're crazy. The intricacy of the ship—ropes to be learned, scrubbings and polishings to be done, cooking and washing and cleaning—could provide years' worth of ego-edges, decades' worth of happiness. Fine looked around at them, his affection mixed with admiration. How solid they were, how responsive. Even his tic, for each of them, was alive with meaning. Many mirrored him, *tic*-ing back. His mates.

Fine gazed out over the railing. What a glorious Memorial Day it was. The morning had come to light through mist, but now, at noon, the weather was holding warm, crisp, and breezy. Fine felt

like a child seeing water for the first time. The sea, the deep blue
of Steph's eyes, was novel and familiar all at once. The sky was
clear but for a curl of high cirrus, edged like the crests of breakers
on a bay. Having celebrated the Bicentennial with a Tall Ships,
Boston was repeating. The immense crowd coated the bobbing
boats in the harbor like refugees, and lined all coasts—except the
sealed-off Long Island and Stow—like prescient stalled lemmings.
The parade path was a gentle long curve between the twin elbowed arms of Deer Island and Long Island. The parade had
begun with the *U.S.S. Constitution*—"Old Ironsides"—firing a
four-gun salute at the mouth of the harbor and being tugged in,
escorted by a spunky fireboat making eight rainbows from jets of
water thrown high into the air. As the oldest ship in the U.S.
Navy passed the biggest—the aircraft carrier *John F. Kennedy*—
Fine and the rest could hear the cheers even far out where they
were, almost to the Brewsters on the edge of the open sea.

"I'm ascared for Aunty Steph!" John James said suddenly,
turning to look at Fine. "Why didn't she come with us?"

"She must have gotten stuck in traffic."

"Is she all right?"

"Sure she is. She can take care of herself."

"No she can't," said the boy. "Nobody can. 'Cause if my da
couldn't, nobody can never! No way!"

"She'll be watching from Stow—we'll see her as we pass by."

"I'm ascared for her, Unky Fine!"

"I know, but I'm not—she's okay. And I'm right here, see?"

Steph was supposed to have come on board. That morning,
she'd driven Belle to the airport, and was going to stop on the way
back to see Nipak Dandi. He, poor man, was in a coma from the
major surgery the doctors had done to correct complications of
the minor surgery on his trick knee, and Steph was to get guard-
ianship to prevent the next operation, a risky experimental proce-
dure used only in extreme cases. Fine, needing to stay with his
patients, told Steph they'd hold off embarking as long as they
could, but had missed her.

Fine's parents, too, had left that morning. As he'd opened the
door of the Olds for her, Anna had stared at him, kindly, and
said: "You know, when you were little, the rabbi talked to me
once. He called you a 'luminous child.' I never understood. Till
now. Good-bye, dear, and thanks." Somehow, before the door

closed, Leo and she had managed to start fighting. Arguing, they'd driven off.

Fine had waved. "Why do people get married?"

Belle had said: "Because, in the night, in the dark, you're not alone." She'd sneezed. "Hay fever! Listen to me—preaching? I stay one more day in this wilderness, I'll sound like a 'Prairie Home Companion'! Come visit in the City—shake the farm mentality, okay?"

Steph and she had gotten into the vintage purple Jag and driven off.

"Yes, er, no," said Mr. Jefferson now to Fine, "and perchance you know how we are able to sail against the wind?"

"Vectors!" said Fine.

"Tricky little buggers, yes, er, no, and yet ever so useful if intuitively known. The sense of the sea. Invisible lines strung through the world of wind and wave, entwining, yes, no, and joining, as if in communion, and, at a time like this, helpful in the extreme—Ahoy there!" He barked orders: "Ten degrees starboard, Jefferson!"

"Jesus!" said the black man, turning the wheel the wrong way. "Michael row the boat ashore!" Mr. Jefferson righted him.

"Hey doc," said Cooter, perched like a hawk in the main-mast rigging, Ron's rifle slung over his shoulder, binoculars at his neck, "we're sailing through this water slicker 'n' owlshit, ain't we?"

"The Tall Owlshits!" said Eli. "Eichmann's dead; get Barbie! Look—is that a U-boat?"

"Hell no, mutha, it ain't mine!" Cooter laughed. "We come from the days of wooden ships and iron men to the days of iron ships and wooden men. We're light as 'luminum 'n' shiny as brass! Hotcha!"

"Live and let live," said Mary, crossing herself, "to each his own. Better safe than sorry. Haste makes waste."

"We've nothing to fear," said Mrs. Bush, "but fear itself."

"America," said Stinko, "ees standink tall!"

"Funny," said Neiderman, "how clichés are trite but true."

Fine smelled the fresh ion odor off the water, licked his lips and tasted salt. He stroked the smooth wood of the railings and looked up the line of march. One after the other the jewels of man's love affair with the sea paraded in and circled back out. John James asked Fine to help him identify the ships. They easily picked out *The Juan Sebastian de Elcano* with its crew of young sailors decked out in red shirts and white pants standing on the yardarms like arrows pointing toward the sky, and then other topsail-schooners and sloops, barks and ketches, full-riggers and jammers and barkentines—all parading like gay ladies decked in linen, pulled by forces known intuitively and only approximated always and yet trusted for being so old. "They'll even sail in space, soon," Fine told John James, "using the sun's photons as wind, tacking and gliding on the high frontier." Crinolines of sail filled with light wind, they glided as if on rollers. Only the white water sounded by the cut of bow into wave and the deep blue-green echo of wake betrayed any motion. To Fine the rising of the Boston skyline seemed so gradual as to be like that of sun or moon or age itself: never a definite start, no distinct steps, no movement, not even a feeling of movement—like the turning of the earth toward night or the tilting of the earth toward winter—and yet, one day, it is all changed, clearly and utterly changed, as each day brings night, and each year, winter.

They passed the tip of Long Island, the site of the gibbet where pirates had been hanged, next to Long Island Light. The island was conspicuously empty, sealed off to the public. As they rounded the point and headed toward the jetty, Cooter scanned Stow with his binoculars, calling out familiar sights. Suddenly he cried out:

"Hey, Doc Fine—there's a dude there looks just like you!"

"What?"

"Spittin' image a' you! Like yo' twin! Here, look!"

Cooter handed down the binoculars and pointed Fine toward the beach below the lawn running down from Jefferson House. Fine saw a figure walking along the shore toward the jetty, sunlight reddening his chestnut hair. Fine raised the glasses to his eyes.

It was as if he were peeping at himself! Like his out-of-body feeling when he seized. Head to toe, gait and arm-swing, it was him! And—the irony!—dressed in loud plaid! Stuart Fine! He was walking—jaunty, jolly—along the beach toward the jetty. Fine seemed able to *read* him, sensing at once his purpose: a wish to see better. Like looking into the vanishing infinites of facing mirrors. How had he gotten here? What an unbelievable coincidence!

As I was to learn later, it was hardly coincidence at all.

Stuart Fine, told to go back to Nebraska, had stayed. From the usual people—hotel clerk, hooker, cabbie—the details of his journey came to light: having cleared the time at home so as not to be back with wife and five kids and Rotarians and swine until after Memorial Day, he'd decided to stay and for once in his life have some fun. "I'm not talking Pima Indians," he'd told the hooker to whom—she reminded him of his eldest daughter—he'd unburdened his heart, "I'm talking *Playboy* magazine fun!" And he had: Legal Seafood to get scrod, swan boats, whore, theater. His urge to sail always having been flattened by the dry rectangular husk called Nebraska, he looked forward to the Tall Ships. He'd read the papers and wanted to meet this other "Dr. Fine." He'd taken a cab to Long Island. At the Stow end of the Curley Bridge the guard, mistaking him for "Doc Fine"—not so incredible, for he was a man often mistaken for other men—had waved him through onto the deserted island. He'd begun watching from high on the hill. Wanting a closer view, he'd waltzed down the lawn to the beach, and then turned up-island.

As Fine watched Fine walk along toward the jetty, he chanced to see another moving figure not far down the shore. The figure seemed to be following. He felt the hair on the back of his neck prickle. Could it be? He tried to focus in on who it was, but he couldn't quite make it out. The time passed slowly. Finally, as the figure closed on Fine—the dallying Fine, who, like a lover or poet or madman was stopping to pick wild flowers—he knew: Sylvia Green! Undisguised, she was tracking him. How had she gotten in? You can't keep them out, or in—not even in the Camps. Fine shouted:

"Mr. Jefferson—bring her into dock—*now!*"

"Yes, but, er, no, the parade route—"

"It's an emergency! Into the jetty! *Right* now!"

"Roger! Starboard tack, Jefferson my man, *now!* All hands on deck, yes!" He barked out orders to set the right tack back. The vessel began coming about, fighting the quartering wind.

And as it did, Fine saw something that made his heart stop: there, entering the driveway of their house, was Steph's purple Jag. She parked, got out, and saw—closer to and down the lawn —the same drama that Fine himself was seeing. Horrified, Fine knew that she'd think it was him. He saw her see it all—the woman following "her" Fine—and then put her hands to her face in shock, wave her arms helplessly, turning around looking for help. And then, finding none, she started running down the lawn toward them. In shock, yet with the utter clarity that comes with shock—seeing history flow up to the present and flow off down away—Fine realized: she is risking her life for me?! Unarmed, she's chasing a killer?! He cried out:

"No, don't! Stop! I'm here, safe! Stop!"

Time seemed to clench. The ship was taking a long time to tack into the wind, back to the jetty. The gap between Sylvia and Stuart was closing. Steph too was closing in. Everything was happening in slow motion and happening too fast. Fine felt sick. The ship was not going to dock in time. He had to act right now.

"Cooter—give me that rifle!"

"Huh?"

"Rifle! Now!" said Fine, savagely, and grabbed the rifle and steadied the gun on the rail. "Hold steady, Jefferson, y'hear?!"

"Aye aye, sir!" The Jefferson stood at the wheel. "Steady as she goes!"

Fine looked through the telescopic sight. Stuart was still walking unaware—whistling! Fine panned to see how close she was—no need—Stuart turned, startled, saw who it was, more startled still. He started to smile, and then his face turned to fright and he spoke. His hands went up—first a ple⸱ then a shield—chest and crotch—and Fine knew this was it. He swung from Stuart to Sylvia—she was aiming a revolver. Her chest was in the crosshairs but then she turned suddenly to look back—at Steph!—and as she turned again toward Stuart, Fine took a breath and—as Ron had told him—breathed out and gently brushed the trigger. He'd hardly felt the jolt when he fired again.

"Yes!" he cried, exhilarated, watching Sylvia drop. "Got 'er!" He looked up. One figure still stood. Which?

Praying, he took the binoculars.

Stuart lay still. Sylvia was down, squirming. Steph, hands to face, was backing away, looking toward the ship.

They docked. With a shout to keep John James on board, Fine ran down the gangplank and up the pebbly beach toward Steph. She ran toward him too, and they met screaming and hugging on the edge of the surf, waves breaking over their ankles. Royce and the others went past them to the site of the carnage. Slowly, they followed.

Sylvia was lying wounded, one arm shattered at the shoulder—white bone sticking through skin—one leg a mass of twitching flesh. Royce and a nurse were tending to her. Stuart, obviously beyond their help, lay on his back, arms and legs outstretched—what huge Corsam shoes!—three rips in his shimmery ultramarine shirt. On his face was an expression of peace and torment, as if saying: "Is this *it!*"

Fine stood still, staring at his double.

Sylvia moaned, in shock. Looking at her, Fine sensed an enormous relief. It's done! She can't escape, ever again—we're safe! Fine looked to Steph, standing with her hands clasped palm over fist on her chest, staring down at the bodies as if in disbelief, and he felt himself being lifted on a wave of joy, tremendous joy. Look —she's not hurt, she's alive—thank God! Tears came to his eyes. She's safe! As if hearing Fine's inner voice, Steph glanced up at him. In her eyes was shock, revulsion. And then, like a flat metal target nicked by a bullet, the other side of what he'd done spun around to face him. A cold spike of horror plunged into his heart and exploded, debris pumping out through the vessels of his body, chilling him to his bones. He shivered, began to shake spasmodically, teeth chattering. He clenched his jaw to stop, and found himself shaking more violently for the clenching. Idiot!—that blood, that glistening white bone, that dead man—these are not films, videotapes—these are *real, all real!* Horrified, with a rising self-loathing, Fine sensed how close he'd come to killing another human being. I'm a doctor, on the side of life, and I tried to kill a patient? *My* patient! Worse!—I sat with her all those hours and never realized? These awful things have happened, all because of a patient of *mine?* Shame swept over him, tumbling him over so that as he glanced around at his Jefferson House patients he was sure he saw, in their shocked, slack-jawed faces, an accusation: *you failed.* Filled with self-hate, Fine stared at the pebbly ground.

They put Sylvia on a stretcher and carried her up the hill to a Stow ambulance. It spit gravel and spun off, wailing, away.

"Well I be dead 'n' done fo!" said Cooter, staring at Stuart. "He looks jes like my ole lady, in them shoes and dippy plaid pants!"

The stark words shook Fine out of his funk. As his other Jefferson Housers began to chatter in their weird argot which made as much sense as any other chatter—more, for its being uncensored —Fine felt himself ease. Sighing, he knew that things now, finally, were over. No more killer. No more fear. He was letting go, coming out of his shock. And yet—as, once, in the aftermath of a car crash with Steph he'd realized just how close he and she had come to being killed—suddenly he was overwhelmed with terror, the terror of "what if": what if I'd missed? Steph would be dead! What if I'd been walking there in his place, as she'd thought? I'd be dead! I could have been killed. It could have been *me!*

"Dead as a bug in a rug!" said Fat Sadie, stomping.

"Holy Mary, Mother of God," said Mary, fingering.

"Holy Moses!" said Eli. "Dr. Fine—he looks just like you!"

"Yes, er, no," said Mr. Jefferson, with authority. "Clearly, we have here, no, er, yes: *a dead ringer!*"

Fine couldn't help but chuckle. His release released the others, and, one after the other, they started to laugh. Their laughter was infectious, ringing on and on. None of them could stop.

"Jesus Christ Almighty!" Jefferson, the big black man, was laughing so hard that he was crying. Big iridescent tears shimmered on his coal-black cheeks. He raised his arms to the heavens and, laughing to beat hell, he said: "It's the big cry, now, Lord, yes, it's the big big cry!"

Fine felt their laughter scrubbing away at his horror, his shame. His skin tingled, as if the pores, cleansed, were opening. And then, for the first time, he realized what he had done. His heart thumped hard—he felt the echo in his temples—Ka-*thunk!* I did it! I did it! Dammit, I did it—I saved the day! Yes! Yes! Yes! Unclenching, breath now coming light and easy, Fine felt sober, powerful. He sensed, in his core, the rightness of his act.

And then, right before their eyes, a seeming miracle occurred: Stuart stirred, belched, groaned, belched, and sat up! He stared at Fine, his eyes rolled up, and again he fainted dead away.

It would turn out that as a government slaughterhouse inspector he'd often been assaulted. One winter in Waco they'd taken a pot shot at him. He'd bought a bullet-proof vest, of new, lightweight Kevlar. Tax-deductible, it had saved his life.

42

TO BE HUMAN is to hunger for heroes and heroines. This hunger is such that in America even a person like Fine would do.

On Memorial Day afternoon Mr. Royce radioed Dr. Pelvin at his Allagash shelter, and told him the news. Pelvin ordered him to "Feed the press—two hundred percent!," jumped into his seaplane, and made it back by nightfall. The media were swarming over Stow-on-Wold, tracking the news, hunting for Fine. They crowded onto his porch, rang his bell, banged on his windows. He opened the door, keeping the screen door latched. The incandescent lights half-blinded him. He said:

"I won't talk to you." They asked why not. "I'm not being phony anymore." He slammed the door. The press loved it. He would be quoted widely. Fine asked Pelvin to shield him, Steph, and the boy. Delighted to be in the spotlight, Pelvin obliged.

Fine was struggling. Against the backdrop of horror of John's death, he was watching his life sink. *His* patient had killed people, *while he was seeing her!* A better diagnostician would've known; Reuben, Serena, and John would still be alive! It was his fault. He was obsessed with guilt. He feared Steph would actually leave for New York, and that he, staying, would get kicked out of the Institute. His lifework would be discredited, he himself shamed, spurned, lost. He felt stunned—knocked down by the universe, trying to pick up his life once again. Pick up his life anew, and gently—as gently as a son who, having been lifted from a crib and carried to a playpen by his father, in the revolution of generations was now lifting his father from a rocker and carrying him to a chrome-railed bed.

Their shared need to ease the little boy's pain was bringing Fine and Steph together. Without saying it, they were putting him first, working hard with each other to provide whatever comfort they could. Again that night they would all sleep in the same bed. Fine told John James to go upstairs and get ready, and that they'd be up in a few minutes. Fine had been wanting to talk to Steph alone, but she seemed to be shying away from close contact with him. Standing in the hallway, she avoided his eyes. Here was his chance, but the feelings were so heavy, he didn't know how to begin. Finally he said: "What you did, today, was amazing."

"What was that?"

"Running down the hill to save me—knowing she was armed. I mean—hell—you risked your life for me!"

"Did I?"

"Why?"

She paused, looked down at the rug. "I didn't think."

"And?" Fine felt a desperation, surfacing.

"I guess it was instinct—like a mother with her child?"

"Really?"

"Who knows? It seemed like the thing to do at the time. Come on—let's try to get some sleep."

"No, I've got to work—tomorrow's the last seminar, and I haven't prepared. Whether or not they kick me out depends on how I do. It's my last chance."

She stared at him in silence. The downturn of lip—always a screen for his projections—seemed to show her skepticism.

"Why? What difference does it make now, Fine?"

"All the difference in the world. One thing I've learned, through all this hell—I *love* being a psychiatrist."

"Oh? Didn't you always?"

"That was a sham; this is real. Now I know what therapy is: my patients feel me there with them, we go to work, grow—it's a miracle! It really does work!" He sighed. "I need the Institute's help, desperately. If they kick me out, I don't know what I'll do."

SAMUEL SHEM

"Why? You *are* a therapist—what do you need them for?"

"Technique."

"Technique? Oh, come on—just go ahead and *do* it—"

"Without basic technique, it doesn't work. Are good intentions enough? Is it enough to say: 'I am here as your therapist, I'm gonna help you change?' No. Never has been, never will. That's where Freud *began*. It's hard as hell to change—just look at us. You can't watch it on TV, you can't read it in a book or put it in your mouth, your arm, you can only change by living for a while *with* someone—not too close, not too far—in the wilderness between human beings." He was embarrassed—it sounded corny. "Anyway—Freud's not perfect, but he's the best so far on technique, especially on transference."

"The technique that squeezed the life out of you?"

"What a jerk I was! Thank God I got shoved out into the mainstream of life, got sucked under, started to open up. I *can* feel empathy, now; but that's only part of it. Nipak's awareness is right for him, but it's only a part of therapy. Strange—the more aware I am of the other person, the more confused I am about how to be a therapist. I've got to integrate things—empathy and thought, intuition and rules, attention and action, past and present, even right hemisphere and left—all I've learned out in the world that made my 'perfectly analyzed self' too limited, with real, taught, historically tested therapeutic techniques."

He had to stop for breath. She waited, and he felt her full attention. He sensed he was saying something else to her, something beyond the content of his words, something to do with yearning, with love. He plunged on.

"I've got so much to learn, and—faults and all—analysts are the best teachers in the world. Learning is like therapy, like living: it can't be done alone, in isolation, it's got to be done with others. I *did* learn, from Fumbles, probably as much as I could at the time. There *are* good people down there, people who care about others, who are trying their best to be with others as therapists, who have a lot more experience than I do. Give them credit—at least they *try* to understand human beings. They refuse to pretend, to be frauds; they know *self*-help can't work; they still believe in the therapeutic *relationship*." Fine felt tense, even angry, and through clenched teeth said: "I've got to do a good job. I've got to convince them to let me stay. I really really care about this,

Steph, it really matters to me. My whole fate as a therapist is on the line. It's a crucial moment in my life."

"Is this the old Fine, then, back again?"

He sensed her hostility. "Is it? You tell me."

"The guy who always put work before play—before people?"

"Look," he cried out, "it's the only thing I've got left!"

Their eyes met, held, but nothing came clear. She broke the glance, turned away. They went upstairs. Fine tucked them in, and went to his office.

Fine worked through the night. He was amazed, again, going back to Freud, to find the beauty of his writing, the depth of his concern, the unflagging integrity in his trying to do the most difficult human thing: become aware of human beings.

By dawn Fine had compressed the world literature into a fourteen-minute lump. It was solid, detailed, and instructive, like, he thought, an organ bottled in formalin, say, a heart. He would be able to stand up before them and read it without passion and with full confidence, and despite all that he had put them through he knew that they would see it as a peace offering and allow him to stay, so that he could, in this community of those dedicating themselves to relieving mental pain and suffering, integrate the conflicted parts of himself, and journey on, to learn his art.

Sometime during the night it had begun to drizzle, and Fine stepped out into a teal-blue dawn. He showered and shaved and got dressed to see Duffy. Shielding himself from the glass mouths of the TV minicams, he ran back to his office in Jefferson House.

Also having had to fight the cameras, Duffy was late. For her to be identified would rock the prime rate. She took it good-humoredly, however, and with a nod and a smile she lay on the couch, ready to work. Fine was relieved to find he still felt such sobriety with her, so connected to her. She began associating, and the session took on the same stark, *in-relief* feel as the last. No seductive hanky-panky, no sadistic withdrawal, just she and he getting on with it.

She too sensed the change. He asked her what had brought it about. She said: "I don't know—with all that's happened, well, it made me feel like a real *person* to you." She considered. "I mean with you I can feel like the person I am—the person I know myself to be. But listen to what happened—daddy wrote me, and—"

Yes: somehow with her, I've given her space to be the person she actually is. Is that all we do?: find the person in the room? Peel off the falseness in each of us that leads to soul-murder? Is relating nothing more nor less than bringing each other into reality?

She went on—repeating almost word for word the stuff she'd told him before—pop, mom, Uncle Savage, the Fed—rekindling her neurotic fires of desire and regret. Yet her repetition was new: stripped down, she was showing them both who she actually was. She was in touch with him, he with her. And she was soon riding the transference into a deeper ring of her pain. So: suffering allows us to be kind; sharing our suffering, sharing our tricks to bear it, we become real. I'm no longer afraid of her loving me or hating me, no.

His tic attacked. He was relieved she couldn't see it, but then he felt phony again. Why relieved? Why hide? Is that the crux of healing?: to be open or to hide? Is it as simple as that?

Using her feelings for Fine, she was trying to face those for her father. Her struggle stirred his compassion for his own father, and his compassion fed hers, and so they moved, back and forth, one to the other, spinning a mutual, felt web of discovery and acceptance. And yet Fine was troubled. He had located her, yes, but what about this transference? She'd shifted back subtly to her vamp-mode, relating to him seductively, even—as she'd done early on—arching her back to show him her breasts! Fine was confused: should he let it build until she herself realized the distortions she was creating, or should he interpret it to her, and have her go on from there? He'd already screwed it up once, laying a mother-interpretation on her that he now saw as motivated not even by his theory but by his discomfort with her sexiness. In conflict, he said nothing. The session ended. Facing her at the door, he felt *present* with her. Suddenly she reached out and caressed his cheek with her fingers, saying: "Know why Duffy Adams keeps doing things that are bad for her?"

"Why?" He was blushing.

"To grow. It's the only way." She stroked his cheek. "Oh Dr. Fine, you're so *fun!*" He felt a little sick. She laughed. "Just *listen* to me—why is it I still so *need* the attention of you men? Ciao!" She left. Fine put his hand to his cheek, feeling a burning there, sensing an ebb, a real loneliness. He'd failed, this session—he should have acted, interpreted. Lots of work still to do with her. And yet, if he got his act together a little better, she would do well. Everyone would do well and all would be well, but me.

After breakfast he, Steph, and John James drove off the island. They dropped the boy at his grandmother's and went to Mass. General to see Nipak. Steph went to the walk-in clinic to check up on something. Fine went to the neurologist's office, to get the results of his CAT scan.

"Negative," said Gersh the neurologist, "you do *not* have a brain tumor."

"Well then," Fine asked, "what caused my seizure?"

"Cause? Hm. Don't know. I read in *Cosmo* something about calcium's role in migraines. Verapamil, a calcium-channel blocker, seems to help. Theoretically, high calcium could cause contraction of blood vessels, bring on migraine. A grand mal seizure can be a migraine-equivalent—maybe your high calcium brought it on, hm?"

Fine realized he hardly felt relieved. He thought: that's how little I love life, now. He got up to leave. Gersh said: "Oh by the way, I read in *Psychology Today*—they studied people like you, with nightmares. You fall into two groups—one was schizophrenics."

"Terrific. And the other?"

"Creative types. Artists, weirdos like that. Nightmares are all biochemical. No wonder your analysis failed to cure them."

Fine went to Nipak's room and helped him pack. Nipak had gotten word that Fine and Dandi, Inc., was booming, the drug companies considering investing heavily, "wanting to make their bets like the hedge." Fine mentioned his proof that calcium's role in learning and memory could never be specific, and warned Nipak about the dangers of high calcium for those prone to migraines or epilepsy. Nipak said: "Ah yes, my fellow, but solely for the bones it is worthwhile—why, the sucking alone will make them happy, like a dog eating a nut." Steph returned, seeming tense. He told her the news, that he did not have a tumor, and even though she seemed relieved, he felt her reaction, like his, to be muted, as if her mind were on something else. Fine asked Nipak what his coma had been like. "Have you been in Arizona?" Fine had not. "Being in a coma is like being in Arizona. Now I am going home."

"Sri Lanka?" asked Fine.

"Brooklyn Heights. There I am living—in Vimila's 'solitude and communion' yes. Remember: life is easy if you stay on the beam. All that is required is to be honest and earnest."

"So then I'll see you Thursday," Steph said.

"*What?*" cried Fine. "You're going . . . ?" He stopped, too shocked to move the words out. She bit her lip, nodded; it was true, real: she was leaving him after all. He felt as if he'd been sucker-punched in the solar plexus. Nipak, trying to stand up, fell down.

"Oh! I am being through the Cuisinart! Put me in a taxi!"

Fine, shaken, sat in the back seat as Steph drove Nipak to the airport. Then they picked up John James, and before going back to Stow, they went food shopping in a huge supermarket in Neponset. Fine hated supermarkets—the glare of the fluorescent lights, the blare of the brand names, the voracious well-fed folk buying food—it made him cringe. Yet this time, waiting in line, as he stared at his fractious, battered co-shoppers, he saw their injuries as medals, merit badges, signs of achievement, of making it through, at least to the checkout line, today. He asked Steph:

"Are all these people as miserable as I am?"

"Are you kidding?" she said, shocked. "Look!"

An old woman was fishing in a change purse to pay for her bananas, King Oscar Sardines, and Shasta Diet Chocolate. One side of her face was gnawed away by skin cancer. Repulsed, Fine looked away, feeling a rush of shame. But then, swallowing his disgust, he forced himself to look again. Imagine what it's like for her! Ashamed, he had an urge to repent—go to her and plant a kiss there, on the raw, furrowed, weepy flesh. "I'm sorry," he said. "I really really am."

They got back to Stow as the mayor's press conference was ending. Because of the drizzle, it was being held in the Carter Pavilion. Pelvin on one side, the expert in malaise on the other, the mayor was ending his oration by calling for a new pilot study:

"*De*-de-de-institutionalization!" he said, as if he had a nervous stutter—understandable, for that morning the U.S. Attorney had subpoenaed his eighty-two-year-old mother to chat about the rumor of laundering money through his wife's birthday party. The press asked what this meant. "It's Mental Hygiene Month! Free the poor mentally ill!"

They left. The place was like a morgue. The oily Rosensdork appeared: "Come do New York—I got for you a commercial and a film—"

"I *am* coming to New York," Steph said, "but no TV or film."

"What?" Rosensdork was aghast. He eyed Fine disdainfully, as if Fine were responsible. "But people *kill* for commercials, for—"

"I don't do dead things." They went off to talk.

Georgina called, saying: "From what I've heard, you've got to be really extraordinary tonight, or else it's *hasta la vista,* Fine." They arranged to meet at seven. Fine hung up and went out on the porch. Wired with anxiety about the seminar, he stared dumbly out into the fog. It had always amazed him that the condemned would actually walk to the gallows. Now he understood.

A large, dark, hump-backed shape was coming up the driveway through the mist. Whale? Whaler? A cigarette glowed, dimmed. It was Detective O'Herlihey.

43

"SHE SAID SHE FELT relieved," said the detective, as they walked the path around the island, in the rain. O'Herlihey had spent the day with Sylvia in the hospital, and had come to go over the case with Fine. "Relieved that she'd been caught."

"So that's why she tantalized us—dropping the cat's eye marbles so I'd find them, showing up at The Comedy Box with the boy."

"Must be. Christ you'da thought we'd'a checked 'er out better, before we hired 'er for the Boston Mounted Police. Know why she was fired from the Central Park Zoo? Shot a Shetland pony—imagine?"

"It fits—but what did she say about the first two murders?"

"When she was laid off the police force in March, her whole world fell apart. She began to drink, do drugs—angel dust, coke—get all tanked up, dress in men's clothes—that wide-brimmed hat—"

"She hadn't a clue, about her gender."

"Right. So she tries to find a shrink. She wants a guy who knows about the kinky stuff, but who isn't kinky himself. So she snoops out this David Wholer and tails him, followin' his every move—to make sartain he ain't a pervert, so's he can help her, y'see? And what does she find?"

"He's bisexual."

"At least 'bi'—maybe 'tri'! She goes batty, calls him up, tells him she's a friend of one of his other patients—she'd tailed them, too—she's expert in all this detective stuff—and convinces him to meet 'er in 'is office on a Sunday."

"How? What would make a psychiatrist work on Sunday?"

"Cash. Tells 'im: 'money is no object.' She gives no name, so she's not in his book. She gets high on booze and dust, kills 'im, writes: 'the rapist.' Turns out she read it in a novel—it meant a lot to 'er 'cause she'd been raped by your double, that bungler Stuart Fine. She did the same with t'other one, this Timothy Myer—a *real* lulu, him!—she saw him one night in a low-cut sequined number in the Zone! Don't they have no quality control for you shrinks at all?"

Fine chuckled. "And why the twenty-eight days in between?"

"Me'n The Uncle hit it right on the head—she's got that new disease—PMS—premenstrual syndrome—plans to use it as defense. Jeez but the law's gotten fooked up, ain't it?"

"What about Reuben, Serena?"

"Right. So she sees in Myer's appointment book that he knows a shrink named Fine, out at Stow. No first name mentioned. How can she stay away? She sees you, is sure you're her long-lost love, Stuart—what a pork chop *he* turns out to be!—and—no ring on your finger—still not married! She gets her hopes up. It's love, man, love! An' you're her shrink, besides! She starts followin' you everywhere."

"To Southie and the Institute May first?" O'Herlihey nodded. "I *did* see a woman nearby, when I screamed at Reuben just before—Jesus!" Fine shuddered. "She killed him for me! Did she follow me to Columbia, to Kinderhook Crik?" Another nod. "Wait—she saw Steph and me together at Stow, Columbia—she must have seen I was married?"

"Said not. Neither of you wear a ring. You each have other lovers—one night you bring home that hefty one—Georgina—the next night someone else, meanwhile Steph's with Johnny, goin' off to gay Paree. You or me would have known it, but her? She didn't see it."

"Denial." O'Herlihey looked puzzled. "She didn't *want* to see it. A psychotic defense."

"Oh, aye." They were at the far end of the island, Long Island Light. Mist rose off the ocean, and the foghorn in the channel off Gallup's Island cried out, one mournful bleat after another. "And then it all gets pretty nasty. The three of ya livin' at Stow upsets 'er, as does your increasin'—how shall we put it, tastefully?— fookin'. This Sunny is one t'ing, but fer a woman raised in the deep South, Serena is anuther entirely, so she knocks 'er off, as a warnin'. It's then, she told me, she started wantin' to get caught. She knew somethin' bad was aboot to happen." The detective stopped, choking back tears. "Poor, dear Johnny O'Day. If only I'd'a been sma'ter!"

"*I* was the one who should've known." They walked on in silence, the detective's huge shoes squishing in the mud. "So she found out I was married to Steph, that Steph, John, the boy, and I were 'living in sin,' and she decided to hurt me. Why didn't she just kill me when she had me cornered, that night on the wharf at 'Old Ironsides'?"

" 'Old Ironsides'? What do you mean?" Fine described it in detail. "I don't recall," said O'Herlihey, "lemme see." He took out a small spiral notepad, his fat fingers riffled to the night in question. He peered at his scribbles. "Now that's foony, in't?"

"What?" asked Fine, feeling a chill.

"She said she took the boy straight to her apartment in Charlestown, and never went out again that night." He looked up.

"But then—" Fine was shocked. The figure coming at him on the dock had not been her. Had there been a figure at all? An apparition? *Was my awakening so close to my going crazy?* "Oh," he said, "I must've dreamed it. Anyway, I guess the rest is clear."

"But for the crucial part—the motive."

"She's insane—isn't that motive enough?"

"Is she? Pretty well put-together, to get along in the world for thirty-four years like she did, let alone pull off murders so neat. If she didn't *want* to get caught, she'd not've—she'd be long gone, roamin' the land unsuspected, mixin' it up with all the other serial killers and mass murtherers out there." He sighed. "So tell us— why'd she do it?"

"Why?" The word echoed in his mind, and, like a word repeated out loud, began to lose meaning. "There is one thing I'm sure of, unique to her: in all the time I was with her, I never felt I was *with* someone, I never found the person in the room. Anyone else I've been with, I made some connection, even through hatred, or contempt. With her I made none—she has no capacity to relate. Now I know what a profound defect that is. Therapy couldn't work—there was no transference." He thought of his Jefferson Housers. "Even psychotics form relationships. She's the sickest of the sick, 'cause she could mask her defect, live in the world, do the most harm."

"And so why was there this defect in 'er?"

Fine tried to be precise. "Was she born defective?—something biochemically wrong in her brain? A deficit of estrogen, a surplus of testosterone? I'd guess yes, but no more than many others. And if born defective, could nurturance have overcome the defect? Yes —it has with others, more severely crippled. But maybe she was born more or less normal—could her defect have come from her childhood? Her mother died before she felt loved by her, leaving her in the care of a butcher of a father, so that cruelty—to animals and humans—became her norm. But her early years were no worse than those of many others, and far worse childhoods have failed to cripple others. Freud was wrong—there are chances all along the way, for development. At a critical juncture, puberty-adolescence, she got crushed—raped by Stuart Fine—maybe repeating a rape by her father—and as she went on in life, it seemed as if at every chance things kept going wrong—she lost an eye, a baby—and none of her therapists helped. A key event was at the time of her first treatment: when her therapist offered relationship, instead she clung to her pain. She never let go and took the chance, *with* someone, of opening up again to love. She dug in her claws, clutched her sick part tight, sealed it over with rage, and let her bitterness eat away her humanity. She withdrew, only to find that isolation made her feel even more dead. She sought cruelty, ugliness—zoos, the worst police cases—creating a world as ugly and cruel as she felt herself to be but couldn't accept. She learned a trade: murder. It was the only thing she was good at."

"But why? Why would she live like that?"

"Why?" Fine thought of Freud, but classic theory—penis envy, faulty internalization of castration anxiety into conscience, etc.— seemed gross, wrong, like medical theories of bloodletting to cure anemia. Repeating her childhood trauma was less to serve a death

instinct than to bring herself to life—aha!—yes!—I too have felt
it: voyeurism. "She killed to *possess* the victim; like her fetish—
horses—she killed to *control,* feel alive. Killing was a 'turn-on.' "

"Aye, I've heard that before. But you know what's the scariest
part? To all who knew her she seemed normal, normal as you or
I."

"Tell me about it—*I* labeled her 'neurotic'! It's frightening—
she's the epitome of our age: style, not substance; image, not essence; outer, not inner; she *looks* great, but all the 'human' has
been leached out. She's self-sufficient; with no relation to others,
others become 'self.' To kill others is to kill herself."

"Why would she want to kill herself?"

"Hate."

"So why didn't she?"

"Fame? Not wanting to miss herself on TV? It's a new sickness
—the video-self—our old logic won't work. Watching TV, we feel
distant and close, *both.* Our leaders will blow us up before we
understand. Without relationship, there's no self; without self, no
conscience; without conscience, no morality; without morality,
nukes, Nagasaki, the nuclear mind, the nuclear age. Even *she*
knew it—sensed herself and others as objects, slick and glassy like
her false eye. She felt trapped—the only way out was to kill herself, or someone else, or go mad. She felt 'live' only when she got
high, stalked, killed, scrawled her logo—'just like on TV.' I bet
even now—"

"Fella named Rosensdork—signed her up this afternoon."

"Incredible! Is there no morality, no limit to vulgarity? Can
they justify *anything?*" He found his arms were raised up to the
sky, as if an answer were forthcoming. He lowered them. "Vidi-
ots!"

"So it was fate, makin' 'er kill? Or was it her own choice?"

"Is there a difference?" he asked, and as if in answer cried out,
"God I hate her!" He tried to calm himself, matching his steps to
the moans of the foghorn. O'Herlihey said she planned to plead
insanity. Great, Fine thought, when the morality of law meets the
determinism of psychiatry, you get farce.

"Rehabilitation?" asked O'Herlihey.

"Her? Forget it. This sickness has no cure—if she can't relate,
there's not a drug or a therapist or a therapy that can touch her—
it's worse than cancer, and it's the sickness of our age. If I *ever*

come across a monster like this again, I call you, fast!" He flushed with rage, craving revenge, thinking it's time we codify what we value—empathy. "Besides, the risk to society is too great. Our errors should be the cost of our safety. This—this—*thing* Green is beyond any treatment. Sure, hate breeds hate; and yes, I do wish I could forgive her—but no." His jaw clenched. "I swear to God I'll do my best to keep her locked up for the rest of her life!"

"I'm glad to hear a professional man say that." He lit a new cigarette from the old. "I myself've been feelin' that yer scales of justice 'ave got to be tipped back, now, toward the victims, the ones who are feelin' the pain." He cleared his throat. "And to the dead."

They walked in silence alongside the sea. There was no wind, and the new growth lay still, luxuriant under the day-long cover of dew. At Fine's house they said good-bye. They'd soldiered through together. Their blindnesses had lost them someone they loved.

"I'd like to t'ink we learned somethin' from this, aboot the whys and wherefores—why she became a killer, why others don't?"

"I wish." More strongly than ever, Fine sensed the overwhelming silliness of the human intellect, which seemed destined to invent concepts like "causation" so as to fail to understand them. "No matter how much we explain, it'll still be a mystery. 'Why' questions are like the monsters kids see in their bedrooms at night —the snake, the lion or tiger or alligator, or the vampire bat that flies off when the light clicks on—monsters invented to bring comfort, to bring those dear people rushing in to tell us that no, that wasn't a snake, only your bathrobe, and that there are no alligators at this latitude, and that lions and tigers roam wild only in Africa. We argue: 'But I saw them, in the zoo! But Africa is pretty close!' And then these kind, loving people tell us all about the strength of the bars in the zoos and the width of the oceans between Africa and us. And our calling has less to do with our fear of our monsters than with our wish to have our loved ones with us. To ask 'why' is a comfort, but a false comfort—unless it turns up something *useful,* like how to find killers *before* they act. The better question is 'what?' "

"Well, we'll keep on asking the questions, nevertheless. I mean what choice do we have, man, after all? God bless?"

Fine watched him vanish in the fog. Why does one become a killer, and another does not? Is it possible to know such things? Look at Duffy—her story's almost as bad, yet she's setting monetary policy for the world. Why? Biology?—was Duffy born with more of the relational stuff—empathy? Psychology?—when Duffy called out at night, someone—mom, dad, her edition of Steph's Aunt Belle—someone must have come to her, and when they came they must have sided *with* her, against the demons of her dark. At least enough so she let go of her pain and kept on risking, having faith in human connection, asking for help so that her bitterness failed to solidify. She never felt trapped; there was always a human way out. In all those WASP enclaves—Palm Beach, the myriad perfect islands, the Adirondacks—her extended "fun" family must have given her some sense of being loved. And being loved, she loved. Is it all as simple as that?

Feeling more and more gloomy, lonely, and fatalistic, Fine found himself alone, high up on the grassy hill overlooking the bay.

The drizzle had lightened, and the mist was rising. The sea and sky were gun-metal gray. The wind whipped in from the Atlantic, the scent of ocean thick, briny. Fine felt he was going under for the last time.

And then he noticed a grasshopper.

It perched on a blade of grass, staring. Could it be? He looked closely, and saw a second, perched, staring, and then a third, a fourth, more—and sure enough, soon they were all around him, standing so lightly on the stalks of grass that the drops of rain clung to the bottoms of the blades, undisturbed. They've come back! He felt a surge of remorse. Fearing that they'd jump at the sound, he whispered: "I'm sorry." They didn't move. "I'm sorry for all the others of you I've killed, for my 'research.' Forgive me." The wet breeze rippled the grass. A large male chirped. Another joined him. Fine watched the exquisitely fashioned, delicately beautiful little creatures of prehistory as they, one by one, hopped down, vanished. Perhaps with calcium I've helped them a little, evolutionarily. After all, freed full-grown so early in the cycle of their one summer, chitin and synapses rich in calcium, schooled in altruism, they had to have a head start. The age of solipsism is over. He sat awhile longer, until, chilled, he got up to see Maurice. The grasshoppers' returning seemed a profound sign, a message to him about what had happened and what had to change for him to go on.

Maurice picked up on Fine's new sense of letting go of self. Proud of Fine's heroics, he told him how much easier it was to come to therapy now that he felt Fine really was his friend. For the first time as he talked about his novel, he keyed more on the writing than the writer. The photo with Liz Taylor was less vital than *l'oeuvre de* Maurice Slotnick. He spread his hands as if reading from *Variety:* "NIX ON LIZPIX, SLOTNICK AVERS!"

Fine laughed. The furry little author lay on the couch. Fine thought: What haven't we been through together?

"What haven't we been through together, eh Fine?" said Maurice. "Starting with that bitch Joann; y'know, I think you were right—she was a butcher—a frigid, castrating cunt—but even if she'd been Liz Taylor I'd have found a way to see my mother in her. So, I did it to myself. Our wives turn out to be whores, our mothers get their breasts eaten away by cancer, and so where does that leave us?"

"Where?"

"In the shit with everybody else. Same shit, different shit—it's all shit, isn't it?" Maurice went on to say that he'd been scared stiff by what they'd gone through together the past month, but had come out feeling that Fine cared about him despite who he was; even *for* who he was. The turning point was that they'd been able to laugh. "I feel like a burden's been lifted! And I feel different about writing—it's not number one anymore! Hemingway said it: 'Writing's a part-time jòb.' And I got clear about *what* I'll write now, too: I'm not going to write the Hollywood-TV-Broadway crap of Neil Simon, and I'm not gonna write the oblique 'watch-your-adjectives' stuff of 'lit.' There are only two ways to write: from your heart, or not; I'm for the heart. It's simple: just trying to write things as they *are*. Try, and fail—always fail, fail every day—but in the failing is the art. I got a new slogan— ready?" Shyly, he said: " 'Joy in the process, faith in the work.' What do you think?"

Fine sensed how much he'd grown to love this guy who—like all his other patients—had become not a drain of his energy, but a source. "Maurice," he said, hoarsely, "I think that's just great."

"Oh . . . oh boy." He fell silent. Fine could feel how touched he was that he'd been taken seriously. "What you just did—making me feel that I *do* have something inside, worthwhile to say—no one ever did that to me before." They sat awhile, without words. Fine sensed all the different Slotnick layers all at once: the adult hunger for fame the same as the voracious infant's snapping at mother's breast; mother's mother, low-slung in Poland, meeting the dancer with the tiny feet and, gun to her head, forced to marry him in New York, he dancing no more but rather bashing metal plates together underground. A life. I sense it, now, past and future, as those who live out their lives in small towns do. Our mothers were the first generation of women betrayed by the American Dream, their frustration breaking through as the art of their children. I feel his hurt, he mine; we mother each other and heal. Maurice asked: "Do all great writers love their mothers? Listen, Fine—I'm making you a promise: I won't write anything, anymore, unless it's *fun.*" He fell silent. "Hey—why *not* write autobiography? I mean all fiction is autobiography, right?"

"And all autobiography is fiction," said Fine.

"I've got it!" said Maurice. "How 'bout *Maurice Slotnick: An American Story?*" They laughed. The writer looked at his watch. "God that went fast! Gotta go!" At the door, eye to eye with Fine, he said: "Oh, I forgot—I'm terminating—saying good-bye."

Fine was shocked. He glanced down to hide his panic. Leave me? I'm not ready! My patients are better and I'm a wreck? It's not fair. Trying to be open he looked up; his face snapped shut—*tic!*

"What's that?" asked Maurice.

"A tic," said Fine.

"Oh. As if you don't have enough trouble already, eh?"

"Is this *it?*" Fine asked, *tic*-ing again. "Is this good-bye?"

"Don't throw a shit-fit—I'll still keep in touch."

Fine was confused—never having been an analyst for a termination, he didn't know whether or not this was premature. Was there more to be done? Had they worked through the issues of saying good-bye? Before he could speak, Maurice had shaken his hand warmly, and left. Fine stared at the empty waiting room. After all this, I hardly know even the basics of analysis. Boy, do I need help.

Downstairs Fine ran into Mrs. Neiderman. "Oh Dr. Fine, you know what's so wonderful about you? You're the same person."

Fine asked what she meant. "In or out of therapy, you're always the same."

"How do you know that?" Fine asked, startled and pleased, realizing now that yes, I'd like to be who I am, wherever.

"I just do."

"But that's a problem with psychiatry—no one knows what happens behind the closed door—no one knows who's any good."

"*I* do. And oh—they still haven't reached the boy's mother in Dublin. She's on vacation somewhere in Egypt, imagine that?"

The three sat at dinner. Fine reached out his hands to Steph and John James, for grace. They closed the small circle, bent their heads. All day long Fine had felt half-crazy with tension about the evening's seminar, and to calm himself he'd been reciting the "Serenity Prayer" from Narcotics Anonymous. He said it again now:

"God give me the serenity to accept the things
I cannot change, the courage to change the things I can,
and the wisdom to know the difference."

The meal was filled with false cheer, long silences. They finished, and Steph got up to clear the table.

"Unky Fine?" John James asked, almost in a whisper.

"Yes?"

"Can we go to see where my da's buried?"

They left at once.

At the cemetery the drizzle picked up, shrouding them in shimmering mist. The dirt path up the hill was slippery, and Fine and Steph, one hand in each of John James's, used their umbrellas for balance. They moved onto wet grass, trudging on up under the leaden darkening sky, shoes soaking through. They found it. A long high mound of wet earth. There were soggy flowers—roses, daisies, lilies. Fine and Steph stopped. The little boy shook free of their hands, and stared. They let him go up to the grave. He didn't walk respectfully, or mournfully, but rather, Fine thought, as if going to a half-wished-for, half-feared meeting with an adult —say a dentist. To see someone not of a kid's world. They watched from the back. He stood there in his dark jacket and new Nikes and then knelt down, praying. They saw his little shoulders shake and knew he was crying. Steph started to go toward him, but Fine held her back. He didn't cry for long. He reached one hand down and took a handful of wet earth. He stared at it for what seemed a long time. The rain came down heavy. Fine shuddered, and took Steph's hand. She was weeping. He put his arm around her shoulder, their umbrellas clashing against each other awkwardly, runnulets of water dripping onto their faces. The water felt cool against his tears. They stared. They heard him saying something. He was singing:

> "Home is the rover,
> His journey's over,
> Yield up the nighttime to old John O'Dreams."

The boy stopped singing and turned around to them, a plea in his eyes. They went to him. They knelt down with him and joined him:

> "Now as you sleep, the dreams are winging clear.
> The hawks of morning cannot harm you here;
> Sleep is a river,
> Runs on forever,
> And for your boatman choose old John O'Dreams,
> And for your boatman choose old John O'Dreams."

They wept and held each other and rose and turned and walked away. Still in the boy's hand was the mud from the grave.

When they got back to the car Fine remembered he'd forgotten to meet Georgina. It was almost eight. If he grabbed a cab, he'd just barely make the seminar. His clothes were soiled, wet. And then he remembered, and a sick feeling came over him. "Oh my God!"

"What's wrong?"

"I left my notes out at Stow! I'm screwed!"

"What do you need your notes for?"

"I'm so tired, nervous—I won't remember a thing. Shit! That's the last straw! All these years—college, med school, psychiatry, the Institute—all of it, right down the drain. Like I wanted to destroy myself!" He sat down on the curb, face in his hands. He felt like crying again, this time for himself. "I give up."

"You can't," she said.

"Who says?"

"Me." She hesitated. "And John."

"What are you talking about?"

" 'He died to bring us alive.' "

The rain came down harder. The drops tapped the car roof, crackling like sparks. Fine shivered. "Yes. Right. But I can't. I'm telling you, I'll just get up there and go blank. I don't remember any of the papers I read last night, on 'Good-bye.' "

"If there's one thing you know about, now, it's 'Good-bye.' You *are* a therapist, you *can* help people, I know it. Go for it."

Fine was puzzled. "You sure have changed. What happened?"

"Last night, I heard you, believed you—and believe *in* you. You won't go blank, if you speak your heart—like you did with me."

"With *them?* Suppose I can't? What the hell do I do then?"

She smiled. "Easy." She giggled. "No problem."

"Yeah, what?"

"Finesse it."

She winked, put him in a taxi, and drove off with John James.

Fine sped off toward the Institute. Why is everything going wrong? I feel like I've been spending my whole life mourning—secretly mourning—as if I've never truly known who died.

44

EVERY YEAR, THE premiere terminal event at the Boston Institute was the final Vergessen seminar: "Termination—Saying Good-bye."

Fine got out on Commonwealth Avenue, under clearing skies, thinking: How much has happened since the first seminar, "The Breast—Saying Hello." Dogwood supplanted magnolia now, and now shrub honeysuckle. The steps of TBI were awash with pale-white-and-purple petals. Georgina was standing at the door, wearing a robin's egg–blue silk blouse. She saw Fine and bobbled down the steps into his arms, saying, breathlessly: "Thank God! I was so worried! Where've you been? They're about to start." She stared at him. "Christ—look at you—you're a sight!"

"Let's go."

"Yeah, but listen—*Metz!*"

"Metz?"

"Frau Metz—here—tonight—awesome!" Fine felt fear wad up in his gut. Georgina said the password—"Jill Flewett." They entered.

The seminar was being held in the large, grand, walnut-paneled Bullitt Room on the ground floor. Fine, feeling embarrassed about his appearance—he wasn't even wearing jacket or tie!—sneaked in

and slithered along the wall to the back, sitting between the floor-
to-ceiling windows. He was startled at the size of the crowd, at the
intense feeling of expectation in the room. He'd blocked out what
a large family the Institute was. Everyone was there. In the back,
the raw analytic recruits, eyes filled with that shell-shocked look
that Fine knew reflected their first encounter with the training
analysts whose harsh silence suggested the trainees' deep, un-
fathomed psychopathology. In the middle, the older eclectic analysts who'd been excluded from power by their drift from Freud,
including a meek brilliant Sullivanian and the soulful Reichian
with whom Georgina was doing body work. Nearer the front sat
the training analysts, in silence—from gargantuan Crusher Gold
and the hysterical expert in hysteria—and Fumbles!—to Vergessen and—yes—Frau Metz! She was old, tiny—even dwarfish—in
Viennese haute couture—with delicately wrinkled skin and cat-
aract-clouded eyes. She sat, hands folded and head tilted, listening. Fine felt scared but relieved that she had come. He sensed
around her an aura of kindness. From the others he felt contempt.
Aside from a nod from Fumbles, no one said hello.

Vergessen arose, asked "How do people change?" and sat
down.

Dr. Pete Gross, his usual stony voice wavering, began:

> "*Die Endliche und die Unendliche Analyse,* 1937: Experi-
> ence has taught us that psychoanalytic therapy—the free-
> ing of someone from his neurotic symptoms, inhibitions,
> and abnormalities of character—is a time-consuming busi-
> ness. Hence from the very first, attempts have been made to
> shorten the duration of analyses. . . ."

Noting Gross's nervousness, Fine realized: yes, this is it, the
tribunal. Metz would be the final judge of whether I would be
allowed to go on with my analytic training. Do I want to? Yes—
intensely! I can't do it alone, I need to be part of this group. Why
had I forgotten my notes? Was it intentional? Am I that unaware
of my unconscious? What will I say? He glanced at Leon.
Wreathed in cigar smoke, his rival was sitting before *his* fourteen-
minute lump of notes, the picture of calm. Fine knew he was in
for it tonight.

Gross dared comment: "In the famous passage that follows,

Freud again returned to his cherished 'dog metaphor'—both as a reaction formation to his own castration anxiety, and as one of the earliest documented postmortems of the concentration camps: 'We should receive admonitions from all sides against the presumption of vying with fate in subjecting poor human creatures to such cruel experiments.' Who has not heard of the 'dogs of war'? Freud was then eighty-one and had had a long-standing love affair with chow dogs. In a 1934 letter to Marie Bonaparte Princess George of Greece he wrote: 'Often when stroking Jofi I have caught myself humming a melody that, unmusical as I am, I can't help recognizing as the aria from *Don Giovanni*: a bond of friendship unites us both.' " Gross went on:

> "If an instinctual conflict is not a currently active one, is not manifesting itself, we cannot influence it even by analysis. The warning that we should let sleeping dogs lie, which we have so often heard in connection with our efforts to explore the psychical underworld, is peculiarly inapposite when applied to the conditions of mental life. For if the instincts are causing disturbances, it is a proof that the dogs are not sleeping; and if they seem really to be sleeping, it is not in our power to awaken them. . . ."

Yes, Fine thought, therapy happens only in the here and now. Next, Leon got up and made a brilliant critique, keying on the quotation:

> "Among the factors that influence the prospects of analytic treatment and add to its difficulties in the same manner as the resistance must be reckoned not only the nature of the patient's ego but the individuality of the analyst."

Leon had chosen to discuss passages dealing with the suitability of analysts for the work. Shock spread through the room—he was on a full-frontal attack of Fine:

> "Analysts in their own personalities have not invariably come up to the standard of psychical normality to which they wish to educate their patients. Analysts are people who have learned to practice a particular art; alongside of

this they may be allowed to be human beings like anyone
else. . . . It is therefore reasonable to expect of an analyst,
as a part of his qualifications, a considerable degree of
mental normality and correctness. In addition, he must
possess some kind of superiority, so that in certain analytic
situations he can act as a model for his patient and in others
as a teacher. And finally we must not forget that the analytic relationship is based on a love of truth—that is, on a
recognition of reality—and that it precludes any kind of
sham or deceit. . . ."

Leon swept on, but the passage sent Fine's mind spinning: art,
yes—being a therapist is an art. Images swam by like schools of
fish, streams mixing, darting in, flashing light, darting out. He
glimpsed the real Freud, the magician beyond the words, the
healer. He stared at the back of Fumbles's head, helmet-shaped.
What the hell—this thing's bigger than me. Whatever I say, so I'll
say.

Yet Leon's finale stunned Fine: Leon held up the morning's
Herald. On the front page was a closeup photo of Fine, the screen
door crosshatching his face: SHRINK HERO NOT BEING PHONY
ANYMORE!

Fine sensed the shock wave pass through the audience—gasps,
murmurs. Leon quieted them: "Freud wrote that we analysts
must meet criteria of 'normality, correctness, superiority.' God
forbid that anyone think this is easy. We each have our problems,
God knows!" He said it kindly, with care. "But there are limits.
And beyond those limits—" he paused, staring at V., then at
Metz—"the countertransference is so pathological . . . it places
the patient *at risk."*

Leon sat. The virulence of the attack made Fine feel like slink-
ing out the door. Georgina prodded him, and somehow he got to
his feet and walked up the aisle through the whispering crowd. At
each step his soaked shoes squished loudly. His legs felt watery—
the same light feeling as when he'd broken his leg, thirty years
ago! Who'll lift me, carry me home now? He found himself, shaking, before them.

What a sight he was! Rumpled white shirt open at the neck,
mud-stained wet trousers, sporting a violaceous shiner, cuts, and

bruises, he was like the crazy cousin who, uninvited, shows up to wreck the wedding. And, to top it all off, he had a tic!

He was so scared, he *tic*-ed a quick quadruple. For an analyst-in-training to have a psychosomatic symptom in front of a room-ful of analysts was the ultimate in failure. And yet, somehow, the bathos of it helped him. What could he do? There was no hiding the truth. So he said: "You may have noticed—I have a slight tic?"

Dead silence. But then Vergessen chuckled, and Fumbles, and a few others too. "I guess this is what it's all about: whether we hide, or open up. We can try to hide behind the couch, but it's not that simple: even face to face we can hide, and even hidden from sight we can open up and connect." He sensed their contempt, and remembered his own. "I'm sorry if I've hurt any of you. It's been a helluva month. Forgive me."

No reaction. His heart beat hard in his throat; scared, he went blank. Stage fright? Oh no! To orient himself he repeated:

"How do we change? Not by thought, or theory. I've let go of *The Fine Theory,* let my grasshoppers go, too. All I can do here tonight is report back from where I've been, am. We *do* change—but *how* we change is a mystery."

The group rustled with discomfort.

"Analysis seeks to understand the self. This nourishes separate-ness, isolation. Why is separation—self-sufficiency—good? Why is dependence bad? How hard it is to recover from an analysis, to get back to relating. Isolation's a killer, and breeds killing. We must attend to 'self-in-relation.' We change in therapy as we *mu-tually* change. Becoming aware—the movement of relationship—*is* change." Fine paused, sensing how clumsy and thick his words sounded. Yet he went on, telling them about his seizure's opening up the female in him, about the altruism of social insects where self *is* other, and about Nipak's showing him, in the surfeit of the West, the starvation of spirit. Failing to connect, he strained: "We change by living. We change in analysis by living it. Yes, let's use what we've learned over the years—the minimal rules framing the experience in trustable time, place, person. But rigidity is death; we must flex. Why lie down *always?* Why not face each other—even touch each other—"

"What?" said Leon. "Freud would never have allowed that!"

"Freud made every mistake in the book—we all know it, why

pretend we don't?—he took his patients on vacation, terminated abruptly, met with families, misdiagnosed, analyzed little Hans by mail and analyzed Mahler in an afternoon! Freud was hardly a classic Freudian. Yet, with him, people changed. Why?"

"The power of the technique," said Gross, "the method."

"The person," said Fine. "Freud had it."

"Had what?" asked Georgina.

"Pzazz, *chutzpah,* soul—whatever. Freud healed despite his theory. He could've cured patients standing them on their heads, or in the back of a speeding truck! So much of Freud dogma is all wet: The psychosocial stages? Maybe. Dreams? Not wish fulfillments at all. Women? Not a clue! The cathartic de-repression of the past? Rarely important, if at all—and we all know it!"

"You are suggesting," said Leon, "that we ignore the past?"

"No! Use it, use everything! But the past is an effigy, and no one's ever healed in effigy. To be faced with suffering in the here-and-now and deflect it into the past is a cop-out."

"Dr. Fine is saying it's not theory, but personality, that heals? History's full of these charismatic men, leading trusting souls astray—Hitler, for one. And, even in modern America . . ."

Fine listened, seeing Leon more clearly: poor guy, locked up in that awkward, acne-scarred body, trying so hard to be good, to do right. Looking around, he saw the same sad craving in the others —these dear deadened souls, making such effort to get back to pop, to mom, to life itself. He felt their sorrow link to his own. And as he began replying, Fine had a strange sense it wasn't he himself talking, but rather some higher power—some prosperous, cheery sage to whom he'd been sent out on assignment—now whispering in his ear:

"Do I like who I am? No. Do you, Leon? Can we help it? Would we trade? Imagine, here, now, being *me?* We each keep doing the worst things for ourselves—marrying the wrong woman, taking the wrong job, wearing the wrong pants, eating the bad herring. Why? Why do we suffer? Freud says we're driven by death instinct—we suffer to die, we repeat painful experience to destroy ourselves. But Freud's life says the opposite: he suffered —did he ever!—ostracism, ridicule, exile—what must it have been like, the long years of jaw cancer, the plate in the roof of his mouth? Imagine his pain! Yet his suffering brought him to life. Suffering, that man lived!"

The room fell still. Fine sensed he'd hit home.

"We suffer not to die, but to live. We have no choice: if we go out into the world opened up, open-eyed, and suffer, we can't help but grow; and if we go out into the world closed off, blind to suffering, *we will suffer,* and grow. Amazing—as if it were meant to be!"

"I take your point," said Leon, voice quavering, clearly moved by Fine's feeling for him, "but many suffer and don't change at all."

"Yes. Suffering alone is not enough. Suffering *with*—shared suffering—brings change. That's where we come in. How do we help? By attending and responding, we become caring. We let them lead us, like children lead their mothers. Back and forth—attend, respond, attend, respond. Our caring, turned on the spindle of transference, brings change. All healing is the same: we feel, in each other, what we feel in ourselves. Not from Freud's 'superior' position, but from a mutual one, from finding in our own hearts the heart of the other. And somehow in this finding, something leaks out, fills the air—aura or vibes or electricity or empathy or spirit—call it what you will, everyone who's felt it knows when it's there and sometimes it happens by mistake or in chance encounters outside the office and women feel it more easily—and we know we can love without being laughed at or having it batted away and be loved and we open up and heal. We find the wisdom born not of neutrality, but of love. We sense our salvation in others. We want to really get to know our patients. We become the people we know ourselves to be. It's religious: love one another." Gross glanced at his watch. Fine plunged on:

"If we're afraid of their love we're lost. If we hide—behind rules, couches, thoughts, past, drugs—we're lost. If our hearts are cold they'll feel the chill. If we sit in rooms leaching out our lives with theory—lost! If Thanatos breeds the fatalism and cruelty we show each other in institutes—forget it! Good analysts are like any good people: throughout history, across culture, healers have worked intuitively—people are always meeting people who change their lives. We analysts are lucky—we *do* have a tradition, experience, technical skills—we've got to keep integrating our rules with our passions, our knowledge with our power, our curiosity with our awe."

Fine saw Fumbles nodding and smiling like a proud father.

"Not everyone can do this. Enrollment here is less guarantee than liability. Institutes kill off so much! We learn to hide our vulnerabilities. Why? Aren't we too the walking wounded? Isn't being open—showing our hurt while still showing up—isn't that life? Our *job* is to be vulnerable! How to learn? Risk, fail—live! Live life to the hilt! A world's out there—a whole wide world! It teems with life! You need to be in it, 'cause at least once in every analysis the time comes to use our *live* selves to touch the other. It's not conscious, we can't plan it, it always happens in every healing relationship, we'll know it's there because it'll feel *right*, sometimes it's in words and sometimes beyond—and it has to happen for real change. It can be a failure of mutual empathy, or a chance 'mistake'—but it's the spur for growth, the cusp of contact—we let go and take the leap together. If we don't, healing may seem to occur, but it'll be sham healing, a shadow. 'Relating' is bringing each other into reality. The magic is that we, with them, become aware of what actually is. We say: well, it's not that we're this or we're that, but just—same as all the other poor souls on the face of the earth—we are. And when that happens it's miraculous!"

Sensing the "vibes," Fine looked around. The room was hushed, attentive. "Is it happening now? I hope so. I really don't know what I'm doing—I'm just beginning to learn. I'm asking for your help."

He imagined they were with him, and went on:

"That's all, that's it. How do we change? We change when we stop funneling the world down into self, step aside and clear the way for the birth of the human spirit, passing through the heart out into the light, as love. We take our contempt and fear, our memory and desire, our pain and rage, open it up and spin it to compassion. Over and over we give birth. We give the greatest gift one gives another—a gift beyond life, beyond death—we give—"

Fine stopped, startled at the word that came, one he'd never recalled having said out loud before. He felt sober, and ended:

"—we give *solace.*"

He sat down. As usual, they went around the room, one comment per person. Fine sat silently, attending, appreciating their effort. He sensed in V. and Metz the same care and attention he'd felt from Nipak, Katey, Steph. Is their analytic silence an aware silence? Are all healers the same? Is the essence of humans this resiliency, this prevailing of spirit? The Nazis did lose. Will they always? Are these two analysts "great" despite analysis? New bumper sticker: SAVE ANALYSIS FROM THE ANALYSTS. Do their patients, safe behind doors, feel this generosity of spirit? Looking around, he sensed a dedication—so rare in an age of drugs and quick cures—to do the deeply human: to care. We're trying to do the hardest thing: to use our art to heal. Good for us. Accepted, I accept.

All were awaiting Vergessen's words. Under their stares, he seemed to open, uncurling like a pale fat flower. His eyes got dewy. And then, first sniffing, then snorting, he began to cry!

A shock flowed through the room. V. took out a sapphire hankie, blew his nose thunderously—"Ka-bahlooomero-ONCKK!" Sniffling, he said: "Yes, yes. We all suffer, and suffer alike, all all alike. Freud would agree. Dr. Fine—don't throw the baby out with the bathwater. You know more than you know of analytic technique. For instance, the 'analysis of the resistance'— hard, close-to-the-bone work that now, for you, has become intuitive. And gift. Gift from God, yes. Useful to apprentice. We do learn, heal. Learn to live with. An amazing fact of life: *when human beings get together, it can help!* Remarkable—as if meant to be." He snuffled. "Freud recommends undergoing a fresh analysis every five years. I think it better to take one year off every two and a half. I won't be back next season." Sensing their shock, the gentle albino said: "I'll be trekking around the world with my family. Good luck." He sneezed. As sheepishly as a boy caught acting like a girl, he blushed scarlet, and smiled.

All turned to Metz. Fine attended to her shrouded eyes, gnarled hands, stiff posture—and pictured her calcified, within and without. She gurgled something in German, like: *"Wo ist zu bist schnell?"* She seemed to be seeking Fine. He sat next to her. She put her hands on his face. Her touch was light, snackly like lightning. She stroked him—noting seizure scar and plump lower lip. Fine sensed that she was making the final decision on his future as an analyst. Odds are they'll kick me the oddball out. Always in the past they had. Unless V. and Metz too had been odd? Metz stopped stroking, sought his hand, found it, squeezed —hers felt to him like a warm bag of delicate, free-floating bones. His heart boomed. She said:

"Fine *ist* Fine."

The analytic year ended. All left. No one said good-bye.

Their good-bye, at Steph's insistence, had to take place at their Crik. Feeling morose, Fine agreed. Separation? He tried to deny the reality, but denial brought attention, and he sensed his spirit dying. Yes, he thought gloomily, this is death.

The three of them drove over from Boston the next afternoon, May thirty-first. Steph would be leaving for New York the next day. She would try, wholeheartedly, to become a comic. Fine would be staying at Stow. The day was clear, hot, suffused with the glossy luminescence of summer. Fine felt the daylight mocking him. He said:

"Summer's here."

"Ah, yes," said Steph, "what is so rare as a steak in June?"

At dusk they were at Kinderhook Crik.

Fine stood alone on the edge of the pool between the stone ramparts of the imagined bridge. He looked up the grotto toward the sun. The two others sat together on Fine's usual rock in the middle. Illuminated by the low slanting sunlight, their heads wore haloes of hair. For an instant it was as if he didn't know her—he saw a beautiful, attentive mother, playing with her child—but then he lugged in his baggage of memory and desire, nicely polluting his vision.

The stream, less swollen this time, flowed gently, curling down from its source deep in the blue foothills of the Berkshires, pooling just past Fine, and then bending sharply down, away, toward its sink. But for a lone jay the birds had quieted, the crickets had yet to begin, and the only sound was the sound of water moving through stone. The scent was of earthy water, and pine. The old Clorox bottle had moved, breeding two smaller others. Fine felt fondly toward them: they are the ones who'll endure. The water was gurgling around his ankles, chilling them so they felt almost warm. He both wanted to go for a swim and did not.

John James shrieked with delight and held up something fishy for Steph to see. They put their heads together, looked, laughed. Fine felt like weeping. Why couldn't the three of them live together happily ever after? He looked away, trying to fathom what he'd learned, from loving her, losing her to John, and since. He realized he'd learned to love her enough to let her go. He felt sad and happy both, the feelings joining him to her deeply. Yet joining can't just happen once, it has to happen over and over, and over again. You can't hold onto it, no. Holding on and letting go, over and over, and over again. Like water.

Steph arose and came toward Fine, slipping and sliding along the stream. In a new baby-blue maillot, backlit by sunlight, she seemed radiant, as if aglow with a secret.

All at once he felt a tremendous surge of love for her, for her as he had known her for so long and for her brand-new. Startled, he was aware of sensing her unknown and known, old and new both, all. His caring felt hot, his heart too leaky to hold it. Thrilled, he sensed his love for her moving like an unseen dancer from a darkened meadow toward the light.

She stood with him. They looked back together at the boy. All waved. Fine, glancing at her, thought she looked fatter. She saw him looking at her tummy. Their eyes met and he knew.

Feelings surged up—hope, then fear. His eyes asked her.

"Yes," she said, "I am."

"Whose is it?"

"Ours."

"But John—"

"Ours."

"Ours?" he asked, in shock.

"Ours," she answered, quietly.

"Oh my God!" Fine felt, deep in his core, a contraction. He reached out to hug her, but then, recalling from his female-phase that what men sense as smooth women sense as rough, he stopped, and, feeling her powerfully, gently touched the crest of her bare shoulder, stroking her lightly with his fingertips.

She shivered with pleasure, and said: "After all this—after all I learned about myself, from John, from comedy, from you— maybe you are my one true love after all—wouldn't that be the bananas?"

"Now's when we should've gotten married."

"Now that you're a human being—a funny one—again?"

"And you! We're so different—we really could learn from each other now—like we did at first, kid, remember?"

"Scary, to think back." She hesitated. "Sad, isn't it? This time around might've worked, I mean if only it could've been new."

Fine's mind was blitzed, confused. For the first time ever he felt related to her selflessly, part of her, as if he himself were about to go off to—aha!—that's it! "Hey! Listen!" He was surprised that he was shouting. "I've got it!"

"What?"

"I'll come with!"

"What?"

"Come with you, to New York! Leave Boston, start fresh! This time, your turf!"

"Who says I want you to come with me?"

"Oh." He felt himself sinking. "Do you . . . want . . . me?"

She hesitated for what seemed a long time. And then her lip skewed into a smile, and a flush crept up her neck and blossomed into an all-out blush, and she said, softly: "Yes."

"Yes?" He shouted, mindless with joy.

"Yes!"

Still he was shouting: "Why?"

She stared at him as if he were a maniac, and then said: "Oh I dunno, I guess I'm just a sucker for daddies." She squeezed him, hard, and then let go, moving off, back. "C'mon, kid, let's go for a swim!" She dived into the pool under the fantasy-span, then surfaced, kicking and splashing like a water nymph.

Fine stalled, fearing the cold water.

"C'mon in! It's fantastic!"

He stepped in deeper, barely balancing on the mossy rocks, his testicles freezing. He stopped, smoothing water on his arms.

"Oh, don't be a baby! Just do it! C'mon!"

He plunged in. The cold took his breath away. He paddled frantically. He knew, then, that the long American adolescence was over. Calming, he looked up and saw her treading water, opening up her arms toward him. "As a rose," he murmured, "all things are as arose."

He swam into her arms, opening his own, mirroring her, and they enfolded each other. They bobbed up and down, kicking, touching lightly, the water a liquor of birth, slippery on their skins, cool and warm and syrupy all at once. Treading water together, they were hanging together almost weightless in the pool of the flow. Fine felt more alive and open than ever before in his life, as if the last quarter of self had dropped off and floated away. He was sensing her sensing the same thing: let us blink in the glare, and begin.

Steph spouted water and said: "Hey, you?"

"Yeah?" he asked, gasping, trying to stay up.

"So tell me," she said, laughing, "Izzy Fine?"

"Yeah!" he said, joining her, laughing. "Fine is."

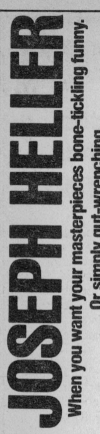